DEAD OF WINTER

DEAD OF WINTER

Annelise Ryan

KENSINGTON BOOKS
www.kensingtonbooks.com

KENSINGTON BOOKS are published by

Kensington Publishing Corp.
119 West 40th Street
New York, NY 10018

Copyright © 2020 by Beth Amos

All Kensington titles, imprints and distributed lines are available at special quantity discounts for bulk purchases for sales promotion, premiums, fund-raising, educational or institutional use. Special book excerpts or customized printings can also be created to fit specific needs. For details, write or phone the office of the Kensington Special Sales Manager: Kensington Publishing Corp., 119 West 40th Street, New York, NY, 10018. Attn. Special Sales Department. Phone: 1-800-221-2647.

Kensington and the K logo Reg. U.S. Pat. & TM Off.

ISBN-13: 978-1-4967-0672-0
ISBN-10: 1-4967-0672-2
First Kensington Hardcover Edition: March 2019
First Kensington Mass Market Edition: February 2020

ISBN-13: 978-1-4967-0673-7 (e-book)
ISBN-10: 1-4967-0673-0 (e-book)

10 9 8 7 6 5 4 3 2 1

Printed in the United States of America

This book is dedicated to all the hardworking healthcare workers I've had the privilege to work with over the years. You guys rock!

Chapter 1

I awaken and peer out of one eye at the clock on my bedside stand, hoping for another hour or two of sleep. Sadly, it is not to be. The clock reads 7:28—two minutes before the alarm is going to sound. I want desperately to close my eyes and go back to sleep, to snuggle down in the warmth of the covers and hide from the morning cold, to cuddle up next to my sleeping husband, bathing in the feelings of love and sanctuary he instills in me. Instead, I reach over and turn off the alarm before it starts clamoring. Bleary-eyed, I ease out from under the covers and sit on the edge of the bed, giving my senses a minute or so to more fully wake up. I listen to the sounds of the house and the gentle snores of Hurley behind me, feeling the coolness in the air, and letting my eyes adjust better to the dark.

Eventually I grab my cell phone and unplug it from the charge cord; then I slip off the last of the covers and tiptoe my way to the bathroom, hoping not to disturb my husband. He's a homicide detective here in the Wisconsin town of Sorenson, where we live, and he works long hours a lot of the time. Plus, we are working parents of a teenager and a toddler, so sleep is a precious commodity for us both.

In the bathroom, I brush my teeth, don a robe against the morning chill, and tame my blond locks as best I can, though a cowlick on one side refuses to stay down, sticking out near my right temple like a broken, wayward horn. I eventually give up on the hair and tiptoe back the way I came, through the walk-in closet, and across the bedroom to the hallway. Our dog, Hoover, is asleep on the floor in front of the fireplace—a fireplace whose warmth I could use right now, though at the moment it's dark and empty—and the dog gets up and falls into step behind me. I shut the door as quietly as I can, and then Hoover and I pad down the hall toward the bedroom of my two-and-a-half-year-old son, Matthew. I'm surprised he isn't awake, because he's proven himself to be an annoyingly early riser who is typically anything but quiet. But when I reach his room, I realize he has stayed true to form and is, indeed, awake; he just hasn't bothered anyone yet. His silence doesn't bode well, and sure enough I find him standing stark naked, busily becoming the next Vincent van Gogh by drawing on his bedroom wall with an assortment of crayons.

"Matthew!" I say in an irritable tone that loses much of its effect because I don't raise my voice. "Why are you drawing on the wall?"

Matthew looks guilty, but not enough so that he stops the scribble he's currently making, something that looks like a giant purple cookie. He doesn't answer me. I shake my head, walk over to him, and take the crayon from his hand, dropping it in a box at his feet that contains an assortment of crayons in all colors and sizes. When I pick up the box and place it on top of his dresser, Matthew lets out a bloodcurdling scream loud enough that a passerby might think he was being physically tortured. Some dark corner of my mind briefly entertains the possibility, before I take a deep breath and slowly release it, coming to my senses.

"I want crayons!" Matthew screams, pounding his fists on the wall.

"Hush before you wake up your father!" I rummage through his dresser drawers and grab some clothing for the day, and then take Matthew by the hand and head for the bathroom down the hall. As soon as we reach the hallway, he pulls free of my grip, runs back into his room, and resumes his crayon mantra, growing louder and more infuriated with each rant. I'm about to pick him up and haul him bodily to the bathroom when my cell phone rings.

"Damn it," I mutter, taking the phone out of my robe pocket. I swipe the answer icon and back out into the hallway so I can hear above my son's screeches. "Mattie Winston."

"Hey, Mattie, it's Heidi." Heidi is a day dispatcher at the local police station.

"What's up?" I plug a finger in my free ear to try to block out the sound of my son's meltdown. I hear the bedroom door open down the hall and see our two cats, Tux and Rubbish, come flying out of the room as if the hounds of hell are on their heels. Behind them, Hurley, or "the hound of hell in our house," shuffles and rubs his eyes. Hurley hates cats.

"The ER has a death to report," Heidi tells me.

"Okay," I say, stifling a yawn. "I'll call them." I disconnect and give Hurley an apologetic look. "Sorry about the noise." I walk over and kiss him on his cheek. His morning stubble feels scratchy on my lips, and I note that he, too, has a cowlick on one side of his head. His, however, looks adorable. But then with that dark hair of his and those morning-glory blue eyes, how could he look anything but?

Hurley looks in at Matthew, who has decided to halt his screams now that his father is here. For some reason, Matthew saves most of his meltdowns for me. "I have to call the hospital," I tell Hurley. "And your son over there has decided he's Michelangelo and his bedroom wall is the Sistine Chapel."

"I got it covered," Hurley says, midyawn. He ventures into the room barefoot, clad only in his pajama pants, and I take a moment to admire his physique.

"I pulled some clothes out for him," I say, setting them on top of the dresser.

Hurley scoops Matthew up in one arm, props him on his hip, and grabs the clothing with his free hand. The socks that are in the pile drop to the floor.

"Damn it," Matthew says, looking down at the socks.

Hurley shoots Matthew a chastising look. "Hey, buddy, we don't talk like that."

"Mammy does," Matthew says, using his unique combination of "Mattie" and "Mommy," fingering me with no hint of guile or guilt.

Hurley looks over at me, eyebrows raised.

I flash him a guilty but remorseful smile, and make a quick escape back to the bedroom, where I shut the door and dial the number for the hospital. A minute later, I'm on the phone with a nurse named Krista.

"Sorry for the call," she says, "but I have a young girl here in the ER who came in badly banged up. Shortly after arriving, she coded, and we weren't able to bring her back. She was dropped off by this guy who was acting really weird. He disappeared sometime during the code and hasn't come back."

I close my eyes and sigh. I had hoped the death would be something straightforward, like an older person with a history of heart disease who came in with a myocardial infarction and died. Something like that I could have cleared over the phone after a quick consult with my boss, Izzy, the medical examiner here in Sorenson. But this death sounds like it won't be a simple one.

"Okay," I say. "I'll be there in fifteen minutes. In the meantime, don't let anyone into the room. If the guy comes back, see if security can get him to stay."

"Got it." She disconnects the call without any further niceties. All business, this dead stuff.

I strip off my robe and pajamas, and don some slacks and a heavy sweater. The February weather has been harsh of late, and I can hear wind howling through the trees beyond the bedroom window. I head into the bathroom, wishing I had enough time to take a shower and wash my hair. Instead, I wet a comb and attempt once again to make my cowlick lie flat. It refuses until I saturate that section of hair thoroughly, plastering it down to my head with my palm. But a few seconds later, it begins a slow rise again, the Lazarus of cowlicks.

I shrug it off, knowing I've gone out looking far worse. My job as a medico-legal death investigator often requires me to go out on calls in the middle of the night, and there have been times when my sleep-addled brain lacked the ability to accomplish basic tasks during those first few minutes of wakefulness. I've gone out on calls with my shirt inside out, wearing mismatched shoes, boasting Medusa hair, and displaying the remnants of makeup smeared beneath my eyes that I was too tired to remove the night before. I'm always fully awake and alert by the time I get into my car and head out, but by then the damage is done.

I find my boys in the kitchen, Matthew standing next to his father, who is tending to something in the toaster. I have a good guess about what's in there, since there is a box of toaster waffles on the counter next to him. The smell of freshly brewed coffee hits me, and I take a moment to relish the smell. Then I indulge in what has become a morning ritual for me of late—I look around me.

Hurley and I have only been in this house for two months, and the newness of it is still a treat for me. We had it built after spending almost two years crammed into his small house in town. As a family of four—Emily, Hurley's teenage daughter from a previous relationship, also lives with us—his house was crowded and uncomfortable. And for whatever reason, it never felt like my home. The entire time we lived there, I felt like a guest who had overstayed her welcome. Almost nothing in the house was mine, or even anything I'd had a say in picking out. I'm not sure why I felt this way, because when I left my first husband, a local surgeon, I abandoned, with nary a regret, all of the furnishings I had purchased and the décor I had chosen. I moved into the small mother-in-law cottage behind the house of our neighbor and my best friend, Izzy, and paid Izzy rent. The place was already furnished, so nothing there was mine, either. But I didn't share it with anyone and it felt like mine, making it different somehow.

After bumping around together with Hurley in his house for a year or so, we bought a five-acre parcel of land just outside the city limits and built a house on a bluff that overlooks the countryside. We were able to move in right before Christmas, and while we didn't have much time to decorate—not to mention an inability to find all the right boxes—I still reveled in our first Christmas here and knew I'd remember it forever. I love our new home; it is a place uniquely ours, a perfect blend of our ideas, tastes, and needs. Despite the fact that it is a large house with an open floor plan, it feels warm, cozy, and comfortable. Part of that comes from the design and décor, but another part of it is the sense of safety and family that it provides for me. Our house is my sanctuary, the place I go to when I need to escape the sadness and the sometimes-hectic pace of my job.

I step around Hurley so I can pour myself a cup of coffee to go. The hospital has coffee, but it's rotgut stuff. I know this because I used to work there. I spent six years working in the emergency room and another seven in the OR. I loved working in the emergency room and had it not been for meeting David Winston, the surgeon who would eventually become my first husband, I probably would've stayed in the ER. But I made the change to the OR so that David and I could spend more time together. Unfortunately, David eventually decided to spend some very intimate time with one of my coworkers instead, and I caught the two of them one night in a darkened, empty OR. As shocking as this was—and it shocked my life into a state of major chaos for quite a while—the fallout from it led to both my current job and, via a rocky, roundabout trail, to my marriage to Hurley.

There are times when I regret making the change from the ER to the OR, though I have to admit that the slicing and dicing I learned how to do in the OR was good preparation for the job Izzy offered me when I fled both my marriage and my hospital job. David's dalliance was well timed in one respect, because Izzy's prior assistant had just quit. And since Izzy was offering me his cottage to stay in, it benefited both of us for him to offer me a job as well. It's hard to pay rent when you're unemployed.

I will be forever grateful to Izzy for taking a chance on me. I wasn't trained in the intricacies of the investigative and forensic aspects of my new job, but I'm a quick study. It didn't hurt that I'm also nosy, and fell into the investigative portion of things quite easily. Now, three years and a number of educational conferences and classes later, I have graduated from my original job as a diener—a term used to describe folks who assist with autopsies—to a full-fledged, medico-legal death investigator, trained in scene processing, evidence collection, and a host of investigative techniques.

As I reach for the coffeepot to fill my cup, I notice something on the door of the cupboard below. It is yet another of Matthew's artistic creations, this time in Magic Marker.

"Matthew!" I say, pointing to the scribbled lines. "Did you do this?"

Matthew looks at the cupboard door, then at me. Without so much as a blink, or a hint of hesitation, he says, "No."

"I think you did, Matthew," I say. "Who else could have done it?"

"Hoovah," he says.

"Really? Well, I guess I better punish Hoover then. What should I do to him?"

Matthew's eyes roll heavenward for a moment, and he sticks his tongue out, a sign that he is thinking. Then he looks over at Hoover, who is lying beneath the table in hopes of a dropped morsel. "Bad dog!" Matthew says, apparently willing to throw Hoover under the bus if it will get him out of trouble. He wags a finger in the dog's direction and repeats his admonition. "Hoovah, bad dog!"

Hoover looks over at me and sighs, as if he knows the kid has just fingered him for a crime he didn't commit. I look at my son, trying hard not to laugh. His antics and quick-on-his-feet lies amuse me, but I don't want him to know it, lest it encourage more such behavior.

The toaster pops, revealing four waffles, and Matthew's attention is instantly diverted, his crime forgotten. The kid inherited his father's dark hair and good looks, but his food fixation is all from me.

"Awful," he says, reaching up with one hand and doing a *gimme* gesture with his fingers.

Hurley takes one of the waffles out, puts it on a plate, and says, "It's hot. Go sit at the table and I'll bring it to you when it's cool enough to eat."

Matthew pouts, mutters, "Damn it," and walks to the table with a scowl on his face.

Hurley shoots me a look. I smile and shrug, and then I give him a kiss on the cheek. "Can I beg one of those from you?" Taking a cue from my son's clever diversionary tactics, I don't wait for an answer. I snatch a waffle from the toaster, plug it into my mouth, and then head for the coat closet.

"Tell Richmond I'll be in around nine if he picks up this, or any other case," Hurley says to me.

"I'm sure he'll be involved with this one," I say, donning my coat. "Sounds like it may be a case of domestic abuse."

I put on boots, gloves, and a hat, tearing off bites of the waffle as I go. It's not much of a breakfast, but it will do for now. As soon as I'm fully armored against the elements, I walk over and grab my coffee cup from the counter, kiss my husband on his lips, kiss my son on top of his head, and head for the garage.

I start up my car—an older-model, midnight-blue hearse with low mileage—and hit the garage door opener. Outside, the sky has a heavy, leaden look to it, a harbinger of what is to come. I flip on the radio and listen as the morning-show host tells everyone that a huge winter storm is headed our way, due to hit our area tomorrow afternoon.

"This one is going to be a doozy," he says with a classic Wisconsin accent. "Expect heavy winds, freezing rain followed by snow, with up to a foot or more of accumulation." Then, after issuing this forecast of gloom and doom, he says in a chipper voice, "Get those snowmobiles tuned up, people. And make sure you stock up on brats and beer."

Despite his cheery tone, he's promising this will be an impressive storm, even by Wisconsin standards. And that's saying something.

I hope it's not an omen for the day ahead of me.

Chapter 2

My job in the medical examiner's office entails understanding how, when, where, and why people die. Sometimes the answers are straightforward and the result of a natural evolution of events. It doesn't make the loss any easier for those left behind, but at least the inevitability of it all, and the knowledge that the deceased had a good life, helps to mitigate the pain. Other times, death comes in an untimely, cruel, and unexpected manner through accidents, diseases, suicides, and murders.

I suspect today's death is one of those latter types, a disheartening, sad, and avoidable event brought about by the brutality of another human being. It's cases like this that make it hard for me to believe that we humans have evolved much because, at times, our capacity for cruelty toward one another seems to know no bounds.

As I enter the ER, it feels as if I never left, even

now, nearly ten years after I worked here. It's a unique environment, a place of rushed urgency, endured suffering, and, hopefully, relief. The people who work in ERs are unique, too, medical personnel who often sacrifice their meal and bathroom breaks, activities with their families, and sometimes their own health and well-being so they can help others. It's a demanding place and pace, one that can go from zero to sixty in the blink of an eye. You either love it or hate it, and, at times, it's possible to experience both—not only in the same day, but in the same hour. The intrinsic high of successfully resuscitating someone who was literally dead on arrival is kept in check by the failures: people who don't survive, people who are given a devastating diagnosis, and people who are gravely and chronically ill.

My victim this morning, a girl whose medical record says she is eighteen, is one of the failures. I know from past experience that the knowledge of this fact will weigh heavily on everyone here. But the staffers have little time to dwell on it, or to deal with it, because the never-ending flow of misery continues, and the staff must put aside their own emotions long enough to care for those who are still living.

I doubt other patients and family members are aware of the sorrow being carried on the shoulders of those who care for them, but I can see it clearly. There is the faintest hint of a droop behind those professional smiles, a certain dullness in their eyes, and a slight slump in their shoulders as they walk away. To me, the sadness is as palpable as the walls around me, because I've experienced it myself.

I know the staff will talk about this case later when they hand off their patients to the next shift, and they'll discuss it several more times in the days to come. It will likely be one of those cases that gets talked about for years, the memories carried in small recesses of the brains of those who were involved, destined to become part of the institution's mythology. Each one of these cases takes a small part of you with it, and over the years they add up to a wound with the potential to erode one's empathy, sympathy, and desire to help. The scarring left behind often leaves its victims a bit more jaded, a bit more cynical, and a bit less trusting of themselves, their power to heal, and of humanity as a whole. Turnover and burnout among ER staffers is high for this very reason.

I check in with the unit clerk behind the desk to find out what room my victim is in.

"Room four," she says, and then she's answering a phone, moving on to the next task.

No one is in the dead girl's room when I enter, and I stop beside her stretcher and stare down at her, wondering about the life she had prior to the tragedy that took it. Her face is battered and bruised, one eye swollen shut, one cheek abraded, her lower lip split. A breathing tube has been placed down her throat, one end of it protruding between her full, bloodied lips. Despite these flaws, it's easy to see that she was very pretty. Her long

strawberry-blond hair is thick, splayed out around
her head. Her eyes are a dark, rich blue, which
makes me think of Hurley, and despite the light
color, her lashes are long and thick. Behind those
full lips is a set of even white teeth, miraculously
unbroken. She is pale—unnaturally so, because of
death—but I can see that her complexion was
blemish-free, her skin smooth and youthful.

I set down the scene kit I brought with me—a
tackle box filled with the tools of my trade—and
retrieve a pair of gloves from a box on the wall in
the room. I don the gloves, and remove a camera
from my kit.

There is a patient gown covering the girl's body,
but she isn't wearing it. It is laid over her, an inad-
equate blanket, an attempt to provide her with
some semblance of privacy and dignity in this last
and most undignified moment of her too-short
life. I snap some pictures of her as she is, and then
after checking to make sure the room's curtain is
fully closed, I pull the gown down to expose the
rest of her body. Her chest is adorned with monitor stickers and defibrillation pads, all of them
placed around young, pert breasts. IV lines have
been placed in both of her arms, and I note that
there are other, older puncture marks on her arms
as well. I reach down with my gloved hand and palpate the forearm closest to me, feeling the hard,
rigid line of one of her veins. It looks like my victim was a user of IV drugs. Had she overdosed?
Had the presence of drugs played a role in her
death somehow? I log these questions into my

brain for later consideration, snap some more pictures, and then continue my exam.

Her belly is flat, and I see bruising in various spots, some of them the fresh purplish blue color of a new injury—which oddly enough makes me flash back on the giant cookie Matthew drew on his bedroom wall—while others are in varying shades of green and yellow, indicating injuries that occurred sometime in the past. I move down the body and see similar markings on her legs, and in her pubic area. I document them all with photos.

The door behind me opens and I quickly pull the gown back into place before turning around to see who it is.

In walks a woman who looks to be about my own age—mid- to late thirties—with shoulder-length blond hair, blue eyes, and a slightly portly figure.

"Hello," she says, showing a tentative smile. Except for the fact that I am significantly taller than she is, since she looks to be about five feet tall and I'm six feet even, we could be twins.

"Can I help you?" I ask in a slightly annoyed tone, irritated by the unexpected interruption. I see that the woman is wearing a hospital ID badge that displays the name HILDY. Beneath that is her title: SOCIAL WORKER.

"You're from the medical examiner's office?" she says, her eyes briefly flitting toward the victim and then back at me.

"I am," I say. "I'm Mattie Winston." I start to extend my hand as an offer to shake, but then withdraw it when I see my gloves.

She acknowledges the withdrawal with a little nod and a smile. "Oh . . . yes. I've heard about you," she says. "You used to work here, right?"

"Right."

"And you were married to Dr. Winston."

"Yes, I was," I say with an awkward but resigned smile. You'd think that after three years the story of my ex and me would have faded into the past. But I can tell from Hildy's slightly embarrassed look that this isn't the case. I fear that our sordid tale is one of those that will live on in hospital history, becoming part of the overall legend of the place. In a small-town hospital, the value of health insurance has nothing over the value of juicy gossip.

"I'm Hildy Schneider," the woman says. "I was involved in this case."

"I see," I say, wondering why. From what I've gleaned so far about the situation, the patient arrived in critical condition and deteriorated rapidly into cardiac arrest. "Is there family here?" I ask, thinking that a social worker might've been called in to help with grieving relatives.

Hildy shakes her head. "No, in fact, that's why I got involved. I think this girl might have been a victim of human trafficking."

"Human trafficking?" I say, surprised but curious. "What makes you think that?"

"Well, she was registered here in the ER as Jane Smith, and the man who brought her in said he was her brother, John Smith." She rolls her eyes at this. "He claimed that she fell out of his car while he was driving, and that's how she sustained her injuries. The staff became suspicious right away and they called me."

"I see," I say, realizing that if the victim is here under an alias, coming up with a conclusive identification for her might be difficult. While I suppose it's possible that her name really is Jane Smith, given all the other suspicious circumstances surrounding her death, it seems unlikely. "Did you talk with the man who brought her in?"

"No. I wish I had, but he disappeared soon after dropping her off, right around the time she started to tank. I did see him, though, so I know what he looks like. And we should have some footage of him on the security cameras. He conveniently forgot to bring any sort of ID with him, or so he said when he was asked. But I'd be willing to bet his name isn't John Smith any more than hers is Jane Smith."

I frown.

"And there's something else," Hildy adds, her eyes looking sad. "I was in the room with the patient right before she coded, and she said something to me." She pauses, and her gaze shifts toward the stretcher. After a moment, she reaches over and straightens one corner of the gown, which had been folded up, revealing part of the victim's upper thigh.

"Please don't touch anything," I say.

Hildy pulls back, flushes beet red, and clasps her hands in front of her. "Sorry," she says. She gives me an apologetic grin that looks more like a grimace. "I have a touch of OCD."

"What did she say to you?" I ask in an attempt to redirect her back to the topic at hand.

In a hushed tone, she answers me. "She begged me to help her little sister, saying he has her, too."

Chapter 3

"Did anyone notify the police?" I ask Hildy, irritated that I'm just now learning this information. The police should have been involved by now. Valuable time has been lost.

In a perfectly timed answer to my question, the door to the room opens, and the curtain is pushed aside. In walks Bob Richmond, one of the detectives for the Sorenson PD. Bob and I have worked together for a couple of years now, and we get along very well—amazing when you consider that I once shot him. He and Hurley share their investigative duties and an office at the police department.

Hildy tilts her head toward Richmond. "I guess that answers that question," she says with a nervous titter. Then she bestows a beatific smile on Richmond: radiant, eager, and . . . could it be . . . flirtatious? I log this observation away in my head for later.

"Hey, Bob," I say. "Are you just getting here?"

"Hell, no. The staff called shortly after the girl got here, right after the guy that brought her in disappeared. A couple of units responded at first, because it sounded like a domestic violence case. Then, when the girl died, they called me. I've been here for nearly an hour already, trying to get a handle on who she is and the man who brought her in."

"Any luck?" I ask, realizing that Richmond finds the circumstances of this girl's death as suspicious as Hildy does.

He frowns. "Naw, the names, date of birth, and other info he gave for both him and her"—he nods toward the dead girl—"were phony. No big surprise there. And I just looked at the hospital security footage. The image is kind of grainy, and it was dark outside, but we have a basic description of the guy from various staff members here, and we know what kind of car he was driving. Unfortunately, we couldn't get an image of the plate, though I wouldn't be surprised to find out that whatever plate was on the car was stolen. This reeks of a professional."

"What about the story the guy told the ER staff about her falling from a moving car? Any truth to that, as far as you can tell?"

Richmond shakes his head, looking frustrated. I notice he keeps looking and then quickly averting his gaze from the victim, something he doesn't usually do. "The guy claimed it happened over on Williams Street, near the corner of Filbert. I sent some guys over there to check it out and there's no obvious evidence of any accident like that—no skid marks, no evidence of any disturbances on the shoulder, no blood, no damaged bushes along the side of the road. There are only two single-family houses nearby, and no one in either of them was awake or heard a thing. The only other buildings in that area are the Safe Harbor house, and that old folks home for Alzheimer's patients. I doubt anyone in either of those is likely to be of any help."

I'm familiar with the area of town he's talking about. Williams Street is a thoroughfare that runs through the middle of town, beginning at one end and ending at the other. Filbert Street is one of a series of crossroads on the north end of town, all of them named after nuts of some sort: Walnut, Acorn, Pecan, and Almond. Oddly enough, this seems somewhat appropriate. I've overheard dozens of times what the cops remark when they get calls to that part of town, calls that generate irreverent comments along the lines of "One of the nuts has escaped its shell again" or "There's a bad peanut in with the mixed nuts."

"Well, I can tell his story is bogus even without your findings," I say to Richmond. "This girl has been physically abused. Her injuries aren't consistent with a fall from a car. She does have a lot of blunt-force-trauma-type injuries, but not all of them are new, and she has bruising around her genital area. There's also evidence of long-term IV drug use. Her veins are severely scarred, and there are numerous puncture wounds, both fresh and old."

There are other reasons why I'm certain the story is bogus. Despite the very chilly weather we are currently experiencing, there isn't much snow on the ground right now. A recent warm spell melted most of it, leaving dirty patches of partially melted snow where the plows and snowblowers had stacked it up. The roads are, for the most part, bare right now, though tomorrow's storm will certainly change that. Without the cushion of snow or even ice, a person hitting the road with any kind of force should have a fair amount of road rash on her body. Our victim has none.

"IV drug use is common with human traffickers," Hildy says. "Sometimes they talk their victims into trying the drugs, sometimes they force it on them. They repeat their efforts until the victims are addicted and easily pliable."

Once again, I see Richmond glance at the girl, but then quickly avert his gaze. Hildy sees it, too.

"Are you okay, Detective Richmond?" she asks in a soothing but somewhat coddling tone. She takes a step closer to him and places a concerned hand on his arm, though I suspect concern isn't the primary emotion behind her actions. She looks at him a bit doe-eyed. "These sorts of things are very difficult, aren't they?" she says. "I'd be happy to talk you through some of your feelings. I do a lot of counseling, you know."

Richmond shudders, though I can't tell if it's from the idea of being counseled, or the situation before us. Or Hildy's touch, perhaps? Clearly, Hildy is interested in Richmond, but I'm not sure the feeling is mutual. Not to mention that the scene doesn't exactly set the stage for building new romantic relationships.

"I'm fine," Richmond grumbles. "It's just that it pisses me off when stuff like this happens." Hildy nods and continues staring up at him. I imagine it's a bit of a strain on her neck, seeing as how Richmond stands a bit over six feet tall. "That girl is so young and innocent," Richmond goes on. "She had her whole life ahead of her. And some scumbag stole it from her."

In an effort to get Richmond to shake off his emotional slump and refocus on the case, I say, "It's too late to do anything for her, other than find the creep who did this. But it might not be too late for her sister."

Richmond shoots me a puzzled look. "Her sister?"

I give Hildy a questioning look, and she blushes, looking guilty. She pulls her hand from Richmond's arm. "I, um, didn't mention that part to the detective," she says, dropping her hand and balling it into a fist.

"Didn't mention what?" Richmond says, his eyes narrowing.

Hildy gives him an apologetic look. "I'm so sorry. When you first got here, I started to tell you, but then the security guard came up, saying he had the video footage cued up. You went with him and I never got to finish."

Richmond lets out an impatient sigh, the muscles in his cheeks jumping. "Tell me now," he says through gritted teeth.

A split second later, Hildy spits the words out, as if saying them quickly now will somehow make up for not sharing them in the first place. "Right before she lost consciousness, she asked me to help her sister . . . said the guy had her, too."

"Crap," Richmond says, squeezing his eyes closed and running a hand through his hair.

"Do we have any idea at all who this girl really is?" I ask.

Richmond shakes his head slowly, woefully. "If this *is* a human-trafficking case, she might not even be from this area," he says. "I've already got someone at the station going through missing persons reports to see if they can find anyone who fits this girl's description. I'll call him and amend the search to include a sister." He takes out his cell phone and punches in a number. As he puts the phone to his ear, he looks at me and his expression brightens. "You know," he says, "the sister's involvement might actually help us."

His call is answered, and he steps out of the room. I half expect Hildy to trail after him, but she remains behind, sighing wistfully as she stares at his retreating form.

"You like him, don't you?" I say to her.

Hildy turns and looks at me with a faint smile, her gaze a smidge starry-eyed. "What's that?" she asks.

"Richmond," I say, nodding my head toward the door. "You like him."

She snaps out of whatever reverie held her, her expression sobering. "Oh, he seems quite capable," she says, trying hard to sound disinterested, or at the least, no more than professionally interested.

I'm not buying it, and my expression says so.

"Okay, yeah. I like him," Hildy says, caving. "He's very masculine . . . so fit, and tall, and strong. And he has caring eyes. You can tell a lot about a person from their eyes, you know."

I nod.

"How well do you know him?"

"Pretty well," I say. "He's one of the good guys."

"Is he married?"

I smile at her. "No, and never has been. He was dating a local woman for a while, but I think that's over. So you might be able to catch him on the rebound."

Hildy contemplates this information, her expression alternating between worry, hope, and curiosity.

"I'd go slow, though," I caution her. "He hasn't had very many relationships in his life. He used to be quite heavy, and something of a recluse."

"Really?" she says, looking thoughtful. "He looks very fit now."

"He lost a lot of the weight a couple of years ago after he was shot in the gut," I tell her, conveniently leaving out the fact that I was the one who shot him. "He visits the gym regularly these days, and he's a new man as a result."

Hildy looks down at herself, running a hand over her slightly rounded belly. "Do you think he'd mind a woman who's a little, um, *un*skinny?" she says, biting her lip and looking at me with a hopeful expression.

"Well, as an *un*skinny person myself, I'd say you never know until you try."

Hildy sighs and turns her attention—reluctantly, it seems—back to our victim. "Do you think we'll be able to find her sister?"

I look down at the bruised young face of my victim, pondering the selflessness that made her devote her last, dying breath to an appeal for help for her sibling. "I don't know," I say honestly. "But we're sure as heck going to try."

"I want to help in any way I can," Hildy says. She looks up at me, her eyes pleading. "And not just because of him." She nods toward the door. "I can be quite resourceful."

"Well, for starters, you can work hard at recalling any other details about the man who brought her in. What was the color and length of his hair? What color were his eyes and skin? Did you notice any mannerisms, birthmarks, scars, or tattoos? Did you pick up on any accents, or peculiarities of speech? Were there any unusual smells about him? What was he wearing? Anything you can remember might help. Write it all down and share it with Detective Richmond. Sometimes the most insignificant detail can turn out to be important."

Hildy nods eagerly, seemingly buoyed by either the opportunity to help or the opportunity to report her facts to Richmond. Maybe . . . probably both, I realize. "I'll get right on it while it's all still fresh in my head," she says. And then she hurries from the room.

I turn my attention back to Jane Smith, wondering who she really is. Where was she from? What was her life like before all this happened? And how had she ended up here?

I continue taking pictures, getting close-ups of

her various wounds. It's the beginning of a long and very intimate process. By the time I get her back to the morgue, and Izzy and I perform her autopsy, I will be familiar with every aspect of this girl's body, both inside and out.

Chapter 4

When I'm done with my photographs, I leave Jane Smith's room and go looking for the ER staffers who cared for her. It's relatively quiet in the department at the moment, though I know better than to comment on this fact. ER workers are a highly suspicious group and there are three things they believe can trigger a shit storm of patients arriving: any mention of the word "quiet," a full moon, and ordering food in. There isn't much that can be done about the lunar cycles other than to gird one's loins and push through it, and I know from past experience that the temptation of delicious, albeit often unhealthy food delivered from some outside source often wins out over the staffers' fears. But if anyone mentions that cursed *Q* word, they are likely to be tarred, feathered, and threatened with a variety of tubes that will fit not so nicely into every one of their orifices.

I make my way to the nurses' station, where

there are three nurses, a physician, a unit clerk, and a technician on duty, all of them seated at various computers. I glance at an electronic board hanging from the ceiling that displays the room numbers and the names and complaints of any patients currently in the department. There are fifteen rooms, and only four of them are occupied at the moment, with one of those being my Jane Smith. I don't recognize two of the nurses, but the third one is a good friend of mine and a longtime presence here in the ER: Phyllis, aka Syph, who got her nickname years ago when I worked in the ER and we spent a shift trying to come up with nicknames for ourselves that were also common maladies. We had a habit—and most ER staffers still do—of referring to patients by their complaint or diagnosis and their room number, rather than their name. It happens in part because of attempts to maintain patient privacy, because there are often visitors or other patients within hearing distance when patients are discussed between caregivers. But it's also the easiest way to identify a patient when you have an ER full of them. Generally speaking, referring to a patient as the "rectal foreign body in bed eight" brings his face and situation to mind much more clearly than his name would.

I also know the doctor on duty, Mike Leonard, not only from when I used to work here, but also because I used to socialize with him and his wife back when I was married to David. Mike has been working in the Sorenson ER for the past twenty years, and his wife, Dianna Muller, is a local veterinarian. I like them both a lot, but haven't seen or spoken with either of them in the three years since my split from David—one of the many things I lost in the divorce.

"Hey, Mike," I say, walking up to his desk.

He turns around and gives me a big smile. "Mattie Winston!" He pops up from his seat and gives me a big hug. "It's good to see you." He releases me from the hug, but holds me at arm's length. "You're looking good," he says, eyeing me closely. "This death work must suit you."

I respond to his comment with something between a grimace and a grin. "I'm not sure how to take that," I say. "But thanks."

"I hear you've remarried and have a kid now."

I nod. "Technically, I have two kids. My husband has a teenage daughter from a previous marriage, and then there's our son, Matthew, who's two and a half."

"The terrible twos and a teenager?" Mike says, looking aghast. "That has to be a handful."

"It is at times," I admit. "How are your kids doing? Casey should be graduating from college soon, no?"

He nods, looking a bit wistful. "He's in his senior year at U of Dub. Seems like yesterday he was a toddler in diapers. Where does the time go?"

"What's his major?"

"He's decided to follow in his mother's footsteps. He's been accepted into the veterinary medicine program at Washington State University, so he'll be moving away next summer."

"And Christine? What is she up to?"

Mike frowns. "She graduated from high school this past June, but hasn't decided yet what she wants to do with her life." He pauses and sighs. "She wants to travel and take some time to *find herself.*" He makes air quotes around the last two words. "Anyway, while it's good to catch up, you're here on business, grim business no less."

I nod. "What can you tell me?"

"The girl was brought in by some guy who said she fell out of the car while it was moving. He estimated his speed to be around thirty when it happened, but I knew almost instantly that his story was bogus. Knew it because she didn't have any road rash, her clothes weren't torn or wet, and her injuries weren't consistent with the story. Plus, she looked scared out of her mind. At first, I thought her fear was because she was in pain, or afraid she was going to die, but it seemed to be targeted toward the man who brought her in. She kept looking at him all wide-eyed and anxious. I started asking him some rather pointed questions, questions that he dodged, and then our girl started to crump, so my attention shifted to her. Apparently, the guy slipped out during our attempts to resuscitate her, so I wasn't able to question him any further."

"Did she say anything?"

"She did, once the guy left the room," Mike says with a sobering look. "My understanding is she said something about her sister, that he had her sister, too. I didn't hear it, but several other people did."

"She didn't give any names or other information?"

Mike gives me an apologetic look. "Not that I heard. Phyllis was the primary. You can ask her if she got any more out of her before I got into the room."

"I did," Syph says from behind me. I turn and give her a wan smile. I'm glad to see her, but wish the circumstances were different. "When I was bent over her, trying to listen to her heart and lungs, she whispered something in my ear. It was just two words: 'lost group.' "

" 'Lost group'?" I repeat, frowning. "What does that mean?"

Everyone shrugs.

I recall what Hildy had said to me earlier. "Maybe she was referring to others in her situation," I suggest. "The social worker seemed to think the girl was a victim of human trafficking, so maybe she was trying to tell us something about the others who had been taken."

Mike says, "I don't know how reliable anything she said will be. Not only was she half delirious because of her condition, the tox screen we did on her came back positive for opiates."

I nod. "I saw the tracks on her arms. Did you get a level? Any chance she died of an overdose?"

Mike shakes his head. "There wasn't enough in her system to kill her. And we gave her two doses of Narcan during the resuscitation attempt. Needless to say, it didn't do anything."

Bob Richmond enters the nurses' station and walks over to me, notebook in hand. "I have a potential ID on our victim," he says, consulting the notebook. "There was an eighteen-year-old girl reported missing from Necedah six months ago, and her younger sister went missing a few weeks after that. The older girl's name was Liesel and the younger one's name is Lily. Their last name is Paulsen. Their father, Kurt, is the only living parent, and he owned and ran a dairy farm outside of Necedah, which had been in his family for three generations, though he recently sold it. The kids' mother died a little over a year ago from cancer."

"Sad," Mike says. "How did they disappear?"

"I haven't had a chance to review the police files, but I can share what's known about the case publicly," Richmond says. "Liesel was a senior in high school at the time of her disappearance. After her mother died, she drove herself and her sister to school every day rather than take the bus. That was so the girls could run errands afterward, like grocery shopping and such, things the mother used to do. Their father was tied up from dawn to dusk with the farm, and it sounds like Liesel took over the role of her mother, cleaning the house, cooking the meals, and taking care of her younger sister. On the day Liesel disappeared, which was a Friday, she took Lily to a friend's house after school and dropped her off for a sleepover. Liesel was never seen again after that."

Richmond pauses for a moment to flip a page in his notebook. "Her father reported her missing later that same night. He said he came back to the house around six and saw no sign of her having returned since that morning. Both girls carried backpacks, and they typically dropped them by the front door as soon as they came home. He waited a while, figuring Liesel was running some errands and would be home soon, but somewhere around eight, he began to worry. He tried calling Liesel's cell phone, but it went straight to voice mail. So he called Lily and talked to her. Lily told him that Liesel had dropped her off around three-thirty, and that she had mentioned something about having errands to run."

Richmond flips another page. "The father called the police around nine, at first just to inquire if there had been any traffic accidents in the area. He talked to a dispatcher, who told him there hadn't been any accidents, and then suggested that perhaps Liesel was with some of her friends and had simply lost track of time. When he mentioned the fact that she wasn't answering her phone, the dispatcher suggested that the battery might have died. A uniformed cop went out to the house and talked to Mr. Paulsen, but he gave him the same set of excuses the dispatcher did. He told Mr. Paulsen to call all of his daughter's friends, and when Paulsen said he already had, the cop told him to wait to see if Liesel came home later that night. If not, he could call again in the morning. The cop did say they'd keep an eye out for her car in the meantime." Richmond pauses, then shakes his head in dismay before continuing.

"Mr. Paulsen then went out in his pickup and drove around for a couple of hours, checking all the roads and areas where Liesel would typically drive, and some that weren't so typical. There was a high school football game that night, so he checked out the school grounds and the surrounding area. The game was over, and most of the people had left. He talked to a few students who were still hanging out, but none of them claimed to have seen Liesel since school let out. So he went back home, hoping she'd be there. She wasn't, and he called the police again, insisting on talking to a different officer this time."

Another flip of a page and Richmond continues. "An officer by the name of Clyde Morrison responded." Richmond pauses and looks up at us. "He's the one I spoke to." He looks back at his notes. "Anyway, Morrison came out to the house and talked to Mr. Paulsen. He admitted to me that he thought Liesel had simply decided to go to a friend's house and perhaps got caught up in some sort of party and lost track of time, since it was a Friday night. Mr. Paulsen was adamant that Liesel wouldn't do that, that she was a responsible, mature child for her age. Morrison took the info, and did broadcast a message to the other officers on duty to keep an eye out for Liesel or her car. Someone spotted her car parked in a motel lot about two hours later. It was unlocked, the keys were in the ignition, and her backpack was on the floor in the rear seat. Her phone was nowhere to be found."

Richmond looks up at us. "Needless to say, that's when things got serious. The cops checked the motel registrants, but there was no sign of the girl. They eventually tried to ping her phone, but they got nothing. The car was dusted for prints and searched for evidence, but it appeared to have been wiped clean. There were security cameras in the motel lot, but all the feed showed was someone in a hooded jacket and gloves dropping the car off, getting out, and walking away. The overall build of this person didn't match Liesel at all. And there has been no trace of her since."

"And the sister?" I ask. "What happened with her?"

"Lily, two years younger than Liesel, disappeared just as mysteriously a little over three weeks later," Richmond says. "According to her father, she was having a lot of trouble dealing with the disappearance of her sister, on top of her mother's death. She dropped out of school and was staying at home. Her father thought she was safe there, but when he came back to the house one afternoon to have lunch and check on her, she was gone. Left her phone behind. Not a trace of her anywhere, either."

"So, one death and two disappearances, all in the same household in a matter of months," I say. "I take it the cops looked into the father thoroughly, as well as any farmhands he had working for him?"

"According to Morrison, they did," Richmond says. "He told me the father was—and still is—completely devastated. As I mentioned before, he has since sold off his farm and now lives in a small house in Necedah. He walks and drives the streets and roads in the area for hours—presumably, looking for his girls—and Morrison said he looks sadder and thinner with each passing day."

"And now we have to deliver the worst news of his life," I say, closing my eyes as dread fills me. This is the part of the job I hate.

"Well, if what Liesel said is true, there is still one daughter out there," Mike says. "Maybe you can find her?" There is a hint of hope in his voice, but also a modicum of uncertainty. I think we all know the odds of that happening are depressingly long.

"So far, the only clue we have is a video image of the car the man who came with Liesel was driving, and an even vaguer image of him, although we do have a description based on eyewitness reports from the staff here. I've got a sketch artist putting something together as we speak."

"We also have Liesel's comment to Syph," I add.

Richmond shoots me a puzzled look, which he quickly shifts in Syph's direction. "Comment? You mean when she mentioned her sister?"

"No," Syph says. She then reiterates what she told us earlier.

"'Lost group,' " Richmond repeats, his face screwing up. "What does that mean?"

Everyone looks blank-faced.

"Whatever it means," I say, "we best figure it out soon, before I have to tell Mr. Paulsen that both of his daughters are dead."

Chapter 5

After the chat in the nurses' station, I call the Johnson Funeral Home, and the CassKit sisters, Cassiopeia and Katerina, arrive to transport the body back to the morgue. The girls, identical twins with long black hair who dress for the job in all black (though I suspect it's as much a fashion statement as it is any type of uniform), are the daughters of the owners of the funeral home. They have embraced the family business with a vigor that some find frightening, though a number of men seem to find their dark sides intriguing, along with their svelte figures, good looks, and aloof demeanors.

They are quiet and mysterious, and there have been times when they have made me arch my brows in confusion. I was originally told that their full names were Cassandra and Katherine, but have since been corrected by the sisters themselves, who informed me that their full names are Cassiopeia and Katerina. I think they made up one set of names, but I'm not sure which one. Did they go through a stage where they hated the dramatic qualities of Cassiopeia and Katerina and decided to normalize themselves by simplifying their names? Knowing what I do of the two of them, I doubt this, since the girls have never been about the plain and ordinary. I think the more likely explanation is that their given names are Cassandra and Katherine, but they decided these monikers weren't exotic or mysterious enough for them. So they upgraded. Whatever their full names are, the "Cass" and "Kit" diminutives are what most people use because the combination of the two nicknames, and the opportunity to refer to them as the CassKit sisters, is all too irresistible.

They help me roll and maneuver Liesel Paulsen, assuming that's who she is, into a body bag. We have yet to confirm her identity, but the DMV picture Richmond showed me on his phone makes me think it's her. I want to believe it's her, not because I want her dead—I'd give anything if that wasn't so—but because some creep has stolen her life and I don't want to believe that he's somehow managed to steal her identity as well.

I've never been able to tell the Johnson girls apart, so I'm not sure if it's Kit or Cass who frowns as we zip the body bag closed.

"What happened to her?" she asks.

"I'm not sure yet," I tell her. "I suspect she's been beaten to death."

"She's so young," Cass or Kit says. She looks across the body at me. "Was the guy who brought her in a boyfriend?"

The quieter of the two sisters pipes up at this

point. "She wants to know because she's dating a loser with a bad temper, despite my warnings to stay away from him."

"Is that true, Cass?" I ask, taking a stab at the identity of the bothered sister.

"I'm Kit," she says with a tired smile, "and he's never hit me or anything like that."

"The key word being '*yet*,'" Cass says with a hefty dose of sarcasm. "But he yells at her all the time, punches holes in walls, and threatens her with bodily harm when their arguments get heated. Plus, he doesn't like it when she wants to spend time with me or anyone else in the family."

"Those are clear danger signs," says a voice behind us. I turn and see that Hildy has reentered the room. She walks over to Kit and places a hand on her arm. "Let's talk about this," she says in a calming voice. Her large blue eyes are reassuring. "Come back when you're done with work today and let's sit down and discuss what's going on, okay?"

Kit stares back at her for several beats before saying, "I have to take call all evening, so I'm not sure when I'll have time."

Hildy takes a card from her pants pocket and asks me if she can borrow a pen. I take one from my scene kit and hand it to her. She uses it to write something on the back of the card, and then hands the card to Kit. "I'll be here until three today, and that number on the back of the card is my personal cell phone. Call me anytime, and we'll talk on the phone if need be, okay?"

Kit takes the card and slides it into the back pocket of her pants. The pants are very tight—she has the figure to get away with it—and I can clearly see the outline of the card when she's done. Without another word, she goes back to her duties. A moment later, we have the body loaded onto the funeral home stretcher, and a blue fabric cover is placed over it all. Cass and Kit roll the stretcher from the room and I follow. So does Hildy.

"Thanks," I tell Hildy in a low voice when we reach the back door, where the funeral home hearse is parked. We watch as the Johnson sisters load the stretcher into the back.

"Make sure she calls me, okay?" Hildy says, her voice barely above a whisper. "This sounds like a dangerous situation."

"I'll see what I can do."

"And let me know if I can help at all with our other victim," Hildy adds. "These lost souls haunt me, you know?"

I do.

My own hearse—a personal vehicle, not a work-related one, even if it is somewhat apropos—is parked not far from the Johnson hearse. The girls wait for me to get behind the wheel, and then I follow them to the morgue, pulling into the underground garage about eight minutes later. Sorenson is not a huge town, and it's located in an area of Wisconsin that is populated by other small towns and a lot of rural countryside. Since my boss, Izzy, lives here and was hired as a medical examiner years ago, our office handles deaths from a wide surrounding area that includes all of our county and, occasionally, some neighboring ones. The bigger cities, such as Madison and Milwaukee, are either an hour or an hour and a half away, respectively.

Because of our small size, a lot of our work gets farmed out to the labs in those cities. But in the three years that I've been doing this job, our abilities and responsibilities have grown. Many parts of Wisconsin still operate on a coroner system, so the presence of an actual medical examiner—a geographic fluke for our area—lends our office a level of professionalism, ability, and importance that some of the other offices in the neighboring outlying areas don't have.

The Johnson sisters use their key cards to access the elevator and bring the stretcher into the elevator, which takes us up to the main floor, exiting into a back hallway near our autopsy room. We have three autopsy tables—a bit of overkill, if you can forgive the pun, given that we only have one ME and only do one autopsy at a time. They help me transfer Liesel's body from their stretcher onto one of ours. Then they sign some paperwork to record the transfer of the body to me so that there is a clear trail of evidentiary possession.

"Thanks, guys," I say.

They nod and turn to leave, but I call out to Kit, this time knowing I've got the right sister because I can see the outline of the business card in her back pocket. "Kit, I hope you'll take Hildy up on her offer to talk. Sometimes it helps to get an objective, outside opinion on things."

Kit says nothing, but she smiles at me. It's not a particularly convincing smile, and I feel a twinge of worry for her. Cass also smiles, hers more an expression of gratitude. And then they are gone.

I wheel the stretcher bearing Liesel's body onto a scale and record the weight in a computer file I start for her. She is small, weighing only 117 pounds, and I feel a flare of anger at whoever abused her, knowing they were likely twice her size. Hell, I'm nearly twice her size, and I feel a tiny twinge of guilt when I realize that Liesel is exactly the kind of girl I used to hate in high school: petite, pretty, and well proportioned.

I suppose "hate" is too strong a word for what I felt, but there was definitely some soul-sucking envy, given that I was already six feet tall when I started high school, was wearing a size-40DD bra, and had feet so big that Jimmy Hoffa could've been hiding out in one of my shoes all these years. When most of my schoolmates were shopping for clothes in trendy, chic little shops, I was thumbing my way through the Lane Bryant racks, wondering why so many of the clothing lines bore the names of Greek and Roman goddesses like Aphrodite, Athena, and Venus—though given that Venus is also a planet, I suppose that one is apropos. There are days when I feel as big as a planet, with moons of fat circling around me.

Oddly enough, my mother is built like Liesel. Clearly, I inherited my physique from my father, who is well over six feet tall, wears a size-fifteen shoe, and tends toward what my sister, Desi, calls "thickness." That's her kind way of avoiding the *f*-word whenever I start bemoaning my figure. Desi got my mother's build, and when we were kids, she had no compunction about calling me any number of stinging names when she was ticked at me, monikers like "lard ass," "thigh-tanic," and "gazonga chest." On one occasion, when I came home with a pair of red flats I'd purchased to go with a new outfit, Desi, who was mad at me over some long-forgotten transgression, snidely asked me if I was trying out for clown school.

Fortunately, age has brought both maturity and kindness to our relationship, but there were times when we were kids when it was like World War III in our house. I didn't let her insults go unrequited. I spent the better part of one weekend stealing items of her clothing and sneaking them over to Jennifer Closker's house because Jennifer knew how to sew. I had her take in the seams and trim them so that when Desi tried to put the clothes on, they'd be suddenly too small. I managed a few other pranks, such as mixing baby oil into her shampoo, and tanning lotion into her regular skin lotion, which made her look like a greasy-haired zebra. Despite these childhood rampages, Desi is my closest confidante and best friend these days, and I'd honestly be lost without her.

As if Desi somehow knows I'm tripping down memory lane, my cell phone rings and I see that it's her.

"Hey, Desi, what's up?"

"I just realized that Hurley's birthday is next Monday. Are you planning a party?"

I utter a silent curse. "Um, yeah, but I haven't nailed down the specifics yet." This is essentially the truth. I thought about throwing a party for him . . . five months ago when we celebrated Matthew's second birthday. Thoughts of Hurley's birthday haven't crossed my mind since, however. The date kind of sneaked up on me.

"Are you inviting friends, or limiting it to family?" Desi asks.

"I think family."

"You think," Desi echoes with a healthy dose of skepticism. "You haven't had time to plan anything, have you?"

"I haven't," I admit. "I've been so busy with work stuff. . . ." I let my excuse trail off, knowing it sounds feeble and like a winning entry for the Worst Wife of the Year award. I figure I can hang the certificate on the wall next to my Worst Mother of the Year award, one I feel I've earned several times since Matthew's birth, this morning included.

When it comes to motherhood, Desi has me beat hands down. Despite her occasional abuses of me growing up, she was born to be a mother, and her kids, Erika, who is fourteen, and Ethan, who is twelve, are sweet, well-rounded, and well-behaved kids. This is all the more surprising, given that their father is Lucien Colter, a local attorney who specializes in criminal defense, but dabbles in other areas as well, such as crass behavior, unfiltered vocabulary, and sartorial disasters. Desi and Lucien met when she was in high school and he was in law school. They got married right after she graduated, and wasted no time at all in starting a family. Desi had Erika when she was just nineteen years old. That blows my mind at times. When I was nineteen, I could barely plan what to wear the next day, much less the start of a family. And since, technically, I didn't plan the start of the family I have now, I think it's safe to say I haven't gotten much better with time.

"Why don't you let me throw something together?" Desi offers. "We can do it here, just like we did with your wedding, and my birthday party. We can have it on Sunday, so no one has to work. I'll invite Dom, Izzy, and Juliana, of course, but we'll keep it just the clan otherwise."

Juliana is the adorable nine-month-old Izzy and Dom adopted six months ago, and she is also my son's best and most frequent playmate, since Dom is my primary childcare provider, though Desi fills in a lot of the time. While Izzy and Dom aren't actually related to us in any way, they, and now by extension Juliana, have always been considered part of our family.

"I doubt Mom will come," Desi goes on, "but you never know."

"Speaking of moms," I say, "if we invite Dom and Izzy, we should probably invite Sylvie."

"Oh, right," Desi says, and it's obvious from the tones we've both adopted that this option is not high on either of our lists.

Sylvie is Izzy's mother, and a difficult woman to like at times, since she is an opinionated, headstrong, stubborn old woman who never misses a chance to say what she thinks. She is also fiercely independent and hasn't taken well to the fact that her health is failing and her strength isn't what it used to be—though woe be it to anyone who ticks her off and is within the swing arc of her walker. Izzy had a cottage built behind his house for Sylvie several years ago after she fell and broke her hip. But after living in it for a year, Sylvie's rehab worked well enough that she was able to move out and into an apartment of her own. This worked well for me, too, since it left the cottage vacant right around the time I fled my home and marriage after catching David in flagrante delicto with a coworker.

Unfortunately, Sylvie's recovery was short-lived, and other health problems eventually made it unsafe for her to live alone. Izzy would have gladly let her move in with him into what Sylvie refers to as the "big house," but she isn't very accepting or tolerant of her son's sexual orientation. Being the natural-born caregiver he is, Dom has done much to win her over, and the presence of Juliana has softened Sylvie even more. But decades of blind prejudice are hard to overcome, and Sylvie still can't resist the occasional judgmental tongue-clucking, or a bit of commentary regarding her son's living situation. The cottage offers the perfect solution by providing Sylvie with the sense of independence she desires, while still being close to her son. And it leaves Dom and Izzy with some privacy, so it's a win-win situation all around.

As I'm contemplating the potential headaches inherent in inviting Sylvie, something occurs to me. "Desi, when you say we'll keep it to family, are you including my . . . our father?"

There is a moment of silence on the other end that gives me my answer. Up until last summer, I always thought Desi was my half sister, fathered by my mother's second husband after my father ran off when I was four. It turns out I was wrong about a lot of things. My father didn't actually abandon us. He entered the Witness Protection Program, and my mother refused to go with him. There were a number of reasons why she refused, not the least of which is her severe OCD and a bad case of agoraphobia. My mother was pregnant with Desi at the time, and in order to protect us, she passed Desi off as the progeny of another man. She did so with such alacrity that even my father didn't know the truth until recently.

Of course, neither did Desi, so I suppose it's understandable that she's now curious about the man who is her newly discovered biological father. I'm curious about him, too, but I've harbored such ill feelings toward him for so many years that I'm having a harder time than she is making nice with the man, now that he has reentered our lives.

"I'd like to invite him," Desi says. "But if it's too uncomfortable for you, I won't."

I sigh. "It's hard for me to tell you no, given that you're offering your home and throwing a party for my husband," I tell her. "How often are you seeing him?"

Aware of how much this subject bothers me, Desi and I have spent the past few months avoiding discussions about our father. Desi has done a good job of making sure our paths don't cross. But I realize it might be time to set my petty differences aside and give the man another chance.

"He comes by about once a month," Desi says. "The kids have really gotten to know him. He spends a lot of time with them, especially Ethan. He's as fascinated with Ethan's bug collection as Ethan is, and it's really helped them bond, since that's something Lucien has never been able to connect with very well."

This is one of those rare occasions when I can

relate to Lucien. Ethan's bug collection is mostly dead specimens, but it also includes a live tarantula, which bears the ignominious name of Fluffy, and a live, three-inch-long, hissing Madagascar cockroach, which is more appropriately named Hissy.

"Does Mom know Dad is visiting you and the kids?" I ask.

"Heck no," Desi says. "She's been stressed out enough about his return, although William tells me she hasn't declared herself terminally ill and taken to her bed for nearly five weeks now."

William (not Bill, he will tell you) is a local accountant whom I met on a blind date that Izzy fixed up for me not long after my split from David. To say our first date was a disaster is a gross understatement, though it wasn't a total loss. Like my mother, William suffers from OCD, though his case isn't as severe as hers. Despite a ten-year difference in their ages, I had a feeling that my mother—who was, once again, single after divorcing husband number four—and William would get along well. And I was right. They're going on their third year together. They share a fear of dirt and germs, making their house cleaner than the OR I used to work in, but William lacks my mother's hypochondria, agoraphobia, and penchant for melodrama. He's also an eminently patient man, a prerequisite for putting up with my mother for any length of time. Whenever my mother gets stressed—which is often, thanks to her many mental illnesses—she goes on a maniacal cleaning binge for a few days, then tells everyone she has some terminal illness, declaring that death is imminent. She then takes to her bed and stays there for anywhere from a few days to a couple of weeks, after which she gets up and goes about her life as if nothing happened. Ever since the reappearance of my father several months ago, and the revelations about events of thirty-some years ago, my mother has "nearly died" at least four times. The fact that she has recently gone for more than a month without declaring herself terminal is a sign she's on the mend.

"Just make sure you tell her you're inviting Dad," I say to Desi. "No surprises. I have enough drama in my life already."

"Oh, I'll tell her," Desi assures me. "That's why I said I doubt she'll come."

"Okay then, dear sister, you are on. And if you can think of the perfect birthday present for Hurley, let me know."

"You're on your own for that part," she says. "Love you."

"Love you, too."

As I disconnect the call, I wrack my brain trying to think of something I can get Hurley for his birthday. We have a new house, he has a brand-new truck in a gorgeous shade of blue that matches his eyes, and aside from some very unromantic ideas, like socks and underwear, I can't think of a single thing he might want or need. My husband is a simple man who takes pleasure in the tiniest of things: the way the sunlight hits the snow and makes it sparkle like diamonds, the sound of his son's laughter, the feel of my body snugged up against his, the rich flavor of a perfectly grilled and seasoned steak. This aspect of him is one of the reasons I love him, but it's also one of the reasons I hate trying to come up with a gift for him.

And I have less than a week to do it. No pressure. No pressure at all.

Chapter 6

The trip-hammer beat of my heart as I struggle to deal with the birthday gift issue seems trivial when I look over at the bagged body of Liesel Paulsen. I feel instantly ashamed and self-absorbed, and I vow to refocus my angst on things that truly matter, like a young girl whose life has been cut way too short, and the sister whose life I might yet be able to play a part in saving.

I hear a door open and see Arnie Toffer, our office's lab rat, enter the hallway, and this, too, helps me refocus. "Whatcha got?" he asks, eyeing the stretcher on the scale.

"A sad one," I tell him. "But it's also one I think you'll find interesting." My implication that the sad death of Liesel Paulsen might be something intriguing to Arnie could sound harsh or uncaring to the average person, but I don't mean it that way. Arnie is a die-hard conspiracy theorist, and the possibility of investigating a human-trafficking ring is something I know he'll enjoy sinking his conspiratorial teeth into. And it might keep him occupied long enough to get him off some of the other, more far-fetched ideas he's following of late, such as the relatively harmless hobby of searching for sightings of cryptozoic creatures like yetis, Nessies, and such, or the more worrisome theories, such as the idea that there is a secret underground city built beneath the Denver International Airport that is designed to serve as home to the New World Order. Crazy as most of these theories sound, Arnie and others of his ilk can put forth arguments in support of them that tend to give one pause, no matter how absurd the original premise seems. And every so often, Arnie's suspicious, conspiratorial mind has proven helpful in solving a case. Because of that, and the sheer entertainment value of hearing him spout his theories and rationale, I not only tolerate Arnie's conspiracy leanings, I occasionally encourage them.

"We have an eighteen-year-old girl who was dropped off in the ER by a mystery man, who then disappeared. Her injuries suggest she was abused and beaten to death, though the story the man gave was that she fell out of a moving car. And to add to the puzzle, one of the last things she said was that she wanted us to help her sister, implying that the man who brought her in had her, too, and it wasn't a friendly arrangement."

"Human trafficking?" Arnie says, his eyes growing wide.

"Possibly," I say, not surprised he made the leap. "Her description fits that of a girl who went missing six months ago. And her younger sister went missing a few weeks after that."

"Wow," Arnie says. "Any leads?"

"Not much, other than the words of the dying girl. She said something about a 'lost group,' which might mean that there are a lot more victims out there to be found."

"I'm sure there are," Arnie says. "These guys prey on young girls and boys—runaways, kids who are estranged or angry with their families, or who have parents who don't give a crap. They befriend them, offer to help them, promise them a better life, lure them in with gifts and money, and then get them hooked on drugs. If the kids wise up and try to leave, the kidnappers threaten them with injury or death, or threaten to kill their family members. Once they have them securely in their grasp, they start farming them out to sexual deviants, drugging them into oblivion, and taking whatever money they can get for them." Arnie frowns and shakes his head sadly. "Most of them end up dead, either from abuse, by their own hand, or from a drug overdose."

"You seem to know a lot about this," I say.

Arnie shrugs. "I saw a lot of it when I was working in LA. There are so many young people who go out there hoping to make it big in Hollyweird, and then the harsh realities hit. They're prime pickings for the type of parasites who engage in human trafficking. I know some guys who track this kind of stuff on the Internet and try to rescue some of the kids, sometimes with the help of the authorities and sometimes not. Either way, it isn't easy. The people who traffic in humans are, understandably, not a very trusting group."

"Scary to think there are people like that out there," I say, imagining Emily, our teenage daughter, or Erika, my sister's teenage daughter, falling into the hands of people like this.

"Have any trace for me to work on?" Arnie asks.

"Not yet. Do you have any online connections who might know anything about human trafficking in this area?"

"Oh, yeah." Before he can expound on whatever conspiracies are current on the matter, the door at the end of the hall opens and Izzy walks in.

"Is this our ER victim?" he asks.

I nod, heartened by Izzy's appearance. He had a heart attack last summer that left him pale, shaky, and a little less confident and assured than the Izzy I've known for the past several years. But he's been doing well lately, and today he looks good. His swarthy coloring is back, there is a definite spring to his step, and his hair, which is normally a ragged tonsorial gathering of black tufts heavily tinged with silver, is neatly trimmed and—amazingly—completely lacking in gray.

"Are you dyeing your hair?" I ask.

He blushes and brushes a hand over one side of his head. "Yeah, Dom talked me into it. Does it look ridiculous?"

"No," Arnie and I both say at the same time.

"It makes you look younger," I tell him. "And it's a good dye job, not one of those cheapo ones. Very nice."

Izzy smiles self-consciously. "I let Barbara do it."

"Really?" I say, a little surprised.

Barbara is a mortuary cosmetologist, though she prefers to refer to herself as a funereal aesthetician. She does makeup and hair for the dead, and works out of the basement of a local funeral home that is the Johnson family's primary competition.

The Keller Funeral Home is run by Irene Keller, an elderly woman who bears a striking resemblance to many of her clients. No one knows for sure how old Irene is, but her paper-tissue skin, age-spotted hands, and dowager-humped back suggest she is older than Tutankhamun. She insists on wearing lots of makeup, but her foundation is always patchy, her eyeliner is often running up her lid or down the side of her face, and her lipstick looks like it was applied in clown school. I'm guessing this is because her eyesight is mostly gone. I don't know why she hasn't had her license taken away yet, but at least she drives slowly. *Really* slowly. I've seen pedestrians walk the blocks downtown faster than Irene drives them.

Despite her seeming frailty, she is still kicking, and doing so quite well, if recent rumors can be believed. There's a story going around about how she recently bloodied the shins and lower lip on some kid who tried to steal her wallet out of her purse at the local grocery store. Apparently, she fell asleep in the little cart she rides in, and the kid thought she was dead and, therefore, easy pickings.

"Have you been to Barbara before?" I ask Izzy. I'm curious for two reasons. The first one is that it was Izzy who first turned me on to Barbara, making a not-so-subtle suggestion that I was long overdue for a makeover, back when I first started working for him and was still reeling from David's betrayal. I was skeptical when he said he knew someone who was very talented with hair and makeup, given that he's basically bald on top with a tonsorial fringe that circles his head like some sort of *Star Trek* alien communication device. My skepticism about his recommendation only grew when he dropped me off in front of a funeral home. I almost blew it off, but then decided to go ahead and give Barbara a try.

My first appointment with her was definitely a memorable one. The girl is a magician, a wizard, a master, when it comes to fashioning hair and applying makeup. But her methods take a bit of getting used to, and this leads me to the second reason I'm curious if Izzy has been to Barbara before.

"No," Izzy says, rolling his eyes. "It was my first time." A shudder shakes him. "I knew what to expect, but I have to admit the actual experience was far more disconcerting than I anticipated. Despite working with dead bodies and the equipment that goes with them on a regular basis, lying down on an embalming table was quite uncomfortable. And I'm not just talking about physical discomfort."

"It does take some getting used to," I agree. "When Barbara told me I was going to have to lie on one of those tables for her to work on me, I nearly walked out. She basically shamed me into it, called me a 'wuss,' or something like that." Both Izzy and Arnie chuckle. "Anyway, once I committed, it wasn't that bad. In fact, Barbara helped me plan out my entire funeral while I was there. She let me look at myself in a mirror while she set different-colored satin pillows beneath my head so I could see what I'd look like when I'm dead. We settled on this lovely pale blue that really sets off my eyes."

Arnie scoffs. "What good is that if you're dead?" he says. "Your eyes are going to be closed."

I stare at him, realizing he's right. This is a little upsetting. What is even more upsetting is the realization that I never figured that out for myself.

Seeming to sense my dismay, Arnie offers up a compromise. "Of course, you could paint blue eyes on some stones and have them set on top of your eyelids."

"You mean like Joffrey on *Game of Thrones*?" I say, wincing. "That's creepy on so many levels."

"It was a common thing to do back in medieval times," Izzy says. "It started with coins, which served both a mythical and a practical purpose. The practical part was that the coins kept the deceased person's eyes closed. The mythical part was that the coins also served as a fare for Charon when he ferries the dead down the River Styx. I think the stones came into play because they could actually be inserted into the body's eye orbits, thereby maintaining a more normal shape since the eyeballs tend to wither quickly."

I shudder. Even though I deal with death on a daily basis, I can still be creeped out. And the eyes have it, so to speak. One of the tasks involved in my job that I dread the most is the drawing off of vitreous fluid, the liquid part of the eye. It's a highly useful sampling because the fluid can provide all sorts of interesting details regarding both the timing and, on occasion, even the means of death. But sticking needles into eyeballs gives me the willies.

"In some ancient cultures, it was also common to put stones in people's mouths when they die," Arnie says, adding his two cents' worth. "Some think it was because it was believed to prevent the spread of plague, while others think it was a vampire deterrent."

"Okay, okay," I say, holding up one hand. "While that's all very fascinating, I don't need any more death trivia today. The two of you can go on and on with this subject for hours, and right now I want to focus fully on our victim. If we can figure out how she ended up here, we might be able to save the life of her younger sister."

This gets Izzy's attention, not an easy thing to do when a discussion revolves around death trivia. Izzy is a walking encyclopedia when it comes to death and the many rituals that go with it. He's given lectures on the subject. And while Arnie is not as well versed as Izzy—at least in real-world applications—he is very well versed on death scandals, rumors, and conspiracies, both modern day and ancient.

"You are absolutely right," Izzy says, all business now. "Let's get to it."

"I need to get her X-rays done, and then I'll bring her into the autopsy suite for you." I reach into the satchel I carried with me to the hospital and pull out a manila folder. It contains several pages and a copy of Liesel Paulsen's DMV photo, which Richmond had printed out at the hospital once he came up with a possible identification for our Jane Doe. I hand the folder to Izzy. "Here's a printout of her medical record. Bob Richmond is heading up the case, but he said he probably won't be here for the autopsy. I haven't downloaded my photos yet, but I will as soon as I finish up the X-rays."

Izzy nods, his expression grim as he studies the smiling picture of Liesel Paulsen. "What's the basic story?" he asks.

I tell him how Liesel came to the ER, how her male companion left in a hurry, and the theory that she, and her younger sister, were both victims of human trafficking. Then I tell him about the girls' father. When I get to the part about how Liesel's final words were a plea to us to help her sister, Lily, both Arnie and Izzy take on a new sense of urgency.

Izzy says, "I'll be dressed and ready to go in a few minutes. Meet you at the table."

Arnie spins on his heel and heads toward the stairs to his lab/office area. The stairwell, like the elevator, requires an ID badge for access. "Let me see what I can dig up from my guys online," he says over his shoulder.

While I wince at his use of the term "dig up," I am heartened by his determination and zeal on the matter. Maybe we can save a life for a change.

Chapter 7

I get Liesel's body X-rayed and then wheel her into the autopsy suite ten minutes later. I'm able to move her onto the autopsy table by myself, given how light and small she is, and by the time I'm done, Izzy has arrived, dressed in his gear and ready to go.

"Give me a couple minutes to get into my scrubs," I tell him, wheeling the stretcher away. "And then I need to download my photos. I shouldn't be long."

Famous last words. There are days when it feels like the world is conspiring against me with everything I do. Today is turning into one of those days. My first clue is when I go to grab a set of scrubs from the locker room so I can change out of my street clothes, and the only sizes I can find on the shelves are smalls and mediums. Our scrubs are laundered by an outside service, and a change in ownership for that service has given us reasons to rethink this arrangement. Izzy is barely five feet tall, and he's a bit on the portly side. Since his heart attack, he has lost some weight, thanks to his partner Dom's watchful eye and skillful cooking, but he's still not what anyone would call slender, or even normal. Since I stand six feet tall, Izzy and I make a comical visual duo when we work together. Ironically, we both wear the same size in scrub pants: extra large. Izzy has to roll up the pants legs several times, whereas I often find that they hit above my ankles. And while the XL tops fit Izzy, my generously endowed bust leaves my tops straining at the seams unless I wear a 2XL.

Izzy has cut back his hours to part-time since the heart attack, and we have another medical examiner named Otto Morton, who fills in on Izzy's days off. Otto is not a small man. In fact, he bears a striking resemblance to Santa Claus. He wears 2XL scrub pants and top. I job share with our newest employee, Christopher Malone; he's just under six feet tall and broad-shouldered, and wears the XLs.

Arnie is only about five-eight, and his slim build fits into the mediums. But Arnie rarely wears scrubs, since he spends most of his time in his upstairs lab, wearing a lab coat over his street clothes. We also have a part-time evidence technician named Laura Kingston, whom we share with the police department. Like Arnie, she rarely wears scrubs—though she will don them on occasion, if she is invited out to help us process a messy scene—and she wears a medium as well. Our only other employee is Cass—short for Cassandra, for sure, in this case—our receptionist/secretary/file clerk, and she is the only person in the office who would wear a small, though I've never seen her wear scrubs.

I try to squeeze my way into a medium-sized top, and end up nearly choking to death when I try to maneuver one arm into a sleeve. Then I find myself struggling to get out of the thing, trapped with my head and part of one arm protruding, while the remainder of the top has me wrapped up like Houdini. As I struggle, I hear a seam rip and finally work my way loose. I toss the top aside, hold up the medium pants for a second, and after realizing I'll never get them past my knees—assuming I could get my snowshoe-sized feet through the pants legs—I toss them aside as well. Resigned to wearing my street clothes, I grab my camera and head for my computer.

My office isn't really an office. I have a desk located in our library, a room that also houses our conference table. There is a second desk in the room, and this one belongs to Christopher. The two of us split our hours much in the same way Otto and Izzy do. Chris is not only a nice guy who bears all the necessary qualifications for the job, he is reliable, funny, and flexible when it comes to scheduling—something I greatly appreciate. But he has a trait that has haunted him in the past, and haunts us in the present. He has some sort of digestive disorder that causes him to produce huge amounts of flatus, which he releases on a regular basis. And it isn't your ordinary, everyday kind of gas. These emissions are the most foul-smelling clouds of noxious odor I have ever experienced, and given that I sometimes work with rotting bodies, that's saying a lot. Arnie once commented that if Christopher had been older, he'd suspect his farts were behind the Bhopal disaster of 1984.

Chris's interview gave us a hint of what was to come, and given that he once filed a lawsuit for wrongful termination against a police department he worked for—a lawsuit he won—we are determined to make the best of the situation. It isn't always easy. We found an underwear product that contains activated charcoal in the lining, and that has helped some. And the library is always filled with a variety of air fresheners that make the room smell like a funeral parlor . . . ironic in a way. But there are still times when it can be quite a challenge to work with Chris, something I fortunately only have to do one or two days a week when our schedules overlap.

Those of us who work with Chris have become proficient at developing euphemisms for his emissions, things like "stepping on a frog," "airbrushing," "cheek flapping," "hummerhoids," "knicker-rippers," and the more delicate "panty whisper." We've even been known to rate them, using what we've dubbed the "sphincter scale." A ten on the sphincter scale will clear a room in five seconds flat.

Fortunately, Chris has a good sense of humor about the whole thing, surprising when you consider his disorder has already cost him two jobs and a marriage. You'd think his problem would make it hard for him to date and hook up with anyone, but as luck would have it, he has struck up a relationship with a local cop named Brenda Joiner, who seems to tolerate Chris's emissions with relative ease. It doesn't hurt that Chris is tall, good-looking, smart, and charming. And with his police background, he and Brenda have a lot in common.

I remove the memory card from my camera and slide it into my computer. As soon as I've started the download process, I head back to the autopsy suite, but Cass stops me in the hallway.

"Mattie? Can you hold on a sec?"

Her voice rings with a British accent, and I see that she is dressed like a 1920s flapper, replete with a cute bobbed wig and a fringed, knee-length dress. Cass belongs to a local thespian group, one that Izzy's partner, Dom, also belongs to. Cass likes to "live my characters." This involves her dressing up and wearing the appropriate hair and makeup all day long—even to work—for whatever character she is currently playing. Izzy indulges this quirk, though it has led to some people believing we have a huge turnover in personnel at our front desk.

"What's up?" I ask.

"That reporter, Irwin Cleese, is out front. He says he heard there was a suspicious death at the hospital, and by the time he got there, you and the body were already gone. The staff there wouldn't tell him anything, so he's here, wanting to know if we can give him any information for the paper."

My gut reaction is to say no, an instinct triggered by my past experiences with other reporters in town. But I stop myself. Unlike his predecessors, Irwin has thus far proven himself to be polite, discreet, and reliable when we ask him to hold back information. Plus, we might be able to use him in this case. Not only do we have a dead victim, but there is a live one still out there, and Irwin might have some resources we can use.

"Ask him to wait while I chat with Izzy," I tell her. She nods and hurries back to the front desk, while I head for the autopsy suite.

"You haven't changed yet?" Izzy says when I enter the room.

"No, and I won't be," I tell him. "We're out of all the large-sized scrubs again. I tried to squeeze into what we had and ended up bursting out of the seams like Poppin' Fresh Dough. I'll just put on a cover-up over my street clothes. But before I do that, Irwin Cleese is out front, wanting to know if we can share any info with him. I started to say no—"

"But then you realized we could probably use his help on this case," Izzy finishes for me.

Izzy has always had a disturbing ability to read my mind, a trait that works both ways. We often finish one another's sentences, and we tend to think alike. We are able to discuss any topic, no matter how painful or awkward, and Izzy is always honest with me, even when I'd prefer he wasn't, like the time he told me my school-bus-yellow dress made me look like I needed a backup alarm. The two of us are amazingly similar and compatible in everything but our physical parameters. We would have made an odd-looking but solid couple if it hadn't been for the fact that we both have a sexual attraction to men.

"You got it," I say. "How much do you want to share with him this early in the game? And should I check with Richmond first? He might not want to involve anyone else just yet."

"Good point," Izzy says with a conceding nod. "Why not give Richmond a call?"

I do so, taking my cell phone out of my pocket. Richmond answers on the second ring. "Hey, Mattie, what's up? Have you got something for me already?"

"No. Sorry. Hold on while I put you on speaker." He waits as I do so, and once I'm done, I say, "Can you hear me okay?"

"I can."

"I'm here in the autopsy suite with Izzy and we have a question for you. Irwin Cleese is here, wanting information, and Izzy and I were thinking that—"

"He might be able to help us?" Richmond finishes for me.

"Exactly, yes."

"I say go for it. We don't have any details at this point that he wouldn't be able to find out on his own eventually, and he might have some resources that could help us find the sister."

"Okay. Anything new on your end?"

"No. As soon as you guys have a definitive ID, I'll go and notify the girl's father." Richmond sounds less than enthusiastic about this plan. "Can't say I'm looking forward to it."

Izzy says, "Given that her hospital ID is probably a phony name, I may need to have the father come in and identify her. I can run her prints through AFIS, but I'm betting she's not in the system. Nor do I have any dental records yet. All I have is a DMV photo of who we think she is."

Richmond makes a pained sound. "Ugh. Poor guy. But if it has to be done . . ."

"Sadly, I think it does," Izzy says, looking down at Liesel's pale face.

"Okay then. The sooner the better," Richmond says. "Any chance Mattie can come with me?"

I look over at Izzy, eyebrows raised in question. Izzy thinks a moment, glances at the clock, and then says, "Sure."

"Thanks," Richmond says, sounding genuinely relieved.

"Give us twenty minutes to talk to Irwin Cleese," I say.

"No problem," Richmond says. "Come on over to the station when you're ready."

I disconnect the call and then head out front to fetch Irwin Cleese. He is a tall, thin fellow with huge feet—a trait that makes me empathetic toward him, particularly since it seems to make him somewhat clumsy, another trait we have in common.

"Hi, Irwin," I say.

"Hi, Mattie. I heard you had something going on with a death in the ER earlier this morning. Got anything you can share with me?"

"We do. Izzy says you can come into the autopsy suite if you want, and he'll talk with you there."

Irwin gives me a look of disbelief. He's never been invited into the autopsy area before. "Are you sure?" His color pales a little.

"I am," I tell him. "Come on and I'll take you there." I turn and head for the back area.

Irwin hesitates a mere second before leaping at

the chance, literally. With his first step, he trips over his own feet and takes a huge jumping step in order to keep from falling. "Sorry," he mutters, regaining his pace.

I lead the way, talking to him over my shoulder. "Have you ever seen an autopsy before?"

"Can't say that I have," he says after clearing his throat.

"It can be a bit overwhelming the first time. Don't be ashamed to admit it if you start feeling queasy or light-headed. There are chairs off to one side you can sit in."

"I'll be fine," he says with forced bravado.

I badge us into the autopsy room and a rush of cold, formaldehyde-scented air greets us. I lead him toward the side cabinets, since they are located a safe distance from the autopsy table and, more importantly, near some chairs.

"Hello, Mr. Cleese," Izzy says.

"Dr. Rybarceski," Irwin says with a nod. These two have always had a very formal relationship. "What have you got today?"

As he asks this, Irwin looks toward the body on the table. Liesel is fully exposed at this point, naked, pale, but still intact. Izzy has removed the various leads and pads that were on her chest, though her breathing tube is still in place, protruding from her mouth. There is a towel covering her genital region, but the multiple bruises on her body—yellow, green, blue, purple—are easy to see. Irwin looks at her and his head tilts to the side. A sad expression comes over him, and for a moment, I think he might cry.

"She's so young," Irwin says, his voice a bit shaky. "What happened to her? Some kind of trauma?"

"Yeah," Izzy says, his voice laced with bitter irony. "The human kind. This girl has been beaten multiple times, and sexually abused."

Irwin's face pinches into a painful grimace, and he looks away for a second, swallowing hard. "Do you know who did it?" he asks, swiping the back of one hand over his mouth.

"Not yet," I tell him. "She was dumped at the ER. The guy who brought her in beat feet almost as soon as they got there."

"Boyfriend?" Irwin asks.

"Not likely," Izzy says. "He gave the staff a fake name, so we're not sure who she is, though we have an idea. We think she may have been a victim of human trafficking."

Irwin perks up a little at this.

"We have reason to believe that her younger sister is caught up in the same human-trafficking ring and is still out there somewhere," I add.

Irwin looks very eager now. "How can I help?" he asks.

"What do you know about human trafficking in this area?" I ask.

"Not much," he says with an apologetic look. "This part of the state doesn't see as much of that as the bigger cities do. I worked in Milwaukee for a little while . . ." His voice fades out, and he takes on a sheepish expression. "But all I did was write obituaries."

"Do you still have connections in Milwaukee you could use?" I ask.

Izzy, who I suspect wants to test Irwin's abilities—or perhaps "sensibilities" is a better word—picks up his scalpel in preparation for making his first cut. He reaches over Liesel's body and places the scalpel just above the distal end of her right collarbone. With a quick, deft slicing motion, he cuts through the skin at a downward angle, stopping midsternum. He then makes a similar cut from the other side, meeting the end of the first one. Finally he places the scalpel at the bottom of the V he has made, and slices down the body toward the pubic bone.

"I . . . um . . . I do know some people there on the city beat," Irwin says, his voice wavering a tad as he watches Izzy's actions with huge, round eyes. "I could put out some feelers."

"You should check with Detective Richmond," I say. "Let him know what connections you can tap. If you coordinate your investigation with him, you could end up with a nice exclusive."

Izzy has undermined the tissue around his incisions and flayed back flaps of skin, exposing the pleural and abdominal cavities beneath. He makes quick work of cutting through the musculature and exposes Liesel's omentum—the tough, fibrous lining in the abdominal cavity, behind which we will find all of the abdominal organs. Two deft cuts later, and the omentum is pulled back, revealing the liver, the stomach, and an intertwining mass of small and large intestine.

"An exclusive would be great," Irwin says, sounding less enthusiastic than he had moments ago. I glance over at him and see that he has wisely taken one of the chairs. His eyes remain riveted on Liesel; his color is pasty.

Izzy picks up the large, scissor-handled bone cutters we use to snip the ribs, effectively creating a removable plate comprising partial rib bones and the breastbone, or sternum. He starts with the ribs on his side of the table, positioning the short, thick blades around each bone and then quickly shoving the long handles together. A loud *crack* emanates with each cut, and just as he finishes with the third one, the *crack* is followed by a resounding crash off to my side.

Irwin has passed out cold, sprawled on the floor beside his chair. Both the chair he was in and the one next to it have toppled over.

I look over at Izzy with a wan smile. "Hey, at least he didn't puke."

After a conceding shrug, Izzy resumes his cuts.

I walk over to Irwin, who has landed on his back, arms and legs akimbo. His mouth is agape, and his eyes are open and staring at the ceiling. For a moment, I'm afraid we've killed him, but then I see his chest rise and fall, and see the pulsation of his carotid in his neck.

"Irwin?" I say, lightly slapping cheeks the color of cottage cheese with the back of my hand.

"Gealzobuck fracas," he slurs. His eyelids flutter and his lips puff out just before more gibberish comes out of his mouth. "Canawanga."

"Wake up, Irwin," I say. I go over to a sink, wet a towel, and bring it back, placing it on his forehead.

"What?" he says eventually, the first coherent thing he utters. A bit of color returns to his face.

He looks around the room with a confused expression before squeezing his eyes closed and covering his mouth. "Oh, man, I'm sorry."

"Don't be," I tell him with a smile. "It happens to the best of us."

He slowly pushes himself up to a sitting position, blinking rapidly several times. His eyes dart toward the table, and just as quickly dart away from it.

"It's probably best if you don't look over there again," I tell him. "Think you can get back up into the chair?"

He nods unconvincingly, but manages to get onto his hands and knees, and from there, to sort of crawl into the chair. After positioning his butt in the seat, he leans forward, elbows on his knees, face in his hands. "This is so embarrassing," he says to the floor.

"Not as much as you might think," I say. "At least you didn't puke or lose control of your bladder. A lot of people do. And once, when I was an OR nurse, I made the mistake of not eating breakfast the morning before a long case and I fainted while standing at the operating table. I felt it coming on and I tried to stop myself from going down by grabbing the sterile drape covering the patient with one hand, and the tray of instruments with the other. I went down anyway, ripped away the entire operative field, and dumped all of the instruments onto the floor. They had to start over from scratch and pray that my breaking of the sterile field didn't compromise the patient in any way. Fortunately, it didn't. But I never lived that moment down. My nickname from then on was 'Avalanche.' "

Irwin gives me half a smile, clearly a little skeptical of my story, but grateful nonetheless.

"I swear," I say, holding up a hand.

"That must have made it hard for you to go to work there every day, facing all those jeers," Irwin says in a way that makes me think he's intimately familiar with such ribbing, and maybe worse.

"It did," I admit, thinking, *But not as much as catching one of my coworkers playing my husband's skin flute did.* I wisely keep this salacious addendum to myself. "Sit there and keep your eyes away from the table. I'm going to go get you a soda."

I leave the autopsy suite and quickly head for the break room, where I grab a cola from the fridge. I carry it back and hand it to Irwin, who holds the cold can up against his temple for a few seconds before popping the tab on it and taking a long gulp. When he lowers the can, his other hand quickly covers his mouth as a loud burp rips loose.

"Oh, geez," he says, looking embarrassed. "I'm sorry. I'm really making an ass out of myself today."

"No, you're not," I say, placing a hand on his shoulder. I feel an odd affinity that I haven't experienced around Irwin before. Empathy? Sympathy? "When you feel like you're able, I'll walk you out."

"I'm good," he says, standing up. He does it so fast it startles me, and I hold my breath, wondering if he'll go down again. But while he wavers slightly, he maintains his stance, and after a few seconds, he starts walking to the door. I shoot Izzy a wary look and then follow Irwin out.

When we reach the front lobby, Irwin stops and turns back to me. "Thanks," he says. "If it's okay with you, I think I'll avoid the autopsy room in the future. But I appreciate the heads-up on the story."

"You're welcome. Get in touch with Detective Richmond, like I said, and he'll fill you in."

He nods, squelches another burp, and then hurries out the door.

I glance back at Cass, who is wearing an amused expression. "I take it he crashed?" she says in a wry British tone.

"Went down like a felled tree."

"Sorry I missed it," she says. And with that, she goes back to working on her computer.

Chapter 8

I return to the autopsy suite, and find that Izzy has removed Liesel's intestines from the body cavity and the chest plate, exposing her heart and lungs. He is standing there looking into her body with a sad expression.

"What's wrong?" I ask.

"This poor girl," he says, shaking his head dolefully. "She was put through hell. Her spleen was ruptured, and her liver was lacerated. She had an intestinal tear, and a bad bruise on one of her kidneys. And to make matters worse, she was pregnant—though not for long—at the time of death."

I squeeze my eyes closed for a moment before looking at Liesel. Izzy has removed the breathing tube and, despite the bruising, the relatively calm and serene repose of her face is a sharp contrast to the violation that is her body. She is as open and desecrated as any person can be, her insides literally exposed for the world to see. Or, at least for

Izzy and me to see. There is nothing I can do for Liesel at this point—her pain is ended—but maybe I can help her sister.

"Did you find any useful trace on her body?" I ask Izzy.

He shrugs. "I took some samples from her vagina and rectal vault that might contain some semen. We'll have to wait for Arnie to analyze them. Maybe we'll get lucky and get a DNA hit. I also took some nail scrapings, though I'm not sure there was anything there that will prove useful." He rolls his neck a couple of times, and sighs.

"Are you okay, Izzy?"

"I'm fine. It's just that this case is hitting home for me. Now that Dom and I have Juliana, it's hard not to empathize with the father of this poor girl. We need to nail the bastards responsible for this. And we need to find her sister."

I'm about to suit up and help Izzy finish the autopsy when the door to the autopsy suite opens and Cass pokes her head in.

"Mattie, there's a woman out front who says she desperately needs to talk to you. She says it's about this girl's case." Cass's British accent is even stronger now.

"Did she give you a name?"

"Yep. It's Hildy Schneider. Says she's a social worker over at the hospital."

Izzy gives me a questioning look. "She was involved in Liesel's care," I explain.

"Then I suppose you should go and see what she wants," Izzy says. "Though I don't know why she didn't just go to the police if she has some new information."

"I guess I'll find out," I say, annoyed that the woman has shown up. I turn to Cass. "Tell Hildy to wait and I'll be out in a bit."

Cass nods and leaves the room. I look over at Izzy, my expression worried. "Are you sure you'll be okay on this by yourself?"

"I'm fine," he says dismissively, if a bit irritably. He glances at the digital clock on the wall, which reads 10:48. "Go. I'll get Arnie to help me if I need a second pair of hands. I'll try to have her ready for her father to see by the time you and Richmond get back."

"Promise me you won't overdo it," I say, heading for the sink to wash my hands.

"I promise," he says with a hint of impatience.

I take my cue and leave. Outside in the hallway, I send a quick text message to Richmond, letting him know that I've been delayed, but that I'm still coming and will have some updates for him. I doubt he'll care that it's taking me longer than expected, since I know he's none too eager to get to the task we have at hand. I wait a few seconds, and he sends me back a quick text that says, **No problem**.

I head up front, where I find Hildy Schneider seated in the reception area. She springs to her feet when she sees me. Grabbing her coat from a neighboring chair, she drapes it over her arm.

"Mattie, hi again," she says, hurrying over to me. "Do you have any more information about our girl?"

"We've only just gotten started on her autopsy," I say, a hint of impatience in my voice.

"Yes, I suppose it is a bit early in the game, isn't it?" She sighs and fidgets with something in the pocket of the coat she's carrying. I give her a questioning look, letting forth with a sigh of irritation. After a brief glance at Cass, she says, "Is there somewhere private where we can speak?"

"Sure, follow me." I turn and roll my eyes at Cass as I badge my way back into the secure section of the office, holding the door for Hildy to follow. I lead the way to my office—the library—and once we are inside, I indicate one of the chairs around the conference table. "Please have a seat."

Hildy does so, but not before eyeing the table and chairs for a moment. She eventually opts for one of the end chairs along the far side, and I watch her as I settle in across from her. She drapes her coat over the back of the chair, adjusting it a couple of times before she seems satisfied. Next she settles into the seat and scoots her chair up to the table, but apparently doesn't like where it is, because she pushes it back and tries again, moving it an inch or so to either side with each attempt. She repeats this three times before she seems satisfied.

I lace my fingers together and set my hands on the table. "What did you want to talk to me about?" I give her what I hope is a friendly smile, even though I'm not feeling particularly amiable toward her at the moment.

"I need to tell you a little something about myself," she says, and it's all I can do not to roll my eyes again. "I know something about that young girl's case that I think might help, but before I tell you what it is, I need you to understand some things, okay?"

I nod, feeling a mix of curiosity and impatience.

"I was orphaned when I was seven," Hildy starts, flicking at some tiny speck of dust on the table in front of her.

I curse to myself, thinking that if she's starting all those years ago, I'm in for a long and tedious story.

"I never knew who my father was, and my mother tried to raise me on her own, but she was . . . well, she wasn't prepared for the emotional and financial responsibilities involved in raising a kid. And she wasn't what one would call a representative of polite society." She pauses, and gives me a hesitant smile. I say nothing, unsure where she's going with this story, but feeling enough empathy, and curiosity at the moment, to give her more time simply because we share a fatherless childhood.

"She was a prostitute," Hildy blurts out.

I try to keep my expression neutral, but know I've failed when Hildy says, "I know, I know. It's shocking, isn't it? But she did it because it was the only way she knew to make a living. She had no formal education or job training of any sort, and her parents were very strict, religious farm people from Iowa, who basically disowned her when she was a teenager because they caught her in the hayloft with one of the local boys. All she had going for her was her looks. She was very pretty," she concludes in a wistful tone.

She reaches into her right coat pocket and pulls out a black-and-white photo that is creased and yellowed with age. She slides it across the table to me and I look down at the picture, which shows a long-legged woman in a pair of very short shorts standing next to a pickup truck. She has pale blond hair cut short in a pixie style that shows off the high cheekbones and oval shape of her face. Her eyes are large and round, her lips are full, her nose is small and slightly upturned, and her complexion and figure both appear flawless.

"Wow, you're right. She was beautiful," I say, sliding the picture back to Hildy. I study the face of the woman across from me, searching for a resemblance to the one in the picture. The shape of the eyes and color of the hair are the same, but there the resemblance ends. Hildy has a square-shaped face, thin lips, and a broad, flat nose. She is not an unattractive woman, but she didn't inherit her mother's beauty or her tall, slender build.

"Clearly, I take after my father, whoever he was," Hildy says with a wry smile, reading my mind and my frank assessment.

"You don't have any idea who he is, or was?"

She shakes her head. "I don't know that my mother knew for sure."

Remembering that she said she was orphaned as a child, I ask her, "How did your mother die?"

"She was murdered." Blunt, and to the point.

"Oh . . . I-I'm sorry," I stammer. "How awful."

"It was," Hildy says with a sober nod. "And the culprit was never caught."

I can't think of anything to say that won't sound trite or patronizing, so I say nothing.

"Anyway," Hildy says, picking up after a brief, awkward silence, "I ended up in the foster system.

My grandparents wouldn't . . . couldn't take me in, and there was no one else, since my mother was an only child. I missed my mother terribly, of course, and as a result, I had a tendency to act out." She pauses and gives me an embarrassed, apologetic look. "I'm afraid I was a bit of a terror, actually. I did some awful things, things I'd rather not dwell on. Suffice it to say, I moved from one foster home to another until I was twelve years old, racking up more than fifteen of them. No family would keep me for more than a few months. I finally got hooked up with a counselor I could relate to, or perhaps it's better to say he could relate to me, and by the time I reached my teenage years, I settled into my new life a little better." She pauses and frowns. "Though I suppose saying 'I grew resigned to it' is a more accurate way to put things." She shrugs and smiles. "Anyway, I spent several of my teen years in a group home with a bunch of other sad sacks like myself and we formed a kind of bond among us that helped me to settle down."

"How awful for you," I say, meaning it. My own childhood was no cakewalk, given that my mother's revolving door of husbands and her severe hypochondria didn't exactly instill me with a sense of security. But at least I had my sister, who, despite some contentious times between us, at least understood where I was coming from. Hildy had no one like that.

"Yes, well, it wasn't ideal, that's for sure," Hildy says. "But I think I'm a stronger person because of it." She pauses, raking her top teeth over her lower lip. "I didn't come out of it unscathed, however," she says, her tone cautionary. "I have a few, um, quirks that evolved as a result of my living arrangements. You see, living in foster homes often means competing with a family's real children, their natural children, for things and attention. And the foster kid always comes out on the losing end. I watched time and again as the *real kids,*" she wraps this term in air quotes, "would get treats I didn't, or get to do things I didn't, or went places I didn't. And sometimes the kids were pretty snotty about it. They'd taunt me, flaunt their booty and their privilege, rubbing it in my face." She hesitates and lets out a snort of derision as her eyes take on a brief faraway look. "In one case, quite literally. It's surprisingly difficult to get peanut butter out of your hair." She grows silent, still gazing off, and I suspect she is briefly reliving whatever moment she is referring to. Eventually she snaps back to the present, looking at me with a hint of embarrassment. "Anyway, things were rarely fair and sometimes, when I did get a little something special for myself, the other kids would often find a way to take it from me. So I found ways to treat myself from time to time. I stole things and hid them, particularly food treats."

Having hidden away a food treat myself a time or two—albeit out of guilt rather than self-preservation—I can relate.

"I sometimes take things that aren't mine," she admits guiltily. "Like your pen this morning."

I think back to my earlier encounter with her and vaguely remember her asking to borrow a pen so she could scribble out her phone number on the card she gave to Kit. It dawns on me now that she didn't give it back to me, though I never really missed it. I carry several pens in my scene kit, so to my mind, it was a minor thing.

Any remaining vestiges of my irritation with her have faded away. I can't imagine a childhood like hers, and figure she must be a very strong and resilient person to have overcome it. Either that, or she's batshit crazy. "I had no idea," I say to her. "If I'd known, I would have been happy to give you a pen."

Hildy smiles. "It's not about my needing a pen," she says, blushing. "It's more about me taking control over my own destiny, having some power over a situation. Or at least that's what my shrink says. It's an almost unconscious thing when I pocket stuff that I fancy for some reason or another. I'm working to get control over it, but it's hard to control something you're not aware of doing."

I stare at her in silence, not knowing what to say. Her history is sad yet fascinating, but I'm also aware that time is ticking by and I should be doing other things.

As if she has somehow read my thoughts, or sensed my restlessness, Hildy says, "And that brings me to why I'm here." She sticks a hand into the pocket of her coat—the left one this time—and removes a candy bar. It's a simple chocolate bar, and she sets it on the table, slides it toward me with a trembling hand.

I look at it, bemused, and then look back at her.

"Turn it over," she says.

I do so, and on the underside of the bar is a small, white circular sticker with the price of fifty-five cents handwritten on it. "I don't understand," I say.

Hildy takes in a deep breath, and eases it out. "I took it from the pocket of the jacket our girl in the ER was wearing." She sucks in her lower lip, straightens her back, laces her hands together and sets them on the table in front of her. She stares at me with a guarded expression, clearly waiting to see how I'll react, and from her posture, it is just as clear she expects me to explode.

I'm too stymied by everything she has said to know how to react. In the end, I keep it simple. "Explain."

Her shoulders sag with momentary relief, but there is a lingering tautness to her posture that tells me she isn't off her guard yet. "I was in the ER when she came in, and I saw the man who came with her. Something about the expression on his face told me that things weren't right, and I checked in with the nurses who were caring for her and they let me know they had the same feeling. The poor girl looked terrified and I went to her to offer some support. It wasn't long after that when she crashed, and then I was pushed out of the room. As I was leaving, I saw her clothes piled on a chair by the door to the room, and the end of that candy bar was sticking out of her jacket pocket." She pauses, pulls her hands from the table, and starts to massage her temples, closing her eyes. "I don't remember taking it, but I do remember seeing it there and I found it in my pocket later, so I know I must have grabbed it." She stops rubbing and opens her eyes, looking back at me. "It's an un-conscious thing," she says in a pitiful tone. "I can't help myself."

"I understand," I say, and I do. I recall the minuscule adjustments she made to her coat when she hung it on the back of the chair, and the similar gyrations she went through once she sat in the chair. Having grown up with a mother who suffers from a severe case of OCD, I have a better than average understanding of these sorts of things.

Looking at me with a pleading expression, Hildy says, "I've worked at the hospital for just over two years and this is the first time I've done anything like this there. It typically only happens when I'm overly stressed, and I think there was something about this girl that got to me."

"I understand," I say again. "But I'm not sure why you're giving this to me, and telling me about it now."

"Because it's evidence," Hildy says. "Look at that sticker. The candy wrapper has a bar code. Practically everything these days has a bar code. And yet that sticker is on there with the price handwritten on it. That suggests to me that the thing was bought—or perhaps taken—from a small mom-and-pop store that rings things up the old-fashioned way. How many of those can there be in the area? If you can find the store, maybe it will lead to something else."

"Good point," I say, nodding thoughtfully. "It's a bit of a long shot, but you never know."

"I'm sorry I took it," Hildy says. "Like I said, it's—"

"No need to explain," I say, holding up a hand to stop her. "I understand. And I appreciate what it must have taken for you to come here and tell me about it."

Hildy sags with relief. "I had to," she says. "I admit,

I didn't want to, but one other thing my history has imbued me with is a strong need for justice, to see the right thing done. And I knew that bringing this to you was the right thing to do."

"You could have taken it to Detective Richmond."

She blushes again. "I know, but I didn't want to have to explain . . . well . . . you know." She shrugs and looks embarrassed.

"You like him and you didn't want to scare him off right away by sharing your history with him."

She nods, her blush deepening.

I consider the situation and the woman before me. I don't know her professionally because I've been gone from the hospital for almost four years now. But I also know that employees who work at the hospital have to undergo thorough background checks, and if she's been employed there for a couple of years, she must be a stand-up person. She didn't have to come to me with this. She could have tossed the candy bar or eaten it, and no one would have been the wiser. Yet she came forth and admitted what she did.

"Tell you what, Hildy," I say. "I'm going to keep this candy bar, and I'll share it with Detective Richmond. I'll tell him you found it in the patient's room on the floor by the chair holding her clothes and you picked it up and pocketed it to get it out of the way. Later, after the girl died, you realized it might be important evidence because of the sticker but felt a little embarrassed that you had taken it. So, you came to me about it and handed it over. I don't think Detective Richmond will be angry. In fact, I suspect he might be impressed by your ingenuity in recognizing the sticker as a clue. Does that sound okay?"

Hildy beams with pleasure. "My goodness, yes!" she says with relief. "I don't know how to thank you."

"Well, you can make yourself available to me whenever I ask. I get the sense that you're a pretty good judge of character, and I might want to consult with you in the future."

Hildy looks like a kid who has just come downstairs and seen the loot beneath the tree on Christmas morning. "Thank you so much," she says, clasping her hands together. She gets up from her chair, picks up her coat, and puts it on. I get up, too, grabbing the candy bar and sticking it in the pocket of my slacks. Then I steer her to the door of the library.

At the threshold, she turns back, looking up at me. She is a short woman. "You've been very understanding," she says, "and I don't want to push my luck too far. But might I ask you for one other favor?"

"You can ask."

"I told you that my mother was murdered, and that the culprit was never caught."

I nod, sensing where this is going.

"It's been over twenty-five years, and I know the odds of finding the person responsible are next to nil. But I did do a little research and digging on my own. I wonder if it would be possible at some point for you to look over what I have and see if there is anything else you can suggest for me to try?"

"Well, twenty-five years makes it a very cold case," I say. "And at the moment, I'm pretty busy."

"Oh, I know that, and I don't mean you have to do it right now. But maybe sometime?"

Her expression is so desperate and pleading that I don't have the heart to tell her no. "We'll see," I say, equivocating and hoping she might forget about it over time. But then I realize that the odds of that happening are about as good as the odds of finding her mother's killer. If I were in her position, I wouldn't let it go.

She looks crestfallen for a moment, but then she rallies. "Thank you," she says with a grateful smile. "I really appreciate it."

Before she can hit me up with any more requests, I lead her back out to the reception area and the front door. "We'll talk later," I say, opening the door and making it crystal clear that we are done for now.

She beams a smile at me and leaves.

"What was that all about?" Cass asks as I head back to the autopsy area.

"She had some ideas about the case," I say vaguely. I go back to the autopsy room one more time and find Izzy still at it.

"What did the social worker want?" Izzy asks.

"She had some ideas about the case. One, in particular, that might be useful."

I show him the candy bar. "It was in the pocket of Liesel's jacket. Hildy, the social worker, said she saw it sticking partway out when she was in the ER." This was essentially the truth.

Izzy barely acknowledges me. He glances at the candy bar I'm holding up, and then just as quickly goes back to his work. "Yeah, so?"

"The candy bar itself is no big deal," I say. "No doubt useless for fingerprints, as there is no telling how many people may have handled it. But there is a price sticker on it that's handwritten. How often do you see that these days?"

Izzy doesn't bother to look at me. He simply shrugs.

"It points toward it coming from some small mom-and-pop kind of store, don't you think? If we could figure out where it came from, it might help us retrace her steps."

Izzy looks at me now, a thoughtful expression on his face. "That's not a bad idea," he says. "Good thinking, Mattie."

"Actually, it was Hildy who had the idea. She said she saw the sticker and thought it might be relevant. That's why she came to talk to me."

"Well, good for her," Izzy says with an approving nod. "Let Richmond know ASAP."

"I'm heading over there now." I glance at the bag from the ER that contains Liesel's clothing and personal belongings and pick it up. "I'll drop this stuff off with Arnie on the way. Have you found anything else that might be useful?"

"Sadly, no. It's just another case of an all-too-young life taken all too soon." He frowns and stares at Liesel's face, his expression morose. "I know the chances of finding her sister are small, but I hope we can."

"So do I," I say. "That could be Emily on your table. Or my niece, Erika. These predators need to be stopped." I take one last look at Liesel's face, which looks deceptively serene. Death has stripped all the emotion out of it.

But it has motivated me.

Chapter 9

Arnie is sitting at his desk, which is a small space nestled between myriad analytical machines, some microscopes, and an assortment of resource books, chemicals, reagents, and other laboratory paraphernalia. Arnie is focused on his computer screen, typing away on his keyboard.

"Hey, Mattie," he says, not bothering to look up at me. "What's up?"

I smile. Arnie has always been able to do this, identify who is walking into his lab without looking at them. In the beginning, it kind of creeped me out. Now I'm used to it.

"I have some stuff from the Liesel Paulsen case for you," I say, walking over and setting the bag down on a small bit of open countertop. "It's her clothing, and something interesting that was in her jacket pocket." I reach into the bag and take out the candy bar, showing it to him with the sticker side up.

Arnie gets the significance of the sticker right away. "You don't see many of those anymore," he says. "I might be able to get a print or some DNA off the back of it."

There are likely to be any number of finger-prints on the outside wrapper of the candy bar, and I realize Hildy's prints might be among them.

"I'm not sure if any fingerprints you find on the outside will be helpful," I say. "I know that at least one of the people in the ER touched it already."

Arnie shrugs this off. "The outside wrapper won't be of much use, but the back of that price sticker might be."

I breathe a sigh of relief, wondering if I'm stick-ing my neck out too far for Hildy. "Can you get me a picture of it so I can show it to Richmond?"

"Sure." Arnie pushes away from his computer and rolls his chair to the other side of the room, where he opens a drawer and removes a camera. He wheels back, snaps a picture of the sticker, and then pushes some buttons on the camera. "I just sent the image to your e-mail," he says.

"Thanks."

I start to leave, but Arnie stops me. "I've been chatting with some folks online about this human-trafficking stuff," he says, turning back to his com-puter.

"And?" I walk over and stand behind him, peer-ing at the screen over his head. I see rows of in-stant dialogue scrolling by on the screen and it all looks like gibberish to me. As Arnie taps away at the keys, I study the top of his head instead. He wears his hair long—shoulder length—but it is thinning on top, and I notice that more of his scalp is showing through these days. I wonder how much longer he'll be able to wear his usual pony-tail, though today he has his hair pulled into a style I hate: a man bun.

"So far all they have to offer are some theories," he says. "But they're going to put out some feel-ers."

"They?"

"It's a group of folks who monitor chat rooms for specific types of activity," he says. "They don't normally visit the kinds of places where you might find the folks we're interested in, but they're expe-rienced at creating online personas and infiltrat-ing certain groups. Mostly, they do it for gaming, or just for fun. But like I mentioned before, there are a few of them who are on the lookout for pervs and such, so they can warn people away, or even tip off the cops."

"I see." Since I'm not familiar with the environ-ments he's describing, I'm not sure I really do see, but that doesn't matter.

"Anyway, a couple of them are going to start hanging out in the places where these traffickers advertise their wares, to see what they can pick up."

"By 'wares,' you mean *children*?" I say in a disap-proving tone.

He sighs and pushes back from his desk, nearly running me over with his chair. "I don't mean to treat the issue lightly," he says, turning around and looking up at me through his thick glasses.

"I know. I'm sorry. It's just that this case is both-ering me more than most. It's hard for me to stay objective."

Arnie nods his understanding. "I get it. And if I

find anything at all, I'll be sure to let you know right away."

Before departing, I give his shoulder a squeeze, my way of cementing my apology and letting him know that I appreciate his efforts.

The police station is only a few blocks away, so I go to the library, grab my coat and gloves, and walk there. I enter through the front door and the on-duty dispatcher, Heidi, buzzes me through to the inner sanctum with a little finger wave as she talks to someone on the phone. I wander down the hallway past office doors until I reach the one that Bob Richmond and my husband share. I find both of them seated at their desks, tapping away at the keyboards in front of their computer screens.

"Hey, handsome," I say, walking over and looping an arm around Hurley's neck. I go to kiss his cheek, but he turns at the last second and we lock lips for a moment.

"Get a room, you two," Richmond grumbles.

"Aw, Bob, are you feeling left out?" I say. I release my hold on my husband and walk over to give Richmond a kiss on the cheek. He blushes a flaming red and rolls his eyes.

"For cripes sake, Mattie," he says, but I see a hint of a smile at the corners of his mouth.

"Should I be worried?" Hurley says, arching his eyebrows at me.

"Naw, just a friendly kiss," I say. "Although there is someone who's interested in giving Bob something more than friendship," I add in a teasing tone.

Richmond shoots me a look that is half frown, half curiosity.

"Do tell," Hurley says. "I hope she's serious, whoever she is, because he's been a real Debbie Downer ever since he split up with that Carpenter woman."

"Rose and I didn't split up," Richmond grumbles. "She just moved a little farther away."

"Southern California is more than a little farther," I say. "Kind of hard to keep a long-distance relationship going with that many miles between you. She might as well have moved to Venus."

Richmond sighs.

"So maybe it's time for you to move on," I say in a suggestive tone. "Remember that cute little social worker at the hospital, the one who's involved in the case of our dead girl?"

Richmond squints at me, looking clueless. It's obvious he didn't notice Hildy's attempts to flirt with him.

"She's in her midthirties, very single, *and* very interested in you."

Richmond shakes his head, frowning again. "I'm not ready for another relationship yet."

"Is that because you're so young you figure you have plenty of time to hook up?" Hurley says in a tone dripping with sarcasm. "I mean, why rush into things, right?"

Richmond says nothing, but communicates his thoughts on Hurley's comments with a bit of one-fingered sign language.

"Is there any chance of you moving to Southern California to be closer to Rose?" I ask Richmond.

He shoots me a look of disgust. "I've been to

Southern California, and you're right. It might as well be Venus. Never mind it being another state, it's like another planet there. It's no coincidence that the term 'road rage' started there. If you ask someone for directions, they tell you how far it is in terms of travel time rather than miles. And when the temperature gets down to sixty degrees, they drag out their sweaters and parkas and stand around shivering in the cold, clutching their ten-dollar, designer-coffee drinks, and wearing those stupid-looking boots with the funny name."

"UGG," I say.

"No kidding," Richmond affirms.

I start to clarify my comment, but decide to let it go. "And is there any chance Rose will move back up here?" I ask instead.

"She says she loves it there," Richmond grumbles. His face screws up in disgust and he adds, "Plus, she bought a house. She sent me pictures of it at Christmas, and it's all palm trees and sunshine. What the hell kind of Christmas is that?"

I get where he's coming from. Our winters here can be harsh and cruel, but Christmas without cold and snow wouldn't feel right somehow.

"Sounds to me like the writing is on the wall," Hurley says. "The only question now is, who's going to take the first plunge and call it off officially?"

Richmond lets forth with a weighty sigh. "I suppose you're right. But I'm not ready to start all over again."

I'm tempted to push the matter, but decide to give poor Richmond a reprieve. "Anyway," I say, "our Ms. Hildy came across an interesting bit of ev-

idence that might give us a lead." I then explain
about the candy bar and show them the picture of
it with the handwritten price sticker. "There can't
be that many stores that use this sort of pricing system," I say.

"It's worth a shot," Richmond says, and Hurley
nods in agreement.

"Arnie has the bar and he's going to see if he can
get a print off the adhesive side of the price sticker.
He's also working on the case from another angle."
I explain his theory about the Internet chat rooms
and what he and his cronies are up to.

"That's not a bad idea," Hurley says, and this
time it's Richmond who nods in agreement. "These
traffickers do a lot of their recruiting online. But
we have the police file from the guys who investigated the Paulsen girls' disappearances, and they
include a forensic analysis of their home computers and their online activities. Neither of them did
much stuff online. They didn't even have Internet
access at their home. That's not how they were
lured in."

"What about school computers?" I ask.

"It's possible, but not likely. The guys who investigated the case talked to students and faculty at
the schools, and their computers have blocks in
place for certain types of Web sites. They did a
search of the Internet histories on them and did-
n't find anything that looked promising."

"What about smartphones?" I ask.

Richmond shakes his head. "Liesel's was never
found. Lily's was, but it didn't show any Internet or
social-media stuff that was helpful. In fact, both
girls tended to be quiet loners. The only social-

media app they used was Instagram, and their participation there was minimal."

"Still, if Arnie can get a handle on the type of people who lure these kids in, maybe it will get us closer to finding Lily," I say hopefully.

"It might," Richmond says, but I get the feeling he's saying it merely to placate me. "I've got some guys I know at the FBI who work with this sort of stuff, looking into local activities. Maybe they'll come up with something. They have a task force of agents who do nothing but create online personas, pretending to be kids, hoping to lure the lurers."

"What are you working on now?" I ask Hurley, looking at the images on his computer screen.

"I've been trying to get video footage from as many traffic cams as we can to try to track the car Liesel was in," he says. "We were able to identify the make and model from the hospital security footage and, so far, we've been able to track the vehicle through town on its way to the hospital. No surprise, there's no evidence of the accident the guy claimed happened. We got a license plate number finally, but as we suspected, it was stolen. I'm trying now to track the car out of town, maybe back trace his route. If he took the interstate, we may be able to spot him, but if he stuck to the back roads, we're probably screwed."

"Fingers crossed," I say.

"Anything turn up in the autopsy?" Richmond asks.

"Possibly. Liesel was pregnant. We can get a DNA profile from the fetus, but I don't know if getting a DNA profile on the father will be helpful or not. Plus, it's likely to take weeks to get the results, and I don't know if Lily has that kind of time."

Richmond looks thoughtful. "It might help us in another way," he says, and both Hurley and I look at him. "A pregnancy isn't a desired outcome for these girls. I'm guessing that if anyone knew she was pregnant, they'd take steps to eliminate it, take her to someone who would abort it."

"But anyone performing that sort of abortion would likely be doing so unofficially," I say. "They wouldn't be able to just check her into a clinic somewhere. The risk of her saying something to someone would be too great."

"Precisely," Richmond says with a hint of a smile. He looks over at Hurley. "Put out some feelers to some of the other agencies to see if anyone can point us toward someone in the area who does that kind of thing." He shrugs. "Who knows? It might provide a lead."

Hurley nods, scribbles something on a pad on his desk, and then goes back to scrutinizing his screen.

"I hate to interrupt what you're doing," I say to Richmond, "but we need to go see Mr. Paulsen, deliver the bad news, and bring him back here to ID the body."

Richmond makes a face. "I hate that," he mutters, his shoulders sagging at the thought. "It seems so cruel."

"Sometimes it's a good thing," I say. "The loved ones need closure, and for some, seeing the actual body is the only way they can wrap their minds around the reality of it all. And at least Liesel's face isn't horribly deformed or anything. There are some bruises, but they're minor."

"Whatever," Richmond grumbles, unconvinced. He gets out of his chair and grabs his parka from a hook by the door. "Let's get this over with."

I kiss Hurley again and say, "See you later," before following Richmond through to the break room and out a back door that leads to the police station's secure parking lot.

The sky outside has changed from pearly gray to the color of tarnished silver, and the wind has picked up in terms of both ferocity and bitterness. It nips at every area of exposed skin I have and I'm grateful when I climb into Richmond's car—a nondescript, twelve-year-old sedan—and shut the door.

"I apologize for the cold," Richmond says nonsensically. I'm about to point out the ridiculousness of his statement when he adds, "I mean the cold in my car. My heater doesn't work very well."

"I'll be fine," I say. "I have plenty of natural insulation."

Richmond says nothing more as he starts the car and pulls out, and he remains silent until we are on a highway outside of town. It will take us about half an hour to get to where Mr. Paulsen is now living, and at this rate, it promises to be a long and awkward drive.

"I hope you aren't upset with me for pushing that social worker on you," I say finally, determined to warm up the atmosphere in the car, even if the actual atmosphere is still freezing.

Richmond pooh-poohs this with a little *pfft* and a spasmodic shake of his head. "No biggie," he says.

"Relationships are hard," I say. "Even when things are generally good."

I see Richmond shoot me a sidelong glance. "Are you and Hurley having problems?"

"No, not really," I say. "I mean, we get along great, and he's a wonderful husband and father. And we love our new house. It's got plenty of room and it fits us well. Plus, it's ours, not his or mine."

"Was that an issue?"

"For me, it was," I admit. "Living in Hurley's house was . . . I don't know . . . a bit awkward, I guess. I always felt like I was visiting rather than living there. Silly, I know, but . . ." I shrug.

"Oh, I get it," Richmond says. There is silence for a minute or so, and then he says, "You know, Rose asked me to move in with her at one point, before she decided to go out to California."

"I didn't know that. What did you tell her?"

"I told her I wasn't ready for that yet. My house is no big deal, but it's mine. I've been a bachelor all my life, and that house is organized and situated the way I want it. It suits my lifestyle, my interests, and my tastes. The thought of giving it up to move into Rose's place, which was just as uniquely hers, with lots of pink and lacy crap . . . Well, it made me break out in a sweat when I thought about it. And the idea of her moving into my place? That was even worse. I would have resented her presence there. I know it."

"It's very astute of you to realize that."

"Oh, I don't know," Richmond says with a shrug and a smile. "I don't think it takes any great degree of insight to know that I'm going to have a hard time adapting to a life shared with anyone else."

"I think we all have a hard time with that," I say. "It seems easy at first because you're so in love with a person, and you feel like you'd be willing to sacrifice anything, do anything, *be* anything, just so you can be with them. But eventually the shiny finish on that new relationship wears off, revealing the rust and dull metal beneath. And after a while, you start to question how much of yourself you're willing to give up to make someone else happy."

"So what is Hurley asking you to give up?"

"Nothing, really," I say, hedging. "I feel like I won the relationship lottery when it comes to Hurley because he doesn't really ask much of anything from me. But that doesn't mean there aren't things I've had to give up or take on that I didn't necessarily want. I mean, I didn't see myself as the stepmother to a teenage daughter, but it happened. If I wanted to be with Hurley, Emily was part of that package. I took it on, and was happy to do so at first. But there were moments . . ."

"Yeah, that kid was a challenge for a while," Richmond says. "But you can hardly blame her. Look how much her life was turned upside down. Look at what she had to give up."

"I know, and while at times it's been a rocky road—one of my favorite ice-cream flavors, by the way—to get to where we are today, it was well worth it. I love that girl as if she was my own."

I feel a certain kinship with Emily because we

were both raised by a mother who was flighty and dishonest. Kate lied to her daughter for the first fourteen years of her life by telling her that her father was dead, and she also lied to Hurley fourteen years earlier when she made him think they were divorced, even though she never filed the papers. Things came to a head when Kate discovered she was dying. She reappeared in Hurley's life by showing up on his doorstep one evening with Emily in tow. Hurley not only didn't know he was still married to her, but he had no idea that they'd had a child together.

My relationship with Hurley was still somewhat new and very complicated at the time, since I'd just discovered I was pregnant. Kate died a few months after she came back into Hurley's life, and Emily found herself without the only parent she had ever known, thrust into a living situation with a father she never knew she had, and the threat of the new family that Hurley was starting with me. Talk about feeling like a third wheel. Emily acted out in a predictable fashion, and at one point, I was a bit afraid of the girl. But some counseling, patience, time, and a near-death experience helped Emily come to grips with her new living situation.

"Something is bothering you," Richmond says. "Is it the kids?"

I let out a little laugh. "I suppose in a way it is," I say. "Not the existing ones, though." Then, with a derisive smile, I add, "Although there are days when Matthew pushes my buttons until I'm ready to go off like a nuclear blast. His latest thing is taking off into another room when I'm distracted for even a few seconds and getting himself into trouble. The other day when I was on the phone, he managed to sneak into the downstairs bathroom and unroll an entire roll of toilet paper. He seems to think mealtime is also free art time, because he likes to fling food around the room. If it wasn't for Hoover cleaning up after him, my kitchen would look like a food abattoir. I bought a couple of those kiddie gates to try to confine him better, for when I'm doing stuff at home, but he figured out how to dismantle them in two days. One of his favorite foods is those goldfish crackers, and he's smashed so many of them into the carpet in the living room that Hoover spends half his day in there, just licking the rug. I've learned not to walk in that room with bare feet, because if you want to avoid the wet spots, it's like trying to play a game of Twister. He's a full-time job, that kid. Finding any kind of private time for Hurley and me is practically impossible. We manage now and then, though perhaps not as good as we could. Sometimes sheer exhaustion overwhelms us and wins the day."

"Well, you've certainly made me feel better about *not* having children," Richmond says after a moment. "Are you happy?"

I give the question some serious thought, but it only takes me a few seconds to come up with the answer. "I'm probably crazy, but, yes, I am," I tell him honestly. "Life is good."

"And yet?"

I shoot Richmond an annoyed look.

"Don't try to deny it," he says. "I may not have a lot of experience in the relationship department personally, but I've been a detective for a lot of years. I know how to read people. And there is something that's troubling you."

He's right, and I silently curse his ability to suss this out. I don't have to discuss it, of course, but I find that I want to. I need to. "You have to promise me, you won't repeat anything I say to Hurley."

"My lips are sealed. Besides, your husband and I don't talk about personal stuff much anyway."

"Hurley wants to have another kid."

There is a tick of silence before Richmond says, "And?"

"No 'and.' That's it. He wants to have *another* kid."

"Oh. And you don't?"

"I don't know," I say. "I'm kind of split on the issue, though I have to admit that the split is about seventy percent *no* to thirty percent *yes*. Actually, it's thirty percent 'I'll think about it.' "

"I see. How hard is Hurley pushing the issue?"

"Not real hard, but he keeps bringing it up. He's been bringing it up since shortly after Matthew was born. At first, I thought he was just mesmerized by the wonder of fatherhood and all that, but Matthew has revealed the ugly behind the mask by now, and Hurley still keeps bringing it up."

"Okay, so he definitely wants another kid. What makes you not want one?"

I blow out a breath that makes my lips vibrate. "Where do I start? To begin with, being pregnant is no real treat."

"I thought you women loved being pregnant," Richmond says. "Getting to eat for two, the whole Madonna thing, the glow everyone talks about—"

"Puking for several months, not being able to drink any alcohol, having to pee all the time, not being able to have coffee, swollen ankles, not that you can see your ankles toward the end when you look like a beached whale."

"Well, there's the wonder of bringing a new life into the world, of feeling it grow and move inside you," Richmond counters, jumping on the pro-and-con wagon with enthusiasm.

His voice is reverent, and it makes me flash back to those moments during my pregnancy with Matthew when I felt him kick, or hiccup, or stretch out, and what a feeling of wonder and joy it gave me. Richmond was there when I delivered Matthew in the bathtub of Izzy's cottage, which is where I lived at the time. I remember him telling me how gratified he was to have had the privilege of seeing it.

"Yeah, there is that," I admit to Richmond. "But pregnancy is not kind to one's body, and when all is said and done, there's this tiny little life that is cute and adorable and the sweetest thing you can possibly imagine, but it also robs you of sleep, good hygienic practices, and your sanity. It's not that I wouldn't want to have another kid with Hurley, it's that I don't know if I want to go through the whole pregnancy thing again, or those early months of infancy. Plus, in case you haven't noticed, I'm not a spring chicken anymore, Richmond. I'm pushing forty and the risk of birth defects increases with every year that goes by. If I could just snap my fingers and have some healthy and delightful little girl appear who is already toilet trained and done with her terrible twos I wouldn't hesitate."

"A little girl, eh?" Richmond asks, arching his eyebrows. "You'd like to have a daughter?"

I shrug. "Not necessarily," I say. "I'd be content with another boy. Though I have to admit, this whole penis thing has been a real eye-opener for me. I grew up with a sister and a mother. I had no idea how early the penis fascination starts."

"Maybe you should consider giving up your job," Richmond says. "The stress of trying to balance motherhood with a career may be part of the problem."

"I don't want to give up my job. I love what I do. And I only do it part-time."

"Does Hurley help you out?"

"He does," I say with a smile. "In fact, I think he helps out a lot more than most husbands and fathers do. He's very hands-on with Matthew, and he's always chipping in around the house with errands and cleanup."

"That's good."

"I know." I let out a deep sigh. "What should I do, Richmond? Should I go ahead and give in? I mean, I don't think Hurley is going to let the matter drop. Clearly, it means a lot to him. Am I being too selfish?"

"Oh . . . no," Richmond says in a cautionary tone. "I can't answer that for you. No one can. You need to resolve this in your own mind. Weigh all the pros and cons, and decide where you fall on the issue. Once you know that, you need to be honest with Hurley about your decision."

He's right, of course. And while I'm no closer to

having an answer than I was when we started our trip, the simple act of talking about it has helped.

Further discussion on the matter has to be waylaid, however, because we have arrived at the house in Necedah where Kurt Paulsen lives, and once again I'm reminded of how petty and unimportant my issues are in comparison to the devastating happenings in other lives.

Chapter 10

Kurt Paulsen looks like a man who has dedicated his life to a family farm. His skin is tanned and weathered, creased like an old leather chair. His hair is dark blond with sun streaks of yellow, and cropped short. One of the fingers on his left hand—the little one—is missing from the first joint up, and I'd bet money that he lost it in a farming accident. His arms are long and sinewy beneath the rolled-up sleeves of a plaid flannel shirt that has seen better days. The jeans he is wearing hang a bit loose on his lanky frame, and I wonder if he's recently lost weight.

While his face bears the markings of a man who has worked hard and spent a lot of time outdoors, it also has the look of someone who is haunted. His cheekbones are sharp and chiseled, the flesh beneath them hollow. The corners of his mouth are turned down, the lower lip sticking out almost defiantly. His eyes are an interesting shade of spinach green, or at least it would be interesting if they didn't look so dead.

What little life might have been hiding in Kurt Paulsen's face flees the moment Richmond identifies himself. He stares at Richmond, not blinking. For a second, I think perhaps he has stopped breathing, but when I look at his chest, I see the faint rise there. A little higher up, I see his pulse throbbing in his neck, and watch it speed up as the seconds tick by. The only other movement I can detect is the twitching of a muscle in his jaw, the result of him clenching his teeth, no doubt bracing himself for the blow I can tell he knows is coming.

"May we come in?" Richmond asks. He has introduced the both of us as being from the Sorenson Police Department, most likely not wanting to broadcast the bad news by announcing the presence of someone from the medical examiner's office. But I can tell it won't matter to Mr. Paulsen. He knows he is about to get some of the worst news of his life.

He hasn't answered Richmond's question, and he hasn't moved, either.

"Mr. Paulsen," I say, reaching over and taking hold of his right hand, which is hanging limply at his side. "We need to talk with you about your daughters." I keep my voice low and even. "Can we go inside to do that?" He shifts his gaze from Richmond to me, but nothing else moves. I take a step closer and then slide past him on the left, still holding on to his right hand. This forces him to either pull loose of my grip or turn with me. He turns.

This little bit of movement seems to awaken

him from his shocked state. He strides ahead of me, pulling his hand free of mine. We follow him down a hallway, past a stairwell on the right, a living room on the left, a bathroom beneath the stairs, and a dining room on the left. At the end of the hallway is the kitchen, and he walks over to an old wooden table in the center of the room and indicates the chairs around it.

"Sit," he says. "Can I get you a drink of some sort?"

Richmond and I both decline, confirming our choices by shaking our heads. We sit—me at one end of the table, Richmond on the side—and once we are settled, Mr. Paulsen pulls out the chair across from Richmond and sits. His movements are controlled and unhurried, and his face is utterly blank, without expression or emotion of any kind. The man is an automaton, a robot, and I know that this is the only way he can maintain control for the moment.

Richmond opens his mouth to speak and gets out, "Mr. Paulsen," before he's interrupted.

"Are they dead?" Paulsen asks. His outer visage may not show signs of stress, but his voice does. It cracks slightly, and I suspect he is only a beat or two away from breaking down.

Richmond hesitates, and I can tell he's rehearsing his response, searching through the many platitudes and aphorisms we are taught to use in times like this. But I sense that Mr. Paulsen needs the stark truth now, blunt and up front.

"Only one of them," I tell him. "And we aren't a hundred percent sure it's her, sir."

He looks at me and his shoulders sag visibly. His eyes close ever so slowly. "Which one?"

"We think it's Liesel. I'm so very sorry."

He opens his eyes and looks at me, his head nodding almost imperceptibly. "I want to see her."

"You may," I tell him. "In fact, we need you to confirm her identity for us. We don't have any dental records or fingerprints we can use. Though if you can point us to a dentist the girls went to . . ."

Paulsen looks away, his expression pained. "We didn't have a dentist," he says. "Did when the girls were little, but when he died, we never found another one." He winces and adds, "Couldn't really afford one."

"Did Liesel have any birthmarks?" I ask.

Paulsen taps a nervous finger on the table, his expression thoughtful. "Sort of," he says. "She has two small moles on her upper belly, one below each nipple. The doc said they were accessory nipples. We used to tease her about being a changeling." He smiles at the memory for a few seconds, and then the smile fades and he looks back at me. His eyes hold my gaze, refusing to release me, searching for the truth. In any other situation, or with any other person, the intensity of that gaze would be uncomfortable. But for whatever reason, Mr. Paulsen's stare doesn't bother me.

"How?" he asks after several seconds.

I wince, and his eyes flit away from mine for a millisecond. I know he senses that what I'm about to tell him won't be easy to hear, but the return of that steady, unflinching gaze tells me he wants to . . . needs to hear the truth.

"Severe trauma," I say as gently as I can. "She was brought into the emergency room, and—"

"Who?" Paulsen asks through clenched teeth, his face a maelstrom of emotion. "Who brought her to the hospital?"

Richmond finally finds his voice. "A man. We don't know who he is, because he gave a false name and left shortly after dropping her off. But we have some leads and we're working tirelessly to find out who and where he is."

Paulsen, his facial muscles twitching and his finger still tapping out a beat on the tabletop, stares at Richmond. Then he drops his gaze and says, "Give me a moment."

He pushes back his chair and stands. Slowly, methodically, he walks around the table and shuffles down the hallway toward the front door. Richmond and I exchange a questioning look, both of us frozen to the spot for the moment. We hear the steady plod of footsteps climbing the stairs, and then the fall of his feet overhead.

"Should we go after him?" I say. "You don't think he'd hurt himself, do you?"

Richmond looks back at me, indecision stamped on his face. We hear the sound of a door closing overhead, then more footsteps. A second later, we hear Paulsen begin his descent on the stairs. In some form of unspoken understanding and agreement, Richmond and I both get up and hurry down the hall to meet him.

Paulsen rounds the newel post and looks at us, a coat draped over his arm. "I just need my car keys," he says. He shrugs his coat on and then reaches over to a small table by the door, where he grabs a set of keys.

"I'd feel better if you would let us drive you," Richmond says. "We'll bring you back home again afterward."

Paulsen looks at him, considering this. I half expect him to object . . . or perhaps explode suddenly. His quiet, robotic movements are unnerving, like the stillness in the air just before a storm hits. But in the end, all he does is nod and open the front door. He steps aside so we can exit the house ahead of him, and as soon as we are out, he follows, pulling the front door closed behind him, and then using the keys he picked up to lock it. He drops the keys into his coat pocket and falls into step behind us. I can see gloves sticking out of his coat pockets, but he doesn't put them on. Nor does he bother to button up his coat. It's freezing outside, but you'd never know it from looking at Paulsen. I suspect he's numb at this point.

Richmond opens the front passenger door, holding it for Paulsen. Without a word, the man settles inside and goes about putting on his seat belt. Richmond eases the door closed and heads for the driver's seat, while I climb into the backseat behind Paulsen.

The first five minutes of our drive go by in a silence heavy with emotion and meaning, like a storm cloud about to burst. Paulsen stares out the side window at the passing scenery, and though what little I can see of his face appears impassive, I sense a churning just below the surface. I can only imagine the thoughts going through his mind and consider letting the silence reign. But after seeing Richmond shoot me an uncomfortable look in the rearview mirror, I decide to try to engage Paulsen. His surface stoicism concerns me; I want to see some level of emotion in that craggy face.

"Mr. Paulsen," I begin in a low, even voice, "I understand you've spent a lot of time looking for your girls." I pause for a few seconds before continuing, studying his profile as he continues to stare out the window. "We'd be interested in knowing what you might have found."

This gets a reaction. His eyes, or at least the one I can see, narrow. A muscle in his cheek twitches, and to my surprise, he smiles, but it's hard and brittle.

"*Now* you want to know what I might have found?" he says bitterly. He turns and glares at Richmond. "The local cops won't even take my calls anymore. They tell me they're doing everything they can, and that I need to trust them to do their job." He spits out a mirthless, sardonic laugh. "So much for trust. Look where it got me. One daughter dead and the other still missing."

Richmond's hands flex on the steering wheel and he shifts nervously in his seat.

"Mr. Paulsen," I say quickly, "I understand why you might feel frustrated and angry."

Like a whirling dervish, he spins around beneath his shoulder belt and glares at me over the back of the seat. "Do you?" he snaps in a tightly controlled tone. The suddenness of his movement makes Richmond flinch, but to his credit, he maintains his grip on the wheel and keeps the car straight on the road.

"How in the hell could you possibly understand what I'm feeling?" Paulsen continues, his voice oscillating like a sine wave. "Have you lost a child? Better yet, have you lost two children and a wife, all in the space of a year?"

I open my mouth to say no, and to apologize, but before I can utter a word, he continues.

"The gall of you people!" he says with such vehemence that a spray of spittle flies from his mouth, landing on the seat back. "You're nothing but a worthless bunch of smug assholes, spewing out promising garbage, but not doing a damned thing!"

Richmond has let off on the gas and I sense he is preparing to pull over, concerned that Paulsen is about to go ballistic. Desperate, I search for something to do or say that will calm the man, or at least break his building anger.

"Your daughters were together," I say quickly. "Liesel spoke of Lily."

Paulsen, whose mouth is opening in preparation for another blast, freezes suddenly, gaping at me. He blinks several times, and then closes his mouth with an audible clicking of his teeth. "What?" he says after a few seconds.

"Liesel was able to speak to the staff at the hospital," I say in as calm a voice as I can muster. Richmond is letting the car coast, and he looks from the road to Paulsen and back again, ready to pull over if necessary. "She mentioned Lily, said we needed to help her because he had her, too, referring to the man who brought her to the ER. So we have good reason not only to believe that Lily is alive, but that the man who was with Liesel might provide a lead to her."

Paulsen's body sags, and he squeezes his eyes shut.

I reach up and place a hand on his shoulder. "We're going to do everything we can to find her," I say. "We weren't able to save Liesel, but we're going to find Lily." I say this with great determination, realizing as the words leave my mouth that I'm sticking my neck out, making a promise I don't know I can keep. But my instincts tell me it's time to go Scarlett O'Hara on this problem and not worry about other possibilities until tomorrow. For now, this is what Paulsen needs to hear.

Tears leak from beneath the man's closed lids, weaving a path down his cheeks. He turns back to face the front of the car, letting his head fall back against the headrest. I feel the car pick up speed, and glance at Richmond in the mirror. He gives me a slight nod.

Even though I can't see his face any longer, I feel Paulsen's shoulder heave beneath my hand and know he is crying. I give him a small squeeze and then let go, sitting back in my own seat, letting him grieve in as much privacy as we can afford within the confines of the car.

Chapter 11

The remainder of our trip goes by without incident. By the time we pull into the underground garage of my office, Mr. Paulsen has regained his composure and is once again dry-eyed and stoic. As soon as Richmond parks the car, Paulsen releases his belt and climbs out. He stands there a moment, looking around the garage. Then he heads for the elevator, intuiting that this is the way he needs to go.

Richmond and I exchange looks of relief and I hurry to catch up to Paulsen, walking alongside him. I summon the elevator and, once it arrives, we all step inside and I use my ID badge to access the first floor. I sent a text message to Izzy to let him know we were close when we were a few minutes out, so I know things will be ready for us.

Our office doesn't have drawers for the bodies. Instead, we have a large, walk-in refrigerator that will hold a half-dozen stretchers if necessary. We rarely have more than two or three bodies in there at one time. It isn't an ideal spot for a family member to view a body, given the cold, the starkness of the interior, and the potential presence of other bodies. Nor is the autopsy suite, with all its equipment and smells. For moments such as this one, we have a small room that was originally designated to be a storage closet located just past the entrance to the library. Izzy had part of the wall knocked out and a viewing window put in years ago, and a curtain hangs on the inside of that window. Depending on the situation, a family member has the option of viewing the deceased from outside the room through the window, or entering the room and seeing the body up close. There is a chair just inside the door, and if a loved one is going to enter the room, we make sure the stretcher is wheeled in so that the head is near this chair and the door, in case a quick escape is needed or desired.

Identification of a body in this manner is certainly not ideal, and we try to avoid it whenever possible. But in the case of Liesel Paulsen, all we have to go on is a driver's license picture.

I steer Mr. Paulsen with a light touch on his elbow to the viewing room, and we stop outside the closed door. Richmond hangs in the hallway several feet from us, within hearing distance but far enough away to give us a sense of privacy.

"Mr. Paulsen," I say, stepping between him and the door to the room, "we have several options. I texted our medical examiner regarding the moles you mentioned, and he confirmed their presence. He said that if you don't want to look at Liesel, he's comfortable enough making an identification based on that information and her DMV photo."

"I want to see her." He was back in robotic mode.

"Okay, then we still have a couple of options. You can look through the glass in this window"—I point toward the glass—"or at pictures we took. Or if you want, you can go into the room."

He looks back at me, surprisingly clear-eyed. "I want to go in," he says without hesitation.

"Then there are some things I would like to tell you before we go in. Dr. Rybarceski has performed an autopsy on Liesel, and because of that she has some incisions in her body."

"I know what gets done," he says in a tight voice. "I'm a farmer, and we raised livestock."

"Yes, but this isn't a cow or a pig. It's your daughter. If you want to lower the sheets enough to see her body I won't stop you. But I don't recommend it."

He nods, but says nothing.

"Also, I want to prepare you for the way her face looks. She has some bruising."

His breath hitches for a second and he squeezes his eyes closed. Then he opens them, looks at me, and says, "Let's do this."

I turn and open the door. The room is equipped with a fluorescent fixture in the ceiling, and the harsh light from it is reflected off the white covering draped over the body on the stretcher. Once again, I steer Mr. Paulsen with a touch on his arm, and we stop at the head of the stretcher.

"There is a chair behind you," I say to him, taking hold of one corner of the covering. "If at any point you feel you need to, please sit down."

He nods, his Adam's apple bobbing frantically. His eyes are glued to the covering, and I sense that he has braced himself for what's to come.

I grab the top edge of the cover and pull it back, revealing Liesel's head and the tops of her bare shoulders. I position the drape just above her collarbone, not wanting to go lower and reveal the autopsy incision.

The transformation on Paulsen's face is stunning. In an instant, the craggy lines soften, the hard muscles relax, and his eyes widen, shining with both love and sadness. He tilts his head to one side and stares at his daughter, his lips quivering. "Oh, little Liesel," he says with a sob. "How did this happen?" Tears flood his eyes and course down his face, dripping off his chin. I stand beside him, letting him look for as long as he wants.

His cry is short-lived. The stoic farmer returns. "Can I touch her?" he asks.

"Of course."

Izzy has taken great care to hide as much of the scalp incision as possible, and despite the fact that I know Liesel's facial skin was peeled off her skull to expose the bone so that Izzy could open it and remove her brain, she doesn't look all that different from the way she did before the autopsy. Izzy has done some of his best work here, but despite it, Liesel Paulsen still looks dead. And I know she will also feel dead. I kind of hope Mr. Paulsen won't touch his daughter. That cold, rubbery feel of dead skin can be devastating.

Holding my breath, I watch as he reaches toward her with a tentative hand. He stops just short of her cheek, the hand hovering there for several seconds. Then he moves his hand a little to the side, caressing her hair where it lies on the cart beneath her. His eyes well up again, and he looks down the length of the covering, his fingers gently stroking through her hair, combing it. After a moment he sucks in a harsh breath, coughs, and quickly withdraws his hand. He swallows audibly, turns, and leaves the room.

I follow him out into the hall, where he is doing his best to compose himself. "I'm so sorry, Mr. Paulsen," I say.

He nods, a spastic gesture, and sucks in a ragged breath. He lets it out slowly, and when he has fully exhaled, he looks at me. "Thank you," he says.

I almost blurt out "You're welcome," out of habit, but stop myself, realizing it would seem inappropriate. So I simply nod and say, "I really am so sorry for your loss." There is a hitch in my voice, my own emotions roiling just below the surface as I struggle to maintain control. I can't control it all, however, and tears well in my eyes. Mr. Paulsen sees this and manages half a smile.

The moment is broken when my phone rings. I glance at the screen and see that it's Hurley, but even though I'm dying to talk with him, I can't bring myself to dismiss Mr. Paulsen so readily, so I swipe the screen to silence the ring and ignore the call. I glance down the hall at Richmond, who is still standing several feet away, leaning against the wall, hands in his pockets. He catches my eye and I give a sideways nod toward Mr. Paulsen. He catches my meaning right away, pushes away from the wall, and comes toward us.

"Mr. Paulsen," Richmond says in a soft voice, "if you're up to it, I'd like to go over some things about the case with you. I know you feel let down by the police up until now, and that's understandable, given what has happened. But I promise you that I'm devoting all of my time and energy to finding out who did this to Liesel, and finding your other daughter, Lily. Will you talk to me, tell me what you know?"

Paulsen has the tired, cynical look of a man who's been lied to, or, at the least, led on, one too many times. He studies Richmond's face, weighing his sincerity. Richmond holds the man's gaze unflinching, stalwart in his commitment. Apparently, Paulsen likes what he sees, because after a bit, he nods, smiles, and says, "Yes, I would like that."

"You can use the library," I say, and Richmond nods. Then he cups Mr. Paulsen's elbow and steers him in that direction.

As soon as they are out of earshot, I take out my phone and call Hurley.

He answers with, "Are you back yet?" forgoing any formal greeting.

"We are. We just finished with the identification. Richmond took Mr. Paulsen into the library to talk with him before he sends him back home."

"Are you okay?"

"As much as I can be. Though I have a strong urge to go home and hug our kids right now."

Hurley makes a noise, somewhere between a grunt and a sigh. After a brief silence, he says, "I don't know if it will help, but I have some good news."

"I could use it. We all could."

"I got lucky with the street cams and I found our guy. A camera caught him getting on I-90 westbound at the Deforest exit. It's a great shot. I can not only see the guy driving, but I can see Liesel sitting next to him."

This *is* good news. "If he got onto the interstate there, the store where they got the candy bar might be somewhere near that exit," I say. "Are there any little mom-and-pop convenience stores nearby?"

"There is. I just called them and the woman who answered said they use the kind of stickers we found on that candy bar."

"I don't suppose they have any security cameras," I say, figuring that if they're old-school when it comes to pricing and scanning, the odds of this are small.

"As luck would have it, they do," Hurley says, and I feel my heart give a little leap of hope. "They just had it installed. The owner told me her grandkids have been trying to shame her into upgrading her technology, and the security cameras were the first thing she agreed to. I'm about to head there now to take a look. Unless Richmond wants to do it."

"I suspect he might," I say. "He's definitely squirming with Mr. Paulsen." I glance at my watch and see that it's nearly three in the afternoon. "Let me go and talk to Richmond to see what he wants to do. I'll call you right back."

"Okay." With no further ado, he disconnects the call.

I find Richmond and Mr. Paulsen seated at the conference table in the library. I crook a finger at Richmond from the doorway, and he excuses himself for a moment, gets up, and joins me in the hall.

"Hurley has some news about the case," I say in a low voice. "He found the store where the candy bar came from and they have security cameras. He wants to know if he should go there, or if you want to."

Richmond looks like a man who's just been given a death sentence reprieve. "I'll go," he says, sounding eager to escape. "Just as soon as I arrange for a uniformed officer to drive Mr. Paulsen home."

We enter the room together, and Richmond announces his plan for getting Paulsen home.

"Actually," Mr. Paulsen says, "I think I'll stay here in town for the night. I'd like to be close by, in case . . ." He drifts off, leaving the obvious unstated.

"I'll have someone drive you to a motel, if you like," Richmond says.

Paulsen nods, his brow furrowed in thought. "I should have brought my car," he mutters.

"The local cab service will drive you anywhere you want in town for two-fifty," I tell him. "And I'm sure that when you're ready to go home, the police department will arrange transportation for you." I give Richmond a questioning look.

"Absolutely," he says. "Let me make some calls."

"Will you call Hurley back?" I say, and he nods. He exits the room, leaving me alone with Mr. Paulsen. "Can I get you something to drink, Mr. Paulsen? A cup of coffee or a soda?"

He shakes his head. "No, thanks. I'm fine." He sighs, and then says, "What will happen to Liesel now?"

I settle into a chair catty-corner from him. "You will need to make some funeral arrangements," I say. "There are a couple of funeral homes here in town I can put you in touch with. They can make the necessary arrangements for you."

He nods, wincing a bit at the thought. He looks wretched and miserable, and it tears at my heart. I can only imagine the pain he is feeling, and I reach over to lay a comforting hand atop one of his.

"Mr. Paulsen, I wish I had some magic words for you, something I could say that would make all this more tolerable, or less painful for you. But I don't. I can't begin to fathom what you're feeling, but even though the loss of Liesel must be ripping you apart inside, I want you to stay strong for Lily. There is hope for her still, and we aren't giving up on her. In fact, we're going to do everything in our power to find her."

To my surprise, he manages a wan smile. If he is aware that these comments are a slight backtracking from the confidence of my earlier ones, he doesn't let on. "Thank you," he says. "I don't suppose . . ." He stops and looks away, swallowing hard. When he looks at me again, the sadness in his eyes has been replaced by a hard glint. "I mean, is there any chance that if they find this man who brought Liesel to the ER I could have a few minutes alone with him?"

My hand is still on his and I pull it back slowly, licking my lips, stalling. While I understand where this emotion is coming from, the tone in his voice and the fierce look on his face are disturbing. Something primal and ugly is still roiling just beneath the surface in this man.

"No, that isn't going to happen," I say carefully, trying not to sound judgmental. "Though I certainly understand the sentiment behind it."

He doesn't look at all dissuaded by my comments.

"You have to understand that the man in question may not have had anything to do with Liesel's disappearance initially, or even with her condition when she arrived in the ER. He has some role in what happened to her, no doubt, but we suspect your daughters were both victims of a human-trafficking ring that is much bigger and more involved than this one man. He might be nothing more than an errand boy, someone's lackey. So while I certainly understand your desire to see this man punished, it's important to keep focused on the bigger issue."

Paulsen's eyes narrow as I speak and he stares off into space, giving me the distinct impression that he is mentally exercising his revenge on some nondescript man. But when I'm done, he refocuses and his eyes soften. His shoulders sag, and I know that the moment has passed . . . for now.

Richmond comes back into the room with Brenda Joiner on his heels.

"Mr. Paulsen, this is Officer Joiner. She will drive you to the Sorenson Motel. We've already booked a room for you there for one night, on us."

Paulsen looks pleasantly surprised by this. He gets up and nods at Brenda before looking at Richmond. "Will you keep me informed of your progress in the case?"

"As much as I can," Richmond says.

Paulsen frowns at this equivocation, but lets it go.

Brenda, in a show of brilliant intuitive timing, chooses this moment to step up and take hold of Paulsen's arm. "Come with me, sir, and I'll get you settled." She deftly steers Paulsen from the room, and as they walk down the hallway, I hear her chatting with him about the coming weather, always a common and safe topic of conversation in Wisconsin, particularly in the winter.

Richmond rakes a hand through his hair, his eyes big. "Phew!" he says. "That was intense."

"It was."

"I'm going to head for that convenience store now," he says. "Unless you need something else from me?"

"No, I'm good. Go ahead. I'm going to finish some stuff up here and then hopefully head home. Let us know what you find, okay?"

"Will do."

* * *

Richmond leaves and I go back to the viewing room to get Liesel's body and return it to the fridge. Before leaving the cooler, I lift the cover on her body and look for the two moles her father had described. They are there all right, and I realize then that some small part of me was hoping they wouldn't be, that it was all a big mistake, and Liesel was still alive out there somewhere. Feeling sadness wash over me, I cover her up and head for Izzy's office to update him.

"All done?" Izzy says when I knock on his opened office door. He is working on the mountains of paperwork that go with his job.

"Yes, we are."

"Was it awful?" he asks, grimacing.

"It was intense, but it could've been worse. I can only imagine the pain that man has gone through."

Izzy nods, and for the next few seconds, neither of us speaks as we ponder the horror of this parental nightmare.

"You did a phenomenal job on Liesel's body, and I think that helped," I say eventually, trying to find something good in the middle of all this sobering sadness. "She looked good, considering."

"Thanks," he says. "I worked hard on her. I couldn't help but imagine that it was me in that man's position, looking at Juliana."

"It's hard not to make comparisons like that," I say.

"This is going to be a tough one, Mattie. You have to realize that we may never be able to figure out who's behind Liesel's death. Our best hope right now is to find her sister. At least that way Liesel's death isn't totally in vain. Have the cops made any progress?"

"Some," I say. And then I update him on the latest findings. When I'm done, I leave his office and go back to the library, settling in at my desk. I wake up my computer in preparation for tackling my never-ending stack of paperwork. This part of my job can be tedious at times, but there are occasions when I welcome it. The boring, by-rote processes involved provide a welcome distraction from some of the harsher, grittier aspects of my job. Today, however, I find it hard to focus. My mind keeps alternating between images of Mr. Paulsen and his grief-stricken, wounded face, and Liesel's beautiful, but bruised and lifeless, face. I muddle through the best I can, trying to turn the dark part of my brain off, but it's like an itch I can't quite reach. A little before five, I give up, shut my computer down, and call Hurley.

"I'm done for the day," I tell him. "Are you going to be home for dinner?"

"I'll grab something here," he says, and I frown with disappointment. I had figured this would be the case, but hope springs eternal. "Richmond should be back soon with the security footage from that store, and I'm working on some contacts to get a lead on docs who do abortions that aren't strictly on the up-and-up."

"Okay. Try not to work too late."

"Give Matthew a kiss for me," he says, letting me know that he isn't planning on being home before our son's bedtime.

"I will. Love you."

"I love you, too."

I hang up and head home, feeling an almost desperate need not only to see Emily and Matthew, but hug them both tightly and never let go.

Chapter 12

I swing by Izzy and Dom's place to pick up Matthew and find him on his stomach on the living-room floor, working on a wooden puzzle that consists of six giant pieces. Juliana is sitting next to him, and every time Matthew puts a puzzle piece in place, she promptly removes it and sets it on the floor.

"They've been doing that for nearly an hour now," Dom says as the two of us stand nearby, watching them. "I keep expecting Matthew to get mad at her, but he doesn't. He's very patient and even laughs sometimes when she takes his pieces out. He's a sweet kid, Mattie."

This tiny bit of praise warms my heart until I remember the temper tantrum Matthew had in the grocery store back in December when I refused to buy the box of sugar-crusted cereal he wanted. The only reason he wanted it was because he liked the picture of the cartoon animals on the front of the box. I'd bought the cereal once before because he asked for it, and he hated the stuff and wouldn't eat it. That didn't matter on this occasion, however. When I said no, Matthew flung himself sideways in the cart seat, a dramatic effort worthy of an Oscar. Then he proceeded to kick his feet, cry, and tell me he hated me. I did my best to ignore this outburst and smile placidly at the shoppers who stared at us, some of them looking annoyed, some of them looking judgmental, and one slightly disheveled woman wearing stained clothing and mismatched shoes, pushing a cart loaded with kiddie food, who looked sympathetic.

Matthew kept up his theatrics, increasing his volume, all the way through the checkout line and into the parking lot. Once he was in the car, he was so exhausted from his efforts that he fell instantly asleep in his car seat, a flushed, sweaty mess despite the cold temperatures outside. It was such a relief to have him quiet, I decided to drive around for a while rather than heading straight home. I didn't want to wake him, but I didn't feel like I could leave him in the car in the driveway in the midst of near-zero temperatures, either. So I'd driven around for half an hour, touring neighborhoods in town and checking out the holiday decorations. When I did finally go home, realizing as I unpacked my groceries that the ice cream I'd bought had melted, Matthew had miraculously transformed into the sweet, leg-hugging, thumb-sucking, "wuv-you-mammy" toddler I adored. Some days, my son was like Dr. Jekyll and Mr. Hyde.

I thank Dom for watching my son, give Juliana a

kiss and a hug, and then pack Matthew up for home. Trying to get his arms and legs into his snowsuit is like trying to thread a needle with a limp noodle. I eventually get it done, but I'm sweating like the proverbial pig when I do. The outside air is a relief initially, but it doesn't take long for the cold to snake its long, icy fingers beneath the sleeves and hem of my coat, freezing my sweat to my skin.

When I arrive at home, I see Emily's car is already in the garage. She's only been driving for four months, and this is her first time on wintry roads. We bought her a four-wheel-drive vehicle with plenty of safety features, just in case, and, so far, she's proven to be a sensible, cautious driver. But the threat of tomorrow's storm, the first big one in what has thus far been a mild winter, snowwise if not temperaturewise, makes me nervous.

I find Emily seated at the kitchen counter, schoolbooks spread out around her. As soon as Matthew enters the kitchen, she drops her pencil, hops off her stool, and squats down, arms open wide.

"There's my favorite brother," she coos, and Matthew runs headlong into her arms, beaming beneath her praise, blissfully oblivious to the fact that he is her only brother. "Let's get you out of this crazy suit," she says, releasing him and unzipping his snowsuit.

"Kwazy shoot," Matthew says, and then he proceeds to help Emily undress him. He helps Emily when she puts him in his snowsuit, too, apparently reserving the noodle act for his father and me.

"How was school today?" I ask Emily.

"The usual," she says. "They're probably going to close early tomorrow with the storm that's coming. If you want, I could stay home with Matthew. I don't have any tests or anything scheduled for tomorrow."

"You shouldn't skip school," I say, though there isn't a great deal of conviction in my voice. Emily is an A student who is meticulous with her assignments. She likes school. Plus, I would feel better knowing she's not on the road.

"It would be safer for me to stay home with Matthew," she says, continuing the debate. "That way, you don't have to drive him anywhere, and I don't have to drive, either."

I consider the idea and it's the appeal of getting up in the morning and going to work without the hassle of getting Matthew up, fed, dressed, and out the door that seals the deal.

"Okay, you win," I tell her.

I'm rewarded for my capitulation with a broad smile from Emily and a cheer from my son, who says, "We win! We win!"

"What do you guys want for dinner?" I ask.

"Mackachee!" Matthew hollers.

Mac and cheese is his most basic diet staple, and one of the few things I can cook. I had a bookcase built into the cabinetry when we designed the kitchen, and after we moved in, I stocked it with a variety of cookbooks. I swore to myself that I was going to learn to cook better—or at all—but so far, I haven't tackled the task, and the space between two of the cookbooks is now filled with take-out menus.

"You had mac and cheese last night, and the night before," I tell Matthew. "Not tonight."

"How about pizza?" Emily offers. "We could order out, or cook up one of the ones in the freezer."

"Let's order," I say. "With the storm coming, we might have to hit up our household reserves, so let's save those for now. In fact, let's order a little extra so we'll have some leftovers."

"Works for me," Emily says.

"Works for me," Matthew echoes with perfect pronunciation.

An hour later, the three of us are seated at the table in the breakfast nook, Emily and I enjoying pizza with tons of toppings, while Matthew works on his plain cheese pizza, the only kind he will eat. Toward the end of the meal, my phone rings and I see it's Hurley. I answer, getting up from the table and moving away so Matthew won't be able to hear. My phone conversations with Hurley often include things that aren't appropriate for little ears.

"What's up?" I say, avoiding any preamble.

"I need you," he says in a sultry tone.

"Your timing sucks."

I hear him chuckle. "I need you to come with me to pay a visit to a certain doctor," he says. "I got a lead on a guy who does a lot of back-room abortions for certain types of women, a strictly cash business. I want you to come with me both to help me interpret if he starts throwing a bunch of medicalese at me, and also to play a potential client."

"You want me to pretend to be a woman looking for an abortion?" I keep my voice low as I ask this, and glance back toward the table to make sure Emily and Matthew haven't overheard.

"Can Emily watch Matthew?" Hurley asks, neatly sidestepping my question.

"I'm sure she can."

"Good. I'll pick you up in fifteen minutes. Bring your earbuds. And try to look like a hooker."

This last request so stuns me that I am momentarily speechless. By the time I find my voice and my indignation, my husband has disconnected the call. Puzzled, but also a little intrigued, I walk back out to the kitchen.

"Em, can you watch Matthew for a few hours?"

"Of course," she says. "But on such short notice, I feel I should charge at least double the usual rate."

She smiles coyly, and I can't help but smile back. The kid is a top-notch negotiator. We started a savings fund for her a couple of years ago, and she put most of her babysitting money into it with the goal of being able to save up enough to buy a car once she was old enough to get her license. Hurley and I then decided to buy her a car, opting for something new rather than anything used, which is all she could have afforded, because we wanted something with all of the latest safety features and a hands-free calling system. As a result, Emily is now driving a cherry-red Jeep Cherokee. She uses her savings to buy gas, pay for her own insurance on the car, and to buy whatever other items she wants, though she tends to be a frugal girl. As a result, her fund now has well over three thousand dollars in it.

I head for my bedroom and sift through my makeup—I'm a bit of a minimalist in that regard, so doing myself up hookerish won't be easy. I put on some lipstick, a heavy dose of blush, eye shadow, and liner, plus three coats of mascara. As a last touch, I tease and spray my hair into something resembling the big-hair styles that were popular back in the 1980s. Then I go to my closet and find the tightest pair of pants I can—taken from the end of my closet that holds my skinny clothes for those rare occasions when I manage to drop a few pounds—and a low-cut blouse that will show off my ample cleavage. It isn't much, and a quick appraisal in the mirror convinces me I look more like a pathetic, middle-aged woman with a bad case of body-image blindness than a hooker, but it will have to do. By the time I get downstairs and don my coat and boots, Hurley is waiting out front.

I climb in his truck—a blue 4x4 that we bought at the same time we bought Emily's car—and he eyes me with one eyebrow arched.

"Oh, my," he says.

"Shut up. This was your idea."

"Do you have the earbuds?"

I dig them out of my pocket and hand them to him. Then I gasp as he takes out his pocketknife and cuts one of the buds from the wire.

"Hey!" I protest.

"I'll buy you a new pair." He hands me back the wire with one bud still attached and slips the severed bud into his coat pocket.

"Where are we going?" I ask once we are under way and I see that we are heading away from town.

"Poynette. We're going to the home of a doctor

who lost his license a few years back for overprescribing narcotics and engaging in some shady billing practices. Apparently, he now runs an illegal clinic and surgery in some part of his house, where he does abortions and a few other medical procedures that people don't want to have done at an official office or medical center."

"How do you know this? Did your FBI contact tell you about him?" Hurley nods, and I shake my head in dismay. "So they know he's doing this stuff and they just look the other way? Why don't they bust him and shut him down?"

"Because the guy has some very valuable contacts in the criminal world, as well as a good safety record for his medical procedures. The people he treats do well, so the FBI looks the other way with regard to the illegal medical stuff, and periodically watches his house to see who might be coming and going." Hurley pauses and shrugs. "I imagine they'll bust him one of these days, but for now he's more valuable to them if they let him continue."

"So the plan for us tonight is . . ."

Hurley looks at me, winks, and smiles drolly. "A bit of role playing. From here on out, I'm Mr. Joe Stevens, and your name is Bambi."

"*Bambi*? Seriously?" I whine. Hurley shrugs. "Isn't that a bit . . . bimboish?"

"Just follow my lead and say as little as possible."

I know Hurley well enough to figure out he isn't going to tell me anything more. After some fifteen minutes of silent driving, I broach a slightly different topic. "Have you heard from Richmond with regard to the security footage?"

"Yes, as a matter of fact. As luck would have it,

the store had cameras installed both inside and out. We now have a better image of the guy who was with Liesel. It's a bit grainy, but Richmond is e-mailing it to Quantico to see if they can enhance it for us. There was one distinguishing characteristic we discovered that we didn't know before, because he was wearing a hat in the ER. Our guy has a round bald spot on the back of his head."

Hurley's phone rings and he uses the hands-free system in his truck to answer it. "Detective Hurley."

"Hey, it's Bob." Since the call is on speaker, I can hear it, too. "We got that photo back from the Fibbies. They do remarkable work. I'm sending it to your phone."

"Great. That will help, once we get to the doc's place."

"They're also running the photo through some facial-recognition software they have to see if it matches any known criminals they have in their database. It's a long shot, but you never know, we might get lucky. In the meantime, I'm looking over the files from the original police reports again. Maybe something there will pop out."

"Let me know if you find anything, and I'll let you know how things go with the doc once we're done." He disconnects the call and his phone dings to indicate a new message. He picks it up from the console and hands it to me. I open the message from Richmond and there is the face of the man who dumped Liesel in the ER. He is pale-skinned but dark-haired, with a sad excuse for a mustache. The picture is a partial profile, and a small section of the bald spot near his crown is visible. His nose has a distinctive bump in it, just below the bridge, and his eyes look dark, though it's hard to tell from the picture exactly what color they are.

I hold the phone up so Hurley can glance at the picture without taking his eyes too far off the road.

"Sketchy-looking fellow" is all he says.

We arrive at our destination a few minutes later, a single-level home on a country lot that is about an acre in size. It is dark, and there are several pine and fir trees growing on the property that allow very little moonlight to get in. The house, however, is lit up with warm light that emanates from the windows and a fixture on the wide front porch. It looks welcoming enough.

Hurley turns off the engine and looks over at me. "Are you ready for this?"

"Ready as I can be," I say.

We get out and walk up onto the porch. Hurley is about to ring the bell when the front door swings open, revealing a short man who looks to be in his late forties or early fifties. He has a paunch that he is trying to hide by wearing a tailed flannel shirt untucked over his jeans. His round face is pale and shiny; his hair is dark and pulled back into a small ponytail. He smiles at us, but it strikes me as a purely perfunctory response because it doesn't appear to be reflected in his eyes, which are a pale shade of blue that looks cold as ice.

"Mr. Stevens?" he says with an inquiring look, and Hurley nods. "Come on in."

Our host steps aside as we enter the house, walking into a living area that is cozy and warm. A fire is crackling in the fireplace, and there is a scent of cinnamon in the air, which makes me want to fix a cup of hot cocoa and curl up in front of the hearth. Instead, I turn and face the erstwhile doctor.

"I'm Stanley Lowe," he says, looking at me with a hint of a frown.

I don't say a word. I assume I'm supposed to be a working girl, brought here under the insistence of my pimp, played by Hurley. So I stay silent and try to look uncomfortable, not a difficult task since I'm genuinely nervous.

"This is Bambi," Hurley says. "The one Sully . . . Mr. Sullivan called you about."

Lowe proffers a hand. "Let me take your coats."

Hurley and I doff our coats and hand them over.

Lowe hangs them on hooks on the wall and then turns back to us. He eyes me once more, his gaze settling on my stomach. "Didn't Sully tell you that the girls need to be no further along than four months?"

"She's only three months gone," Hurley says.

Lowe arches his eyebrows at this and looks pointedly at my midsection. "That tummy looks more like five months to me," he says.

Belatedly I try to suck in my gut while I silently curse Lowe with some choice words and the threat of a plague. Hurley glances over at me, and I can tell he's trying to suppress a laugh. I shoot lasers at him with my eyes.

"She's naturally a bit round," Hurley says. "Some men like that." He gives me a wink and a swat on the butt that's hard enough to make me take a half step forward and glare at him. "I swear to you she's barely three months along."

Lowe looks at me. "Is that correct?" he asks, and I nod. His eyes narrow, and he looks unconvinced. "When was your last menstrual period?"

Fortunately, I anticipated this question, since it's a standard one asked in any medical situation involving something like this. I'd asked it of patients hundreds of times when I was working in the ER, and was already doing the math in my head. "November nineteenth," I say. Since it is now mid-February, this answer satisfies Lowe.

He nods, and tells us to follow him, leading us to his kitchen and then to a door that goes down into his basement. We follow along dutifully, Hurley appearing as cool and calm as the proverbial cucumber. I, on the other hand, am conjuring up scenes from any number of horror movies I've watched where the characters follow someone into a basement, and I then yell at the screen to let them know what stupid morons they are, ultimately declaring their idiotic decisions an example of Darwinism in action.

Lowe's cellar looks like any other basement in Wisconsin: a large open room with concrete walls that holds a washer, a dryer, and a wooden table. There are several other rooms opening off this one, including a smaller canning room, a workshop, a storage area, and a mechanical room for the furnace, water heater, and water softener. Lowe heads for the workshop area, where I feel certain he will use his chisels, hammers, and power saws to kill and dismember us both. Instead, he walks over to a bookcase and reaches into it. A second later, the entire bookcase swings aside silently, revealing a gleaming surgical suite.

I'm admittedly impressed. Lowe has managed to outfit his little operating room with all the latest equipment. The bed, trays, overhead lamp, and side tables look to be the same make and models as the ones that were used in the hospital OR when I worked there. There is an autoclave off to one side, and trays of wrapped surgical instruments appropriately labeled with a date. There is also a suction machine, several oxygen tanks, and a small cart with a monitor defibrillator on top and several drawers, which I suspect contain airways, drugs, and other emergency equipment. A portable heart monitor that can also measure blood pressure and oxygen levels stands near the bed. And in a glass cabinet hanging on one wall, I see a supply of drugs, all carefully labeled, most of them sedatives of some sort.

What is missing is any sort of anesthesia equipment, but it isn't necessary to use full anesthesia during an abortion. A little something to sedate the patient and take the edge off the pain is often sufficient, and if the sedation proves a little too effective, it appears that Lowe has the appropriate reversal agents and the necessary resuscitative equipment close at hand.

"This is where it will be done," Lowe says. "You will have the procedure here, and after a brief recovery time, you will need to have someone take you home and stay with you for the next twelve hours or so."

"I have that covered," Hurley says.

"Do you do the procedure yourself?" I ask.

"I'm the only medical person involved with the procedure, but I have a woman who serves as an assistant." He looks at Hurley and adds, "She's very trustworthy. She's been with me for years."

"Will I be asleep? Or knocked out in some way?" While I'm impressed with Lowe's setup, it's clearly not an official setting for such procedures.

"I don't use anesthesia," Lowe says. "But I will give you a drug that will calm you and cause some retrograde amnesia, so you won't remember anything."

I'm familiar with the types of drugs he's talking about, as we used them all the time when I worked at the hospital. But any time we sedated a patient, we always had several staff members on hand in case things went wrong. It didn't happen often, but when it did, it was often more than one medically trained person could safely handle.

"What do you do if something goes wrong?" I ask, looking around the room wide-eyed. "What if I start to bleed heavily, or something like that? I've heard it can happen."

"I've never had any problems with any of my patients," Lowe says, niftily avoiding an actual answer to my question. "And I'm quite capable of handling any emergencies, should one arise."

This isn't true. There are any number of things that could go wrong, some of them potentially fatal, and I'm certain Lowe knows this. But admitting that I also know it would raise questions as to how it is I possess that knowledge, questions I'm not prepared to answer at the moment.

Hurley nods and says, "Looks good. Are we set for doing this in the morning?"

"I can fit you in," Lowe says. "There is the matter of compensation still to discuss."

"What is your going rate?" Hurley asks.

"I thought Sully would have told you that," Lowe says, narrowing his eyes at Hurley.

Hurley shrugs. "If he did, I don't recall the amount."

"Five K," Lowe says after a moment's hesitation. "If there are any complications, the rate doubles automatically."

"Five K for a simple abortion?" Hurley says, wrinkling his face in distaste. "That seems rather high."

"It's not simple," Lowe says. "You are paying for both my expertise and my discretion."

This is all Hurley needs to hear. Hurley reaches into his pocket, takes out his badge, and shows it to Lowe, giving him a moment to absorb it.

"Are you kidding me?" Lowe says with a roll of his eyes. "I'm being busted by some small-town local yokel?"

Hurley tips his head down toward his chest and says, "Did you get it all?" He then raises a hand to one ear, where I see that my decapitated earbud is firmly nestled in place. Hurley looks down at the floor for a second before saying, "Great. Good work." He looks at Lowe and smiles, his eyebrows raised suggestively. I'm sure I look as shocked as Lowe does right now, since I know Hurley isn't wired.

Seconds pass as the two men engage in a stare-off, and then Lowe looks heavenward and mouths something unrepeatable. He looks at me, his expression annoyed. "I take it you don't need a D and C?" he asks.

"I do not," I say.

"I should have known," Lowe says with distaste. "You're not the right type."

"For what?" I ask, feeling oddly insulted.

"Am I under arrest?" Lowe asks, ignoring my question and turning his attention back to Hurley. He takes a cell phone from his pocket and proceeds to start tapping at the screen. "I need to call my lawyer."

Hurley reaches over and places a hand over the top of Lowe's phone. "I'm not here to arrest you, though I will if you don't help me."

"Help you with what?" Lowe asks, looking suspicious but hopeful.

Hurley takes out his cell phone, taps at the screen, and then shows Lowe a picture of Liesel. "I'm looking for this girl," he says.

Lowe stares at the phone long enough to get a good look, then shakes his head. "I'm certain I've never seen her."

Hurley pulls his phone back, swipes at the screen, and then shows it to Lowe again. This time, the screen is displaying the enhanced picture of the man who brought Liesel to the ER. "How about this guy?" Hurley asks. "We think he might be with her."

Lowe is a terrible liar. The change in his face is subtle, but it gives him away nonetheless. One eyebrow arches slightly, and his eyes dart away from the screen for a nanosecond before going back to it. He licks his lips and looks at Hurley. "Don't know him, either. Sorry."

With a laser stare, Hurley looks at the man. He doesn't speak, doesn't blink, doesn't move.

After another very long, very pregnant pause, Hurley takes his phone back, removes a pair of handcuffs from his jacket pocket, and says, "Stanley Lowe, you are under arrest for—"

"Hold on! I—I might have seen that guy," Lowe says, talking fast. He licks his lips again. "Yes . . . yes . . . I remember now. He brought someone here once before, but it wasn't that girl you showed me, I swear."

"Who is he?" Hurley asks.

Lowe makes a *pfft* sound and gives Hurley a dismissive wave of one hand. "He's a nobody. Some flunky errand boy."

"What's his name?" Hurley asks, opening one of the handcuffs to punctuate the question.

Lowe eyes the handcuff warily and licks his lips yet again. They are faintly rimmed in red, making me think this is a common nervous habit of his, and that he ought to invest in a few tubes of Chap-Stick. Wisconsin winters are notoriously hard on lips, hands, and skin in general.

"All I know is his first name," Lowe says. He looks at Hurley and pulls his head back a smidge, as if he is expecting to get hit for his answer. Judging from the look on Hurley's face, I'd say the odds are pretty good. When Hurley doesn't react immediately, Lowe tosses the name out there. "It's Kirby."

It could have been worse, I tell myself. The guy

could have had the name John, or Bill, or Tom, or any number of other names that are shared by thousands of men in Wisconsin alone. At least Kirby is a somewhat unique name. Plus, I'm pretty sure Lowe is lying about only knowing the man's first name.

"I need more and I think you're holding out on me," Hurley says in an ominous tone. "Who's he a lackey for? Who pays the bills?"

"Kirby does," Lowe says, ignoring the first question. "He always pays in cash."

"Always?" Hurley repeats with a *gotcha* smile. His head moves closer to Lowe's face, and Lowe, realizing his mistake, backs up a full step. "How many times has he been here?" There is a low, underlying growl to Hurley's voice that is full of menace and threat.

Lowe is starting to sweat. "Look," he says, his voice cracking slightly. "The guy brings me a lot of business. If I give him up, I'm done for."

"If you go to prison for twenty to life, you'll be done for," Hurley counters.

Lowe laughs this off, momentarily buoyed by bravado. "The penalty for what I do isn't anywhere near that," he scoffs.

Hurley takes a step closer to Lowe, forcing the man to back up yet again. He now has his back to a wall, and his eyes dart around, looking for an escape. Hurley leans in and places his hands on the wall to either side of Lowe's shoulders, the cuffs dangling from his right hand. Lowe realizes he is trapped, and he stares up at Hurley, frozen and bug-eyed, like a rat whose leg is caught in a trap and facing down a mean, hungry cat.

"Listen to me, you slimy, snake-oil charlatan," Hurley sneers. "I have an eighteen-year-old girl in my morgue, and this Kirby creep is responsible for her being there. If you don't give me what I want, I will see to it that you are also connected to her death, whatever it takes. And I promise you, you won't see the light of day for at least a quarter of a century, if ever. Got it?"

Lowe nods, a spastic movement that makes him look like one of those bobblehead dolls.

"But if you help me, I'm going to walk out of here and pretend I never came, that I have no idea what kind of horrible crap you're doing here, and you'll be free to go about your business. No one needs to know where my information came from. Understand?"

Another spastic nod.

"All right then," Hurley says, straightening up and lowering his arms. "I'm sure you have some sort of contact information for this Kirby guy. I want it."

Lowe weighs his options for a few seconds. "If I give you what you want, you swear you won't bust me? You'll leave me be?"

"Promise," Hurley says.

I frown at this. Letting this hack continue providing illegal abortions seems wrong. While I will admit that he has a nice setup here—it's leagues higher than most of the back-alley setups that still exist—it's still several steps lower than your standard hospital setting. Of course, it isn't the actual procedure that's illegal, just the way it's being done.

"Fine," Lowe says, clearly irritated but seeming resigned. He turns and heads back upstairs, makes his way down a hallway on the main floor to a back room, which is clearly being used as an office. I watch from the doorway as he goes over to what appears to be an electrical outlet in the wall. He pushes on the reset button at its center and the outlet pops out of the wall a couple of inches. Lowe reaches into the opening behind it and comes out with a key.

Then he walks over to a safe built into the hardwood floor and hidden under the edge of a rug. As he unlocks the safe and reaches down into it, my mind envisions him coming up with a gun and shooting both of us dead. A quick, worried glance at Hurley assures me that he, too, has considered this possibility. He has his gun out and at the ready.

"No funny stuff," Hurley says.

Lowe looks up at him and registers surprise at the sight of the gun. "I'm just taking out an address book," he says, slowly raising the hand that has dipped into the safe while holding his other hand up in a gesture of transparent cooperation. Holding a book in one hand, Lowe slowly gets to his feet and walks over to the desk, never taking his eyes off Hurley.

"Go stand over there," Hurley says, waving his gun toward a corner of the room away from the desk and the safe. Once Lowe has obeyed, Hurley walks over and peers down into the open safe. A smile creeps over his face and he looks over at Lowe with disdain.

"I'm glad you decided to play things smart,"

Hurley says, kneeling and reaching into the safe with his free hand. He picks something up and my heart skips a beat when I see that it's a handgun. "I'm betting this particular weapon isn't registered to you, am I correct?"

Lowe doesn't answer, which in and of itself is an answer of sorts.

Hurley moves over behind Lowe's desk and opens the drawers. Then he bends down and peers beneath the desktop. Satisfied, he shoves a pad and pen toward Lowe. "Give me Kirby's contact information."

Lowe approaches the desk after Hurley backs away from it. He opens the book he is holding, flips through several pages, and then takes up the pen. After scribbling something down on the notepad, he tears the sheet off and holds it out to Hurley.

"Mattie, can you get that?" Hurley says, keeping his gun aimed at Lowe.

I step forward and take the proffered sheet of paper. Written on it is *Kirby O'Keefe,* and a phone number. I hold it up so Hurley can see it.

"This name and number better produce some results," Hurley says, holstering his own gun and then removing the clip from Lowe's. He pockets the clip, ratchets back the slide to check the chamber, and removes the bullet he finds there, pocketing it as well. Then he tosses the empty gun into a nearby chair. "If it doesn't," he goes on, "if I find out you've tried to dupe me, I will be back. And I won't be nearly as understanding next time. Understand?"

Lowe glares at Hurley with a mixture of fear and contempt.

"Do you understand?" Hurley repeats, and Lowe grudgingly nods.

Hurley looks at me, nods toward the door, and says, "After you."

We leave Lowe's house at a quick pace and get back in Hurley's truck. I glance over my shoulder a couple of times to see if Lowe is coming after us, but there is no sign of him. As we pull away, I see a curtain drop back into place in a window, and I imagine Lowe is breathing a sigh of relief.

"Why the fake wire?" I say once we're under way. "Why not do it for real? Shouldn't we be busting this guy?"

"Part of the deal I made with the undercover FBI contact who gave us Lowe's name, location, and introduction was that I wouldn't hurt the operation in any way. They've been monitoring him for nearly two years now, but as I explained earlier, they don't want to arrest him or shut him down yet. Technically, the only law he's breaking is practicing medicine without a license, and he'd most likely get a slap on the hands and a fine, and then be back at it somewhere else."

"What about that book he had in his safe? If Lowe got busted and someone got their hands on that book, wouldn't that go a long way toward shutting down these human-trafficking rings?"

"The FBI has infiltrated some of those groups by tracking people who bring girls here," Hurley explains. "But Lowe's clientele also includes some prostitution rings and the occasional lone woman who has heard about what he does via word of mouth. Women without insurance will come to him because he's cheaper than any clinic or hospital. The price he quoted us is what he charges the *professionals*." He lifts the first two fingers of each hand from the steering wheel and makes air quotes when he says the word. "Besides, according to the FBI, he's good at what he does. His patients don't experience much in the way of complications. Shut him down and they'll end up going to some hack somewhere else."

"He does appear to have a nice setup there," I admit. "But just because nothing bad has happened, so far, doesn't mean it won't."

"That's true of any setting where abortions are performed, isn't it?"

He has a point. Resigned, I give up the argument. "Are you going to call this Kirby O'Keefe fellow?"

"Not yet. I want to do some research first, see if we have anything on him. I suspect Lowe was right. O'Keefe is just a lackey, an errand boy. If we can get a bead on him and watch him without him knowing it, he may well lead us to someone higher up the food chain. And I think that's where we're going to have to go if we're to have any hope of finding Liesel's sister."

"So what's next?"

Hurley yawns widely. "Home and bed," he says when he's done. "I'll give Richmond a call to update him, but I need to catch a few z's. I can't think straight when I get too tired. I'll start fresh again in the morning."

This sounds ideal to me. I'm exhausted, and my idea of heaven right now is me stretched out in our comfy bed with Hurley curled up beside me and the warm glow of a fire coming from the fireplace. I'd love to be able to put this case out of mind temporarily, but I know it will be next to impossible. In fact, as Hurley pulls into our driveway and heads up the hill to the house, I find myself wondering if Kurt Paulsen ever has a good night's sleep anymore.

Chapter 13

Despite our weariness, we don't head to bed right away. Both Emily and Matthew are upstairs asleep. Hurley hasn't had dinner, and after scoping out the fridge, he reheats the leftover pieces of pizza from earlier. I'm hungry, too, and after my turn scouring the fridge, I find a half-eaten container of tuna salad and fix myself a sandwich.

Hurley has a copy of the file on the missing girls with him, and the two of us sit at the island counter looking it over for an hour or two before we finally turn out the lights and head upstairs. I fall asleep quickly, the emotional drains of the day sapping me both physically and mentally.

I awaken a little later as a wave of nausea rolls over me. My guts cramp and roil uncomfortably, and bile rises in my throat. I fling back the covers and hurry into the bathroom, shutting the door behind me so I won't wake Hurley. I barely man-age to get the toilet seat up before my stomach squeezes painfully and I vomit up bitter bile. My body feels hot and cold at the same time, and now the cramping is in my lower gut. No sooner has my stomach emptied itself than I feel an urgent need coming from the other end. I whip around, yank my panties down, and sit in the nick of time. All I'm wearing is a T-shirt and panties—my usual nighttime attire—and the bathroom feels freezing. I reach over and grab a towel hanging on the rack, and drape it over my shoulders in an effort to get warm.

After a time, the cramping subsides some and I get off the toilet and shuffle over to the sink. I brush the sour taste from my mouth, and then crawl back into bed. But my guts start to revolt again, and I hurry back to the toilet, once again positioning myself on the porcelain throne. I grab a nearby trash can, in case things decide to come out both ends again. Every time I think things have settled down, another wave of nausea hits me and I'm wracked with cramps and spasms. Eventually I stop upchucking—there is nothing left in my stomach to come up—but my lower half continues its attempts to empty me out.

A glance at the clock next to my bed when I first awoke told me it was a little after two in the morning. By the time Hurley wakes and comes into the bathroom to find me pale, shaky, and utterly miserable, I've been sitting on the toilet for two hours straight. I can barely feel my legs, I have a permanent ring imprinted on my butt cheeks from the toilet seat, and I am weak as a kitten.

"Jesus, Mattie, are you okay?" Hurley says when he sees me.

I shake my head miserably. "I think I have food poisoning," I tell him. "Every time I try to get off the toilet, it hits me again. It's like my colon is Mount Vesuvius and my butt cheeks are the hills of Pompeii."

"I'm sorry," he says. "What can I do?"

"You could grab me my bathrobe for starters," I say, my teeth chattering. "I can't seem to get warm." He retreats into the bedroom and returns a moment later with my robe, which he helps me put on. I see him wrinkle his nose at the smell, but he says nothing. He kisses me on my forehead, and then strokes my head with his hand.

"On the back of the top shelf on my side of the closet, there's a metal box with a lock on it," I tell him. "The key to it is in the medicine cabinet over there. Will you get it for me? I have some medications in it that I think might help."

Hurley nods, goes to the medicine cabinet, grabs the key, and once again retreats into the bedroom. The box I told him to get contains a variety of medications, including some that require a prescription. I have nausea pills, as well as an antidiarrheal, meds I saved from previous prescriptions and over-the-counter purchases for just such an emergency. I keep them locked up to make sure Matthew can't get to them. He's a nosy, curious little bugger—a trait I think he inherited from me—and this is the best way I could think of to keep him safe.

Hurley returns a minute later, carrying the box. He opens it, probably a good thing since my hands are shaking, and gives it to me. I rummage through the various medications and find what I need. Meanwhile, Hurley goes over to the sink and gets me a glass of water.

Once I have myself as medicated as I can be, I hand him the box. "Put it back on the closet shelf," I tell him, "but leave it unlocked. I have a feeling I'm going to need it again."

"I can stay home this morning and work from my office here," Hurley says, giving me a worried look.

I shake my head. "Emily is staying home from school today because of the snowstorm. She can keep an eye on Matthew. You go on into the station and do what you need to do. I think I'll be better in another couple of hours."

"You're not planning on going into the office, are you?"

"I don't know," I tell him, and he scowls at me. "I need to see how I feel, but I think the worst of it may have passed."

Hurley lets out a resigned sigh. He has learned that it's not worth the effort of arguing a matter once I have my mind set. "I'll have my cell phone with me at all times," he says. "Call me if you need anything, okay?"

"I will. Now go on. You'll need to use the other bathroom to get ready. Sorry."

He moves around the bathroom, gathering up his toothbrush and some shaving supplies. When he's done, he walks over and kisses me on top of my head again. "Promise you'll call me if you need anything."

"I promise. But I'll be fine. The nausea is better already. I've got Emily here to help me, and if worse comes to worst, Christopher will be in the office at noon. This is our overlap day."

Looking reluctant, Hurley leaves. As soon as I hear the bedroom door close, I pry myself loose of the toilet seat and walk over to the shower. I feel a little light-headed, but my legs are steady.

A minute later, I've got the shower going as hot as I can stand it. I climb in, shut the door, and stand under the stream, feeling the warmth move through my body. The combination of heat and washing refreshes me to some degree. And the fact that I'm able to take an entire shower and wash my hair without another attack of the runs is encouraging.

Half an hour later, I'm dried off, wrapped in a flannel nightgown, and cozy beneath the covers of my bed. In a matter of seconds, I fall asleep.

I awaken a bit later, once again stirred from my slumber by painful, warning rumblings in my lower belly. A glance at the clock and I see that I've managed to sleep for nearly two hours, a very encouraging sign. I make another trip to the porcelain throne, but this time, I can tell things are winding down. A few faint waves of nausea hit me, but they're minor and fade quickly. I even feel the beginning pangs of hunger. It takes a lot to make me lose my appetite.

I make a test run with a glass of water, the ice-cold fluid a welcome balm to my dry, irritated throat. I'm not sure if it's going to stay down, and wait with some trepidation. But not only does it stay down, my body is telling me to give it more. Just to be safe, I go back to the bedroom, grab the medicine box from the closet shelf, and repeat the dose of the antidiarrheal medicine. Then I venture downstairs to the kitchen.

I find a sleepy-eyed Emily and a bright-eyed Matthew both seated at the table in our kitchen nook.

Emily looks surprised to see me. "You're not supposed to be down here," she says. "Dad said you looked like death warmed over and would probably spend the day in bed."

"I thought I might at one point, but I'm feeling better now. In fact, I want to try to eat a little something."

Emily hops out of her chair. "Sit down," she says. "I'll fix you whatever you want."

"Thank you, Em," I say with genuine gratitude. My legs are still a little shaky so I'm happy to take the seat, though I have to step over Hoover to get to it. "Maybe just a piece of toast with a little bit of strawberry jelly, and a cup of tea. If I do okay with that, I might try to graduate myself to a cup of coffee."

Matthew, who up until now has stayed unusually quiet, looks at me with innocent, wide-eyed concern. "Mammy sick?" he says.

"A little," I say with a smile. "But it's getting better."

It *is* getting better. The tea Emily makes for me feels warm and soothing as I drink it, and the toast settles my stomach. There are still some ominous rumblings lower down in my gut, but for the moment, Mount Vesuvius doesn't seem inclined to erupt. I feel good enough, in fact, I decide to go into work. The urgent need to find Liesel's sister, Lily, is uppermost in my mind. That, and the horrible, dead expression on Kurt Paulsen's face. I know that if I try to stay home the case will haunt me all day long.

I go upstairs and dress, slipping a couple of doses of the medicine into the pockets of my slacks. Though I'm reasonably confident the cause of my GI upset was the tuna I ate last night, I decide not to kiss Matthew good-bye, just in case it turns out to be something viral. I blow him a kiss instead, do the same to Emily, and head out to the garage.

It's cold enough in the garage to make me gasp, so it comes as no surprise that the hearse gasps a little, too, when I try to start it. I let it warm up for a minute or so with the garage door open before pulling out, and check out the weather on my cell phone while I wait. The threatened storm is still on its way, due to arrive this afternoon, with predictions for somewhere around a foot of snow, galelike winds, large drifts, and a teeth-chattering high temperature of twelve degrees. With the wind chill calculated in, that twelve will feel more like minus twenty.

I'm barely down my driveway, about to pull onto the main road, when my cell phone rings. It's Izzy, and I curse before answering, thinking that it must be a death call.

"What's up, Izzy?"

"My car won't start," he says irritably. "I would take Dom's car, but he has some kind of theater thing going on this afternoon, so I don't want to leave him stranded. He can drive me in, but it means bundling Juliana up and loading her into the car, and I thought maybe you could at least give me a ride into the office if you're not there already."

"Your timing is perfect," I tell him. "I'm just turning onto the county highway now. I'll be at your house in ten minutes."

"You're a lifesaver."

"Used to be," I reply. "But thanks to you, I now get to figure out the life enders."

I disconnect the call and pull out onto the highway. Picking up Izzy requires a slight detour from my normal commute, and I end up driving past the entrance to the driveway of my old house, the one I used to share with my ex-husband, David, although the house we lived in no longer exists. It burned to the ground a couple of years ago, not long after I moved out. Fortunately, the house was well insured, and the settlement helped to provide me with a nice cash payment in the divorce. The settlement also provided David with a new wife, as he started dating and eventually married Patty Volker, our insurance agent.

As I pass the driveway, I see a car waiting to pull out onto the road. Behind the wheel is Patty. She waves at me and smiles as I go by—thanks to the hearse, I'm sure she knew it was me when I was still several hundred feet away—and I return the gesture with a wave and smile of my own. Even in the short amount of time it takes me to pass, my limited view of her, and the distance between us, I can easily see the changes that have taken place in her recently. She is pregnant—due to deliver any day—

and has the round, slightly puffy, almost moon-shaped face of a woman on the verge of motherhood.

I pull into the driveway to Izzy's house, located several hundred feet farther down the road, and watch in the rearview mirror as Patty drives by. I hope she and David will be happy, because I genuinely like Patty. But I also know things are a little tense for them right now, for some reasons Patty is aware of, and some I suspect she isn't.

My ex, David, who is currently the only general surgeon in town—though recruitment efforts are about to pay off with the addition of a woman general surgeon—has been navigating a rocky road through life lately. Hurley and I investigated a series of deaths several months ago that turned out to be connected to one another, and to some deaths that happened thirty years ago, deaths that involved my father. Over a period of time and with the help of an eager young news reporter, a group of pharmaceutical company executives were recently exposed, indicted, arrested, and prosecuted for hiding complications associated with certain drugs they were pushing. A number of physicians, legislators, judges, and other government personnel were swept up in the mess, too. David, more or less unknowingly—I've given him the benefit of the doubt here—received some well-disguised kickbacks for prescribing one of these drugs, a weight-loss medication that had the potential for some serious and often fatal side effects. One of his patients died because of it, and when I learned about the cover-up, its history, and David's involvement—which I realized also involved me at one point, since I traveled with him twice on trips that might have been hidden bribes—I convinced David to go to the authorities, throw himself on their mercy, and offer to be their whistleblower.

He wasn't keen on the idea at first, but when I caught him making a little too nice with his new office nurse, I basically shamed and then black-mailed him into doing it by threatening to reveal his latest dalliance to Patty. He reluctantly com-plied, and the resultant fallout had been nothing short of spectacular, in a bad way. The investiga-tion rapidly made it from the local news into the national and international news, and the net cast by the authorities was a wide one. The guppies in-volved, people like David and some of his associ-ates—other doctors who presumably participated in these kickback schemes without fully under-standing the ramifications—were tiny bites low down on the food chain. They were punished with minor reprimands that consisted of hand slaps and fines, with the hope that these bottom-feeders would then lead to some of the bigger fish in the pond.

The investigation rocked the medical world, and there were, and still are, some very unhappy and suspicious swimmers in that cesspool of a pond. There was an assumption that someone, some-where, started the ball rolling by stepping up as a whistleblower, and while the identity of that per-son is as yet unknown—at least as far as I know—the acrimony expressed by those swept up in the net was, and still is, nothing short of incendiary. Speculation has been constant, and a lot of people have stuck their suspicious noses into Sorenson's medical business because of the deaths that happened here, and some of the local people who were indicted.

I've spoken briefly with David a few times since it all came out, and he's as nervous as a blind man navigating a floor covered with thumbtacks, worried that he'll be outed. I'd feel sorry for him if it weren't for the whole cheating-on-his-new-wife thing. I thought he'd learned a lesson when he cheated on me, but, apparently, that old adage about the leopard and his spots is true. At least he's making an effort once again, or appears to be doing so. He fired the nurse involved and hired a new one named Myna, who has all the charm, warmth, and personality of a T. rex. No one knows for sure how old Myna is, but her face has more creases in it than a crumpled piece of paper, the staffers call her Methuselah behind her back, and I overheard someone say her driver's license was written in hieroglyphics.

I don't know if Patty knows about the office-nurse affair, but I figure Myna will eliminate some temptation for David. Of course, temptation can be found anywhere—particularly if one is as much of a hound dog as David seems to be—and given David's track record thus far, I wouldn't be surprised if he strays again. He swears he's turned over a new leaf, and I hope it's true for Patty's sake, but I fear it's Eve's fig leaf he's turned over so he can get to what's underneath.

I honk my horn once I've pulled up behind the garage to Izzy's house and he hurries out a moment later, his head hunkered down inside his coat against the cold. He whips open the passenger door and drops into the seat, bringing a blast of frigid air with him. Then he practically falls out of the car while reaching for the door handle so he can pull it closed. It finally shuts with a solid *whump* and Izzy shivers so hard that I can feel it through the bench seat.

"Old man winter is revved up something fierce, isn't he?" I say with a smile.

Izzy doesn't answer. Instead, he cups his hands over his mouth and blows into them, eyeing me with a sardonic tilt of his brows.

"How is Sylvie dealing with the cold?" I ask as I back the car around and head down the driveway.

"She's managing," Izzy says, lowering his hands and holding them out in front of the heat vents instead. "Though I think she's trying to cook herself. She's constantly cranking the thermostat in the cottage up as high as it will go. The other day, I found it set at ninety." He rolls his eyes, lets out a loud sigh, and shakes his head woefully. "Her mental faculties are really starting to slide," he says in a sad voice. "These days, she's a few clowns short of her usual circus."

"I'm sorry," I say, pulling out onto the road. "Maybe she'll mellow some with senility."

Izzy scoffs at my suggestion. "I doubt that. She's ticked off at Dom again because he won't let her babysit Juliana. She can't seem to understand why we're upset over the fact that she was trying to tune in NBC on the stove the other day, or why it should bother us that she forgets to bathe for a week or more."

"Is she aware?" I ask. "What I mean is, does she know that she's losing it?"

Izzy shakes his head. "No, and I guess that's something."

"I'm truly sorry, Izzy. I know how difficult this is for you. Let me know if Hurley or I can help in any way."

"Thanks."

My stomach, which has been behaving for the past ten minutes, gives a threatening rumble that makes me rub it and catch my breath. Izzy doesn't miss the gesture.

"What's wrong?" he asks.

"Food poisoning," I say with a grimace. "I ate some leftover tuna I probably shouldn't have last night. I think the worst of it is past. The nausea is almost gone, but I'm not sure my gut is done cleansing itself." As if to confirm this, another rumble rolls through me, and this time I'm seized by an uncomfortable feeling low down. "Oh, crap," I say, a bit breathless, an expletive that is ironically apropos. I tighten my grip on the steering wheel while simultaneously tightening my sphincter muscles.

"Are you okay?" Izzy asks, looking alarmed.

"I think so," I say with half-clenched teeth. I hit the gas as I turn onto the main drag, eager to get to the office. The speed limit here is only twenty-five miles an hour, but there is little traffic this early in the morning, and I only have a few blocks to go.

The Fates, who have a history of screwing with me, decide to have some fun again today. The light in front of me turns yellow. It's an intersection where I need to make a left turn, and I gun the gas a little. Izzy, sensing what I'm about to do, braces himself the best he can, though there isn't much he can do, since his feet barely touch the floor and his arms aren't long enough to reach the dash with the seat as far back as I need it to drive. He clutches his seat belt strap with one hand and grips the armrest with the other.

The light turns red just as I reach the intersection. There are no cars coming from the opposite direction, and while there is a car to my right waiting to go through the intersection, he hasn't started to move yet. I turn the steering wheel to the left, brake slightly, and fishtail into the turn.

Unfortunately, there is a lingering patch of ice near the far curb of the street I'm turning onto. Plowed remains of the last snowfall have accumulated and then melted, thanks to steam coming up from a nearby sidewalk grate. The resultant puddle has refrozen in the frigid night air, and the rear tires of the hearse hit it. I feel a sickly sliding sensation in my gut and I'm not sure if it's the movement of the car causing it, or something else.

I hear Izzy say, "Christ, Mattie!"

And then the rear end of the hearse slides up onto the sidewalk, hitting a lamppost. The jolt of the collision is jarring and sudden, but it stops the car's momentum.

I quickly shift the car into park and look over at Izzy; then I look past him out the window. The police station is less than fifty feet away, our office a mere two blocks past that. *So close.*

"Are you okay?" I ask Izzy, after letting out the

breath I didn't realize I was holding. But as I take in a new one, it comes with a fetid, nauseating odor—a definite ten on the sphincter scale.

He nods and starts to speak, but then clamps a hand over his mouth, his eyes bugging out. "What is that smell?" he says, his words muffled behind his hand.

My brain, in an initial postcrash haze, was working hard to convince me that I had merely expelled some gas. But I can feel it now: hot, lava-like liquid seeping between my thighs and up my back. "Oh, God," I say, letting my head drop forward, chin on my chest. "I think I crapped my pants."

Izzy, kind, supportive friend that he is, snorts back a laugh. "You did not," he says, his tone clearly amused.

"I did," I say, feeling like I want to cry, or die of embarrassment. "What a great start to the day."

"Well, it's about to get a whole lot worse," Izzy says, his tone sounding oddly jocular considering his words.

I lift my head and give him an inquisitive look, unsure what he means. His eyes aren't focused on me, and as I follow his gaze out the passenger side of the windshield and see two uniformed police officers approaching us on foot at a rapid trot, his meaning becomes all too clear.

"Get out!" I tell Izzy.

He looks back at me, puzzled.

"Get out of the car and stall them," I explain. "Keep them occupied. Answer questions. Keep them away from me."

"But you're the driver," Izzy says in the same tone of voice I've heard him use to explain something to my son when he doesn't understand basic logic. "They're going to have to talk to you."

I squeeze my eyes closed, curse under my breath, and feel my face grow hot. When I open my eyes again, I see the two officers—Patrick Devonshire and Brenda Joiner—mere feet away. Biting my lip, I roll down my window and lean out.

"Brenda, come here," I say. "Patrick, can you check on Izzy to make sure he's okay?"

My maneuvering works and the duo is cleaved down the middle, with Patrick going to Izzy's side of the car. "Get out, Izzy," I say under my breath. "Please."

With a chuckle that makes me want to give him an extra little shove, Izzy climbs out of the hearse. I turn back to my window and Brenda. There is no way to escape some embarrassment over what has happened, but at least with Brenda, it's another woman I'll be sharing my shame with, and for whatever reason, that seems preferable. Plus, Brenda is dating Christopher Malone, and given that he has so many hot-air emissions that he might be solely responsible for global warming, I figure the woman must have a higher than average tolerance of the odors that go with such things.

"What happened, Mattie?" Brenda says as she reaches my window. "Are you okay?"

"I'm not okay," I say in a low voice that is a hair above a whisper. "I have just crapped my pants."

Brenda stares at me for several seconds, the corners of her mouth twitching as she tries to decide if I'm being funny or not. Then her eyes grow wide and I see her nostrils flare. "Oh, geez, Mattie," she says. She gets my dilemma right away, glancing around to see who else is nearby and what they're doing.

"Remnants of some food poisoning," I say in my sotto voce tone, speaking fast. "I felt it coming on and I was trying to get to the office. I took the corner a little fast, hit a patch of ice, and the rear end fishtailed. We're okay. I'm sure the car is okay. It's as tough as a tank, thanks to those reinforced panels Hurley added onto it a couple years back. And I don't think the lamppost suffered any permanent damage. Please don't make me get out of the car. And please don't let Patrick near me."

I stop, and suck in a deep breath as I've exhausted my lungs' reserves with this rapid-fire explanation, all uttered in one whispered breath. Brenda, bless her, gets the situation immediately and takes things in hand.

"Hey, Devo," she says, using the nickname I've heard other cops use for Patrick, presumably a play on his last name. "Car and lamppost okay over there?"

Patrick nods. "It's fine," he says. "The car isn't even dented. There's a tiny paint scrape on the rear-quarter panel, but that's it. And the lamppost is solid." Just to prove his point, he wraps his gloved hands around the lamppost and tries to shake it. It doesn't move.

"Great," Brenda says. "Can you steer traffic around us then, until Mattie gets back on the road? I don't see any need to do a report here. No one is hurt."

Patrick, who is well known for hating the myriad bits of paperwork that accompany his job, even more so than most cops, is all too eager to comply.

He steps out behind the hearse and waves on the few cars that have stopped to gawk. I hit the power button for the passenger-side window and lower it.

"Get in, Izzy," I say.

He bends down—though he doesn't have to go far, given his height—and leans in the window. "If it's all the same to you, I think I'll walk the rest of the way."

I narrow my eyes at him, glaring. "Really? That's how you're going to play this? You, who have smelled things ten times worse, like week-old summer decomp!"

"It's nothing personal," he says. "I need the exercise."

I am not fooled by his attempt to soften the blow, but I'm anxious enough about escaping this whole scene that I let it go. "Fine. Don't slip on the ice and break your ass," I mutter as I power the window back up, thinking evilly that a little fall, just enough to make his butt hurt, would be justice attained.

Brenda steps back and checks for traffic, then gives me a nod and a *come-on* gesture with her hand. I slip the hearse back into gear and gently tap the gas. The tank glides off the curb with a small jolt, and I am back on the road. I give Brenda a smile of gratitude and mouth the words "Thank you" to her as I drive by.

Less than a minute later, I pull into the relative safety and shelter of our underground parking garage. I park as close to the elevator as I can and climb out of the car. I look back inside and see a large brown area of wet nastiness on the leather seat. I can feel my pants clinging to my backside, and then I feel my stomach rumble ominously. That gets me moving, so to speak, and I slam the car door shut, badge my way into the elevator, and head for the main floor, praying that I won't run into anyone.

Chapter 14

As I said before, the Fates like to mess with me and clearly they aren't finished with their shenanigans for the day. I take off my jacket in the elevator, hoping it has escaped the damage my clothes have sustained, and examine it. Fortunately, it's a waist-high jacket, and the lava doesn't appear to have made it quite that high. I drape it over my arm and hold it away from my body as I hear the little *ding* that announces I've reached my floor.

I start to barrel out of the elevator car as soon as the door slides open, but I'm forced to stop because someone is standing in my way. Startled, I step back and slap a hand to my chest. Then I recognize the face of my blocker. It's one of the twins from the Johnson Funeral Home.

"You startled me," I say with a smile. Then I remember my predicament, and as the elevator door starts to close, I'm tempted to let it and head back down to the garage. But I step forward, catch it, and exit into the hallway, my embarrassment momentarily forgotten as the details of the face before me start to sink in and make me suspect that the woman in front of me is Kit, not Cass. She is bruised under both eyes; there is a cut across the bridge of her nose; her lower lip is bleeding and swollen. "Are you okay, Kit?" I ask as the door closes behind me.

She starts to answer, but ends up clamping a hand over her mouth instead. I figure it's because she just got a whiff of me, and I start to explain and apologize for my situation. But then the girl bursts into hard, heaving sobs, turning away from me. For a brief moment, I wonder if the rank smell of me is what brought her to tears, or if it's something else. Then I remember that this is Kit Johnson, a woman I've watched scoop up the liquid remains of a putrescent corpse without so much as wrinkling her nose, and I come to my senses.

"Kit, what happened?" I say, putting a hand on her shoulder. "Is it that guy you've been dating?"

She sucks in great gulps of air, trying to get her sobs under control. Unfortunately for her, the air she is currently sucking in is redolent with the smell of poop. Her eyes grow big, and the hand over her mouth clamps a little tighter. She stares at me, a questioning expression on her face.

Wanting to address the stinky elephant in the room so we can move on, I do a quick pirouette, point to my butt, and say, "Sorry. I've got food poisoning and I had an accident. That's what you smell. Why don't you come with me to the locker room so I can get cleaned up?"

Her sobs have abated somewhat, and the expression I can see in her eyes over the top of her hand changes. The hand drops, and I watch as the fattened lip starts to curl up at the corners.

"You pooped in your pants?" she says, her tone a mixture of disbelief and amusement.

"I did."

She makes a funny movement with her chest that looks like the start of a convulsion, and then she bursts out laughing. She laughs hysterically for a moment, tears rolling down her face, and just as I become convinced the red-hot shame crawling up my face is about to make me burst into flames, the laughter reverts to sobs. It's unnerving to see this normally cool, reserved, and collected woman cycling between emotions with such instability.

"Come on, Kit," I say, taking her elbow and steering her toward the locker room. She comes along without protest, her sobs transforming into hiccups that make her elbow bounce in my hand. I push open the locker room door and steer her toward a bench seat along one wall. I leave her there a moment and head for the scrub closet, giving a silent prayer of thanks when I see that the laundry service has been here during the night with their delivery. I dig out the necessary items, and then head back to Kit.

"I need to hop in the shower," I tell her. "You sit here until I come out, okay?"

She nods, but does so in a half-handed, glazed sort of way that makes me doubt the veracity of her answer. In the end, I opt for showering with the curtain open so I can see her, not caring if she can see my nakedness, though I'm not sure she's seeing anything at the moment. Her eyes are staring off into space with an eerie emptiness.

I peel off my fouled pants and toss them and my undies in the trash. Then I wash my hands and remove the rest of my clothing, which is fortunately uncontaminated. I step into the shower, scrub myself clean from the waist down, and then step out and dry off, keeping a watchful eye on Kit the entire time. She doesn't move. In fact, she is so still, I find myself staring at her chest to ensure myself that she's still breathing.

I dress quickly, momentarily cursing the fact that I have no clean underwear and will have to go commando. I'd gladly put on an adult diaper right now if I had one—the embarrassment of wearing one mild in comparison to the shame I'd experience with another accident.

Once I'm done, I settle on the bench beside Kit. She is still staring, and doesn't acknowledge my presence. I have a sense that her mind is off somewhere else, and this is confirmed when I touch her arm and she starts, looking at me with wide-eyed surprise.

"Kit," I begin softly, "do you want me to call your sister? Or anyone else?"

She shakes her head and shifts her gaze to the floor. "Cass was right about Ernie," she says. "And knowing her, she won't be able to resist telling me so, over and over again. I don't think I can deal with that right now."

"I take it Ernie hit you?"

"He did that," Kit says with a humorless laugh. "I told him that I wanted to go to the movies with my sister tomorrow night, just the two of us, and he went berserk. He gets insanely jealous and he kept saying that he didn't believe me. He thought I was going to meet some guy rather than my sister. I told him he could call Cass to verify it, but he only got madder, saying that Cass would lie for me because she doesn't like him." She pauses and looks over at me with a wan smile. "He's right about that," she says. "Anyway, I told him he was being ridiculous and overbearing." She pauses again, starts to rake her upper teeth over her lower lip, but stops, wincing, as her teeth touch the split there. I wince in empathy, both for the pain she is feeling in her lip, and for what I suspect came next in her encounter with Ernie. "He didn't like that at all," she says with a slight hiccup. "He hauled off and slapped me in the mouth so hard that I saw stars."

She splays her hands on her knees, staring at them for a moment, and then she lifts them and rubs them together. "I hit him back because I was so angry," she says, looking abashed. "So I guess I had it coming."

"You did not!" I say in as stern a tone as I can muster. "It is never right or acceptable for a man to hit a woman, and he hit you first, without provocation."

"Oh, I provoked him," she says with a sardonic grin. "With my words. I knew it would make him angry."

I shake my head, frowning at her. "Kit, I don't care how harsh your words were. There are no words in the English language that can justify him hitting you."

She shrugs, clearly not convinced. Her attitude about all of this worries me. I've seen it before in women who are abused; there's an exuberance of forgiveness for their partners' violent behavior, a willingness to accept some of the blame for the abuse, and a blanket of excuses and denial that they wrap around themselves like a cloak. It can become a vicious cycle. Kit needs professional help.

"Did you follow up with that social worker who gave her card to you?" I ask Kit. "Hildy Schneider?"

Kit shakes her head and looks over at me with red, tear-stained eyes. "I didn't have time. Everything happened so fast. And it escalated." She swallows hard and looks away for a moment. "He has a gun," she says in a quiet, quavering voice. "And he threatened to use it on me." She risks a look back at me then, gauging my reaction.

"Did he aim it at you during your fight?"

She shakes her head. "He never got it out, but I think he would have if he'd had the chance. After I hit him back, he hit me some more. I kept trying to get away from him, or get him to stop, but he wouldn't. I finally grabbed my keys from the hook by the door and used the pepper spray I carry on my key ring. It stopped him momentarily, but he was thrashing and bellowing like a mad bull. I've never seen him so mad, so I ran out of the apartment to get away and give him some time to cool off. I got in my car and pulled out of the lot, but I didn't know where to go. I was afraid Ernie would come after me, and I felt certain he'd come with his gun. I thought about going to the funeral home and my parents, but I didn't want to risk anyone else getting hurt. The police station was an option, but I was afraid they might try to confront Ernie, and if he had his gun, he might . . ."

She let the rest of that thought go unspoken, but I knew what she was thinking. Given what I had learned about Ernie and his temper, a showdown resulting in a shoot-out was a highly likely outcome.

"I knew Ernie would check my sister's place first thing," Kit went on after a brief silence. "Then I thought of here. I figured I could badge myself in downstairs, and even if no one was here at the time, I knew someone would be soon. And he wouldn't be able to get in."

"That was smart thinking," I tell her. And it was. The sisters had their own key cards for accessing the elevator, since they were the designated transporters for any bodies that needed to be brought to our morgue. And this early in the morning, our office was locked up and reasonably secure. "How long were you here before I arrived?"

"Only about five minutes," she says.

"Has Ernie tried to contact you?"

"He couldn't," she says. "I left without my phone. But I used one of your phones when I got here to call my sister and warn her, in case Ernie showed up there."

"And he hadn't?"

"I don't know," she says, fighting back tears. "She didn't answer. She sometimes does that on our days off, and today we have a part-time employee covering pickups."

"What's Ernie's last name?"

"Roberts," she says.

"I'm going to call Hurley. He's at the police station and can be here in minutes." I rise from the bench and walk over to where I'd dropped my jacket and purse just inside the locker room door. I dig out my cell phone and place the call. As I'm waiting for the connection to go through, I look over at Kit. She looks troubled, her face screwed up with worry, her hands wringing, one foot tapping nervously on the floor.

"What's up, Squatch?" Hurley answers. "Are you okay? Do you need me for something?"

"I'm okay," I say, opting not to share the fact that I'm less toilet trained than our toddler at the moment. "But I do need your help. Not for me, for Kit Johnson. She's here at my office. She came here after running away from her boyfriend, Ernie Roberts, early this morning after he slapped her around and then threatened to shoot her."

"Shoot her?" I can tell from the stringent tone of Hurley's voice that I have his full attention. "Did he actually aim a gun at her?"

"She says no, but that's probably only because she didn't give him a chance to get it. She pepper-sprayed him and ran. But he has a gun, and she said he threatened to kill her."

"Does she know where he is now?"

"No. But she feels certain he is going to come after her."

"Okay, hold on a sec." I hear him holler out "Devo!" but it's muffled, making me think he has his hand over his phone. Apparently, Brenda and Patrick have returned to the station from the scene of my earlier accident. I hope they haven't told Hurley about it. A few seconds later, I hear Hurley issue orders to Devo to check on the whereabouts of Ernie Roberts, and to bring him in if he can find him. Then he caveats his instructions with a warning that Roberts may be armed and dangerous.

"Okay, Squatch," he says, returning to me on the phone. "I've got Devo and Joiner out looking for the guy. I want you and Kit to stay there at your office and make sure nobody lets this guy in. Got it?"

I nod, realize Hurley can't see that, and say, "Got it." Then I remember Izzy, who should have arrived here not long after I did. It would have taken him only minutes more to walk the few blocks from the scene of the accident to our office. "Are you going to come over here and talk to Kit?" I ask. I feel exposed and vulnerable all of a sudden, and I can't help looking over my shoulder toward the locker room door.

"I will, but not just yet. You should be safe there. Don't go anywhere, and call me if anything happens."

"Okay. I will." I disconnect the call and glance at the clock on the wall. It's 7:38, and Cass, our receptionist, typically comes in at eight. I need to let her know what's going on, and check on Izzy.

Chapter 15

I take Kit to my office, aka the library, settle her in at a desk, and tell her to stay put. Then I head back the way we came to check Izzy's office and see if he is there. He is, settled in behind his desk working at his computer.

"Ah, I see you've managed to clean yourself up," he says with a wicked gleam in his eye.

"Yes." My answer is short and clipped, making Izzy frown. "But I still need to do something about my car."

"Call Not a Trace, that biohazard company that cleans up death scenes," Izzy suggests.

"Good idea. I trust you enjoyed your walk."

"I did. It was very . . . refreshing." He bites back a grin.

I don't return the smile and his quickly fades when he hears the worried tone of my next question. "How did you come into the building?"

"Through the garage. Why?"

I fill him in on my own arrival, Kit's situation, and the current status of things. "I trust there wasn't anyone suspicious-looking outside when you came in?"

"Not that I noticed, but I confess, I wasn't really focusing on that."

"Hurley has officers looking for Roberts, and I doubt he'd think to look here. But it's always possible."

"Where did Kit park? I don't recall seeing any other cars in the garage besides yours."

I think back to my own entry into the garage, and realize I didn't see any other cars there, either. I had to admit, though, I was otherwise distracted. And, I realize, I have no idea what Kit's personal car looks like. Every time I've seen her and her sister, they've been driving a hearse.

"Good question," I say. "This boyfriend of hers might be able to find her car. I'll ask her."

"Keep me posted."

Next I head out to the front reception area. It is fifteen minutes before eight, and Cass has a habit of showing up at eight o'clock on the dot. I walk over and check the front door to make sure it's locked securely, and then I head for the desk while taking out my cell phone and dialing Cass's number. She answers on the first ring.

"I'm just about to leave the house," she says, forgoing any formal greeting.

"That's fine," I say. "Take your time, and I need you to be careful when you get here." I then fill her in on the situation. When I'm done, she asks what Roberts looks like, so she can keep an eye out for him. That's when I realize I have no idea. I tell her so, and that I'll see if I can find out; then I suggest that she keep an eye out for anyone who looks out of place or suspicious, and if she sees such a person to keep on driving. I disconnect the call and log into the computer at the front desk to see if Arnie is logged in yet. He typically comes to work at seven, and sure enough, he's already checked in.

I head back to the library and find Kit exactly where I left her. She doesn't appear to have moved an inch. Her eyes are staring off into space, and I can only imagine what sort of movie reel is playing in her head.

"Kit, are you okay?" I ask in a soft voice, not wanting to startle her.

She jerks violently anyway, whipping her head around to stare at me. After a moment, she calms and nods slowly.

"I need to ask you a couple of questions," I say, grabbing a chair and pulling it up beside her. "To start with, can you tell me what Ernie looks like?"

She stares at me for several seconds without answering, her brows furrowed into a frown. "Are the cops going to hurt him?" she asks finally, ignoring my question.

She seems overly concerned for his welfare, and her attitude irritates me. If a guy had done to me what Ernie has done to her, I wouldn't care if the bastard was hurt. In fact, I'd be inclined to hurt him myself. But I know that victims of this type of domestic abuse are often torn and confused about their feelings for the abuser, and I tamp down my own ire. Presumably she had cared about this man enough at some point to make him a significant part of her life, and perhaps she was struggling with the memory of this version of the man as compared to the current one.

"I don't know," I say honestly. "I know they'll try not to hurt him, but if he is armed and confrontational, things could get ugly."

Kit looks down at the floor and nods slowly. Tears well up and streak their way over her lids and down her cheeks.

"Can you give me a description of Ernie, please?" I ask again.

She looks at me, swipes irritably at the tears on her face with the back of one hand, and then looks at the computer that is sitting on the desk in front of us. "Can I use the computer?" she asks. "I can show you a picture of him."

I nod, awaken the computer, and log into it. Then I turn the controls over to Kit. She manipulates the mouse deftly, types in a few things, and then turns the screen toward me. I see that she has logged into her Facebook account, and on the screen is a picture of a much happier Kit and a man who is tall, dark, bearded, and, notably, not smiling. He has an arm draped over Kit's shoulders, his fingers wrapping around her upper arm in a tight, possessive-looking grip. Kit is a tall woman, not as tall as me, but taller than most. I gauge her height to be somewhere around five-ten, and since she appears to be wearing flats in the picture on the screen, and Ernie stands a good six inches above her, I figure his height is somewhere around six-four. His shoulders are broad, as is his chest. He is a mountain of a man, and I feel a momentary twinge of worry for the cops who are looking for him.

"He's a big guy," I say to Kit. She nods, and I notice that she is avoiding looking at the screen. I reach over and take the mouse and keyboard, and quickly save the picture. Then I send it to Cass's cell phone. "I don't recall seeing another car down in the garage when I pulled in this morning," I say as I'm working. "Where did you park, and what does your car look like? I assume you didn't drive the hearse."

"I have a Toyota pickup with a cap on the back," she says in a robotic-sounding voice. "It's white. I parked on the street between here and the police station because I was going to go there, but then I changed my mind and came here instead." She pauses, swallows hard, and continues. "I didn't want to trigger . . . anything."

I know what she's implying. She's afraid Ernie might be mad enough, crazy enough perhaps, to go into the police station, gun waving, and get himself shot. She hasn't parked that far away from the station, so the possibility of that happening isn't ruled out entirely. "What is Ernie driving?" I ask.

"A black SUV. It's a Ford of some sort."

Great, I think sardonically, *a car that looks like one-third of all the other cars on the road.* I get up and walk around the room, feeling anxious. I send a text to Cass with a description of the car, and then I dial Arnie's number. He doesn't answer, so I leave a voice mail message telling him what's going on, with a description of both Ernie and his vehicle. When I'm done, I look back at Kit, who is once again staring off into space.

"I'll be right back," I tell her, and then I head for Izzy's office again, intending to update him on the situation. The second I step out into the hall, my phone rings. I see it's Hurley and answer, "Have they got him?"

"No, and things have taken a turn." I can tell from the level of anxiety in his voice that this turn is one for the worse. "He's been to Kit's sister's apartment."

I continue down the hall, and as I approach the elevator, I hear it rumbling its way up from the basement level. I breathe a sigh of relief, knowing that Cass must have made it here safely.

"He threatened to shoot her if she didn't tell him where Kit was," Hurley continues. "He'd already been to the funeral home, so he knew she wasn't there." He pauses, and takes in a deep breath. "Squatch, he pistol-whipped the parents and then beat up Kit's sister pretty good."

"Oh no! Are they okay?"

"I think she will be, but he messed the parents up pretty good. And there's something else."

The elevator *ding* announces its arrival. I hear my phone beep to tell me there is another call, and when I glance at the screen, I see it's Arnie. I let it go to voice mail, knowing I can call him back as soon as I'm done talking to Hurley. I turn around as the elevator door slides open and Hurley continues his update.

"Apparently, Kit called her sister from your office, and Roberts saw it on the caller ID on the sister's phone. He took her key card to your office, so he may show up there."

Indeed, he might, I think. *Indeed, he has.* I gawk openmouthed at Ernie Roberts as he steps out of the elevator, gun in hand.

"Squatch?" Hurley says. "You need to be careful. I'm on my way over there now, but stay alert, okay?"

"Not another word," says Roberts. His voice is low and calm—barely above a whisper—but I'm not fooled by it. I know this is only so Hurley won't hear him. The cold glint in his eye and the barrel of the gun he's pointing at me tell me that he is anything but calm on the inside. "Hand it over." He does a *gimme* gesture with his free hand, and as soon as I hand him the phone, he disconnects the call with his thumb and drops the phone in his jacket pocket.

Ernie takes another step toward me, his huge size looming over me. I detect the reek of alcohol on his breath, and it's emanating from his pores. "Where is she?" he demands.

My mind quickly races through my options. The gun, which is inches away from my chest, eliminates most of them. In a bizarre segue of thoughts, I wonder if the ample size of my bosom might prove to be an advantage, should I get shot. Maybe all that flesh will slow down the bullet's track enough before it hits anything vital. Best not to get shot at all, of course, so I decide to try to buy some time by playing dumb.

"Sir, I don't know what it is you want, but it's difficult for me to help you with that gun pointing at

me. It makes me very nervous." I say this in as calm
and reasoned a tone as I can muster, though I hear
the quaver in my voice.

"Where the hell is she?" he asks again, tilting his
head to one side and moving the gun a hair closer.
His tone is much more demanding this time.

"I'm sorry, sir, are you looking for someone who
has died?"

"Kit Johnson," he says through gritted teeth.
"Don't play any frigging games with me, lady. Where
is she?"

"Kit?" I say, trying on an apologetic expression.
"Oh, she was here, but she left a few minutes ago.
You just missed her."

"Bullshit!" he barks, spraying spittle at me and
making me jump. I take a step back away from
him, but he quickly closes the distance. "I know
you're lying. Now you can either tell me where she
is, or I can kill you right here and go look for her
myself." With this, he raises the gun, aiming it between my eyes.

Not enough extra flesh there to save me, I think
idiotically. And even Barbara's magical ministrations, using all the makeup in the world, won't be
able to fix up what would be left of my face.
Humpty Dumpty would never get put back together again, even with all the king's horses and all
the king's men. The elevator makes a clunking
sound and then starts to move, going back down to
the garage. The noise brings me back to my senses.

Hurley, I think, hoping. But then I realize it
might also be Cass, arriving to work unaware that
the danger I'd warned her to watch for outside was
currently inside. And even if it is Hurley, he'd be a

sitting duck when the elevator doors opened. The simple fact that our last phone call ended abruptly might not be enough to alert him. Calls get dropped all the time in our office.

I need to get Ernie on the move, away from the elevator.

"Okay," I say, a bit breathless. I hold up my hands like a traffic cop. "Just relax and I'll take you to her." I hear the elevator doors slide open below us.

I turn away and head down the hall, half expecting to feel a bullet in my back at any second. After a few steps, I turn and enter a smaller hallway, at the end of which is a large metal door. I hear Ernie behind me, but don't turn to look at him. When I reach the door, I punch in a number code on the lock, hear the click, and open the door.

"What the hell?" Ernie says as I step inside the morgue refrigerator. He surveys the contents of the large, cold room with eyes suddenly grown huge. There are only two bodies in here at the moment, both of them lying on a stretcher and covered with sheets. One of those bodies is that of Liesel Paulsen. The other is a large man in his fifties, who we determined died of a heart attack, and who was from out of town. We are waiting on the family to make arrangements to have the body transported to Minnesota. No need to look at toe tags to tell who is who in here. The huge mound beneath the sheet on one of the carts is the equivalent of about three Liesels.

Off to one side of the refrigerated room is a second door, this one leading into the autopsy suite. I head for it, talking over my shoulder. "Sorry to go through this way," I say, "but Kit was going to put a body in here, so I thought I should check it first. She must be in the autopsy suite." With brazen boldness, I push open the second door and step into the autopsy room. Only then do I turn and look back at Ernie.

I admit I was hoping he would be too intimidated by the dead people in the fridge to follow me, but I quickly see I was wrong and realize how stupid it was of me to hope for it in the first place. The man is dating one of the Johnson twins, after all, the creepiest women in town. And he's clearly blinded by rage, in the throes of an obsession that has taken over his mind. He's right behind me, and he looks pissed. It doesn't take him long to figure out that Kit isn't in this room.

I try to think fast, searching both my mind and the nearby parts of the room for something I can use as a weapon. Ernie looks angrier now than he did before, and I fear I'm a goner. My mind races through a few scenarios, trying to plan an escape, but there is nothing I can think of that would be faster than a bullet. Any second now, Ernie is going to shoot me and then head back out to the main part of the office, where everyone else is. I need to stop him, or warn the others, but how?

I hear a ringing sound then, and realize it's my cell phone in Ernie's pocket. It distracts Ernie from me for a second or two, and as he goes to reach into his pocket, I react on blind instinct. My mind registers the slight waver of his aim with the gun, so that it's pointing to the left side of my head now. My eyes dart to my right and spy the metal

Mayo stand next to the autopsy table. In the same second, I bend to my right, grab the top of the metal stand, and fling it with all my might at Ernie.

His reactions are quick. The gun swings around as the Mayo stand slams into his free arm. I hear a loud explosion by my left ear, hear the reverberating clang of the Mayo stand's top as it separates from the frame and hits the ceramic floor, and I feel a white-hot burn on my left arm near my shoulder. Next I hear a muffled curse, and I look around frantically, trying to determine where Ernie is and, more important, where's the gun. I see him standing mere inches away, behind me and to my right. The gun is pointed at the floor, and Ernie is struggling to maintain his balance. I whirl toward him and shove as hard as I can. He falls to the floor, and I make a mad dash past him and run into the fridge. As I make my turn toward the other door, I pause long enough to grab the leg of the body closest to me, that of the large man. Mustering up all my strength, I wrap my right arm around his leg and heave him toward me. The brakes on the stretcher are locked, so I succeed in dragging the man's body off the stretcher and onto the floor, where it lands with a sickening thud. I spin around and hit the second door on the fly, knowing Ernie is probably right behind me. As soon as I'm past the door, I start to yell for help at the top of my lungs, but can't because I run straight into a mass of solid flesh.

"Hurley!" I say, both frightened and relieved. "He has a gun. He's right behind me."

I risk a glance over my shoulder and see Ernie come barreling into the refrigerator like a mad bull. He sees the body on the floor at the last second, but his attempt to leap over it fails. He trips, the gun fires, and the echoing sound of the subsequent ricochet is deafening.

Hurley pushes me aside and steps through the door I just came out of, his gun aimed and ready. He stops near Ernie's head and yells, "Don't make a move, asshole!"

A hand clamps down on my shoulder from behind me, and I let out a yelp as I whirl around. It's Kit.

"Is that Ernie in there?" she asks. Behind her, I see Arnie come around the corner at the end of the hallway, his eyes huge.

"Arnie, call the police!" I holler. "Get them over here *now*! Tell them we have an active shooter situation, but it's contained."

Arnie nods and disappears in a flash. Kit tries to push past me to go into the fridge, but I restrain her, triggering a sharp bolt of pain down my left arm.

Hurley has managed to take Ernie's gun away, and he handcuffs the man's hands behind his back, leaving him on the floor next to the Minnesota man's body. Enough of Ernie's adrenaline has worn off at this point that he's starting to realize the naked body next to him is dead. He wriggles away from it, crawling across the fridge floor like the worm he is.

Hurley exits the fridge and hurries over to me, his face pale. With one hand, he grabs the neck of my scrub top and yanks it down toward my left shoulder. This causes an electric current of pain that makes me yell out. I look down at the area of the pain and see blood, lots of blood. That's when I realize I've been shot.

"Mattie, are you okay?" Hurley asks, his voice trembling slightly.

"I don't know," I say, focused on nothing but the source of my pain and the hole in my left shoulder. My adrenaline is starting to wear off, too, and my body begins to shake. "I think I've been shot."

I look at Hurley, then back at my shoulder. So much blood. And then the world goes black.

Chapter 16

My mind registers the sounds first: lots of people talking, the stomp of running feet, shouts, doors banging. I open my eyes and see Arnie staring down at me. Above him, and me, is the ceiling, and I realize I'm lying on the floor.

"Are you okay, Mattie?" Arnie says.

"I think so," I say, doing a quick bodily inventory. I can feel everything, some things too much so. "What happened?"

"You fainted."

The memories rush in then, and I make a frantic effort to get up from the floor, crab-walking backward away from the morgue fridge.

"Whoa," Arnie says, pushing down on my injured shoulder. "It's okay. They got the guy. They're taking him over to the police station now."

I squeeze my eyes closed with relief. "Thank goodness. Did anyone get hurt?"

"Just you, unless you count the bullet that hit the body in the fridge in the head. I imagine we're going to have a challenge explaining that one to his family."

My left shoulder is throbbing painfully, and I realize then that Arnie is pushing on it. "That hurts," I tell him, wincing and putting a hand up next to his on my shoulder. I realize my top has been torn to provide better access to my wound and some nonsensical part of my mind bemoans the fact that there will now me one less 2XL scrub top in the inventory.

"Sorry, but I have to," Arnie says. "You were hit in the shoulder. Izzy looked at the wound and it appears the bullet tunneled into your skin, but didn't hit any bones. There was a tiny artery that was nicked, but with a little pressure, we have it contained. It looks and probably feels worse than it is because of all the blood."

Izzy comes around the corner, carrying a bag. He squats next to me. "Let me see," he says, prying Arnie's hand away. "Ah, yes. Looks good. The bleeding is under control for now. I'll put a dressing on it."

He removes supplies from the bag he is carrying and goes about placing gauze pads over the wound and then wrapping it with rolled gauze under and around my arm.

"Where's Kit?" I ask, wincing as Izzy's ministrations trigger tiny shocks of pain.

"She's in the library with some police officers," Izzy says, taping the last bit of dressing in place.

"There's an ambulance on the way to take you to the hospital."

"I don't need an ambulance," I say irritably. "Help me up."

Both Izzy and Arnie start to object, so I use my good arm to get to my knees, and from there, onto my feet. I feel a little woozy at first and lean against the wall as the two men eye me warily, but after a few seconds, my head clears.

"You need to go to the ER and get that wound cleaned properly," Izzy says.

"I'll drive over there."

"The hell you will," Izzy says. "First of all, you fainted not that long ago, so there's no way you belong behind the wheel of a car. And secondly, I don't think your car is a good way to get there." He raises his eyebrows at me and I belatedly remember the mess in my front seat.

Arnie looks at Izzy curiously, but, fortunately, all Izzy says is "Let the ambulance take you."

"I don't want or need an ambulance," I say irritably. "Can't someone drive me?"

"I can," says a voice behind me. It's Hurley. He walks over, wraps a strong arm around my waist, and pulls me close. "You scared the hell out of me, Squatch. When I saw all that blood on your chest and arm, I thought . . ." His voice trails off and I see him swallow hard.

"It's just a flesh wound," I tell him. "Hurts like hell, but it's not fatal."

Hurley nudges me forward, his arm rock solid around my waist. "Let's get it looked at."

We walk together to the main hallway and after

a quick detour to fetch my coat, we take the elevator down to the underground garage. "Your car or mine?" Hurley says as the elevator door opens.

"Yours," I say quickly, realizing Brenda and Devo must not have shared the information about my earlier accident. As if my gut is having a simpatico reaction to the memory of the morning's earlier events, it rumbles and shifts. I squeeze my eyes closed, praying that it's nothing more than a lingering bit of borborygmus, aka bowel sounds.

We make it to both the car and the ER without further incident. Hurley talks the entire time, filling me in on some of the details of Ernie's arrest. "I don't think we'll have to worry about him for a long time to come," he concludes. "Good thing, I think, because Kit is all concerned about him, upset that he's been arrested. She keeps saying it's her fault. I think if she had the chance, she'd go back to him in a heartbeat."

"Stockholm syndrome, or something like it," I say. "Sadly, not that unusual in victims of domestic abuse."

We arrive at the ER, and we're ushered into the back with great haste when Hurley announces that I've been shot. It's an overreaction, but I'm in enough pain that I don't care and don't bother to clarify things. I'm placed in a bed, promptly stripped of all my clothing, and within minutes of my arrival, there are two nurses and a doctor standing at my bedside. I have a full set of vital signs taken and am put on a cardiac monitor. This initial flurry of activity dies quickly, once they remove Izzy's dressing and realize my wound isn't life threatening, and Doc Leonard checks me over from head to foot.

"Looks like you were lucky," he says when he's done. "I'll have a nurse clean and bandage that wound on your shoulder. I'm going to put you on an antibiotic as a precaution, and I'll give you a script for a few pain pills."

"Sounds great," I say. "Can I get some ibuprofen for now?"

"Sure. Want something stronger?" Leonard asks.

I shake my head. "Not now. I still have work to do today."

Hurley huffs out a breath of annoyance. "You need to go home, Squatch. You weren't feeling well this morning as it was. And now you've got this to add to the mix."

"I'm fine," I insist. "Or I will be, once I get some ibuprofen."

"On it," says Dr. Leonard, and he disappears from my room.

Hurley sits down in a chair beside my stretcher and leans forward. I know from both his posture and his expression that he is ramping up for an argument on whether or not I'm going home for the rest of the day.

"Save it," I say before he can speak a word. "I'm going back to the office. Chris will be in at noon and I can head home then. Okay?"

He narrows his eyes at me, studying my face. Something in my expression convinces him that further argument would be a waste of time, effort, and breath. He sighs heavily.

A nurse named Becky comes into the room then,

armed with a medication cup, some water, some cleaning solution, and dressing supplies. She administers the ibuprofen to me, and then prepares to clean my wound. I brace myself, knowing it isn't going to be fun.

Ten minutes, and a slew of colorful cusswords later, my wound is cleaned and redressed. Before Becky leaves, I thank her and ask if Hildy, the social worker, is on duty.

"She is."

"Would you mind calling her and asking her if she can come talk to me for a minute?"

Becky's brow furrows with curiosity, but then she shrugs and says, "Sure."

"What do you want with the social worker?" Hurley asks.

"I want to talk to her about Kit. That girl is going to need some counseling."

Hurley opens his mouth to say something, but his phone rings. "It's Arnie," he says. He answers with, "What's up, Arnie?" He listens for a few seconds, looks at me, smiles, and says, "She's fine. She'll be back in the office within the hour." He listens some more, and I can see from his expression that whatever Arnie is telling him has him excited. Finally he says, "Sounds promising enough. I'll be there as quickly as I can."

Even before he disconnects the call, I'm leaning toward him, eager and curious. "What's he got?"

"He wouldn't tell me specifics, but he said he's made a computer connection that might give us a strong lead in the Paulsen case. Apparently, some of his cronies—"

He's interrupted when the door to my room slides open and Hildy Schneider walks in. "Hello, Hildy," I say. "Good to see you again . . . well, sort of."

"Oh, my, what happened to you?" Hildy says with a frown.

"I got shot," I tell her. "It isn't serious, just a flesh wound. Remember that young woman you talked to with the abusive boyfriend?"

"Yes, Kit Johnson." Hildy's eyes grow big. "This was him?" When I nod, she says, "Wow! That escalated faster than I thought it might."

"I think it happened faster than anyone thought it might," I say. "And Kit, the girl in question, really needs some counseling. Can you help?"

"Of course," Hildy says without hesitation. "I run a domestic abuse group along with some other therapy groups . . . substance abuse, grief and loss, that sort of thing. But given what's happened here, I'm thinking Ms. Johnson might need some one-on-one time first."

"I agree," I say, feeling something niggle at my brain. For a moment, I chalk it up to the pain pill I took, but then I remember that it was nothing more than ibuprofen.

Before I can explore it further, Hildy asks, "Where is the man in question?"

Hurley fields this one. "We have him in custody. He won't see the other side of the bars for quite some time."

Hildy nods approvingly. "That may make things

easier," she says. "Though it will all depend on Ms. Johnson's frame of mind. Should I call her?"

"If you have the time, I'd prefer it if you could see her straightaway. She's over in my office."

Hildy frowns. "I'm on duty here at the hospital until three, and can't really leave the premises. I could see her after three, or if there's a way to bring her over here right away, I'll make time for her in my office."

"Her parents and sister are here," Hurley says. "Kit's boyfriend did a number on them, too. It would be easy to bring her over here to see them, if you think that would be appropriate."

I'm caught a little off guard by this news. Only now do I recall Hurley telling me during the earlier phone call that Ernie pistol-whipped Kit's parents, and beat her sister as well. "Are the Johnsons okay?" I ask.

"Oh, the Johnsons," Hildy says with sudden dawning. "I didn't realize they were related. Seems every other person who comes in here is either a Johnson, a Nelson, or an Anderson. The ER staff said they were victims of a home invasion. That was the boyfriend also?"

Hurley and I both nod solemnly.

"Well, now, it seems this Ernie fellow is quite the *drittsekk,*" Hildy says. I arch my brows at this, unsure what the term means, but gathering the general meaning nonetheless. "I heard the daughter was here, too, but I haven't spoken to her," Hildy goes on. "Truth be told, I haven't spoken to the parents, either, because they weren't in any condition for it yet. I planned to come back to them. If I remember right, Mrs. Johnson is being admitted to the hospital, but Mr. Johnson is likely to be discharged. The nurses said their daughter would get discharged home, too."

"I hope Mrs. Johnson is okay," I say, worried.

"I think she's okay," Hildy says. "My understanding is that she's being admitted only as a precautionary thing because she's on a blood-thinning medication. They want to watch her overnight."

"Oh, good," I say with relief, figuring that any serious, long-term repercussions to the family will only complicate Kit's emotional well-being and counseling.

"I'll have an officer bring Kit over here," Hurley says. "Will you stick around so we can hook you up with her?"

"I'm here till three, like I said," Hildy replies. "I'm a simple phone call away if I'm not here in the emergency department."

We thank Hildy, and she leaves. Hurley gets on his phone and drifts from my room to make the necessary arrangements. My nurse returns with my discharge instructions, and I make quick work of this exchange, eager to get back to the office with Hurley to see what Arnie has dug up on the Paulsen case.

And I'm gifted with a new, intact 2XL scrub top from the hospital's supply to replace my torn one. That almost makes it worth the trip.

Chapter 17

Remembering that I need to call a cleanup company to come and take care of my car, I realize that I don't have my cell phone. Then I remember Ernie taking it from me earlier and putting it in his pocket.

"Hurley, my cell phone was in Ernie Roberts's pocket. I don't suppose you have it?"

He shakes his head and takes out his own phone. By the time we reach the car, he has made arrangements for someone to bring the phone to my office, though it may take a while because it was tagged as Roberts's personal property.

When we get back to my office, I'm glad to see that Kit is gone. Hurley informs me that Brenda Joiner has taken her to the hospital so she can see her family. "Brenda knows to try to hook her up with the social worker," Hurley tells me. "Let's hope it does some good."

"Let me check in with Izzy before we go up to see Arnie," I say.

"No problem," Hurley says. "I'll wait here in your office. I've got a few phone calls to make, and I need to get Richmond over here to see what Arnie has."

I leave Hurley and head for Izzy's office. I find him seated behind his desk buried, as usual, in paperwork.

"What are you doing here?" Izzy says, peering up at me over the top of his glasses when I knock on his open door.

"I'm fine," I tell him. "Chris will be in at noon, and if anything changes before then, I'll go home. But for now, I'm good. I want to keep working on this case. The thought of Liesel's sister still being out there . . ." A shudder runs through me. "It haunts me."

"I hear you," Izzy says, nodding solemnly.

"Besides, my car isn't exactly drivable yet."

"Right," Izzy says. He then starts scrolling through the Rolodex on his desk, stops at the *N* tab, and removes a card. "Call these guys. They'll take care of it for you." He hands me a Rolodex card with a business card stapled to it for Not a Trace.

"Thanks. Do you mind if I use your desk phone and call them from here? I don't have my cell phone."

"Have at it."

I dial the number and make the necessary arrangements, letting the company know that they can get my car keys from the receptionist. When I'm done, I hand Izzy back the card and he sticks it back in its proper place.

"Thank you," I say. "They said they'd be able to get to it within the hour."

"Good. What are you going to do in the mean-time?"

"Arnie called while we were in the ER and said he has something that might help. So Hurley, Richmond, and I are going up there to see what he has."

"Okay, but don't overdo it, Mattie."

"Pot, kettle," I say with a smile.

I leave it at that and go up front to give my car keys to Cass, and explain the situation. With that done, I head back to my office to fetch Hurley.

We opt to take the stairs rather than the elevator up to the second floor, and as we exit the stairwell, we hear the sound of raised voices coming from Arnie's lab and office area. Everyone's nerves are on edge after the morning's events, particularly mine, and I pause in the hallway, listening. Seconds later, I relax a smidge because I recognize the voices as belonging to Arnie and Jonas Kriedeman, the po-lice department's evidence technician. Arnie and Jonas have a lot of overlapping duties, and they generally work well together, divvying up the vari-ous tasks, evidence analysis, and crime scene data between them.

In addition to their work duties, they've also been sharing Laura Kingston for the past two years. Laura joined our staff a couple of years ago, and her position ended up being split between our office and the police department. She spends half of her time working for us, and half of her time working for them. Most of the time, the "us" and "them" in this scenario are Arnie and Jonas. Both men have taken a liking to Laura, and both men have been courting her with varying degrees of success. As I listen to the heated words coming down the hallway, I realize that Laura and the objects of her affections are the subjects at hand.

"She can go wherever she wants to!" I hear Jonas yell. "She doesn't need you enticing her with promises you can't keep."

"Oh, I can keep them," Arnie taunts. "I don't know why you're even bothering to try anymore. Laura made her choice, and you're out, bro."

"The hell I am," Jonas snaps. "I had her over for dinner just the other night," he says in a *so-there* tone. "And my daughter adores her."

"Oh, sure. Play the cute-kid card," Arnie scoffs. "You're using your daughter to get laid. That's pretty low, dude."

"I'm not using my daughter for any such thing," Jonas says. "You take that back."

There is a tightness in Jonas's voice that makes me look at Hurley in panic. He returns the look and we hurry down the hall toward the lab.

"Make me," Arnie taunts.

We reach the door of the lab in time to see Jonas lunge forward and shove Arnie, forcing him backward several steps. After catching his balance, Arnie charges back at Jonas, one fist raised. Jonas rears back just as Arnie lets his fist fly and it misses its mark. Arnie overbalances and starts to fall to the floor, though he manages to catch himself on a chair back and halt his descent. Jonas, seizing the moment, raises a leg and kicks Arnie in the ass. Arnie yells out, "That's it!" and charges at Jonas, head down, coming at him like a raging bull.

Jonas, in classic matador style, deftly steps to one side after grabbing both sides of Arnie's head between his palms and steering him off to the side. So far, Jonas seems to be winning this battle, but that changes in the next few seconds as Arnie lunges across the floor at Jonas's feet, wrapping his arms around Jonas's ankles, and then logrolling.

Jonas goes down hard. Unfortunately for Arnie, he lands on Arnie's legs, forcing a string of colorful curses from Arnie. Both men roll apart, taking a moment to catch their breath and assess their respective injuries.

Arnie's hair, which is again in a man bun, is hanging in threads around his red, sweaty face.

Jonas, who probably outweighs Arnie by a good fifty pounds—though most of that weight is flab—is looking equally exhausted and is breathing hard. He reaches into his pants pocket, pulls out an inhaler, and gives himself a quick squirt.

I take advantage of this momentary lull in the action to say, "You know, there is a lot of very expensive equipment in this room."

"Mattie's right," Arnie says, watching Jonas get to his feet and take another blast from his inhaler. "This equipment is too delicate and expensive to risk damaging any of it."

I'm mentally patting myself on the back for making these two come to their senses when Arnie ruins it for me. "Let's take it out in the hallway," he says.

Jonas nods, stuffs his inhaler in his pocket, and starts to head that way. Arnie picks himself up from the floor to follow. They push past us, and once they reach the hallway, they face off about six feet apart and start circling, both of them hunkered down like wrestlers.

"I'm willing to fight for my woman," Jonas says in his best caveman voice.

"Don't call her *your* woman," Arnie says irritably, shoving his hair back off his face. "She doesn't belong to you."

"You guys," I say in a chastising tone, shaking my head. But I might as well be talking to the walls.

"You talk big, now let's see if you can back it up," Jonas says.

"Bring it on," Arnie says with a sneering curl of his lip and a *come-on* motion of his hands.

With a look of fatalistic determination, Jonas takes a step toward Arnie. Arnie does the same, and then they start circling again.

I give Hurley a pleading look. "Are you going to stop this?"

"Do I have to? It's kind of entertaining. Besides, I'm not sure I should. This ritual is as old as time itself." He shrugs. "Let them fight it out."

I stare at him in disbelief as he smiles and leans back against the door frame, folding his arms over his chest.

In the hallway, the men keep circling, mirroring pugilistic postures and expressions.

"Oh, for Pete's sake," I say, rolling my eyes. "You two are both idiots." I step into the center of their circle and stand there, looking from one to the other.

A chime announcing the arrival of the elevator distracts everyone momentarily. We all look down the hallway and watch as Richmond steps out of the elevator. He starts to walk toward us, but then stops, staring at the weird tableau before him: the two men with their fists raised and me in between them.

I take advantage of the distraction. "If you two idiots really want to beat one another up, I'd suggest you go to a boxing ring somewhere and do it sensibly—though, to me, that's an oxymoron. But before you decide one way or the other, there is something you should probably know."

I'm whipping my head from one side to the other in order to look at both men, and it dawns on me that I tower over and outweigh both of them. If I wanted to put an end to this, I probably could. Then again, little guys can be scrappy and tough, and I only have one good arm. I decide discretion is the better part of valor and continue with my verbal attempts instead. I take a deep breath, and spill: "Laura is dating Patrick Devonshire behind your backs."

Both men's faces instantly change from their angry, pugilistic expressions to looks of confusion at first, then skepticism.

"I don't believe you," Arnie says.

"Believe her," Hurley says. "She's been out with Devo at least a half-dozen times in the past month."

The two men look at Hurley and then, in unison, shift their gazes toward Richmond, who simply nods and shrugs.

Jonas drops his hands to his sides. "I thought it was weird when she told me she couldn't come over for dinner the other night because her tummy was upset, and then she came into work the next day looking fine and ordering spicy beef from Peking Palace for her dinner."

Arnie drops his hands as well. "She told me she had a migraine last night, but when I drove past her house, I heard loud music coming from inside. I figured maybe her headaches were different from most and responded to that sort of thing." He narrows his eyes in thought. "She *has* been hanging out at the police station a lot lately." He looks over at Jonas. "I assumed it was because she was spending more time with you."

Jonas shakes his head. "Haven't seen much of her for the past few weeks, except for during shift change, when she's coming in and I'm getting ready to leave, and the one dinner. She was in a hurry to leave after we ate, claiming she was tired. And now that I think about it, Devonshire was down there in the lab with her on two mornings that I know of. I didn't think anything of it at the time. I just assumed he was inquiring about some evidence on a case or something."

"She's been playing you guys off one another for a long time now," I say. "I think it's time you two wised up, made up, and moved on."

I watch as the expressions on their faces change

from determination to hurt anger, then to disappointment. They finally settle on a sad, resigned expression that I suspect will be a precursor to loneliness. Neither guy has much experience with women, other than Laura, and I know it won't be easy for them to let go of their hopes for their respective relationships with her.

"There are plenty of other fish in the sea," Hurley tosses out nonchalantly.

I wince, knowing that his words, while meant to be encouraging, will likely rankle the two men. Hurley, with his tall good looks, killer blue eyes, and hot body, has women fawning over him all the time. I doubt the man has ever had a problem getting a girl in his entire life. Arnie and Jonas, on the other hand, are more in a class with Richmond and me: not butt-ugly by any means, but certainly not members of the beautiful elite. Neither man is handsome in the classic sense. They are both short; Jonas is pudgy, and Arnie is skinny. Arnie is balding and trying to make up for it by wearing his hair long, and Jonas has an angry mop of hair, which I suspect he cuts himself. Arnie is a bit out-there, personalitywise, with his conspiracy theory tendencies; Jonas, while certainly more down-to-earth, has the extra baggage of being a single parent to an adorable little girl who is seven years old. While I don't think his daughter will scare a lot of women away, it will deter some of them, and his need to care for her and to hold down a full-time job makes his available dating time difficult to come by.

Sure enough, as soon as Hurley utters his plati-
tude, the two men look at one another and roll
their eyes. I feel bad for both of them, and start
thinking I might need to put out some inquiries
and start to play matchmaker.

"Can we get back to work?" I say to no one in
particular. "We have a very pressing case to solve,
and I, for one, would like to do so as soon as possible." I look over at Arnie. "You said you had something for us?"

"I do," he says, making another effort to smooth
back his escaped strands of hair.

Arnie walks into his office and heads straight for
his computer. He pulls out his chair, plops down
into it, and grabs his mouse. The rest of us filter
into the room and form a semicircle behind him,
looking over his shoulders. Richmond nudges me
and then hands me my cell phone.

"That was quick," I say in a low voice.

"There are some advantages to working for a
small-town police department," he says. "We have
a little less bureaucracy to deal with."

I check the phone for missed calls and see that
there was one from Hurley, right around the time
that Ernie and I were facing off in the autopsy
suite. After making a mental note to tell Hurley
how timely his call was, I slip the phone into the
pocket of my scrub pants.

"One of my online buddies hooked into something in a gaming chat room he visited," Arnie begins, tapping away at his keyboard. A moment

later, he has a personal e-mail account up on the screen.

"Gaming chat rooms are rife with pedophiles looking to dupe some young boy or girl into meeting them somewhere. My buddy has befriended a couple of these skanks, and he monitors who it is they're chatting with, though they change usernames all the time so it's hard to keep up with them. He's spent enough time observing their chat behavior, syntax, and lingo that he can usually mark them when they change names. If he suspects some kid might be getting suckered in, he warns them.

"I told him I was interested in finding someone who might be involved with human trafficking in this area, and he gave me the name of a gaming chat room he knows is trolled all the time by someone from this general area, someone who is either a pedophile or a scout for one.

"So, I created an e-mail account just for this purpose and a username of Luv2game247. And just so you know, my persona under that username is that of an eleven-year-old boy. I wasn't in that chat room more than ten minutes when I was contacted by someone claiming to be an eleven-year-old boy also, though I'm pretty sure he isn't."

"How can you tell?" I ask.

"My buddy gave me some key things to look for," Arnie explains. "And he's been monitoring this particular username for about two weeks now. I think when you see the e-mails he sent me, you'll understand. They'll make your radar go off."

Arnie opens the first in a series of e-mails from

someone going by the name Games4ever2018. We read it over his shoulder. It's a basic, getting-to-know-you kind of e-mail with nothing salacious or suspicious in it. Arnie clicks on four more e-mails that follow, all of them of a similar nature where the two "boys" share some facts about their lives, discuss what games they like to play, and ask a few personal questions. Games4ever2018 asks more questions than Arnie does, and by the time they've exchanged four e-mails apiece, Arnie has revealed that he is an eleven-year-old male, latchkey kid with blond hair and a slight build who lives in central Wisconsin.

I'm stunned, but also impressed, by how Games4ever2018 gets this information out of Arnie with seemingly innocuous conversational threads about how tedious parents can be, how bullying some kids at school can be—particularly the big kids—and complaints about how all the girls Games4ever2018 likes are bigger than he is.

In the fifth e-mail, Games4ever2018 starts complaining about how expensive the games are to buy. Arnie agrees in his reply, bemoaning the fact that he can't afford to buy any new games because his old ones are getting boring. Games4ever2018 then asks Arnie if he's a good player, and Arnie replies with some boasts about his scores. Games4-ever2018 then asks Arnie if he'd like to learn of a way to play some new games, and not have to pay for them. Arnie's reply follows that, of course, he would.

Arnie turns around at this point and looks at all

of us. "There are more of these to read, but it should be noted that another online friend of mine is also in communication with Games4ever2018," he explains. "There are several people involved, and they're coordinating the effort from different venues. Anyway, this particular friend has visited several different chat rooms over the past year or so that are often used to shop for, um, human companionship. And he has let it be known that he functions as a broker or middleman for others who want to find a certain type of companion."

"You mean pedophiles," I say with disgust.

"Some, but not all," Arnie says. "Some of the people in these rooms are adults who are into kinky-sex stuff and want to find someone else who shares their interests. Anyway, this guy traces the ISP addresses of the people who respond to him, which is how we know that Games4ever2018 is also known by another username elsewhere in this other chat room. And when Games4ever2018 posted in the companion chat room, using some online code words that he might have a young, prepubescent boy to be had, my friend jumped on it."

"*Online code words?*" Richmond says, scratching his head. I imagine he's having trouble following all of this, given that he's something of a Luddite when it comes to technology. He still struggles with basic e-mail applications.

"Yep," Arnie says. "There are certain terms, certain words, that when used in the right context can be interpreted to mean someone who is looking for young boys, young girls, or either. There are certain symbols that are used as well."

"I've heard of that," Hurley says. "When I was working in Chicago, there was a guy from the FBI who came and did a presentation on human trafficking and pedophiles. If I remember right, the symbol for someone looking for young boys is a triangle inside another triangle. For girls, it was a heart inside of a larger heart."

"Correct," Arnie says. "And some of the words that are used are seemingly innocuous, everyday words, like 'pasta' or 'lollipops.' I don't want to go into the details, but if you want to go wading in the muck, do some online research. It will give you nightmares and make you want to lock your kids in the house forever."

I feel a shudder build and try to suppress it, but it races down my spine anyway. Hurley, standing next to me, feels it and reaches over to wrap an arm around my waist, pulling me closer. This sort of stuff is distasteful and hard for a parent to face, but I also know that ignorance isn't necessarily bliss. As disgusting and frightening as it all is, it's all too real a danger, one that I, as a parent, need to be cognizant of.

"So, anyway," Arnie goes on, "the next few e-mails from Games4ever2018 tell me about a friend he knows who works for a company that develops computer games. He claims that this friend needs kids who are good at playing computer games to beta test the new ones for bugs, and if I want to do that, he can provide me with free copies of dozens of games before they even hit the market. And not only will I get to keep the games, I'll also earn a small stipend for each one I complete. I was all over that like white on rice, begging him to let me do it.

"So then Games4ever2018 told me I was in, but that I would have to do a test case first to prove that I could play as well as I say I can. He said I can't tell anyone about the arrangement—not my friends, not my mother, nobody—because what I'd be doing is in violation of the child labor laws. He said I would have to meet the gaming guy face-to-face, just to prove I am who I say I am, and he will give me the first game. I think it's safe to assume, given that Games4ever2018 is already advertising me in the companion chat area, that once I agree to meet this guy, they will either try to kidnap me outright and drug me shortly thereafter, or the other way around."

"How can you be sure they'll move that fast?" Hurley asks.

"Well, the friend in the companion chat area has been there a long time and has plenty of fake online IDs that he sets up as pretend customers, who then provide recommendations for him. He does it for fun," Arnie says with a shrug. "He likes trolling the trolls. But because of it, he has a reputation for being safe and reliable, which in this case means exactly the opposite of what most people think 'safe' and 'reliable' represents. When my friend indicated he was looking for someone that fits my made-up self-description, Games4ever2018 jumped on it and indicated that he could provide the goods."

Arnie opens the next series of e-mails, wherein Games4ever2018 invites him to meet the game man at a local pizza restaurant after school so they can talk about the gaming event. Arnie's e-mails do a good job of showing hesitancy and concern about getting in trouble with his mom, but eventually Arnie succumbs to the lure of the meeting for a chance to make money and get some free games. He agrees to meet the games man the following day at three forty-five, and Games4ever2018 even promises Arnie that the mystery man will treat him to a couple of slices of pizza.

"So what are we hoping to gain from this?" Hurley asks.

"Well, if Games4ever2018 is what I think he is, he's a headhunter of sorts for some trafficking ring that's working in this area. And if we assume our victim, Liesel, was taken by this group, there's a good chance her sister was, too."

Hurley shakes his head and frowns. "I don't know, Arnie," he says. "I mean, I'm all for busting this guy if he is what you say he is, but I'm not sure it's going to lead us any closer to the Paulsen girl. For one thing, I reviewed the old investigation files into the disappearance of those two girls. They didn't have any kind of computer access at their house. It was too far out in the boonies and there isn't any cable or other kind of Internet service available out there."

"Their involvement likely came about in a different manner, I'll grant you," Arnie says. "But these trafficking cabals are a tight, incestuous little group—forgive the awful imagery—with a select class of clients. They are constantly trading off their victims to satisfy the peculiar and particular whims of their clients. If we can get an in with someone who knows anything at all about these groups, we might be able to turn him and get some information on other groups. And who knows? Any one of those clues might lead us to Lily Paulsen."

Hurley's lips thin into grim doubt. "It's a hell of a long shot," he says. Richmond nods in agreement.

"What else have you got?" Arnie counters.

The lack of an answer, ironically, is one.

"What about Kirby O'Keefe?" I ask. "Anything on that yet?"

Richmond says, "I haven't found anything on him in any of the criminal databases. I did find an address, a rental house in the Dells, and I have some officers up that way seeing if they can spot the guy."

"What about the phone number Lowe gave us?" I ask.

"It's a burner," Richmond says. "I plan to try to trace where it was bought, but I haven't gotten to it yet. That whole thing with Roberts occupied most of our morning."

I shift my attention back to Arnie. "If we meet this games guy, how are we supposed to recognize him? And since we don't have an actual kid to play the role of your online persona, won't we scare him off? It's not like Arnie can pass for an eleven-year-old in real life."

"I told the contact I always wear a red knit cap," Arnie says. He sees us all staring at him questioningly and he shrugs. "He asked how he'd know me, so I made something up on the fly."

"I have an idea how we might get it to work," Hurley says. He tosses his thoughts out there for the rest of us to consider, and when he's done, we have a consensus of sorts. Next he makes a phone call, and within the hour, we have the whole thing set up.

Chapter 18

Once our plans for the next day are finished, Richmond goes back to the police station to work on the other leads, and Hurley walks me back downstairs to my office. I'm surprised to see that it's only eleven-thirty in the morning. I feel like this day has lasted twelve hours already. Christopher will be in soon, and I start to rethink my commitment to staying here for the rest of the day. Not only is the storm coming in, I'm feeling pretty beat. Between my nighttime escapades, getting shot, and the emotional drain of the Paulsen case, I feel like I've been working for days straight. My bed is sounding really good to me about now.

I'm about to say as much to Hurley, and then my cell phone rings. When I look at the number and see that it's Izzy's partner, Dom, calling, I feel a worm of worry wriggle in my gut, thinking that something might be wrong with Matthew. Then I remember that Matthew is home with Emily today rather than with Dom, and I hope the wriggle isn't the hallmark of something else going on in my gut.

"Hey, Dom, what's up?"

"Mattie, I need you. I need your help right away. Something awful has happened."

My heart lurches. "Is it Juliana?"

"No, no, sorry. She's at your sister's house. I'm down at the theater. We had a dress rehearsal today and I dropped Juliana with Desi so I could come down here for a few hours."

"Then what is it?" Hurley is staring at me, brows raised in curiosity.

"It's Roger Dalrymple," Dom says. I have no idea who Roger Dalrymple is. "He's here, and he's dead!"

"Did you call the police?"

"No, I called you first. I tried to call Izzy, but I got his voice mail."

"Okay, okay," I say, thinking. "Stay where you are, and make sure everyone else stays there, too. Don't let anyone leave, and don't let anyone touch anything. Hurley is here with me. We'll be there in two shakes, okay?"

"Okay," Dom says, his voice quavering like he's about to cry. "Please hurry."

"I will." I disconnect the call and fill Hurley in on what Dom said.

"Who is this Roger Dalrymple person?" Hurley asks when I'm done.

"I have no idea. I don't really keep up with Dom and his thespian group activities. But our receptionist, Cass, is involved with the group, too. Maybe she knows. Should we call Richmond back?"

"No," Hurley says, shaking his head. "I'm up next anyway. Let him stay focused on the Paulsen case and I'll take this one."

I pick up my desk phone and dial Cass's extension. After the phone rings six times, I'm starting to think Cass must not be there, and I prepare to hang up rather than leave a voice mail. Then she answers.

"Medical examiner's office," she says. Her tone is not its usual, chipper self, and there's no hint of her earlier British accent.

"Cass, it's Mattie. I just got a call from Dom and he—"

"Yeah, I just hung up from him," she says. "Roger Dalrymple is dead!"

"Who is Roger Dalrymple?"

"He's the playwright for the play we're currently working on, and a bit of an ass. Dom said his death looks suspicious. If someone killed him, your list of suspects is going to be a long one."

"Are you here in the office?"

"I am. I was about to forward the phones and head down there after Dom called. And then you called."

"It might be best if you stay here for now," I tell her. "Hurley and I are on our way there. Can you fill Izzy in on what's going on? He'll probably want to be there, too."

"Will do."

I disconnect the call and go to the locker room to get my coat. Then Hurley and I take the elevator to the garage level. Hurley tries to call the station along the way, but the call won't go through.

"Dead zone," I remind him, and he chuckles at the pun. "Let's take your truck," I say, once again remembering the state of my own.

As we are pulling out of the garage, we pass a van with NOT A TRACE on the side of it pulling in.

Hurley makes a call on his cell the instant we have cleared the garage and arranges for some help to meet us at the theater. "Junior Feller will join us there," he says when he's done. "If we need more help than that, I'll call in some units once we get there."

"Sounds like a plan."

Hurley gives me a quizzical look. "Did you guys call Not a Trace to clean up the Roberts mess? I didn't think it was that bad."

"Um . . . no. That's not why we called them," I say, silently cursing Hurley's miss-nothing detective skills. "I had a little accident in my car on the way in this morning."

Hurley's brow furrows with worry. "An accident? Geez, Mattie, what else can you add on to this day? Are you okay?"

"I'm fine," I say with a dismissive wave of my hand. "It wasn't that kind of accident. Well, um, it was, but that part was minor. The hearse is built like a tank and it took it like a pro."

"And what's that got to do with Not a Trace?" Hurley asks, looking at me in confusion.

I take in a deep breath. "I kind of had a personal accident as well," I say, hoping he'll let the matter drop. But it's a futile hope, and I know it.

"A *personal* accident?"

"I pooped in my pants, okay?" I blurt out.

At first, this pronouncement is met with several seconds of silence. Then Hurley bursts out laughing.

"Wow," I say with heavy sarcasm. "Your sympathy is overwhelming." I scowl while Hurley struggles to get himself under control. I shake my head in dismay. "Boy, between you and Izzy, I . . ." I drift off, straightening in my seat. "Oh, crap," I say, and this makes Hurley's laughter build again. I ignore him. "I forgot about Izzy. He doesn't have a car today."

As if he heard me, my phone rings and I see that it's Izzy calling. Hurley pulls up and parks in front of the theater just as I'm answering.

"I'm sorry, Izzy," I say, forgoing any greeting when I answer the call. "I forgot you didn't have a car."

"Where are you?"

"We just arrived at the theater. We can come back and get you."

"Don't bother. Christopher is here and he said I can ride with him. We'll meet you there in a few minutes."

Before I can say anything else, Izzy disconnects the call. I curse under my breath.

"You drove Izzy to work?" Hurley says.

"I did. His car wouldn't start."

"So-o-o he was with you when you had your . . . *accident?*" The corners of his mouth are twitching with barely contained amusement. I nod. "Man, you've had a rough day of it, haven't you?"

"Not one of my best for sure," I say, opening my door. I don't wait for an answer. I get out of the truck and grab my scene-processing kit behind the seat. I have two of them, one for the hearse and

one for Hurley's truck. I used to have only one,
but it became a hassle at times to make sure I had
it with me because I often ride to scenes with Hurley.

I close the truck door a little harder than necessary because I have some pent-up frustration to
vent, but the action makes my left shoulder scream
at me, and I instantly regret it. I shrug that arm
ever so slightly, and turn to look at the theater's
façade while I wait for Hurley.

The building is an old movie theater built back
in the 1950s, but it hasn't shown a movie for at
least two decades. Back around 2000, it was slated
to be torn down, but a group of wannabe thespi-
ans and the local historical society took on the re-
sponsibility of salvaging the place and turning it
into a live theater. With time, some financial assistance, and a lot of donated construction talent,
the place was eventually brought back to its original, Art Deco–inspired glory. It's been used for
plays ever since, with a new one put on every few
months by a local group of interested actors, writ-
ers, costumers, and set designers. The performances are typically offered only on the weekends,
with matinees on Saturdays and Sundays, as well as
evening performances on Friday and Saturday
nights. From what I've heard, the audience may be
anywhere from a handful of people to a full house,
depending on what play is being performed and
the time of year. Not surprisingly, the crowds tend
to be bigger in the winter, when there isn't much
else to do.

There are large windows on either side of the front door, and there is a small marquee overhead. Inside the windows displayed beneath pairs of theater masks are the pictures and names of all the actors and others who belong to the local group, known as The Drama Factory. On the marquee is an announcement that the latest production will be opening one week from this Friday. Perhaps ominously, the name of the play is *Final Curtain*.

Hurley tries the front door, but it's locked. I peer in through the glass, but I don't see anyone out in the main foyer area. "There's another door around back," I tell him, and he heads that way in silence. He looks chastised and repentant for his laughter at my expense, but I'm not mad at him. His dark, often warped sense of humor, so like my own, is one of the things that attracted me to him initially, and it keeps me attracted to him now, even when I'm the butt—literally in this case—of his jokes. I know that if the roles were reversed, I would have busted on him as bad as he did on me. Maybe worse.

I consider saying something to let him off the hook, but decide to wait. It's not the proper time and place, and besides, what's the harm in having him feel a teensy bit indebted to me for a few hours more?

Behind the theater is a parking lot that can hold fifty cars, and it's about half full. I don't think all of them belong to the theater group—or at least I hope there aren't twenty-plus people in there to interview and question—as there are also a couple of small shops and restaurants on the block, and customers often park back here rather than on the street. I recognize Dom's car, but no others.

The back door is an unmarked and unremarkable entrance that is, fortunately, unlocked. Hurley holds it open for me and I am hit with a blast of welcome heat as I step past him into a darkened interior. Hurley is right behind me, and as he lets the door swing shut, I'm momentarily blinded by the sudden blackness. I halt my progress and Hurley runs smack into my backside.

"Ooomph," he mutters as our bodies bounce off one another, making my shoulder screech again. "Sorry. What is it?"

"I can't see anything," I say, blinking my eyes rapidly in hopes that this will somehow make them adjust faster. "Give me a sec."

Hurley's body once again comes into contact with my backside, slower this time, until I can feel the warmth of his breath on the back of my head and neck. He parks there for a moment, and one arm snakes around my waist, pulling me into him tighter. "I'm willing to give you all the time you need," he whispers in my ear.

Ah, yes, a little sense of indebtedness has its perks.

Then he lets out a woeful sigh and releases me. "But not here, not now."

I let out a matching sigh of my own and reach back with my hand. As my eyes adjust better to the darkness, I find one of his hands and give it a squeeze. We are in a hallway with overhead lights, though they aren't on at the moment, and I reach over to the wall and grope around until I find a switch to flip. The darkness disappears as a flickering wave of fluorescent lights struggle to life. Most of the fixtures eventually glow steady, though a couple of them continue to sputter. We follow the hall past closed doors: One is marked JANITOR; another says STORAGE; some aren't marked at all. Near the end, there are two bathrooms, side by side, one for men and one for women.

The hall comes to a T, with the right side leading to a set of stairs that go up to the second floor. I've been here before and know the upper level houses offices directly above us, and at the opposite end of the building, there is a narrow, enclosed space that used to be the reel room, where the movie spools were loaded and played. To the left of us is an open backstage area, with a ceiling that is three stories high; a maze of scaffolding, ropes, and pulleys; and a curtain that provides a backdrop to the main stage.

A low murmur of excited voices has been audible ever since the back door closed, growing louder with each step. And as we turn left at the T, we finally reach the source of those voices, and our victim.

Dom is dressed in a black suit with a white shirt and black bow tie. His strawberry-blond hair is slicked straight back, glued into position with some sort of pomade. When he sees us, he rolls his eyes heavenward. "Oh, Mattie, thank goodness!" he says, swiping the back of one hand across his forehead. I would assume the move was a dramatic gesture coming from anyone else, but I've seen Dom do this many times in the past when he's stressed. And, clearly, he's stressed now, given that there is a dead body at his feet. Dom is normally quite fair-skinned. At the moment, between what I assume is his partially shocked state of mind and the harsh light from overhead, he looks practically translucent.

Several other people come into view, and I do a quick scan to assess the crowd. Standing to Dom's left is a heavyset woman wearing a purple feather boa, a matching purple wide-brimmed hat, and a garish yellow dress with matching shoes, all of it circa 1920s. I try to guess at her age, but it's hard to tell because of all the heavy makeup she has on her face. Her dark hair is generously laced with silver, but I'm not sure if it's her natural color or done up for her role. Her arms are in front of her, and she is grasping her left wrist with her right hand, an attempt, I think, at folding her arms over a chest and belly that are too large to accommodate the gesture. One bright yellow foot is tapping impatiently, and she huffs loudly several times in a period of a few seconds, just in case we missed the first one or two signals indicating her high level of irritation.

Standing next to her is a middle-aged man who is tall and quite thin. His cheeks are hollow, his eyes sunken, his graying hair sparse, and his shirt and pants hang off his lanky frame like clothing on a scarecrow, the pants held up by a pair of suspenders. My nursing alarm starts to clamor, but as we draw closer, I see that while the thinness of his body is real, it's not as severe as I originally thought. Some very artful makeup has created hollows and depressions on his face, and the clothing he is wearing is purposefully sized much larger than he is. Beneath that makeup, I see a few zits trying to sprout, and a pair of lively, dynamic eyes. I realize then that the man isn't a man at all, but rather an adolescent boy momentarily trapped in that awkward gangliness that occurs between puberty and adulthood.

Seated in a folding wooden chair next to the boy-man is another woman, mid-thirties, with shoulder-length black hair. She is very pretty and, from what I can see, has a very nice figure. She is wearing a snug-fitting T-shirt—snug enough that I can tell she isn't wearing a bra—beneath a blue angora cardigan sweater. Her outfit is finished off with a pair of gray corduroy pants and ankle-high blue suede boots. Despite the fact that no smoking is allowed in public buildings, she is puffing away on a cigarette she is holding in one hand, and flicking the ashes from it into a plastic cup of some liquid she is holding in the other hand. She looks like she's been crying.

Standing behind these three are two others: a bespectacled man, who's probably in his thirties, dressed in a pullover sweater and jeans, which may or may not be a costume. He is whispering to a third man, who might be gay, judging from his posturing, facial expressions, and mannerisms. Though I do have to concede to myself that my judgment might be clouded a smidge by the fact that he's dressed in women's clothing: a flapper-style skirt, which hits just below the knee, with a long-sleeved, straight-hemmed white blouse over it, and a pair of sensible pumps. Between the hem of the skirt and the pumps is a pair of very hairy legs encased in stockings. Long blond hair waves down over his shoulders, but I'm certain it's a wig, thanks to the very dark five-o'clock shadow on his chin and cheeks. He is wearing makeup—eyeliner, eye shadow, mascara, foundation, and lipstick—but it's poorly applied, making the sight of him an incongruous one.

I finally shift my attention to the only other person in the room: our victim. He is lying on the floor in a prone position, though his head is turned slightly to one side, revealing half of his face. With the exception of the small pool of blood that has seeped from his mouth, he looks oddly peaceful, as if he simply stretched out there on the floor for a nap and is now enjoying a dreamy REM state. Of course, the fact that both of his legs are bent in directions they were never meant to go destroys the effect somewhat, but if one were to keep her eyes above the waist, things didn't look so bad.

I know that the broken legs alone wouldn't have killed him, though the pain might have been severe enough to make him lose consciousness, so I kneel down and study him closely, just to make sure he isn't breathing. I see no movement, and after donning a pair of latex gloves, I feel along his neck for a pulse. I don't find one, but I do find a significant step in his cervical spine—a deformity that occurs when bones in the spine are displaced—and realize our cause of death is likely a broken neck. On his left wrist is a watch, its face broken, the second hand still, giving us a precise time of death. I take out my video camera and start filming, beginning with the watch.

Hurley takes out his little notebook and a pen. "Has anyone touched the body?" he asks with a frown.

Dom starts nervously. "Not since I've been here," he says. "But there were others here before me."

"Why didn't any of you call 911?" I ask. "How did you know he was dead?"

The people in the group exchange a bunch of nervous glances. Finally the heavyset woman with the purple hat says, "I was the first one here. I used to work as an EMT. I could tell just from looking at his neck that he was dead and there was no point in calling for an ambulance."

"Did you touch him?" Hurley asks.

Heavy purple lady shakes her head. "There was no need. I wasn't that far away when he fell. I heard him hit the floor. And when I got here, the catwalk above us was shaking slightly."

Everyone looks up toward the catwalk for a moment, and then in unison, as if someone had given them a cue, they all shift their gaze to the dead man on the floor.

Hurley gives me a questioning look, and I nod. The story makes sense. But what we have to figure out now is how and why he fell.

"Let's start with some identification," Hurley says, pen poised.

I finish filming the body and begin filming the people in the room. This earns me a few dirty looks and one pose—not surprisingly from the heavyset woman—as a result.

"Dom, I know who you are," Hurley goes on. "Who is our victim?"

Everyone starts talking at once and Hurley holds up a hand, squeezing his eyes closed. This earns him a few eye rolls and looks of disgust. As soon as everyone is quiet, Hurley opens his eyes and zeroes in on Dom. "Dom, can you please tell me the name of our victim?"

Dom nods, a spastic movement. "His name is Roger Dalrymple. He wrote this play we're working on, and he was trying to direct us as well."

"Okay," Hurley says, scribbling in his notebook. He looks over at the heavyset woman in the purple hat. "And you are?"

"Darlene Fisher," she says in a smoky, British-accented voice. She unclasps her wrist and flings one end of her boa over her shoulder. "I am the matriarch of the Fisher family," she adds, casting a glance at the others. "Mother to this entire ragtag band of misfits."

Hurley and I both stop what we're doing for a moment, though I leave my camera rolling and aimed in the general direction of Fisher, and we stare at the woman, gauging her. Then I look over at Dom with my eyebrows raised in question. Dom rolls his eyes and shakes his head.

"We're not here to play games, ma'am," I say to the Fisher woman, my tone irritable. "This is a death investigation, not a play. The death is very real. We need your real name, not your character name." Out of the corner of my eye, I see Hurley look over at me, his brow furrowed.

The woman stares back at me with a haughty expression before letting out a heavy sigh and shaking her head with dismay. "You people are no fun," she whines, her voice suddenly several notes higher on the scale and lacking the British accent.

I give her a chastising look. "Untimely deaths aren't generally fun."

"Whatever," she says, clearly unimpressed. "A little whimsy couldn't hurt." She looks at us, gauging our reaction to this comment. Apparently, it's not what she hoped. "My name is Helen Niehls." This is uttered quickly and flatly, and she then starts to pick at one of her fingernails. Hurley asks her to spell her last name, and she does so with a huff of irritation.

"How long ago did you find Mr. Dalrymple? How did you find him? When did you last see him? What were you doing when you found him? Who else was nearby?" This rapid-fire series of questions is a tactic I've seen Hurley use before. He claims it rattles the interviewee to some degree, and that whichever question they answer first is often telling.

Helen claps a hand to her chest and smiles. "Oh, my, so many questions. Let's see . . . I found him when I was on my way to the bathroom. It's down the back hallway there." She points over Hurley's shoulder to the hallway we used coming in. "I was walking across the stage and heard the horrible sound of him hitting the floor. When I pushed aside the curtain, there he was." She makes a fist with one hand and bites the side of it, her expression suddenly distraught and distressed. "It was awful, just awful," she utters breathlessly. Her British accent has suddenly returned, and it's met with a series of groans from nearly everyone in the room.

"Oh, come on," Helen whines. "The accent works. It just does. Just because Dalrymple didn't like it, doesn't mean it isn't so. The rest of you don't need to use one. We can use a story line that has me from England, like Cass's character, but the rest of you born here." She pauses, looking bright-eyed and hopeful at the rest of the group. Her cluelessness is beyond the pale. Either that, or she's a complete sociopath. Whichever it is, Hurley quickly shifts Helen's attention back to the matter at hand.

"You and the victim were having some sort of disagreement?" he says, his voice laden with innuendo.

Helen shoots him a wide-eyed look. "Nothing serious," she says dismissively. "Just artistic differences." She looks affronted all of a sudden and claps a hand over her ample bosom. "What are you suggesting?"

Hurley looks up toward the scaffolding over our heads. "Based on your story, the piece of material I can see stuck on that railing up there, and the tear in Mr. Dalrymple's shirt tail, a shirt that appears to match the material above, it would seem our victim fell from that catwalk. I'm guessing someone pushed him, because that looks like a high enough railing to make an accidental fall unlikely. And if someone wanted to commit suicide, I'd imagine there are a number of better ways to do it. A fall of this distance isn't guaranteed to be fatal, even though it appears it may have been in this case. So I'm thinking Mr. Dalrymple might have had a bit of assistance with his fall."

Hurley watches the group as this sinks in.

The gangly kid is the first one to speak. His face breaks into an eerie smile and he casts a glance back toward the people behind him. Then he turns back to Hurley. "You're saying you think Dalrymple was murdered?"

Hurley doesn't answer.

"Looks like life is going to imitate art, instead of the other way around," the kid says.

"How so?" Hurley asks.

"Well, Dalrymple wasn't happy just writing and directing the play, he had to have a part in it, too." The kid pauses, and Hurley thrusts his head toward him, eyes wide, brows arched in question. "Come on, you have to admit it's a bit ironic," the kid goes on. "Dalrymple's play is a murder mystery. His role was that of the victim. And all of us are the suspects."

Chapter 19

Christopher and Izzy arrive at the scene, with Junior Feller in tow. After asking where everyone's coats and such are, Hurley sends Junior to scrounge them up while he herds the potential suspects out front to the seating area of the theater, separating them so they can't gossip and compare notes. Dom gives Izzy a desperate look before following the others.

"Go and talk with the detectives," Izzy says to Dom, his voice calm. "Just tell them the truth."

"But I don't know what happened," Dom says, looking like he's about to cry. "I came in the back door and walked in on Helen and the others all standing here staring at Da—"

Izzy holds up a hand to stop him. "Dom, listen to me. I don't want you to tell me any of this before you talk to the detectives. We need to make sure everything is strictly by the book on this, okay? Go on, you'll be fine."

Dom rolls his lips in and nods, though he doesn't look convinced.

"Come on, Dom," I say, my voice soothing. "This is all standard procedure."

Dom, his shoulders slumped, his face toward the floor, shuffles off after the others. I look over at Izzy. "He'll be okay," I say.

"I know," Izzy says. "It's just that he gets so worked up over things sometimes. I'm going to be trying to calm him down for days, maybe weeks over this." He pauses, and takes on a dreamy, far-away look. "You know, there is an upside to this," he says after a moment. "Dom tends to want to cook a lot when he gets upset, and he leans toward comfort foods during times of stress. That means there may be some good food coming down the pike instead of this healthy crap he's been fixing ever since my heart attack."

"But that healthy crap has you looking and feeling pretty good," I say, although I'm as excited, if not more so, than Izzy over the prospect of Dom's cooking. Some of his standout, specialty dishes are from my favorite food group: Italian. And I have no compunction about inviting myself over for dinner. "And you've lost some weight."

"Yeah, yeah," Izzy says with a dismissive wave of his hand. "A little indulgence now and then isn't going to kill me."

"We just need to learn moderation," I say, and he nods, rolling his eyes. Izzy and I both struggle with our weight, so this rah-rah, team-building speech is one we've engaged in numerous times in the past. We're far better at the speeches than we are on the follow-through.

Christopher chooses that moment to loudly pass some gas, and the smell quashes the visions of sugarplums—or, rather, stuffed manicotti—dancing in my head. It's a good six on the sphincter scale.

"So where do you want to begin with Mr. Dalrymple here?" I say, switching subjects. "I've already done a brief preliminary examination, and it appears he has a pretty serious neck fracture along with two broken legs."

"You've done pictures already?" Christopher asks.

"Video," I say, with a nod toward the body. "But I suppose I need to do some up there." I look up at the catwalk.

Izzy looks above us with a ponderous expression. "Why don't you do that, and Christopher and I will start bagging his hands and getting him ready for transport."

I head off toward the far end of the backstage area we're in, searching for a way to get to the upper level of the scaffolding and catwalk. I finally find a doorway leading to a set of stairs and take them up to what is essentially the third floor of the building. Here there is access to a narrow catwalk made out of metal mesh, which gives me the heebie-jeebies when I step onto it. Not only can I see through the floor of the catwalk to the stage below, the whole thing wobbles a bit as I move along it. My shoulder isn't very happy about the climb, either, since I'm gripping the side rail for all I'm worth.

I turn the video camera on and hold it in front of me with my good hand while I grip the side rail-

ing with the other. The railings are high—nearly
to my waist—and that means an accidental fall is,
indeed, unlikely, just as Hurley said earlier. But
railings aside, the catwalk is not for the faint of
heart or the acrophobic. Heights are not my favorite thing, and I have to force myself to focus on
the mesh floor in a nearsighted way that doesn't
let me see through it to the stage below. I nearly
drop the camera at one point, and my efforts to
catch it make the catwalk sway even more.

I finally reach the area directly above Dalrymple's body and see the swath of material Hurley
had pointed out earlier. It's snagged on a small
piece of wire on the outside of the railing that was
used—ironically—to attach a small metal caution
sign to the inside wall of the catwalk.

I make the mistake of looking down below,
where I see Izzy and Christopher squatting beside
Roger Dalrymple. The dizzying height makes me
squeeze my eyes closed momentarily, and I grip
the side rail tightly. But then I find that with my
eyes closed, I can feel the slight movement in the
catwalk and that gets my adrenaline pumping. I
open them again and force myself to stay focused
on the items in my immediate vicinity and not
look down.

I start to shoot video of the surrounding ropes,
pulleys, and scaffolding, all of which control various lights and scenery boards, but as I look through
the lens, I notice the image is cloudy and blurred.
I turn the camera around to examine the outside
of the lens and see that there is an oily smudge on
it. Puzzled, I look at my gloved hands and discover
the same oily substance on several of the fingers

on the left-hand glove, the one I was using to grab the railing. I have no idea what it is, but figure I must have gotten it on my glove on the way up here.

I clean off the camera lens with the hem of my shirt and then I slowly backtrack the way I came, filming my excursion, and examining the railing that is now on my right, but would have been on my left before. I find the source about five feet from where Dalrymple went over. There is a smear of a flesh-colored, oily substance on the railing that I surmise is probably stage makeup.

I shoot some close-up video of the makeup smudge on the railing, and when I'm done, I stand for a moment, imagining how the fall could have occurred. It wouldn't have been easy to get someone over the side, and Dalrymple wasn't a small man. I figure he is somewhere around six feet tall and weighs in the neighborhood of two-fifty.

What was he doing up here? I study the ropes and pulleys, and notice a backdrop suspended nearby that is lower than the others. Had Dalrymple reached for the rope to lower this particular piece of scenery? If so, it wasn't beyond the realm of possibilities that he could have leaned out over the side railing far enough to lose his balance and fall, or been easily pushed.

I go back down to the main floor and venture over to where Izzy and Christopher are. I remove my makeup-smeared glove, placing it in an evidence bag.

"Why are you bagging your glove?" Izzy asks.

I explain about the substance I found on it and on the railing. "Any chance our victim is wearing anything like that? Some stage makeup, perhaps?" I ask.

Izzy shakes his head, and then takes another closer look at Dalrymple's face, and then his hands, which Christopher is about to bag. "Nope, nothing," he announces.

"I think we're all leaning toward the idea that Dalrymple didn't just fall from that catwalk," I say. "And the makeup suggests that someone else was up there recently. I don't see how we can prove it was at the same time, though."

"You should go and clue Hurley and Junior in on what you found and determine who in our group of suspects is wearing stage makeup," Izzy says. "Before they have a chance to remove it."

"Got it, though I won't be surprised to discover they're all wearing it." I remove a bunch of swabs from my scene kit. "First I need to go up there and get a swab sample. Who knows? Maybe we can get some DNA from it?"

"Go for it. We have the body recovery under control," Izzy says.

I nod, gather some supplies, and don a fresh pair of gloves, then stuff some extras in my pocket. Then I go back up onto the catwalk. I get two swabs of the substance on the railing, just to be safe. After sealing and labeling them, I retrieve the snagged and torn piece of material and place it in an evidence bag. When I'm done, I climb back down, hand off my evidence to Izzy and Christopher, and head out to the front-stage area to find the others.

All of the suspects, except Dom, are seated out in the audience area, with Junior pacing back and

forth in front of them. The actors are purposely
separated by enough seats to keep them from
chatting with one another.

"Where's Hurley?" I ask Junior.

"He's talking to Dom out in the front lobby
area. He said he's going to talk to each person out
there eventually. I'm babysitting." He says this last
with a grumbling tone and a pouty face.

"How would you like to collect some evidence
for me?"

This appears to cheer Junior. "What do you
need?" I haul him off several feet away from the
others so I can hopefully speak to him out of their
earshot. Realizing that the acoustics inside the theater may make this difficult, I decide to whisper
into Junior's ear and explain to him about the
makeup. When I'm done, I look at him to see if he
understood me.

"Got it," he says. I hand him the swabs and then
leave him to it, while I head out to the foyer area
to find Hurley and Dom. Dom is sitting on the
floor, his back against the wall, looking up at Hurley, who is squatting in front of him. There is a
poster of the upcoming play over Dom's head, and
it shows a knife dripping with blood pointing directly down at him.

Hurley hears me and rises to his feet, meeting
me halfway, while Dom pulls his knees up, crosses
his arms over them, and buries his face. "What's
up?" Hurley asks.

"Is Dom okay?"

Hurley glances back at him. "He's fine, or he
will be. I've pretty much ruled him out at this
point. He said he was in charge of buying some

props this morning and wasn't at the theater until he came in and found Helen and the others standing over Dalrymple's body. I'm guessing the others will verify his story, plus he says there are some bags of stuff he bought that he left back there by Dalrymple's body. He had the receipts in his wallet and showed them to me. I took pictures of them and bagged them for now."

Between the receipts and the time of death indicated by the broken watch, I realize we have a good, solid timeline for Dom, a good thing given the potential conflict-of-interest issues there are with him. "Why does Dom look so glum if you've cleared him?"

"I think he's just in shock over the whole thing. It's one thing to live with someone who deals with death like this on a regular basis. It's a whole other thing to experience it firsthand yourself."

I tell Hurley about the oily substance and the need to swab everyone. "I don't see anything that looks like that substance on Dom," I say. "But just to make sure we play fair and cover our butts, I should probably swab him. We don't want a defense lawyer down the road saying we showed favoritism for the ME's husband." I hand him the video camera. "You should be using this."

Hurley nods, studying Dom's forlorn form on the floor, and takes the camera. "Swab him, and then I'll let him go. Do you want to listen in while I question the others, or do you have to go back to Izzy?"

"Christopher is helping Izzy, so I get to stay with you."

"I like having you by my side," Hurley says in a

low voice laced with a hint of less-than-professional innuendo. He punctuates the comment with a wink and then reaches down and gives my butt a surreptitious squeeze. I frown at him and scoot away, walking over to Dom and squatting down in front of him.

"Dom?" Off to the side, I see Hurley turn the camera on and start filming.

Dom raises his head to look at me, and I see that his eyes are red-rimmed. "Oh, Mattie, this is such an awful mess," he whines. "I can't believe Roger is dead. And to think someone might have killed him?" His expression morphs into one of fear. "Have I been working side by side with a killer all this time?"

"It kind of looks that way," I say. "At least you're in the clear, from what I hear. That's good news."

Dom shakes his head. "I don't know how you and Izzy deal with this kind of stuff day in and day out," he says. "It's so sad, and so . . . so . . . unnerving."

"It certainly can be," I say. "Listen, Dom, I need to do something with you, some evidence collection kind of stuff. And as soon as I'm done, Hurley says you can leave."

Dom stares at me, confused. "Evidence collection? What kind of evidence? What are you saying? Are you suggesting that I might have had something to do with this?" His voice rises with each question, until he is on the verge of hysteria with this last question.

"Dom!" I say in my best stern-mommy voice. It's the one I use on Matthew when he does something worse than his usual menu of transgressions. "Listen to me." I grab his arms near his elbows and hold them tight, making my shoulder stab yet again. "I need to swab your face and hands because we found something on the catwalk railing. I think it's stage makeup. You don't appear to be wearing anything like that."

"I'm not," he says frantically. "I didn't have time to do makeup yet."

"That's great. But in order to make sure we do everything by the book, I need to swab you the same way we're going to swab the others. We don't want anyone suggesting that we showed you any favoritism." I pause, squeeze his arms a little tighter, and give him a light shake. "Do you understand?" I say, moving my head closer to his and looking him straight in the eye. "No one thinks you had anything to do with Roger's death."

Dom stares back at me, his breaths rapid and heaving at first, but then gradually slowing. Finally he nods. And then he smiles. "Sorry," he says. "Izzy is always telling me I overreact to things. I guess he's right."

"Well, in this case, I think your reaction is justified," I tell him. He rewards me with a grateful smile. "Let's get this over with so we can get you out of here, okay?"

Five minutes later, I have Dom thoroughly swabbed, the specimens appropriately sealed and labeled, and both my and Hurley's initials on the packages, just to be safe, since there is a potential conflict of interest here. It's still not ideal, but it's the best we can do for the moment, along with the video.

I tell Dom he can go, and we let him leave through the front door, locking it behind him. I turn and look back at Hurley with a wan smile. "It's going to be a long day."

"That it is," he says. He walks over and gives me a light kiss on the tip of my nose. "Having you here with me makes it much more tolerable, though," he says, his voice low and husky.

"Ditto," I say. We share a long look, our faces nearly touching; the heat between us is palpable and sizzling. But we both know this is the wrong place and time, a theme that seems to recur a lot in our lives. And then I completely kill the moment.

Chapter 20

"Hurley," I say, a bit breathless, "has it occurred to you that we seem to get turned on by murder investigations?"

He rears back, his dreamy-eyed expression morphing into one of bemusement. "What are you talking about?"

"Think about it. In our past, how many times have we shared moments like the one we just did at a crime scene, or during an investigation?"

He gives me a look that tells me he finds the idea ludicrous, but I can see his wheels turning, and a moment later, he looks troubled. Then he looks off to the side, and I can tell he's resurrecting past crime scenes in his mind.

"Damn," he says after a few seconds. He looks at me as if he's begging me to tell him it's not true. I arch my eyebrows at him. "It's the adrenaline," he says. "It's normal to feel a little revved up physically, and that can easily manifest itself sexually, right?"

"I suppose," I say, unconvincingly. "Or maybe it's just a need to reaffirm life . . . our lives . . . in the face of death."

"I'll take that one," Hurley says, still looking mildly disturbed. He takes a step away from me, as if he was just caught doing something naughty, or I was, and he's trying to distance himself.

"Who's next on our list of suspects?" I say, thinking a quick change of subject is called for.

Hurley bites on the bait like a starving fish. "I'm going to make that annoying Helen Niehls woman wait until last," he says, suddenly all business. He consults a page in his notebook. "Let's do Corey Ferguson next. Can you go and get him?"

"I can if you tell me which one he is. I don't know the names of any of those people other than the Niehls woman."

"Right, sorry," Hurley says with an appropriately apologetic smile. "Ferguson is the kid made up to look like an older man, the tall, skinny fellow."

"Got it." I head back into the main theater area, walk halfway down the aisle, and stop at Junior. "We're going to talk to Mr. Ferguson next," I say. "Have you swabbed him?"

"I have," Junior says.

I turn around and say, "Mr. Ferguson, will you come with me, please?"

Ferguson pops up from his seat, carrying his coat, and comes toward me with long, energetic strides, while the rest of the group frowns, grumbles, mumbles, and makes gestures of frustration.

I see Junior briefly squeeze his eyes closed and then shake his head. I give him a sympathetic smile of understanding, and then turn to lead Ferguson out to the front lobby and Hurley.

It's obvious that Ferguson is wearing stage makeup, lots of it, in fact. It's on his forehead, his neck, his cheeks, and his hands, which I notice have smudges of the makeup on them. I hope Junior swabbed all those areas.

While I take over the video camera, Hurley steers Ferguson toward an office chair he has dug up from somewhere and does a preliminary introduction for the camera, stating the time, date, and who it is he's talking to, and then starts questioning Ferguson about the events leading up to the discovery of Dalrymple's body.

"When did you first realize something had happened to Mr. Dalrymple?" Hurley asks.

"When we heard Helen scream. It was real bloodcurdling," Ferguson says with an expression that is somewhere between admiration and disgust. "Although I think it was a bit of acting on her part, since she didn't seem all that upset when I got to her."

"Did Helen scream words, or just make a noise?" Hurley asks.

"Just the scream," Ferguson says.

"And where were you when she screamed?"

"I was in the prop room looking for a pipe." Hurley's eyebrows arch at this and Ferguson doesn't miss it. "The kind of pipe you smoke," Ferguson clarifies. "It wasn't scripted for my character to have one, but I thought it would work and add a level of sophistication that Dalrymple might like. What do you think?"

Based on Hurley's expression, he thinks Ferguson is an idiot. He ignores the man's question, and comes back with one of his own. "Where is this prop room?"

"Stage-left area, or house right, depending on your perspective, over past the stairs that go up to the catwalk."

"Did you go up those stairs at all?" Hurley asks.

Ferguson shakes his head. "I don't like heights," he says with a shiver. "And I can be a little clumsy at times. My feet are too big." He screws up his face, looking pained. I have a pretty good idea of what he's feeling, and the kind of past he's had with his feet. Since I wear a size twelve—although ever since my pregnancy, it's more like a twelve-and-a-half shoe—I can relate to the issues that go along with big feet. They do tend to make you clumsy. The world is organized and structured in patterns designed for normal-sized people and normal-sized feet, and I don't meet either one of those definitions.

"I try to avoid going up on the catwalk at all," Ferguson says. "Don't really have to, most of the time."

"Was anyone with you, or did anyone see you going into the prop room?" Hurley asks.

Ferguson thinks for a second and shakes his head. "Nope, don't recall anyone."

"Was anyone else with Helen when you got to her?"

Ferguson shakes his head. "I got there first, but

the others arrived within seconds of me. They all came from different directions: Rebecca from the front-stage area, Mickey from the stage-right area, and Brad from the back hallway."

"In that order?" Hurley asks, scribbling away in his notebook.

"I think so, yes," Ferguson says, squinting in thought.

"And exactly where was Helen in relation to Dalrymple's body?" Hurley asks without looking up from his notes.

"Standing by his head. She didn't look as upset as I thought she might, given the scream she'd let out. In fact, she looked . . . amused."

"*Amused?*" Hurley echoes, finally looking up.

"I know," Ferguson says with a grimace. "That sounds wrong in so many ways, but that's the best description of her expression I can come up with."

Hurley switches gears and gets some more demographic information from Ferguson. Turns out he's older than I thought, though not by much. Ferguson is twenty-one, works part-time as a bartender at a local pub, and lives with his parents. He is taking general, prerequisite classes at a local community college, with the idea of eventually getting a college degree in English or something equally as generic, assuming he can't get into some sort of acting school.

"I spend my summers down around the Chicago area doing summer stock," he tells Hurley. "There are some big names that show up from time to time, like J. K. Simmons, or the Cusacks. You never know when you might get lucky."

Hurley eventually lets Corey Ferguson leave out

the front door, providing us with a glimpse of the
storm building outside. A gust of wind grabs the
door when Hurley opens it, nearly ripping it off its
hinges. And snow has begun to fall . . . wet, sloppy
stuff.

Next on our list is Rebecca Haugen, the pretty,
thirtysomething woman with the long black hair
and killer figure, if you'll pardon the expression. I
go back into the theater and make sure Junior has
swabbed her. Then I call her name and watch as
she sashays her way up the aisle toward me, her
coat draped over her shoulders. I feel an almost instant and puzzling dislike of her, for reasons I can't
pinpoint, though the simple fact that she is wearing corduroy pants is a good start. Only women
who have thigh gap can wear corduroy pants without risk of humiliation and potential injury. The
rest of us end up chafed and hot, thanks to the
friction created by those wales rubbing together
all the time. Whenever I try to wear them, I end up
making a sound like the percussion section for a
New Age band when I walk. Plus, corduroy isn't exactly a slimming material. Putting on corduroy
pants is like putting on ten pounds, a definite fashion *don't* for girls built like me.

Not only can Rebecca Haugen walk quietly while
wearing corduroy pants, and do so without risk of
starting a fire, she looks fantastic in them. My ego
takes another hit when I glance at her perky, per-
fect-sized breasts—hard not to do, since they are
practically waving hello beneath the thin T-shirt
she is wearing, the tiny, blue, unbuttoned cardigan

sweater she has on over it framing everything nicely. As soon as we enter the lobby area, I see Hurley's gaze briefly flit there—though, to his credit, his eyes don't linger. I suppose I should feel a twinge of jealousy, but I don't. It's not like anyone could *not* look at Rebecca Haugen's chest. Her nipples are standing up beneath the thin shirt material like flags atop mountain crests, as if someone has just staked out that desired territory and claimed it as his own.

I straighten up and roll my shoulders back in an effort to lend my own chest a bit more perkiness, but I can feel the heavy weight of my double-D cups resisting the effort. I'm fighting a war with gravity, and doing about as well as Custer did at Little Bighorn.

And if Rebecca isn't making me feel insecure enough as it is, I fix on those cute little blue suede boots she's wearing, on what I would guess are size-seven feet, fashionable footwear that I'm certain doesn't come in a size twelve and a half. If they did, they'd look like a 1960s Volkswagen van parked at Woodstock. I look down at my own feet, encased in athletic shoes that I bought in the men's department because I couldn't find any in my size in women's, and sigh.

I shove my insecurities aside and focus on Rebecca's face. That's when I realize her eyes are two different colors. The right one is hazel green and the left one is brown. I stare at her corneas, looking for the telltale rim of contact lenses, but I don't see any.

"Yes, they are naturally that way," Rebecca says, seeing my scrutiny. "The right one will darken some at times to more closely match my left eye, but for the most part they are distinctly different."

Hurley looks at her eyes, shrugs, flips a page in his notebook, and jots something down.

I turn the camera on and watch as Hurley starts his questioning with the usual introductory information, and then asks Rebecca for her personal information. We learn that she works as a loan officer at the local branch of a statewide bank, is divorced, and lives in a house she bought on the east side of town two years ago with money from her divorce settlement. Rebecca's version of events matches Ferguson's closely. She says she heard Helen's very loud and dramatic scream and came running from the main area of the theater, where she had gone to make a phone call on her cell.

"Who were you calling?" Hurley asks.

Rebecca rolls her lips inward, appearing reluctant to answer. Then she says, "My father," with a hint of embarrassment that I find puzzling.

"Was there anyone else out in the main area with you at the time Helen screamed?" Hurley asks.

"No. I went out there because, well . . . for privacy. I was supposed to be getting dressed in my costume, but I wanted to talk to Dad first."

There's an undercurrent here that I sense, but don't yet understand. While my original intention was to let Hurley do all the questioning, I have an irresistible urge to jump in.

"Do you routinely call your father in the middle of the day?" I ask.

She looks at me, abashed. "Depends," she says with a shrug.

"On what?" Hurley asks, shooting me an annoyed look that I ignore.

"On how things are going here," Rebecca says.

"Here, meaning *here?*" I say, making a circle in the air with one finger. "Here at the theater?"

Rebecca nods. I can tell she doesn't want to offer any more than she has to, but something— perhaps the curious and determined look on my face—wears her down. She sighs. "My father is financing this play, or at least most of it," she says. "He provides backing for a lot of the plays I act in."

Hurley, suddenly seeing some wisdom to my line of questioning, perks up. "Who is your father?"

"Stig Dahl," she says, looking sheepish.

"As in the Stig Dahl who owns the chain of banks you work for?" I ask.

"Yes." She rolls her eyes, obviously irritated. "Look, I know what this looks like. Daddy finances the plays, and, in return, his daughter has to have everything done her way. But that's not how it is. The stuff I asked Dalrymple for wasn't dependent on any of the financing, even though I think he sometimes saw it that way."

"What sort of requests have you made recently?" Hurley asks.

"Nothing major," Rebecca says dismissively, looking around the vestibule area we're in. "Some little rewrites on lines, or a costume change here and there. That sort of thing."

"How did you and the others get along with Dalrymple?" Hurley asks.

Rebecca rolls her eyes. "He isn't . . . wasn't the easiest man to work with," she says. "And today he seemed more irascible than usual." She runs a hand down her side, as if she's searching for a pocket. Realizing she doesn't have one, she sighs and finally looks Hurley in the eye. "I could really use a cigarette," she says in a pleading tone. "It's a nasty habit, I know, but it helps calm me. Would you mind terribly if I have one?"

"I would mind," Hurley says. "And I'm almost done anyway. You can get by for another few minutes, can't you?" He stares at her with those intense blue eyes of his, the faintest hint of a smile on his face.

I can tell she wants to be irritated with him, but in the end, she can't quite pull it off. She smiles at him and says, "Sure. Okay."

Hurley then deftly questions her about who was already by Dalrymple's body, and who arrived from where, once she got there. Her answers match Ferguson's with one exception: She swears Helen was standing by Dalrymple's feet, rather than his head. Hurley then asks her if she has gone up onto the catwalk for any reason.

"Sure," she says. "We're a small group and we all have to chip in and do things outside of our normal job descriptions from time to time. Depending on who is in a given scene, we all take turns handling the lights and scenery boards up there on the catwalk. I don't think I was up there today, though."

"You don't *think* you were?" I say. "I would think you'd remember doing something like that."

She looks at me with a hint of annoyance, like I'm a pesky mosquito buzzing around her head. "The days all blur together after a while," she says. "But I'm pretty certain I wasn't up there today."

Hurley thanks her and lets her go with a warning not to discuss the case with any of the others.

"What's your take on her?" he asks after Rebecca has left.

"She's a bit full of herself," I say. "Possibly a daddy's girl. Beyond that, I'm not sure." I leave out the part about how I envy her thighs and feet. "Who's next?" I ask.

"Let's do our cross-dressing fellow." Hurley consults his notebook, flipping back a bunch of pages to the front. "His name is Brad Levy."

"Really?" I say, looking surprised.

I went to high school with a guy named Brad Levy. If this is the same guy, I didn't recognize him. Then again, the Brad Levy I knew nearly twenty years ago didn't dress in women's clothes—at least not that I knew of.

This questioning session could prove interesting.

Chapter 21

By the time I fetch Brad, he has ditched his wig and the pumps he'd been wearing. Now that I know his name, I look at him more closely and see that he is indeed the same Brad Levy I had known in high school. The eyes are the same chocolate-brown color, and I remember the mole I can now see just in front of his left ear. The hair on the wig had hidden it from view before.

"You're Mattie Fjell, aren't you?" he says, using my maiden name as I escort him out to the lobby.

"I am, though I go by Mattie Winston now," I tell him. I say this in a low voice, because it's a bit of a touchy subject between Hurley and me.

Now that Hurley and I are married, it makes sense for me to take his last name and get rid of David's. But I haven't done it yet for two reasons.

The first is basic laziness and a desire to avoid the bureaucratic claptrap involved with changing one's name. I learned a hard lesson about financial independence when I left David, because everything we had was either in both of our names or David's alone. I had no credit, no assets, no nothing in my own name, and it left me in a financial quagmire for a while, which I swore I would never be in again. I established bank accounts and obtained credit cards after the split, using the name of Winston, and after nearly three years, I've managed to establish a decent credit rating and some financial independence. I fear changing everything now might gum up the works and affect the credit I've worked so hard to build.

The other reason I haven't changed my last name is because it's awkward when Hurley and I are working together. For some people, having the same last name implies a certain lack of impartiality, which we don't want people to fear. As it is, Hurley and I have to be careful during any investigations we work together to make sure we document everything to the letter. We use videos whenever possible as a record of events, and often end up playing devil's advocate with one another whenever we discuss a case.

All that aside, Hurley says that maintaining my ex's last name is something of a slap in the face to him. I understand why he feels that way, but it hasn't pushed me into doing anything about it yet. Then I get an idea. Maybe that's what I could give him for his birthday, finally changing my last name and taking his. I like the idea of it. It would make a unique gift and be a romantic gesture. But when I think about what's involved with actually doing it, I start rethinking the whole thing.

"What have you been up to, Brad?" I ask, tabling the idea for now. "Last I heard, you had moved to California, or New York, or somewhere like that."

"Yeah, I lived in LA for about fifteen years, trying to make a go of it in the acting biz." He shakes his head, looking woeful. "It's tough out there, very cutthroat."

His comment reminds me of what Arnie said about all the young people in LA trying to break into the entertainment business, and I wonder what Brad went through.

"I gave it my best shot and it wasn't good enough. So I went to school and got a degree in English and a teaching certificate. I came back home two years ago and now I teach at the elementary school here. I do this kind of stuff"—he waves a hand from his face to his midsection—"to satisfy my creative side." He gives me a meager smile. "Kind of sad, isn't it?"

"Not really," I say. "Life seldom works out the way we plan it. Mine certainly didn't."

"Yeah, I heard that you'd gone to nursing school and then married a doctor. I take it you aren't doing nursing anymore?"

"Nope, I work for the medical examiner's office these days. No nursing, and no doctor husband anymore, either. I'm married to a cop now, the one you're about to talk to, in fact. And we have two kids. So, see? Life has its own ideas about where it's going to take us. We're just along for the ride."

"Well, you look good. And happy."

"I am happy," I say. "How about you? Married? Any kids?"

"No, and despite appearances today, I'm not gay," he says. "I've had a few relationships, but nothing seems to stick. My last girlfriend told me I had Peter Pan syndrome. The one before that said I had serious commitment issues. They all seem to want the ring on their finger and the happy-little-family scenario." He pauses, giving me a wan smile. "That's just not my scene, at least not at this stage in my life."

"To each his own," I say. "I think it's great that you're self-aware enough to admit to that, and not give in to peer or societal pressure."

"Not to mention family pressure," he adds with a roll of his eyes. "My mother is determined to get a grandkid out of me. She might, but I doubt it will be through any kind of marital arrangement."

"What about your sister? What was her name? Vicky?"

"Valerie," he says. I watch a veil of sadness descend over him. "She was killed in a car accident in Arizona four years ago. She moved there with her husband. They were only married for two years and didn't have any kids yet."

"Wow. Sorry to hear that." The door to the lobby opens and Hurley pokes his head into the auditorium.

"What's going on?" he says with a pointed look at his watch.

"Sorry," I say. "Catching up on old times. I went to high school with Brad." I steer Brad toward the lobby and ask him if Junior has swabbed him yet. Brad, whose makeup is heavier than anyone else's so far, nods and widens his eyes. "That guy came at me with so many swabs, I kept waiting for him to tell me to drop my drawers and bend over." He laughs, and places a hand on my shoulder when he does so. I wince when he hits my wound, but I manage to chuckle along with him. Hurley does not.

Once that awkward moment has ended, I direct Brad to the chair and take up the camera. Hurley starts his questioning with the usual introductory information, but then, surprisingly, his first few questions are off script.

"Are you married, Brad?"

"Nope," Brad answers with a smile, apparently oblivious to the undercurrent I can feel.

"And you knew Mattie back in high school?"

"I did." Brad looks over at me, smiles, and winks. "In fact, we went to a school dance together once."

I shoot a glance at Hurley and see his scowl deepen. "Did the two of you date?" he asks Brad.

"Nothing official," Brad says, bestowing another wink on me. "We were basically just good friends back then. It was a small school, so there was a lot of cross-dating, and pretend dating. But Mattie and I never hooked up or anything."

I wince at his choice of words and bite my lower

lip. "Brad," I say, "I forgot to mention that I'm video recording this."

My comment is more for Hurley than Brad, a not-so-subtle reminder that everything he's asking is being recorded on videotape, a tape that might be looked at by any number of other people. Hurley seems to get the message. He looks over at me, then at his feet, clears his throat, and squares his shoulders. When he finally looks up, he starts asking Brad the same questions he asked everyone else, staying on focus.

Brad's answers are in keeping with the others'. He says Helen was standing beside Dalrymple's head when he saw her, and that the others all arrived at the scene around the same time he did. When asked if anyone had any big issues or problems with Roger Dalrymple, his face clouds over for a moment.

"Roger wasn't an easy guy to work with at times," he says. "Though I think maybe he was worse than usual today. I saw him right after he came back from lunch, and he looked kind of pissed off. And I think he'd been drinking."

Hurley asks Brad if he was up on the catwalk today, and he says he wasn't, but had gone up there yesterday.

The possibility that the makeup I found on the catwalk railing might have been left on a day other than today renders it of minimal value as evidence, and I wonder if there's a way to prove when the makeup smear was created.

When we're done with Brad, we let him out the front door and check on the status of the storm.

The wind has died down some, but I suspect it's a temporary respite. The wet snow is still falling, but not as hard as it was earlier. Main Street has emptied itself in the time we've been here, everyone heading home to settle in for the storm.

Next I go out to the auditorium to fetch Mickey Parker, who is apparently the group's multitasker. He does hair and makeup for the actors, as well as scenery and costume design. Mickey isn't wearing any makeup, at least not in the usual sense, although he has smears of it on his shirt, his arms, his hands, and his pants. Not surprising, given that he must have applied it to the others.

"You must be a very busy man," I say to him as I walk him back toward the lobby beneath the death glare of Helen Niehls, who has made it clear she does not appreciate being left for last. "I understand you perform several jobs for the group."

"I do what I can," he says. "It gives me an outlet for my artistic side, and since my paintings don't seem to be earning me any recognition or money, this stuff keeps food on the table and a roof over my head."

I have to admit that Mickey doesn't fit into my idea of what an artist should look like. If I'd had to guess his occupation after bumping into him on the street, I'd have gone with accountant. In his thirties, he is of average height, with short brown hair that he combs over from a side part, and glasses. He is dressed in jeans and a pullover sweater that has seen better days, judging from the holes in the elbows and the stains all over the front of it, some of which appear to be paint, while I suspect others are makeup. Beneath the sweater is a pale blue, collared shirt, and his jeans—also well stained— are a generic, knockoff brand. His feet are encased in a pair of old loafers that are so covered with paint that I can't determine their original color.

"Mr. Parker," Hurley begins, after the usual introductory spiel as soon as I've started the camera, "I need to get your version of the events that happened here this afternoon regarding Mr. Dalrymple."

"Hurley, excuse me, but do you mind if I ask him a question?" I say, eyeing the plethora of stains on Parker's clothing. Hurley gives me a nod. "Tell me something about this makeup you use," I ask. "How long does it take for it to dry?"

"Depending on how heavy it is, it can take as long as half an hour or more. When I clump it up on my palette, it stays pliable for up to two hours beneath the surface. It might crust over on the outside, but it's a thin crust and the stuff underneath stays nice and moist. And it's easy enough to make it wet again if you apply or mix in the necessary remover solutions. Why?"

I don't answer him, though I'm relieved to learn that the smear I found on the catwalk will be somewhat time-sensitive. "Did you apply makeup to all of the actors here today?" I ask him, checking out the splotches on his arms, hands, and clothing. Most of them look dry, but there is no way for me to know how old they are.

"I didn't do Dom, because he wasn't here. I did

everyone else, except that snobby bitch, Haugen," he says. "She always insists on doing her own, and then she never applies enough of it. I keep trying to explain to her that it needs to be overdone for the stage so that the audience can see it, but she won't listen to me. She says she doesn't want to look like a whore, and that she's pretty enough without a ton of makeup." He scoffs and gives Hurley a sidelong glance. "Did I mention she's also very modest?"

"I take it you and Ms. Haugen don't get along," Hurley says.

"Nobody gets along with her," Mickey says. "She's a manipulative, egotistical control freak."

"Don't mince your words," I say with a heavy note of sarcasm.

"Sorry, but it's true," Mickey says. "Her father finances these plays all the time, and because of that, she feels like she can dictate anything she wants. And trust me, she always gets her way. Though I have to say, Dalrymple typically puts up more of a fight than some of the others we've worked with."

"Were there tensions between Dalrymple and Ms. Haugen?" Hurley asks.

"*Tensions?* I don't think 'tensions' is a strong enough word for it. It's been all-out war most of the time between those two."

"Give me some examples," Hurley says.

"Well, for starters, Dalrymple wanted Helen to play the role of the daughter rather than the family matriarch, because he wrote the daughter as someone with a weight problem who is self-conscious about her body. And Helen, while irritating in her own way at times, at least has no illusions about her body. She was perfect for the role. But Rebecca insisted she had to have it, and she refused to play the matriarch role, claiming that she couldn't be convincing as some old lady. When Roger told her she'd have to wear a fat suit if she took the role of the daughter, Rebecca refused. Then she proceeded to rewrite the character the way she wanted her to be." He gapes at us, wide-eyed with disbelief. "Can you imagine the gall? I mean, come on. This play is Dalrymple's work, his vision. What kind of 'nads does it take to insist on rewriting it?" He shakes his head in dismay.

"Dalrymple caved, I take it?" Hurley says.

"He did this time, though he's stood up to her before, but I don't think he was up for it today. He was in a bad mood when he came back from lunch, and I think he'd had a few, you know?"

"Meaning what?" Hurley asks.

"Meaning a liquid lunch," Mickey says. "Can't say I blame the guy. I mean, the poor bastard really wants to see his play produced, and with Rebecca's father footing the bill, he's kind of over a barrel with Rebecca's demands, you know? Hell, Rebecca's not even that good of an actress. Dalrymple is going out of his way by just letting her be in the production."

"And you think Mr. Dalrymple might have been inebriated this afternoon?" Hurley asks.

Mickey waffles with a waggle of his shoulders and a sigh. "I don't know if you could say he was drunk, but he definitely wasn't feeling any pain. He kept stumbling over his words, and he was walking kind of heavy, you know how some people do when they've had a little too much?"

"How did the rest of the crew get along with Dalrymple?" I ask.

Mickey makes a face. "Dalrymple isn't the easiest person to work with," he says after a moment of contemplation. "He's very picky about a lot of stuff. And he isn't a particularly patient man."

"Has he had arguments with other members of the cast?" Hurley says, scribbling away in his notebook.

"Of course," Mickey says with a shrug. "But for the most part, it's just the usual crap that always happens when these big egos and creative types try to work together."

"Did you observe any disagreements today?" I ask.

Mickey thinks for a few seconds, and then nods. "Well, I didn't hear what was said, but I know that Rebecca and Roger had a tense discussion of some sort this morning. And then Roger and Brad got into it this afternoon, because Brad is insisting that he wants to play his character as more of a Klinger type, you know, the guy who kept trying to get sent home on a Section 8 in the TV show *M*A*S*H*?"

I nod. Hurley is busy writing.

"Roger wants him to play it as someone who is gender confused. They argued about the beard, and the amount of makeup to use, and the way Brad would walk and talk. Brad tried to do it Roger's way, but today he went off on him and said it just wasn't working, and he'd have to do it his way or not at all."

"Did Dalrymple cave?" I ask.

"No," Mickey says. "In fact, he threatened to fire Brad. I think Roger was tired of being bulldozed by Rebecca and took it out on Brad. Anyway, the two of them stormed off in opposite directions, and Dalrymple turned up dead about half an hour later."

Chapter 22

Things aren't looking good for Brad Levy or Rebecca Haugen by the time we get done talking to Mickey. It turns out he knows a lot about each of the people involved, since his position as their stylist often creates long periods of time where talk fills the awkward silent voids. People confide in him, much the same way women tend to confide in their salon stylists, and as a result, Mickey is a fount of information.

We learn that Rebecca, with her demands and her air of privilege, is universally disliked by everyone else in the group; Helen and Roger were rumored to be having an affair; young Corey has a crush on Cass, our receptionist; Dom is considered by everyone to be one of the best singers, as well as one of the best actors, in the group; everyone, to a man, dislikes the murder victim, who is, or rather was, in Mickey's words, "a pretentious, nitpicky asshat."

We also learn that none of our suspects had any inkling of where the others were at the time of Dalrymple's death, or if they did, they weren't letting on, though everyone agreed they heard Dom come in the back door after the body had been discovered. While this makes things look good for Dom, it doesn't rule him out completely, as Hurley points out to me after Parker leaves. Dom could have, in theory, come in the back door, climbed up onto the catwalk, and pushed Dalrymple, then gone back down and out the back door so he could come in again a short time later with an apparent alibi.

Our final witness is Helen Niehls, who by now has grown apoplectic at being the last person talked to.

"My time is worth something," she snaps at me when I come to fetch her. "Do you really think I have all day to just sit around here waiting on you people?" She storms past me, heading up the aisle and out to the lobby area. I see Junior roll his eyes and shake his head.

When Helen reaches Hurley, she stops, cocks one hip out to the side, and plants a hand on it, arm bent. "Would you mind explaining to me why I'm the last person you're talking to, when I was the first one to find Dalrymple's body? I should think my story would be the most important one. I'm your key witness, am I not?"

Her attitude is one of obvious annoyance and impatience, but that dissipates fast when Hurley comes back at her with, "What you are is a key *suspect*."

Helen looks appalled, then disbelieving. "*Sus-*

pect? Are you serious? Why the hell would I be a *suspect?*"

"Because you disliked the victim," I say, my camera already rolling.

"Everyone disliked Roger," she says in a Captain Obvious–sounding tone, giving me a brief glare before turning her attention back to Hurley. "Just because I'm the one who found him doesn't mean I had anything to do with his death. And, frankly, I'm insulted that you would think so."

She drops her arm to her side and straightens her hips. "Can we get this over with, please? I have places to go and things to do." She taps at the wristwatch on her right arm. "Ticktock, time's a-wasting."

I can tell from the expression on Hurley's face that he greatly dislikes Helen Niehls, and I suspect if he could figure out a reason to do so, he would arrest her right now and throw her in jail, just on general principle. Instead, he takes a slow, bracing breath and starts in with his official questions.

"Can you please tell me where you were in the minutes leading up to you finding Mr. Dalrymple's body?"

"I was on the main stage," she says. "I was out practicing my lines and needed to use the bathroom. I heard that horrible noise, came backstage, and found him there. Then I screamed."

"Did you hear anything, or see anyone else, when you were on stage?" Hurley asks.

"No."

This strikes me as odd, since Rebecca Haugen had said she was also out in the main auditorium right before Helen screamed.

"And when you saw Roger on the floor, did you try to touch him, or talk to him at all?"

"I already answered this question," she says irritably.

"Humor me," Hurley says.

Helen emits a sigh of disgust. "Like I said before," she says with barely contained anger, "no, I didn't. I used to be an EMT, and I could see from his neck that he was . . . well . . . I knew it was bad."

"Okay," Hurley says. He purses his lips and stares at her for a few seconds. I've seen other people wither beneath that scrutiny, but Helen just stares right back at him, looking as exasperated as ever. "When you screamed," Hurley says, "did you scream a word, like 'help'? Or his name?"

Helen's brows knit together. "I don't know," she says after a few seconds of thought. "Maybe I screamed, 'Oh, my God' or something like that." She pauses and shakes her head. "No, I don't think I screamed that. That's too many words. It doesn't feel right. And I'm pretty sure I didn't say his name." She stares off into space, one finger tapping at her lips. "I might have said 'help,' but that doesn't feel right to me, either." She gives Hurley a frustrated look. "Isn't that silly? I honestly don't know what I said. Did you ask the others? What did they say I said?"

"Speaking of the others," Hurley says, deftly avoiding her question, "who was the first to arrive at the scene after you?"

Once again, Helen's brows knit together, her eyes narrowing in thought. She doesn't answer right away, and other than shooting me an annoyed glance, she doesn't look at either of us. "You know, I'm not sure." She looks at Hurley apologetically, but also with a hint of worry. "When I try to picture it in my head, it seems as if everyone was just there all of a sudden. I can't remember any one person arriving. One minute, no one was there, and the next, they all were there."

"So you can't tell me where any of them came from?" Hurley asks.

Helen shakes her head, looking both surprised and a bit miserable.

"Did you go up on the catwalk for any reason today?" Hurley asks next.

"I did," Helen says. "First thing this morning, when I got here. I went up there to adjust some lights for Roger."

"Did Roger typically ask you or the other actors to go up and do things on the catwalk?"

Helen shrugs. "He asked periodically. I don't know if I'd call it typical."

"Have you worked with Roger Dalrymple before?"

"Yeah, we all have. He's a prolific playwright."

"Does Rebecca's father often subsidize your plays?"

"He's done a lot of them. I haven't kept tabs."

"Who else supports your group?"

"Well, there are other individuals who donate time and money, and we have received grants over the years. And then there are the students from U-Dub who come and volunteer from time to time."

"Were you and Roger Dalrymple having an affair?" Hurley asks this question with the same level and tone of voice he'd used with all the others.

Helen opens her mouth to answer, but freezes, saying nothing. She cocks her head to one side and narrows her eyes at Hurley. "Who told you that?" she says finally.

"Were you?" Hurley repeats.

"No." Helen tries to stare Hurley down with her answer, but this time, his blue-eyed intensity is too much for her. I suspect it's because she's lying. She looks away and makes a pretense of covering a cough—a theatrical gesture if ever I saw one.

"So you've never dated Mr. Dalrymple?" Hurley says.

Helen bites her lower lip. "Well, we might have gone out for a drink or two, at one time or another. Roger likes his drinks." Something about the way she says this, and the expression on her face, gives me an idea.

"You wanted something more, but Dalrymple wasn't giving it," I say.

Helen shoots me a look of incredulity. "Don't be ridiculous," she scoffs.

Hurley and I both stare at her, saying nothing.

"Okay, fine," she spits out. "I liked the guy and made a move on him. What of it?"

"Did he take you up on it?" I ask.

Once again, she opens her mouth as if to answer, but stops herself. She sighs heavily and does another one of her coughs.

"How many times?" I ask.

"What?" Helen snaps, looking confused and irritated.

"How many times did he sleep with you before he broke it off?" I see Hurley look at me with a bemused expression.

Helen is gnawing at the inside of her cheek, fussing with the cuffs of her sleeves, and tapping one foot anxiously. After an interminable amount of time, she looks at me with this wounded, angry expression and says, "Men can be such assholes sometimes, can't they?"

Chapter 23

We let Helen leave without getting a final answer to our question, though it's clear to us that she was a scorned lover to our victim, which keeps her high on our list of suspects.

"What do you think?" I ask Hurley once she's gone.

"I think we're going to have to talk to all of these people some more," Hurley says. "Dom included. There are some dynamics here they haven't made us aware of, and I think those dynamics might have played an important role in all of this. But I want to wait and see what the autopsy turns up, if anything."

I glance at my watch. "Why don't we check in with Richmond and see what he's managed to accomplish with the Liesel Paulsen case."

Hurley nods, takes out his phone, and jabs at the screen a couple of times before putting the phone to his ear. After nearly a full minute, during which I assume he's going to be sent to voice mail and have to leave a message, he says, "Hey, Richmond." He listens a moment and says, "Okay"; then he sighs. Covering the bottom of his phone with his free hand, he says, "He asked me to hold on for a minute."

I nod, and then hear my own phone ding out a tone that tells me I've received a text message. I look and see it's from Not a Trace, informing me that my hearse is clean and the keys are with our office receptionist.

"Yeah, I'm still here," Hurley says. I watch his face as he listens to whatever Richmond is saying, wishing he'd put the call on speaker. His expression gives away nothing, and the only things he says are "Really?" very early on in the basically one-sided conversation, and then "Too bad," a minute or so later. And finally: "Gotcha. I'll meet you back at the station later and we can plan our next step."

He finally disconnects the call and I wait eagerly for him to fill me in. "Come on, Hurley, give. What did Richmond have to say?"

"How bad do you want to know?" he teases.

"Hurley," I whine impatiently, my expression darkening. "I'm not in the mood for games."

"Okay, fine. Come on, I'll fill you in on the way."

We gather our stuff and head for the stage area. "Richmond was able to get a search warrant for O'Keefe's place in the Dells. It makes sense in a way that the guy lives there. A vacation spot like that would be prime pickings for kid snatchers. But his house is a rental, and when the local guys served the warrant, no one was home, so they had to have the landlord let them in. And it looks like O'Keefe has flown that particular coop."

"That stupid doctor probably tipped him off," I say.

"Probably," Hurley agrees. "Too bad I couldn't have arrested the guy for real. At least the Feds are watching his place, so if O'Keefe shows up there, we'll get him."

When we reach the auditorium, we see it is empty, and when we check the backstage area, we discover that Dalrymple's body is gone and the area has been cordoned off with yellow police tape. Junior is there, finishing up the processing of the crime scene. Over by the wall, I see a large collection of evidence bags and boxes containing swabs.

"Who picked up the body?" I ask Junior. "The Johnson family is kind of waylaid today."

"Yeah, I heard," Junior says. "Izzy ended up calling the Keller Funeral Home. There was some new girl who showed up. Kind of cute." He wiggles his eyebrows salaciously.

"Don't let Monica hear you say that," I caution him.

"Monica and I broke up."

"Oh no! When?"

"Officially, a few days ago, but it's been coming for a while."

"I'm sorry," I tell him, adding him to my mental list of men who need to get fixed up with someone, though I put Junior at the bottom. He and Monica have been an item for a long time and he'll need time to recover.

"Thanks," Junior says with a weary smile. "How did the interviews go?"

"They were interesting," Hurley says. "The only person we were able to rule out, more or less, was Dom, since everyone agreed he hadn't been here until after Dalrymple's body was found. I mean, technically, I suppose, he could have done it, but it would've required a lot of precise timing. And I don't see Dom for this."

Junior nods his agreement.

"Anyway," Hurley says, "I suppose I'm going to have to chat some more with all of these people down at the station at some point." He looks over at Junior. "How's your schedule looking?"

"I have some things on the burner," Junior says, though I suspect he's stretching the truth a bit. His primary area of investigatory focus is vice-related stuff, which in most cities means things like gambling, pornography, and prostitution. In Sorenson, most of the gambling that goes on is friendly bar bets related to sporting events, and the purchase of lottery tickets. As for pornography, I suppose the pictures some of the local farmers pass around of their bulls, stallions, and boars during breeding season might qualify, but these days most pornography makes it through the doors of homes via the Internet. A small police force like ours doesn't have the type of resources necessary to make much of a dent in the online porno industry. Prostitution occurs, but not all that often, and the most likely sex-for-money deals that take place in town typically involve the breeding of farm animals.

We do have our share of burglaries, drug offenses, and vandalism, and most of the time that's what Junior spends his time working on. He is available, if needed, to assist with death investigations, however, anytime Hurley or Richmond asks for help. And I suspect the man is desperate to be involved. His girlfriend, Monica—or ex-girlfriend, now—told me a few months back that Junior was so bored with his current job that she wouldn't be surprised if he became a serial killer just so he could have something more interesting and exciting to do. Hurley's inquiry now, with its implied promise of involvement in a homicide investigation, is job crack for Junior.

"I could use some help looking into these theater people," Hurley says. "Not to suggest that Roger Dalrymple's life isn't just as important as anyone else's, but I really want to stay focused on this Paulsen investigation."

"I'm happy to help with anything you need," Junior says, looking an awful lot like my dog, Hoover, whenever I open a bag of dog treats. "I can even take lead on it, if you want."

"Let's see what the autopsy shows," Hurley says. He looks at me. "Think Izzy will do it right away? It's four-thirty already."

"Let me call him and ask," I say. "I don't want him to overtax himself," I add as I place the call.

Izzy answers on the second ring. "Hurley wants to know what the time frame is for the Dalrymple autopsy," I say.

"It won't get done until tomorrow, if then. Otto is supposed to be taking over for me tonight, but I got a call from him a little while ago. He got caught in this storm and ran his car into a ditch. He got picked up by someone, but he thinks he broke his arm and he isn't going to be able to make it into the office for a few days, maybe longer. Not sure if he's going to be able to do autopsies until his arm heals."

"Oh no!" I say. "Can we get a temp in?"

"No need," Izzy says. "I can cover for now."

"Izzy," I say in my best reprimanding tone. "You're supposed to be part-time and semiretired at this point, remember? Your heart attack wasn't that long ago. Don't overdo it."

"I won't. That's why I'm going to wait until to-morrow, assuming I can even get in. This storm is building fast, and from what Otto said, the stuff yet to come our way is nasty. I'd stay here in the office tonight, but I think Dom needs me."

"I'm sure he does. I'll be there in a little bit and drive you home. Let's hope the weather will keep people on their best behavior tonight so we don't have to go out on any calls."

"You won't need to. Christopher is staying here overnight."

"Smart thinking on his part," I say. "See you soon."

I disconnect the call and fill Junior and Hurley in on the conversation.

"I suppose we should all get sheltered as soon as possible," Junior says. "What do you say we call it a night? I'll lock up here. I got the keys from that Haugen woman."

"Sounds good," Hurley says.

* * *

With that, he and I head for the back door. When we open it, we are met with a winter maelstrom of swirling, stinging snow; frigid gusts of wind; and an early darkness thanks to the cloud coverage. We make it to the truck without blowing away, but there are a few dicey moments.

"Man, this thing is really revving up," Hurley says. "I'm going to go back to the station and help Richmond, but why don't I drive you home first? You can pick up the hearse in the morning."

"I need to take Izzy home," I remind him. "And I need to report off to Christopher. I'll be fine. That hearse handles well in the snow."

Hurley looks displeased with my answer, but he offers no argument. He white-knuckles the drive to our office, which, fortunately, is only a few blocks away.

"Are you planning on staying all night at the station?" I ask as he pulls into our underground garage. The sudden escape from the elements makes me realize how tense I was during the ride. I relax, but I can feel an ache in some of my muscles from being clenched up.

"Probably," he says. "Are you okay with that?"

"I'd rather have you home, but I understand. And I suppose you can work on finding more info on this O'Keefe guy. Has Richmond run him yet to see if he has any priors?"

Hurley looks over at me with a big smile.

"What?"

"You're getting good at cop-speak," he says. "It's kind of sexy when you talk like that."

I give him a look of disbelief. "Seriously, Hurley? I'm starting to worry about the things that turn you on."

"*You* turn me on, Squatch," he says, his voice suddenly low and sultry. He reaches over and starts to play with my hair. "You always have. Right from the first moment I saw you."

I stare at him, unsure how to take this. On the one hand, I'm flattered, but on the other, I recall that the first time he saw me was at a crime scene, one involving the murder of the woman who had been having an affair with David. And not only was it my very first crime scene investigation with Izzy, I ended up being a suspect. Then there was the quirky turn of events that led to my underwear getting tagged as evidence.

"I remember seeing you walking behind Izzy," he says, "looking all scared and vulnerable. You were clearly unsure of yourself, even though you were trying hard not to show it. And the way you blushed with that whole underwear thing . . ." He trails off, his eyes gazing off into the past. "I don't know what it was exactly, but something about the way you looked and acted that night had me all hot and bothered." He gives his head a little shake and focuses on me again. "It nearly broke my heart when I realized you were a suspect. I didn't think you had anything to do with it, but I had to keep my distance until I knew for sure."

I'm stunned by this revelation. I knew there had been an attraction between the two of us early on, but I had no idea how early, or how strong it was on Hurley's part. For me, it was nearly instantaneous. One look at Hurley with his dark hair, vivid blue eyes, and those long, lanky legs so tidily wrapped up in a pair of tight-fitting blue jeans . . .

I reach up and give his arm a squeeze. "Are you happy with our life, Hurley?"

"Very," he says without hesitation. Then his brow furrows. "Why do you ask? Are you happy?"

"I am," I say, and I mean it.

He smiles warmly at me. "I will admit to one thing I'd like to see different, though," he says.

My mind reels in panic. Is he going to tell me he wants me to do a better job at keeping the house clean? Or that I need to learn to cook something other than hot dogs and mac and cheese? Or that I need to lose about twenty-five pounds? Or that he wants to have more sex? Or less sex? Or sex in different places? Or . . . heaven forbid . . . sex with other people? I start to ask him to clarify, but my mouth is so dry I can't get it to work. It turns out I don't have to. Hurley provides the answer for me.

"I'd really like to think about us having another kid."

I'm both relieved and dismayed. *This again.* My mind strobes images of all the reasons why I think this is a bad idea, a montage of leaky breasts, huge bellies, morning sickness, swollen ankles, and me looking and feeling utterly exhausted. And then I see an image of Matthew smiling at me, hugging me, talking to me, calling me "Mammy," his unique combo of "Mattie" and "Mommy." It makes me feel all warm and squishy inside, and I smile.

"I'll think about it," I say. "There are some things we need to consider."

"Such as?"

"Such as the fact that I'm not a spring chicken anymore. I'm thirty-seven, Hurley. I might not be able to get pregnant."

"You certainly didn't have any trouble with Matthew."

True that. Matthew was a surprise, one that occurred while I was on the pill, though I admittedly hadn't been as religious about taking them as I should have been. Nevertheless, Hurley and I seemed eminently compatible in that regard.

"My eggs are looking a little gray around the edges," I say. "The risk of birth defects greatly increases with the age of the mother."

Hurley shrugs. "I don't care. If it's our kid, we'll love it, raise it, and give it the best life possible."

"That's an idealistic view of things, Hurley. It's a serious consideration and it's irresponsible to simply dismiss it out of hand. Give it some thought."

"I have, Squatch." He takes my hand in his and gives it a squeeze. "I love Emily and Matthew, and our family makes me happy. But something inside me keeps clamoring for another one. I don't know what it is, but it won't let me go."

"It's your biological clock ticking," I tell him. "I've felt it, too, but I'm worried that in my case my biological clock has already sprung a few sprockets."

"Women have babies well into their forties these days," Hurley argues.

He is adamant on the subject, and I can tell from the tone in his voice and the set of his jaw that he is determined on this matter. More so than I realized.

"You really want this, don't you?" I say.

He tucks a strand of hair behind my ear, and says, "I do. I love you, Squatch. I love us. I love our family. And more than anything, I want to make another little person who is a combination of you and me." He shrugs. "I can't explain it any better than that."

Tears well in my eyes. " 'You had me at hello,' " I say, my voice hitching.

Hurley's brow furrows. "What?" he says. "I didn't say 'hello.' "

"No, silly, it's a line from a movie, *Jerry Maguire.*" Hurley shrugs and shakes his head. "Never mind." I lean over and kiss him before getting out, and as soon as I shut my door, he pulls around and leaves the garage, heading for the police station two blocks away. I have the weirdest urge to run after him.

Chapter 24

I take the elevator up to the first floor and head straight for my office, where I find Christopher seated behind his desk.

"This storm is getting crazy," I say when I walk in. "Can I report off to you so I can drive Izzy home?"

"Sure. I'm staying here at the office tonight. That way, I know I'll be able to get to work in the morning."

"Yeah, Izzy told me. I think that's a smart idea, given that you live out in the boondocks."

Christopher was renting an apartment in Sorenson when he was first hired, but he recently decided to buy an old farmhouse, which he's living in while he fixes it up. It's a charming place, with several acres of land, an old barn with a fieldstone foundation, and a stream that runs through the property near the house. But the charm ends there. The amount of work needed on the place is huge. The wiring is old knob-and-tube stuff with fuses,

and the plumbing leaks bad enough that most of
the pipes have to be replaced. The roof is estimated to be about fifty years old and it leaked like
a sieve when Chris first moved in. Thanks to the
leaking roof and pipes, as well as the ravages of
time, and the work of some homesteading rodents,
the walls and floors had been heavily damaged in
places. The house was barely habitable when Chris
bought it, but he replaced the roof first thing and
courageously—or foolishly—moved in, sharing the
abode with an extended family of mice, a small
township of chipmunks, and a raccoon that hung
out in the basement. After only a week, he informed
us that the wildlife had flown the coop, and Izzy
and I privately speculated on whether Chris had
an exterminator come out, or if the quantity and
quality of his daily emissions drove the critters away.

His most recent project is the replacement of
the electrical wiring. After wisely purchasing a
high-end, gas-powered generator, he hired an
electrician to come in and rip out all the old knob
and tube and replace it with modern-day wiring.
Unfortunately, he hired Billy Conroy to do this,
and while Billy does a bang-up job—in the most lit-
eral sense at times—and knows his stuff, he has a
bit of a drinking problem, which makes him a tad
unreliable. I took care of him twice back when I
worked in the ER because he managed to shock
himself good enough to throw his heart into a
funky rhythm. I know of at least six other occasions since then when he came into the ER with
the same complaint. The one consistent factor in
each of these incidents was that Billy had decided
to work with a hangover. And Billy's hangovers

aren't your garden-variety headache-and-nausea kind of stuff.

Billy is a binge drinker, someone who will go days, even weeks, without touching a drop of alcohol, and then decide one night to get so liquored up that he can barely function. His binges typically last a week or more, and he treats his hangovers each morning with the hair of the dog, to the point where the dog bites him in the ass.

Billy's binges are the stuff of legend in Sorenson. On one infamous occasion, the police found him naked doing the breaststroke on someone's front lawn while the sprinklers were going. Another time, he was found naked curled up in the corner of a coat closet in the house of a perfect stranger. Yet another time, he was found—yes, naked again—sitting on a bench downtown trying to "drive" with a Frisbee in his hands. Billy's penchant for getting naked when he binges has led to the police keeping a spare change of clothes for him down at the station.

Billy was between binges when he was hired to redo Chris's wiring, and he managed to stay sober long enough to rip out most of the old stuff and start running the new wire. But then one of his binge cycles kicked in and he hasn't been back to the house in over two weeks, so Christopher has no power other than what he can run off his generator. He's been using candles for light, his fireplace for heat, and an old kerosene stove to cook on. Since he doesn't have hot water, he's been using the office bathroom and showers for his daily ablutions. And once a week, he hauls his laundry to the local Laundromat to wash it.

It's a lifestyle that might do in the hardiest of souls, but Christopher has taken it on with good spirits and a sense of adventure. The coming storm, however, might be too much for even his pioneering spirit, since his house's location gives him a half-hour commute on winding, narrow country roads, and his car is a beat-up old VW Bug, with tires that have about as much tread on them as an inner tube. I figure sleeping on a stretcher in a morgue that has power, heat, and running water will probably seem like Shangri-la to him at this point, even if he is sharing the space with a few dead people. At least they won't be bothered by his gastric problems.

"Let me know if you need any help," I tell Christopher. "If you get a call, that car of yours isn't going to do very well. Hurley's truck has four-wheel drive, as does Emily's car. And Hurley has a plow he can hook up to the truck if necessary."

"I will. Thanks," Christopher says. "Hopefully, I won't get any calls and can stay here. I brought an overnight bag with toiletries and such in it, and I can just wear scrubs for a change of clothes." His statement is punctuated by a quick whistle of wind that escapes from his backside. "Sorry," he says almost automatically.

"You don't need to apologize," I say. "I'm used to it. You can't work as a nurse for any length of time without learning how to tolerate nasty smells. And the same tends to go for this job. Not to mention potty training a toddler. I'm pretty much immune to such things by now."

I figure I have no right to be critical of Christopher's issues, given that I managed to outdo his emissions this morning, a fact I wisely decide to keep to myself, though I wouldn't be surprised if Brenda Joiner lets the story slip when she and Christopher get together.

Chris smiles. "You and Izzy have been very kind and understanding about it," he says. "I appreciate it."

"How's the gluten-free thing going? Is it helping any?"

"Doesn't seem to be making a difference," he says.

"Sorry to hear that."

"By the way, I heard you had some excitement here earlier," Chris says.

I panic for a moment, thinking Brenda has already spilled the beans and he's referring to my earlier Code Brown. Then I realize he's talking about the shooting and Ernie Roberts. I spend a few minutes sharing all the gory details with him—having insider info on a juicy story like this one is practically better than money here in Sorenson—and then give him a brief update on the Paulsen case and the Dalrymple case.

When I'm done, I call the house to see how Emily and Matthew are doing.

"We're having fun," Emily says. "We built a blanket tent in the living room and Matthew says he's going to live there forever."

I smile at this, recalling how Desi and I used to build blanket tents when we were kids and spend hours in them. I update Emily on my ETA for home, and tell her that her father won't be home until very late, if at all.

* * *

With that done, I pack up my things, bundle up, and go to Izzy's office. As the two of us head down to the garage, I'm curious to see how good a job Not a Trace did on my car. I've seen the amazing work they can do on crime scenes, some of which I would've thought had to be burned to the ground to get rid of the odors and detritus left behind by dead humans.

When I unlock the car door, I'm pleased to see that the seat looks as good as new, better, in fact, than it did before my accident. I doubt the hearse has been this clean since it was driven off the lot. And the smell inside is a fresh linen sort of scent. I hit the power button and unlock the passenger door for Izzy. He pokes his head inside warily, sniffing and examining all the surfaces.

"They do good work," he says finally, settling himself into the seat.

"Yes, they do," I agree, turning the key. The car starts with only a minor hiccup, and we fasten our seat belts. "Okay," I say, flexing my hands on the steering wheel. "Let's see how bad the roads are."

They are horrible. The snow is drier now, but it's coming down hard and fast, and blowing sideways. The wind is so strong that the hearse is buffeted sideways as soon as we leave the protection of the building. The rear wheels slide a smidge with Mother Nature's zealous exhalation, but they quickly regain their grip and the hearse plows along, its heavy weight providing both a solid base and decent traction. The plows are out, clearing and salting, but the storm has taken on such fury at this point that they are hard put to keep up. The main streets downtown have been cleared once, but already they are covered again with the wet, slick whiteness.

As the wind howls its banshee calls, drifts of snow build and blow, snaking their way around the corners of buildings, eddying in pirouettes on the sidewalks, and darting between the few cars still parked on the street. It's like a dance troupe of ghosts putting on their winter performance, and it's both mesmerizing and terrifying.

I take it so slow that Irene Keller could have whizzed by me. I navigate my turns at a snail's pace, and keep an eye out for the occasional stray drift. When we get to the outskirts of town and turn onto the road Izzy lives on, we find it virgin and untouched, a couple of inches of snow already piled atop a base of frozen rain. As I approach the entrance to Izzy's driveway, wondering if I'll be able to navigate the climb of it, I see headlights appear up ahead, skewing wildly from side to side. They disappear momentarily, replaced by a flash of red taillight before they return again, the light beams suddenly still and pointed toward the sky.

"Did you see that?" I say to Izzy.

"I did."

"Should we go and see if they're okay?"

Izzy, clearly torn, makes a face. "I suppose we should," he says.

I've slowed the hearse to a near stop, and I gently press the gas. The rear wheels spin for a second, but then they take hold and I ease the car farther down the road. As we close in on the lights, I see that there is a car in the ditch, the back end down, the front end pointing toward the sky. The vehicle

looks familiar and, sure enough, when I look at
the trail it left in the snow, I see that it came down
and out of David and Patty's driveway. After shifting into park, I leave the engine running, turn on
the emergency blinkers, and get out of the hearse.
I clamber down the bank and into the ditch, the
wind hitting my body hard enough to upset my already precarious balance, and stirring up loose
clouds of snow that make it difficult to see. The
windshield is already halfway obscured with falling
snow and I can't easily reach it, so I navigate my
way around to the driver's-side door and look
through that window.

Inside I see Patty behind the wheel, her eyes
closed, her hands on her belly, her face screwed
into a pain-wracked grimace. I grab the door handle and give it a yank, making my shoulder scream
yet again, but it's locked. Pounding on the window, I yell at Patty.

"Open up! Patty? Can you hear me? It's Mattie.
Unlock your door!"

Her eyes open and roll toward me, filled with
fear and pain. I start to yell again when some semblance of sanity surfaces, and Patty punches the
lock release. I grab the handle and, with a huge effort, manage to open the door. But the position of
the car makes the door more of a hatch cover.
Gravity is pulling on the weight of it, and it's all I
can do to keep it open. I'm forced to prop it with
my left shoulder, and I grit my teeth against the
pain.

Patty lets out a moan, her face tight with agony.

"Where are you hurt?" I ask.

"I think . . . I'm in . . . labor." She grunts this

out, and suddenly I understand. I place my hand on her belly, and even through the thickness of her coat and clothing, I can feel the rock-hard surface of her belly, tight with a contraction.

"Where's David?"

"In surgery." The contraction eases some and she pants, looking at me with a sardonic smile. "Someone who was in a car accident. Go figure."

"Okay," I say, thinking. "Can you get out of the car? If you can walk up the bank here, my hearse is right above us."

"I'll try," Patty says. She throws her left leg out of the car while I struggle to brace the door open. She shifts slightly in her seat, turning toward me, and then she lets out a scream, clutching her belly again. "Oh, God," she says through clenched teeth.

I grab her arm and try to urge her out of the car, but with the weight of the door on me, I can't get enough leverage. Plus, my feet are threatening to slide out from beneath me with every move I make, no matter how subtle.

Something catches my eye off to the side, and I see Izzy slide—literally—down the hill. He comes down on his butt and then half walks, half crawls, over to me. "What's going on?" he asks.

"It's Patty. She's in labor."

This explanation proves unnecessary a second later when Patty again lets out a scream and says, "Get it out of me!" while rubbing her huge belly.

"We can't do anything with her like this," I say to Izzy. "We need to get her out of her car and up to the hearse. Can you hold this door for me?"

Izzy slips and slides his way over to me, and takes my place at the door. Trying to squeeze my body,

Izzy's, and Patty's very pregnant belly into the space created by the open door proves to be an exercise in frustration and ingenuity, because, somehow, we manage to get Patty out of the car and standing beside it. With Izzy on one side of her and me on the other, we start hauling her up the hill to the road above. Halfway up, Patty stops, doubles over, and lets out a yelp. Izzy and I both slip, Izzy managing to maintain his stance, while I fall onto my knees and slide back down to the car. When I look up at Patty, I see that the insides of her pants legs are soaked and realize her water has broken. I scramble back up to her and grab her arm.

"Patty, up the hill. NOW!" I use my sternest voice and yank hard on her arm. I've got a sick feeling that Patty is going to drop that kid any second, and I'll be damned if she's going to do it out here on the snowy, icy hillside.

The urgency in my tone motivates Patty, who manages to scramble the rest of the way up the hill in a matter of seconds, leaving Izzy behind. I walk around and open the tailgate of the hearse and usher Patty inside. "Lie down," I tell her.

She does so, just as another contraction hits. I glance back to make sure Izzy is managing okay, concerned that the effort might prove harmful to him on the heels of the heart attack he had just months ago. But he has topped the hill and looks okay, his breath exertional but not struggling.

"I have to push," Patty says through gritted teeth.

This is not good. Her delivery is likely imminent. I had hoped we could make it to the hospital before that happened, but it doesn't look like that's the case. It would take forever to drive there—and who knows how long it would take for an ambulance to get to us?

"Take your pants off," I tell her. While she slides her wet pants down over her knees and to her ankles, I grab the scene-processing kit I keep in the back of the hearse and start rummaging through it. Izzy reaches us and immediately grasps what is happening.

I look at Patty, who is now naked from the waist down to her ankles. Her perineum is bulging and I can see a large circle of fuzzy, light hair down there. "She's crowning," I tell Izzy. "We could call an ambulance, but they're not likely to get here very fast in this weather. We're going to have to do this here."

"Got it." Izzy is all cool calmness. Granted, his job doesn't normally entail births, but he is a doctor, and he has delivered a baby in the not-so-distant past—mine. Between the two of us, I feel certain we can manage.

We have Patty scoot herself up as far into the car as she can. It still leaves Izzy and me with our backs in the storm, but we are able to lean deep enough into the back of the car to keep Patty and her baby out of the elements. Within a minute or two, we have a body bag unfolded and spread out beneath Patty, and a pair of scissors and some hemostats—clamps—at hand, ready to use. I also have towels in the car—I keep a stash on hand so I can use them on Matthew or, occasionally, on Hoover—and with these minimal items, we wait.

We don't have to wait long. Patty gives one more mighty push and the head pops completely out.

"Good girl," Izzy says. He supports the baby's head and gently lifts and rotates its body as Patty gives one more push and spits out the rest of the kid.

"It's a girl," Izzy says, and Patty half laughs, half cries. Her legs are trembling, and so are mine.

Izzy clamps the cord and cuts it, and we wrap the baby girl in the towels, clean her as best we can, and then hand her to Patty. The baby lets out a lusty cry, and Izzy and I high-five one another.

"I'll ride back here with them," Izzy says.

I nod and shut the tailgate on Patty and her new life in an area meant for hauling dead people. Then I get behind the wheel and prepare once again to do battle with the roads and Mother Nature's temper tantrum.

Chapter 25

Before starting the drive, I call the hospital—amazed that cell service has survived the storm thus far—and inform them of the delivery and our intent to bring both patients in. Izzy delivers the placenta a few minutes into our trek, and we make what is typically a ten-minute drive in a little over half an hour. I call again when we are only minutes away, and there is staff waiting for us in the ambulance garage when we pull in. Because the birth happened outside of the hospital setting, Patty's baby won't be allowed in the nursery with the others because of the risk of infection, but both mother and child are examined in the ER, both by the ER doc on duty and an OB/GYN doc, who is staying in the hospital overnight because of laboring patients and the storm.

David, we learn, is still in surgery, tending to a patient who has a ruptured bowel from an earlier car accident. I'm disappointed that I can't see his reaction to the news of Patty's delivery, because I'm curious to see how it affects him as an individual and how he interacts with both Patty and the baby. I'm not sure why I want to see these reactions. I suppose it's part simple curiosity, and part a desire to see if the future I imagined when I was with him is even close to the actual reality.

Having turned our patients over to the hospital staff, I call the house to let Emily know that I'm okay and going to be later than expected. Izzy and I are about to leave, and tackle the roads in an effort to get back to our respective homes, when Izzy's phone rings.

"It's Dom," he says after checking the screen. "Give me a minute?" I nod, and he steps off to one side to take the call.

I wander toward the nurses' station, where I see the social worker, Hildy, behind the desk. All of the nurses—two of them, since one was unable to get in because of the storm—are busy. When Hildy sees me approaching, she smiles broadly and waves me over.

"How is the case going?" she asks. "Any progress on finding that missing girl?"

"Some, but nothing concrete yet," I tell her. "That candy bar you noticed turned out to be a helpful lead."

"Oh, good," she says with a big smile. "I hope you can find the sister."

"Me too," I say. "What are you doing here this late in the day, and with the weather like it is?"

"I have my grief support group scheduled for

tonight," she says. "I canceled it, of course, but I wasn't able to reach everyone who usually comes. I doubt anyone will brave these elements for the group, but I thought I would stay in case someone shows up. Besides, the ER unit clerk was unable to get in, so I told the hospital supervisor I would stay down here and help by answering phones and such. In exchange, the hospital is giving me a bed for the night. What are you doing here?"

"Dr. Rybarceski and I just delivered a baby. In my hearse," I add with a sly smile, suspecting Hildy will appreciate the irony of bringing a new life into the world inside a car meant for carrying the dead to their final resting place.

"That was you?" Hildy says, grinning back at me. She is about to comment some more, but David rushes into the nurses' station. He sees Hildy first and says, "Where's my wife?" Then he sees me, stops short, and takes on a look of utter confusion. "Mattie? Why are you here?"

"I just helped Izzy deliver your baby," I say, smiling.

His furrowed brow furrows deeper. "Here? In the ER? Are you working here again?"

"No, she didn't have the baby here," I tell him. "She had it at the base of your driveway, in the back of my hearse. Patty tried to drive herself here and her car slid into the ditch. Izzy and I happened to see it and went to help her. Minutes later, your daughter was born. Congratulations."

David still looks confused, but after a moment, he breaks into a smile. "I have a daughter?"

"You do," I say, biting my lower lip as I realize I

may have stolen some of Patty's thunder. "I thought you knew already, so maybe you can act surprised and let Patty tell you it's a girl?"

"Oh. Sure," he says. He looks off to one side, shakes his head, and his smile broadens. I've seen him do this exact same thing many times before, back when we were married and he was puzzling out a particular case or diagnosis. What I just saw was his "Aha!" moment, and I suspect its cause now is the dawning reality of his new status as a father.

"Where is she?" he asks.

"Bed six," I tell him.

"They're okay?"

"They seem to be. The OB doc has been down here already to examine them both."

David nods, his expression a mix of awe and happiness . . . with perhaps a hint of fear. A common reaction to new parenthood. He starts to head toward Patty's room, but stops after a few steps and looks back at me.

"Thank you, Mattie," he says, and he has the kindest and most sincere look on his face that I've seen since the day I left him. "And can you please tell Izzy 'thank you' as well?"

"I will. And you're welcome. Congratulations to you both."

I watch him scurry off and then turn and look back at Hildy. She is smirking at me. "What?" I say.

"You handled that very well," she says. "And what a tangled web has been woven there, eh?"

"I suppose," I say.

"You know," Hildy says, "sometimes the sense of

loss experienced through divorce is on a level with that experienced by those who lose someone to death. Many of the emotions are the same—loneliness, a feeling of abandonment, sadness, the realization that the life you had is lost to you now, and the need to retell your story so that it can be colored by the latest events. I've had some divorced people in my grief-and-loss group before. If you ever want to sit in—"

"Wait, what did you just say?" I ask, grabbing Hildy's arm and interrupting her explanation.

She sputters for a second. "Um, I, uh, was talking about—"

"You said 'loss group,' " I tell her, interrupting again. I look at her, waiting to see if she makes the same connection I just made.

"Yes, well, I call it a grief-and-loss group. And if you ever . . ." She trails off, seeing that my mind is focused elsewhere.

"One of the nurses who cared for Liesel said the girl whispered the words 'lost group' to her, right before she died," I say. "But maybe she misheard it. Maybe she said 'loss group'?"

"Yes, it certainly could have been that," Hildy says after a moment of silent contemplation. Her eyes grow wide, and the corners of her mouth creep up into the start of a smile. "And it makes perfect sense," she says. "Their mother died, right?"

"Right. Do you know of any support groups like yours up in the area where they lived, around Necedah?"

"I don't, but I can find out," she says, sounding excited.

"Do you think you could find out something about groups in that area tonight?" I ask her. "Like now, even?" I bite my lower lip and look at her expectantly, eyebrows raised.

"Heck, yeah," she says, and without another word, she hustles off.

Excited by my new idea, I take out my phone and call Hurley.

He answers, saying, "Are you okay?" sounding mildly panicked.

"I'm fine," I assure him, and then I fill him in on the events with Patty.

"Wow, you've had an exciting evening so far," he says when I'm done.

"Yes, I have, and I'm not done yet. I had a possible brainstorm about the Paulsen case. Is Richmond there with you?"

"He is."

"Can you put me on speaker so he can hear me, too?"

"Sure." I wait for a few seconds and then hear Richmond say, "Can you hear me, Mattie?"

"I can. Can you hear me?"

"Loud and clear. What have you got?"

"Remember what Liesel said to Syph, right before she died?"

"You mean about the guy having her sister?"

"No, what Syph heard was just two words, which she reported to us as 'lost group.' But what if she really said 'loss group'?"

There's silence on the other end, presumably while Hurley and Richmond both try to parse this out. "I guess I'm not seeing the distinction you are," Richmond says finally.

"The girls' mother died six months or so before Liesel disappeared. And Hildy, the social worker over here at the hospital, was telling me about her grief-and-*loss group* meeting, which she had to cancel tonight." I say the words "loss group" slowly, enunciating the syllables with great care.

Hurley gets my meaning almost immediately. "Of course," he says. "You're thinking the girls might have been involved in some sort of bereavement group."

"Exactly."

"Oh," Richmond says with slow dawning. "That does make sense. It would be the perfect picking grounds for anyone looking to snatch up some vulnerable women," he muses.

"That's exactly what I was thinking," I tell them, feeling my excitement grow. "Hildy is already looking into what groups might have been available in that area around the time of the girls' disappearances."

"Make sure she passes on to me any information she learns," Richmond says.

"Oh, she will," I say. I have no doubt that Hildy will jump at the chance to report to Richmond directly.

"So, are you going home now?" Hurley asks.

"Hopefully. I'm waiting on Izzy to get off the phone."

"Do you want me to come and get you with my truck? It might be safer with my four-wheel drive."

"No, the hearse did fine, and the plows are out working in earnest. We'll be all right."

"Call me once you're safe at home, okay?"

"I will."

I see Izzy walking toward me as I disconnect the call, a tired look on his face. I meet him halfway and say, "Ready to go home?"

"I am," he says. "Dom is in quite a state over this Roger Dalrymple thing."

"I'm sorry."

Izzy gives me a sly look. "He burst into tears several times while I was talking with him." He utters this almost casually, but with a hint at some deeper meaning. I get what he's thinking almost immediately.

"Ooh, tears usually mean something sweet and sugary," I say, licking my lips.

Dom is an excellent baker and cook who tends to express his emotions through his culinary creations. The shed of actual tears almost always results in a baking spree, whereas anxiety is represented by rich French food, and anger by something down home and simple (though always delicious) like a pot roast dinner or a big pot of stew. If he's fixing Italian food, it generally means he's happy and content. Fortunately for me and my food predilection, Dom is a fairly happy person much of the time.

Izzy says, "He's already baked up a Dutch apple pie, and at the moment, he's in the midst of whipping up a batch of those pecan tassies he makes."

"Yum," I say, closing my eyes and imagining the taste. The pecan tassies are like tiny pecan pies in cookie form, and one of my favorite desserts. "How close is he to actually baking them, do you know?"

"He was filling the little pastry cups while we

were talking," Izzy tells me. His smile broadens and he shoots me a conspiratorial look. "I'd say they'll be ready right around the time we arrive at the house."

I lick my lips and sigh. "Let's get to it then, shall we?"

Chapter 26

The roads are still treacherous and the going is slow, but the plows are working diligently and the main city streets are navigable. As we get closer to the edge of town and Izzy's house, however, things get dicier. The hearse slogs through it all with ease, though, and the only hiccup in our travels is a moment of slippery hesitation as I negotiate the slope of Izzy's driveway. Well, that and the lingering smell of blood and amniotic fluid coming from the back of the car.

"You should call Not a Trace again," Izzy says, reading my mind. "They'll get it cleaned for you."

"I'm sure they will, but I can't say I'm looking forward to having to call them again. They aren't cheap."

When I'd retrieved my car keys from Cass, she also handed me the bill of service, which nearly made me poop my pants all over again. Now I was not only going to have to pay again, I couldn't help but wonder what the company's employees would think of me. Cleaning up poop one day, and delivery excreta the next, would leave them wondering just what it was I did in my hearse.

"Make David pay for it," Izzy says. "He can afford it."

It's a good idea, and I log it away for later consideration.

When I pull up behind Izzy's house, I don't wait for an invitation to come inside, and Izzy doesn't offer one. Based on experiences shared in the past, the assumption of my doing so is simply there. The kitchen smells like heaven, the rich scents of apples, pecans, cinnamon, nutmeg, and brown sugar all blending together in a mouthwatering lure. Underlying these aromas is the scent of chili powder, and I see a large pot of chili simmering on the stove, and a pan of unbaked corn bread ready to go into the oven.

Clearly, Dom had no doubt about whether or not I'd stop in, either, because he already has a container of warm pecan tassies prepared for me to take home, and a huge chunk of apple pie in another container. His eyes are red-rimmed, a clear sign that he's been crying, but at the moment, he appears calm and content, albeit busy as he bustles about the kitchen in his apron.

Juliana is seated in her high chair at one end of the table, eating a small piece of sugar-dusted piecrust, and Izzy goes over and kisses her on her forehead. This elicits a huge smile from Juliana, followed by her attempt to push a piece of her piecrust up Izzy's nose.

"Those containers are for you," Dom says to me.

"I can fix you up another one with some chili in it, or if you want to stay and eat with us, you can do that."

"Thanks, Dom," I say, giving him a kiss on the cheek. "My thighs hate you, but the rest of me adores you. I'd love to stay, but I really want to get home to Emily and Matthew."

"Juliana missed him today," Dom says. "When I picked her up at your sister's, she kept looking around for him."

"Aw, that's sweet," I say, giving Juliana a loving look.

"Speaking of your sister, she invited us to Hurley's birthday party on Sunday," Dom says, stirring the chili. "I was thinking of getting him a nice bottle of wine. Think that's okay?"

"No gifts necessary," I tell him, knowing he'll feel obligated to get one anyway. "And, yes, the wine will be fine." The smell wafting up from the stove is making my mouth water, and I'm rethinking my need to hurry home. Maybe just a small bowl before I go.

I'm about to say as much to Dom, but then he says, "Any idea yet if someone killed Roger?"

Izzy and I exchange a look. Dom, fortunately, is studiously stirring the chili, not looking at either of us.

"We have to be very careful about discussing any of this," Izzy says to Dom.

Dom gives him an exasperated look. "Maybe it wasn't any of us," he says, tears welling. "Someone could have come in from the outside. Maybe Dalrymple was upset over something or someone not even related to the theater group. Everyone said he came back from lunch drunk, so couldn't something have happened to him outside our group?"

I realize Dom is grasping at straws, unwilling to consider the possibility that one of his fellow actors might be a murderer. His scenario, however improbable, isn't impossible—the back door *was* unlocked when we got there—but the timing of the events as reported makes it unlikely.

Hurley had said at one point that we couldn't rule Dom out totally because it was within the realm of possibilities that he could have done it. In theory, he could have entered the building, gone straight up onto the catwalk, shoved Roger, and then just as quickly exited the building, only to reenter a moment later and make it look like he was just arriving. None of us considered Dom as a serious suspect, but in an effort to rule him out more permanently, I made a point of looking at the time stamps on the receipts Dom had given to Hurley. Between the time on those receipts and the time of his phone call to me, only twelve minutes had gone by. When you took into account the amount of time it would have taken him to drive from the stores in question back to the theater, park, and go inside, plus the time taken to assess the situation when he found the others crowded around Roger Dalrymple's body, it was hard to believe he had managed to do what he said he did, much less commit a murder on top of it.

As for some stranger doing the deed instead, based on Helen Niehls's story, there likely wasn't time enough from when she heard the thud of Roger's body hitting the floor, to the time of her scream, for someone to have fled the scene without Dom seeing him or her exit the building. Of course, that's assuming Helen Niehls was telling the truth.

Whether or not Dom wanted to face it, the odds were good that if Roger Dalrymple was murdered and didn't just stagger off that catwalk, drunk, it was someone in the theater group who pushed him.

"Let's wait until we have a chance to do the autopsy before we get too worked up, Dom," I say. Then, in what I hope will be a distraction sufficient to get Dom off the subject, I ask, "How's Sylvie doing today? Is she coming over for dinner?"

Dom shoots a guilty look at Izzy. "I fixed a plate up a little while ago and took it over to her. I hope that's okay." He pauses, puts the back of his hand on his forehead, and stares at the ceiling for a moment. "I just don't think I have the strength to put up with her snide comments tonight."

Izzy, who knows all too well how deeply his mother's barbed comments can wound, walks over to Dom and hugs him. "It's fine," he says.

He's rewarded for his efforts with a sobbing Dom draping himself over his shoulder. There are times when I find such emotional drama entertaining, but now isn't one of them. I take two seconds to weigh my need for escape with my desire for some chili, and for once, food doesn't win out. Of course that's probably because I have other food besides the chili.

I clear my throat loudly and gather up the containers of food Dom has fixed for me. "I'm going to go before the roads get any worse. Thanks again for these, Dom." I make a hasty retreat without waiting for a response, and I'm behind the wheel of my hearse less than thirty seconds later.

The country roads still haven't been plowed, and it makes for slow going for two reasons. The first is that the snow is accumulating fast. There is a good four inches of new stuff on the ground, and it's still coming down hard and fast. This makes it hard to see where I'm going and hard to see where the road ends and the fields begin. In addition, the wind gusts have created some unusual and unexpected drifts. Twice I nearly go off the road when I hit drifted accumulations of snow that are a foot or more deep. But the hearse plugs along through it all, and forty minutes after leaving Izzy's, I find myself at the turn for my driveway. Getting up it proves challenging, but after a few wheel spins and sickening sideways slides, I make it to the top and pull into the garage. After turning off the engine, I send Hurley a text to let him know I'm home safe, and then I sit for a minute to give myself time to unwind.

It's been a hell of a day, starting off with my Mount Vesuvius incident, being shot in the arm by Roberts, the death of Roger Dalrymple, the progress we made in the Paulsen case (though I would have liked to see more of that), and the delivery of Patty's baby. As my mind replays an abbreviated version of all these events, I feel my body grow wearier with each passing image. I'm exhausted, I realize, and suddenly my legs feel too tired to move.

I look over, see the containers of pie and tassies, and grab the pecan treats. I pop the lid and take a big whiff, hoping a little sugar inspiration will get me moving. It works, but not in the way I think. The smell of the pecan treats mingled with the lingering smells coming from the back of the hearse makes me nearly gag. I snap the lid back in place, gather up the other container, and haul my butt out of the car and into the house.

There's no sign of Emily and Matthew downstairs anywhere, though the blanket tent is still up in the living room, strung between a chair, the couch, and the coffee table. I glance at my watch and see that it's going on eight, and figure Emily is upstairs getting Matthew ready for bed. I set my goody containers on the counter, shuck off my boots, and then strip off my coat and scarf as I'm walking to the front hall closet. When I reach the base of the stairs, I hear Emily upstairs talking to Matthew.

"Mom is going to be so mad at you," she says in a voice that is sympathetic rather than chastising.

This has my curiosity piqued, and I tiptoe up the stairs. I hear water splashing and see the light on in the bathroom and figure Emily must be giving Matthew a bath. Still tiptoeing, I approach the bathroom door, which is halfway shut, and push it fully open.

I'm partially right. Someone is getting a bath, but it isn't Matthew. He and Emily are standing next to the tub, which has several inches of water in it. Inside the tub, in the water, is Hoover, looking like a drowned rat. Then I have to rethink the image because the dog in the tub looks like a Dalmatian.

"What in the world?" I say, making Emily start.

She drops the sponge she's using on the dog, whirls around, and claps a hand to her chest. "Oh, my God, you scared me!" she says, her voice a mixture of relief and annoyance.

Before I can apologize for my sneakiness, Hoover makes a mad dash to escape, scrambling out of the tub, and causing a mini tsunami of water and soap. Emily yelps and tries to grab him, but the dog is quicker, despite his paws doing a cartoon scramble on the bathroom tiles. He's also collarless and slippery. The second his feet get a holding, he darts past her and me, and hauls butt down the hallway, leaving a trail of sudsy water in his wake.

"Damn it," I hear Emily say, and she goes after the dog.

"Damn it," Matthew echoes, and then he, too, takes chase.

Hoover gallops down the stairs, both kids in pursuit. I stand in the bathroom, looking at the mess, and trying to understand why my yellow Labrador retriever is now covered with black spots. Shrieks rise up from below, and then I hear both Emily and Matthew laughing. There is the sound of running, of furniture getting shoved, and more shouting and laughter.

I weigh my options, and then grab a towel from the bathroom cabinet. I head downstairs in no particular hurry, and when I reach the front hallway, I see Hoover go hurtling by from the living room into the kitchen. Close on his heels is Emily, who is holding a blanket from the now-destroyed tent. Three seconds later, I see my son go running by, his face bright with laughter.

I want to be angry. I'm much too tired to deal

with the mess I'm going to have to clean up, and my dog doesn't look right. But the ongoing shrieks of laughter are contagious, and before I realize what I'm doing, I've joined the chase, the towel held in front of me with both hands.

In the kitchen, Emily has Hoover somewhat trapped between the island and a wall of cabinets. Every time Hoover tries to escape, Emily heads him off. If she went around the island to Hoover's side, he could easily make a run for it, so the two of them stay on their respective sides doing the doggy version of a Mexican standoff. Matthew is standing at one end of the island, watching and telling his sister whenever Hoover moves in one direction or the other.

"Emily," I say, walking up to the scene slowly. "You go around the far end of the island and I'll take this end. We'll flush him out."

Emily looks at me and then nods.

I speed up my approach a little, and when Hoover sees me, he freezes for a moment, tensed and ready. "Hoover, come on," I say, speeding up some more. That's enough to make him spring into action. He spins away from me and heads around the opposite end of the island.

"Here he comes!" I yell to Emily.

Matthew squeals with delight and claps his hands, jumping up and down.

Emily throws the blanket at the dog, wrapping one arm around his shoulders, and wrestling him to the ground. Hoover struggles to get upright, and I can see Emily is in danger of losing her grip, so I hurry over to help. I fling one leg over the dog, straddling him, and issue a stern command. "Hoover, sit!"

Amazingly, he does, the blanket still draped over his body. Emily gets herself into a more stable position and repositions her grip on him. Between her and me, we have him held for the moment, her sitting on the floor beside him with her arms wrapped around his neck, me bent over with my arms wrapped around his torso right behind his front legs.

We need to get his collar back on him, and I'm about to ask Matthew to get it, when I hear him shriek with delight. I catch movement out of the corner of one eye and look to see my son barreling toward me.

"Get Hoovah!" he yells, and then he leaps, flinging his entire body at me.

My first instinct is to try to stop him so he doesn't hurt himself or the dog, and I release my grip on Hoover and put an arm out to slow Matthew's flight. Matthew hits me with a full-body slam on my left side, making me yelp in pain when he hits my injured shoulder. The dog, sensing a distraction in his prison guards, heaves himself forward. Emily loses her grip on him, and Hoover knocks one of my legs to the side in his scramble to escape. Seventy-five pounds of dog muscle is hard to contain, and he's gone in a flash. I grab Matthew around his waist to keep him from falling to the floor, gritting my teeth against the pain in my arm, and then do a demented version of the Watusi as I try to keep myself upright. It's a valiant effort on my part, but my balance is too precarious. I go down, breaking my fall the best I can with my good hand, knocking Emily off her knees, and pulling Matthew along with me.

Emily and I end up in an ignominious heap on the floor, breathless and panting, with Matthew sprawled on top of us, laughing.

"Are you okay?" I ask Emily, rolling my head toward her.

She nods. "Are you?"

"I think so." I wiggle some appendages and squirm a little to make sure everything moves. My shoulder is throbbing, but aside from that, nothing hurts too much.

Matthew shifts his position so that he's straddling my waist. "Horsey!" he yells.

"No, no horsey," I say, picking him up and setting him on the floor beside me. Overhead I hear the gallop of Hoover's feet running down the hall toward my bedroom. I pray that he stays off the bed with his wet, soapy fur. I look over at Emily, eyebrows arched in question.

"Yeah," she says with a guilty smile. "It's a long story."

"Wrong story," Matthew says beside me. Then he leaps toward me again, landing in my lap. I wrap my arms around his wriggling body and hold him tight.

"Give me the short version," I say to Emily.

She rakes her top teeth over her lower lip and gives Matthew an exasperated look before she begins. "I was doing some homework in my room, and Matthew was in there with me, on the floor, coloring."

Upon hearing his name, Matthew stops squirming and rivets his attention on Emily.

"Hoover was in there with us, too," Emily goes on. "I had to go to the bathroom, so I told Matthew to keep coloring and went down the hall. I wasn't in there that long, I swear. And I had the door open the whole time. When I got back to the bedroom, I saw that Matthew had gotten up on my desk, grabbed my black Magic Marker, and was using it to draw spots on Hoover's fur."

"Spots for Hoovah!" Matthew says with a big smile.

"No, Matthew, we don't do spots on Hoover," I chastise.

"Spots for Maff-you!" he tries instead, uttering the words with great seriousness.

"No, we don't do spots on Matthew, either," I say, a bit more sternly.

"Uh-huh," Matthew argues, pouting a little. Then he lifts up his shirt. There, all around his navel, is a big black circle, drawn on his skin with Magic Marker.

"Matthew, no!" Emily says, clearly shocked. She shoots me a confused, somewhat fearful glance, then shifts back to Matthew with a scowl. "You are a naughty boy," she scolds. "How on earth could you have done all that so fast?"

"Maff-you fast!" he says, and he starts to scramble off my lap. Sensing the potential for more mayhem, I grab him, ignoring the pain in my arm, and start kissing him on his neck, his face, his head, and then his belly. He laughs, wriggles, squirms, and squeals, and before I know it, we are on the floor, rolling and wrestling, laughing and yelping. The play session lasts a few minutes before all of us run out of gas. The three of us stretch out on the floor—me on one side, Emily on the other, Matthew between us—and stare at the ceiling, our chests heaving a little less with each breath, contented smiles on our faces. Eventually I roll over onto my side toward Matthew, propping my head in one hand. I lift Matthew's shirt, looking at his black hole.

"Matthew, markers aren't to be used on people, or animals, or walls, or furniture," I say. "It makes Mommy mad and also sad when you do that, because it doesn't come off very easy, if at all. So no more markers for you, young man."

I half expect him to throw a tantrum, or pout, or argue the point, but he rolls over, instead, on his side and mimics my position, one arm propped beneath his head to hold it up. Our faces are inches apart, and he looks directly, and deeply, into my eyes. "Okay. I sorry," he says.

My heart melts, and I can't help but smile. "I love you, buddy," I tell him, and then I lean over and kiss his nose.

"I wuv you, Mammy," he says back to me.

"It's bedtime, okay?"

"No." This is said matter-of-factly, without any whining or pouting. "TV first." He gets up from the floor, scurries into the living room, and picks up the remote control. A few seconds later, he's flipping through channels.

As Emily and I get up from the floor, she says, "Mattie, I'm really sorry. I swear I wasn't in the bathroom that long."

"Don't worry about it," I tell her. "Believe me, I know how fast that little devil is. He unrolled an entire roll of toilet paper the other day in the time it took me to brush my teeth. And then, while I was cleaning up the mess of paper and putting on another roll, he proceeded to paint the bathroom sink with toothpaste."

"Are you sure it was Matthew who unrolled the toilet paper?" Emily asks. "I caught Rubbish in the bathroom the other day doing the same thing. That cat is fascinated with the toilet paper roll."

"No, it was Matthew. And don't tell Hurley about Rubbish doing it. He hates those cats enough already."

Emily mimes locking her lips and tossing the key away.

I smile at her, and then hug her. "I love you, kiddo," I say. "And your dad and I are so appreciative of what you do for us, particularly with watching Matthew. I hope you know that."

She is a bit stiff in my arms for a second, but then she hugs me back. "I do. I love you guys, too," she says, and I hear a faint hitch in her voice.

We have come such a long way with this child, now almost a woman, and I feel my heart swell over it. Before the hug can get too awkward, I release her, and she turns away quickly, swiping at her face, not wanting me to see her tears.

"Hey, I'll make a deal with you," I say. "If you'll get Matthew into his jammies and into bed, I'll start cleaning up the mess in the bathroom. Let me know when he's tucked in and I'll come and kiss him good night."

"Deal," she says, and then she fetches Matthew

from the living room, turns off the TV, and leads him upstairs.

I stand in the kitchen for a moment, surveying the wet splotches and smears on the floor, the dining chairs and island stools knocked askew, the area rugs scrunched up and wrinkled, and the trampled remnants of the blanket tent. It can all wait until morning, I decide, and I make my weary way upstairs.

An hour later, my son is tucked into bed and already asleep—the evening's events exhausted him, as well as me—and the bathroom is reasonably clean, straightened, and dry. There is no sign of Hoover when I go in my bedroom, and, fortunately, the bedcovers are dry and intact. I undress and slip into one of Hurley's T-shirts and then slide between the sheets, stretching out luxuriously beneath the blankets. Despite my exhaustion, I toss and turn, my mind busily replaying scenes from the day, and worrying about Lily Paulsen. I always sleep better when Hurley is beside me, and I wish he were here now.

After an hour of restless tossing, I decide to turn on the TV and make another stab at watching a British murder-mystery series on Netflix, which I've been trying to watch for two months now. But I only watch it in bed so there is no risk of Matthew seeing it, and I always fall asleep in the middle of an episode. Tonight I'm actually hoping that will happen.

It doesn't work. But it does distract me from all the other thoughts and images that keep racing through my mind, so I let Netflix count down for another episode, and then another, and then one more, binge watching the show. Finally Netflix stops the automatic loads and checks to see if I want to continue.

How sweet—at least someone is checking up on me tonight. I tell Netflix I'm still among the awake and living, but when the next episode starts, I pause it. I'm hungry, and I remember the treats Dom sent home with me. I get out of bed, grab my robe for warmth, and go downstairs to the kitchen. The containers aren't on the counter where I left them, and in my sleep-deprived state of mind, I take a moment to play back my arrival. Had I put them somewhere else? No, I distinctly remember putting them here on the counter.

Maybe Emily found them and moved them. I search the cupboard, the refrigerator, even a drawer or two, though I can't imagine anyone with half a brain putting the containers in them, but to no avail. I stand there, tapping my foot in irritation, trying to puzzle it out. Outside the house, the high-pitched keen of the wind rattles the walls, making me shudder, even though I don't feel cold. I wonder if I only imagined bringing the containers in, visualizing it in my mind, but leaving them in the car. The idea of walking barefoot into the unheated garage makes me shudder a second time, but deter-mination, curiosity, and the lure of a pecan tassie—or four—wins out.

Looking in the car proves to be a huge mistake. As soon as I open the door, I catch a whiff of the lingering smells inside: blood, amniotic fluid, and something else I don't want to identify. The containers aren't there and I slam the door hard in ir-ritation and hurry back inside.

Resigned to not having anything, I start to head upstairs. As I pass the living room, I hear a sound like someone whimpering. I look toward the noise and see Hoover, curled up in a ball in the corner. He is sound asleep, the black ink spots on his fur dark and irregular, his legs twitching, an occasional whimper emanating from him as he dreams.

I have no idea what he's dreaming of, but I have a good idea what's fueling it. Beside him on the floor are the chewed-up remnants of the dessert containers. He hasn't left so much as a crumb.

"Well played, Hoover," I say, eyeing the sad remains. "You got your revenge. Except I'm not the one who turned you into a Dalmatian, or gave you the bath."

I want to cry, but I'm too tired. Instead, I trudge upstairs and crawl back into bed, letting Netflix woo me once more.

Chapter 27

When I awaken the next morning, the bedroom is brightly lit with sunshine coming through the window. I glance at the clock on my bedside stand and see that it's already after eight. A quick look to the other side tells me that Hurley didn't make it home during the night, and the TV is glowing Netflix's worried message, wondering if I want to continue.

It's my day off, and the thought of luxuriating in bed tempts me. But when you're the parent of a toddler, those luxuries come at too high a price. I fling off the covers, grab my robe, and put on some socks and slippers. After disconnecting my phone from the charger, I check it and see there are two text messages, one from Hurley and one from Hildy Schneider. Hurley's message, sent at a little after three in the morning, says simply: **Sweet dreams, luv you**.

Hildy's message is much longer, providing me

with the name and phone number of a person
who runs a grief support group in Necedah, except that while the group is advertised by doctors
and others in Necedah—a small village with a pop-
ulation of less than a thousand people—the actual
sessions are held in Mauston, a town some fifteen
miles away. At the end of the message she adds,
**There is supposed to be a meeting tonight at seven,
assuming the weather cooperates**. Below that is the
address where the meeting is being held.

My bladder demands where my first stop will be,
but once I'm done with that, I head down the hall
toward my son's room. His bed is empty, and I experience a brief moment of panic, until I see that
the door to Emily's room is open and her bed is
empty as well. I move toward the stairs and hear
their voices from below.

For a moment, I seriously consider going back
to bed, but even though it's my day off, there are
things I need and want to do. Best to get a somewhat early start.

When I reach the main hallway downstairs, I
peek out the window in the top of the front door.
Outside is a winter wonderland of glittering whiteness: The ground is humped and drifted with
peaks here and there, like the frosting on a cake;
the branches of the trees are dusted in flour; sugar
crystals are everywhere, sparkling in the sunlight.
It reminds me of the desserts I never got to eat,
and my stomach rumbles with hunger.

Out in the kitchen, I find Emily and Matthew
seated at the table. It is located in a nook that has
windows on three sides, and the light is so bright
around them it's almost blinding. The sky outside

is cloudless and a vivid blue that makes me think of Hurley's eyes. Amazing that so much beauty can come out of all that meteorological fury.

"Hi, Mammy," Matthew says. "We gonna make snowman!"

"Are you?" I say, heading for the coffeepot and pouring myself a cup.

"I promised him I'd take him outside to see if we can build one," Emily says. "It's the first decent snowfall we've had this winter and I think the snow is heavy and wet, so it should pack well."

"Sounds like fun," I say with a smile, sliding into a chair next to Matthew.

"Fun!" he says, thrusting his spoon-wielding hand into the air. A stray clump of oatmeal flies off the utensil and lands in my hair.

"By the way," Emily says, her expression suddenly serious, "I think Hoover got into some more mischief last night."

"I know," I say with a mournful sigh, scraping the oatmeal out of my hair. "I came down last night, looking for a snack, and found him in a food coma in the living room, the chewed containers on the floor beside him."

"What was in them?"

"Pecan tassies in one, and apple pie in the other. Dom made them."

"Oh, I love his pecan tassies," Emily says with a little moan. "Darned dog."

"Me too." I look around for the food thief. "Speaking of 'darned dog,' where is he this morning?"

"In the laundry room at the moment. I shut the door because he was farting up a storm. When I let him out this morning, he pooped like three times."

I smile, but it morphs into a frown. "I hope none of the ingredients in what he ate will hurt him," I say. "I should probably call the vet and check on it."

"So Dom made cookies *and* pie," Emily muses. "That's a lot of baking. Is he upset about something?"

I smile. Emily is a keen observer and a sly eavesdropper. She doesn't miss much. "He is," I say. "Something to do with his theater group. It will probably be in the paper next week."

Knowing I'm not going to share any more details, Emily lets the matter drop.

"I'm going to try to go into the office for a while this afternoon," I say. "It's my day off, but there's some stuff going on with a case I'm working, and I really want to be there for it. Assuming I can get in. Are you okay with watching Matthew? For the usual pay, of course."

"Absolutely," she says. "We're going to make a snowman, and later we're going to have hot chocolate. Right, Matthew?"

"Hot chock-it!" he cheers, once again raising his spoon. This time I manage to deflect the dietary debris.

From outside, I hear a scraping sound and the rumble of an engine. I get up and walk into the living room, carrying my coffee cup with me. I look out the window just in time to see Hurley coming around the last curve of the driveway in his truck, the plow hooked onto the front. Belatedly I see tire tracks leading to the shed and realize he's likely been out there for a while already in order to come up the drive, hook up the plow, and then clear the driveway. I see now that this is his second pass on the driveway, and when he's cleared the last bit, he turns and heads back to the shed.

A moment later, he comes walking along the sidewalk out front, pushing a shovel in front of him. I rap on the window and he looks up and smiles. After smiling back, I hoist my coffee cup in the air and point to it with a questioning look on my face. He nods eagerly.

I go back to the kitchen and prepare him a cup of coffee in an insulated to-go cup, and then I go to the hall closet and don boots and a winter coat. When I finally venture outside onto the front porch, he is in the process of clearing snow from the stairs.

"Did you sleep at all last night?" I ask him, handing him the mug.

He takes a sip before answering me, letting the hot liquid roll around in his mouth before he swallows. He closes his eyes to relish the taste and warmth for a few seconds.

"No," he says after he finally swallows. "But I'm fine. And this helps," he adds, proffering the mug. "As does the sight of you." He bends down and kisses me on the mouth. His nose is frigid against my cheek, but his lips are warm and coffee flavored.

"I missed you last night," I tell him once we part.

"Believe me, after being up all night with Richmond, I missed you, too."

"Did you guys come up with anything on the Paulsen case?"

He shakes his head and makes a face. "No sign of O'Keefe. He's gone to ground, and with this storm we had, who knows where that might be?"

"Are we still on for this afternoon with the meeting of Arnie's online perp?"

Hurley smiles at me over his mug. "I love it when you try to talk cop."

"Yeah, whatever. Are we?"

"Someone is a little grumpy this morning," he teases.

"You would be, too, if you had the night I had. Don't be surprised when you see Hoover. He's apparently changed breeds overnight."

Hurley gives me a quizzical smile as he swallows another swig of coffee. "Care to explain?"

"Later. Are we on for this afternoon or not?"

"Richmond, a couple of FBI agents, and I are," he says, narrowing his eyes at me. "That's the only *we* involved."

"Aw, come on, Hurley," I whine. "I want in on this."

"Only cops," he says. "We're letting Arnie come along so he can listen in on the wire, but that's only in case the guy shows up and asks questions we can't answer. He was up most of the night exchanging e-mails with this guy to make sure the meeting would still take place. He'll be in a van parked a few blocks away from the pizza restaurant."

"Why can't I be in the van?"

"For one thing, I believe you're supposed to be off work today, no?"

"Technically, yeah, but this is my case, Hurley. The thought of that young girl still out there haunted me all night. I barely got a wink of sleep. I need to be involved. I need to do something."

"It's too dangerous," Hurley says, shaking his head and then taking another drink of coffee.

"You've let me participate in other stuff that was dangerous."

Hurley stares at me over the top of his mug, a frown creasing his brow, steam coming out of his nose as he exhales in the frigid morning air. "Let me think about it," he says.

I break into a big smile. I know that this tiny capitulation is just the first step in his conceding the battle. Before he can think about it, or talk about it anymore, I change the subject. "How are the roads this morning?"

"They're fine in town, but the outlying roads are spotty. The guys on the plows have been working hard all night, and we didn't get quite as much snow as they predicted. But the drifts are impressive. I actually ran a couple of miles on our road with the plow this morning to clear it."

I think about Izzy then, and his car that wouldn't start. "I should go and call Izzy to make sure he has a way into the office this morning. I'm guessing that if his car wouldn't start yesterday, it's not going to start today, either. He might have Dom's car to drive, but maybe I should check and see. He'll need to go into the office to do the autopsy on Roger Dalrymple."

"Why don't you let me call him," Hurley suggests. "If he needs a ride, I can pick him up in my truck. At least it has four-wheel drive."

"Thanks, but I'd rather take the hearse into town. I need to have it cleaned again, what with

Patty delivering her baby in the back of it last night and all."

Hurley sighs, creating a cloud of steam around his head. "I assume Emily is okay with watching Matthew all day?" he says.

"She is. They have plans to go outside and build a snowman, and then have hot chocolate in front of the TV later. Matthew is quite excited about it."

Hurley nods approvingly. He takes one more swig of coffee, draining the mug, and then hands it back to me. "Thank you. I needed that. I best get to it."

An hour later, Hurley has gone back to the police department, and I am showered, dressed, and on the road headed for my office. The roads aren't great, but they are leagues ahead of the condition they were in last night. I called Izzy before my shower to see how he was doing, and he was already in the office, having taken Dom's car.

By the time I arrive at the office, Izzy and Christopher are in the autopsy suite and are working on Roger Dalrymple. I make my first order of business a call to Not a Trace, informing them that I am once again in need of their services for my hearse. This time, I tell them I will leave the car unlocked in the garage and ask them to call me when they are done.

Next I call the number Hildy Schneider gave me for the grief support group in Necedah. The contact is a woman named Michaela Watkins, but when I get her voice mail I decide not to leave a message, and to try again later. With that done, I head up to Arnie's lab area to see if he is there. He is not, so I go back down and enter the autopsy suite to see how things are coming along there and to ask if anyone needs any help.

"What are you doing here?" Izzy and Christopher both ask at the same time.

"I figured I'd take advantage of Emily's snow day and come in to get some paperwork caught up while she watches Matthew. Need help with anything?"

"We're okay for now," Izzy says. He looks at me over Dalrymple's body, narrowing his eyes. "Why are you really in here?" he asks after a moment.

"I told you. Paperwork." He gives me a look that says he isn't buying a bit of it. "Okay, I'm also here because we're organizing a sting of sorts this afternoon that we hope will catch one of the guys involved in a human-trafficking ring."

"We, who?" Christopher asks, intrigued.

"Well, Richmond and Hurley, of course, but there are also some FBI guys in on it. In fact, they have a female FBI agent with a small build who wears her hair super short, and she's going to play the role of an eleven-year-old boy. Arnie arranged the whole thing by exchanging messages and chats with a bunch of people online. He gets to go, too, assuming he shows up. He wasn't in his office."

"He's home taking a nap," Izzy says. "He told me he was up all night helping the cops with something and needed to go out with them today, though he didn't give me the specifics. He should be in around eleven."

"It all sounds very exciting," Christopher says, punctuating the comment with a whistling sound that emanates from his backside. "What are you going to be doing?"

"Just observing from a van somewhere," I say. "That's where Arnie will be, too. Hurley didn't want me to go along, but I basically nagged him into it."

"Nagging is definitely one of her strong suits," Izzy says to Christopher, eyebrows arched in warning.

"Find anything on Dalrymple yet?" I ask, ignoring Izzy's dig.

Izzy answers with an equivocal nod. "So far, we have the expected fractures in the legs, some compression fractures in the spine, a radial fracture in the left arm, and the big fracture in the neck at C2. But there's very little bleeding around any of them. Not sure why, but once we open his head, we might have a better idea."

"Okay, then," I say. "Holler if you need me. I'll be in the library."

For the next two hours, I focus on my backlog of paperwork, making good progress. I check my phone every ten minutes or so, waiting for the final word from Hurley that I'm good to go with them to the sting this afternoon. If he doesn't cave on the matter, it will be the first time I've gotten him to capitulate partway without eventually getting the Full Monty.

When noon rolls around, and I still haven't heard from him, I decide to give him a call. Just as I pick up my phone, Christopher comes into the library.

"Hey," I say. "What did you guys find?"

"Interesting case," he says. "Dalrymple had a

major head bleed. Looked like it might have been an aneurysm, but he also had head trauma in the same area, so Izzy said he wasn't sure. He wants to wait until the tox screen comes back, and take some time to look at some tissue slides."

"So no definitive cause of death yet?"

Christopher shakes his head. "We do, however, have a lead on a suspect if it turns out to be murder. That smear of makeup you swabbed up on the catwalk? It had some sort of biological material in it."

"'Biological material'?" I repeat the term, askance. I ponder the information for a moment. "What kind of *biological material*?"

Christopher shrugs, and with it comes another of his leaking emissions, and this one a squeaker. "We're waiting on Arnie," he says. "He's looking at it now."

I get up from my desk, gather my belongings, and head for the door. "I'm going to meet someone for lunch," I lie. "You can have the room to yourself."

"Okay, see ya."

Once I'm out in the hallway, I call Hurley. He doesn't answer and I don't leave a voice mail. Instead, I head upstairs to Arnie's lab. I find him with his face bent over a microscope.

"Hey, Mattie," he says, "What's up?"

"That's what I planned to ask you. Christopher said you found some biological trace in the makeup smear from the catwalk in the theater case?"

"It's botanical," he corrects. "That's what I'm looking at now. Want to see?" He straightens up and waves me over.

I put my eyes to the lens and peer through. It takes a second for my vision to adjust, but when it does, I see a small bit of brown something with lines in it. "What am I looking at?"

"A tiny piece of dried leaf."

I raise up and look at him, waiting.

"I'm not sure what it is," he admits. "I've got Laura coming over to look at it."

Two-timing Laura has equivocated on careers in the past, the same way she's been equivocating on the men in her life. She has an MBA, and she's a whiz at forensic accounting. One of the other areas she specialized in was forensic botany.

Arnie glances at his watch. "I have to go. Is there anything else you want?"

"No. Where are you going?"

"I need to run over to the police station," he says, getting up and grabbing his parka from a hook on the wall.

"Oh, for the sting, right?" This is a guess on my part. "I'm going, too."

Arnie's brow furrows. "You're involved in the sting?"

"Not involved, at least not directly. But Hurley said I could come along and be inside the van with you to watch." This isn't quite the whole truth . . . okay, it isn't even quite part of the truth. But I figure if I'm there when they're ready to head out, it will be harder for Hurley to tell me no. "Let me run downstairs and grab my coat and I'll meet you out front."

Arnie shrugs, and I make a mad dash downstairs to grab my coat and hat from the locker room. I don't even stop to put anything on, hurrying up front to the reception area, and trying to get my arms in the sleeves of my coat as I go. Cass is at the front desk, and she looks at me with a puzzled expression.

"Why are you here today?" she says.

I see Arnie standing outside by the front door, dancing in place to keep himself warm.

"I'm not," I tell her with a smile. "I'm outta here." I meet Arnie and tug my coat closed in front, not bothering to button it. I shove my hat into a pocket—my gloves are in the other pocket—and say, "Shall we?"

I thought the walk to the police station would be short enough that I wouldn't have to worry about dressing up fully, but it turns out I'm wrong. I grossly underestimated how cold it is outside. And it's slow going because while the sidewalks have been cleared to some degree, not all of them have, and there is an icy layer of skim at the base.

By the time we reach the station, I feel like a Popsicle and my fingers are numb. We go in through the front, and the dispatcher buzzes us on back without question. When we reach the office shared by Hurley and Richmond, we find both of them inside, along with three other people I've never seen before. One of them is obviously the agent who is going to play our eleven-year-old boy, and if I had any doubts about a grown woman's ability to pull off such a charade, they are now instantly erased. Her limbs and overall stature are small, her hips are narrow, and her facial features are androgynously ambiguous. As had been reported, her blond hair is cut close, cropped like a boy's would be. At the moment, she is dressed in boy's clothing: blue jeans, boots, and a T-shirt with a gaming logo on it. Despite her small stature, I can tell she is strong and muscular. The short sleeves of her shirt reveal sinewy muscle in her arms, and her neck has a definite masculine look to its musculature.

The other two people in the room are both men, and it's not hard to tell where they're from, since they're both wearing FBI T-shirts, unnecessary in my opinion since they both scream federal agent with their military-style haircuts, rigid posture, khaki cargo pants, and broad shoulders—not to mention the guns they're both sporting.

Everyone in the room looks at Arnie and me as we walk in. All expressions are curious and friendly, except Hurley's. He scowls at me and I flash him a smile, trying to look as if nothing is wrong. My heart is racing—a trip-hammer thud in my chest—as I wait to see if he's going to call me out in front of the others.

Richmond, apparently unbothered by my presence, does the introductions. "Mattie, Arnie, welcome. These are Agents Corey Black, Mike Anderson, and Jen Nolan. Agents, this is Mattie Winston and Arnie Toffer with the ME's office. Arnie is the one who snagged this online meeting, and Mattie happens to be the wife of Detective Hurley."

There are murmurs of greetings and a lot of head nods, while Hurley continues to frown at me.

I decide to ignore him and compliment Jen Nolan on her impersonation of an eleven-year-old boy.

"You are very convincing," I say. "Is this kind of impersonation something you do often?"

"As a matter of fact, yes," she says, and she even sounds like a boy.

"Don't let her size fool you," Agent Black says. "She is wicked strong. She's taken me down before." This is impressive, considering that Agent Black is six feet tall and looks to weigh somewhere in the two-hundred-pound range. "Now that we're all here, let's review the plan."

Over the next hour, the seven of us discuss and plan out in minute detail how the operation will go down. Jen is fitted with a tiny microphone that looks like an emblem on her red knitted cap—the color hat Arnie told the online persona he would be wearing—and an earbud that is all but invisible so that the agents can talk to her. She is also wearing a wristwatch that is supposed to double as a camera.

"She can aim the face of the watch at something she wants us to see," Agent Black explains. "By using normal body movements—scratching her cheek, adjusting her hat, folding her arms over her chest—she can capture just about anything or anyone without being too obvious. Everything she sends us is captured digitally and saved. That way, we can look over the people in the restaurant and the surrounding area at leisure, both during the operation and after the fact."

Agent Black, clearly the one in charge in this group, gives us a demonstration of the watch's capabilities, using a small laptop computer. Agent Nolan moves her arms about in seemingly normal ways, catching everyone in the room on camera within a matter of seconds.

"We have some known entities in this trafficking business whose faces we might recognize. And then there's this O'Keefe fellow to watch for, too," he adds with a nod of approval toward Richmond.

"Arnie," Agent Black goes on, once the watch demo is finished, "you will be in the van with us wearing a headset like this one." He hands the headset, which has a mike attached, to Arnie. He then hands out similar headsets to Richmond, Hurley, and me.

"Put them on," Black instructs, and we all do so. "You should be able to hear anything Jen says or hears, and you'll all be able to speak to her directly through her earbud, if need be. Let's give it a test. Agent Nolan, why don't you go outside to the front of the police station."

Agent Nolan dons a coat and departs, and while we're waiting, Agent Black puts on a headset and says, "You'll be able to hear everyone who has a headset, and since there will be several of us with them, be mindful of unnecessary chatter. We'd prefer no chatter at all, except from Arnie if we need some facts filled in. We've reviewed your e-mail and online exchanges with this guy quite thoroughly, but it's always possible that some question will arise that Jen can't recall the answer to. If that happens, she'll clear her throat like this."

On cue, Agent Nolan clears her throat. I hear it as if she were standing right next to me. These FBI guys have some fun toys. Even Hurley has forgotten his irritation with me—for the moment—as he admires the gadgets and their capabilities.

"Arnie, say something to Agent Nolan," Black instructs.

Arnie, looking like he's died and gone to heaven, says, "Are you single by any chance?"

The two male agents snort back laughs; Richmond and Hurley grin and shake their heads. I manage to stay quiet, but so does Agent Nolan. After an awkward few seconds of silence, Agent Nolan finally answers.

"I am," she says good-naturedly, "but I bat for the other team. Thanks, though. I'm flattered."

Arnie blushes so hard that the top of his bald head turns flaming red. Agent Anderson, who, up until now has stayed quiet, smiles at Arnie. "Better that you have tried and failed," he says.

Agent Black looks at his watch and has us remove our headsets. "Let's get on-site and set up," he says. "I assume you guys will follow us?"

Richmond and Hurley both nod. "I'm going to take my own vehicle," Hurley says. "Arnie, you can ride with Richmond."

The assumption here is that I will be riding with Hurley, or at least that's the assumption I guess all the others have made. I, on the other hand, fear Hurley has yet to play his final card. Will he say something to me? I wonder. Or will he simply try to ditch me?

As soon as Jen returns, the group of us don our winter wear and head for the parking lot behind the police station. Hurley says nothing to me, but he doesn't look at me, either. I follow him to his truck and half expect him not to unlock the passenger-side door as I'm standing next to it, waiting. But he does, and I get inside, bracing myself for the storm I suspect is coming. Last night's winter maelstrom is likely to pale in comparison.

"What the hell, Mattie?" Hurley says the second I shut my door. He starts the car and waits for the Fibbies to get into their van, which has no windows, save for the front compartment, and is boasting the logo of a cleaning service on both of its sides. "You have no business coming along on this."

"Yes, I do," I argue. "It's my case, and I have as much of an interest in finding Lily Paulsen as any of you do."

"But I told you not to come," Hurley says, his jaw tight.

"No, what you said was that you'd think about it."

"And did I give you any reason to think I'd changed my mind?" he asks, his tone escalating. "Did I, at any point in time, say it was okay?"

"Not in so many words, but you never said I couldn't, either."

"The hell I didn't," he snaps.

"Not after you said you'd think about it. And I—"

Hurley holds a hand out toward me, his face contorted with anger. "Don't," he says through gritted teeth, pulling in behind Richmond's car in our mini convoy. "I don't want to hear it, and I don't want to discuss it anymore. I'm seriously pissed right now and badly sleep deprived, and I'm afraid of saying something I don't mean, or can't take back. You're here. Enough said."

I sink back into my seat, frowning. The drive to our location will take a little over half an hour. At the moment, the temperature inside the car is much more frigid than outside, and I pull my coat closed at my throat, more a move of withdrawal than one intended for warmth. Several times during the ride, I think of things to say, everything from conciliatory apologies to defenses of my position. But I voice none of them. Hurley and I have had disagreements and arguments before, and we've been angry at one another before. But this is the maddest at me I've ever seen him, and it frightens me a little.

In the end, I opt for channeling Scarlett O'Hara yet again and deciding that tomorrow is another day. We'll sort it all out then. For now, I have a sting to focus on.

Chapter 28

Arnie's arranged appointment at the pizza restaurant was for three-thirty, and by two forty-five, everything is set up and in place. The FBI van is parked in the lot of a convenience store in the block behind the restaurant, and both Hurley and Richmond have parked their respective vehicles on a nearby side street in a residential neighborhood. The school Arnie claimed he attends is four blocks away, though that's now a moot point since it was closed for the day due to the weather. Fortunately, Arnie also claimed that he lives in the neighborhood near the restaurant, though he was able to avoid providing a specific address, saying that his mom told him never to do that online.

The video and audio equipment has been tested and retested, and Jen is sitting in the front passenger seat of the van, restless and fidgety. The rest of us are crowded into the back of the van, each of us wearing a headset. There are two of the small laptops, one on either side of the cargo area, the first one manned by Agent Black, the second one by Agent Anderson.

Just before three, Agent Black tells Jen to go. "Our guy might well show up early to scope things out and watch the kid come in, so we best be earlier still."

Jen hops out and assumes the hands-in-pocket, hunched-down swagger of an eleven-year-old boy. She walks a block over so that she is on a street of houses, and then turns toward the pizza restaurant.

When she reaches the parking lot, she glances at her watch, giving us a fleeting view of her red-nosed face, and then she meanders some, doing sliding skids on some icy patches, and scraping up snowballs here and there that she lobs at empty parking spaces. This is so she can get a video feed of all the cars and their plates currently in the restaurant lot. At three-fifteen, she heads inside the restaurant, stopping for a moment near a podium with a cash register. The light inside the building is much darker than the outside, and it takes a moment for the camera to adjust. When we are able to make out the interior, we see a dining area set up with booths around the perimeter, and tables and chairs through the middle. There is a counter area at the front for waitstaff orders, and the kitchen with the pizza ovens in full view is behind it. There is a separate area to the right of the podium for orders called in for pickup. Between the front counter and the dining area is a long salad bar.

The place isn't crowded, not surprising given

the hour and the weather, and Jen heads for a booth near the windows bordering the parking lot. She sits facing the door, the watch on her left arm aimed toward the seating area.

A waitress approaches almost immediately. "Can I help you?" she says, her tone rife with skepticism. Jen lifts her arm, showing us the waitress's face. The girl looks barely old enough to have a work permit, and she's frowning at Jen.

"I'm waiting for someone," Jen says. "Is it okay if I sit here, or do I have to wait by the door?" I'm impressed by Jen's boyishly appealing tone, a mix of politeness and nerves. The waitress is apparently impressed, too, because her expression softens immediately.

"Normally, we'd ask you to wait in the foyer area," she says. "But we're not that busy, so you can stay here for now."

"Can I get a Coke?"

The waitress seems to weigh this request, and I guess she's wondering if the kid has the money to pay for it, should his other party not show up. "Sure," she says finally. "Be right back."

In the two minutes it takes for the waitress to return with the drink, Jen manipulates her arm to provide us with a better view of the other diners. We see that there is a woman seated across the dining area in a booth by the opposite window, but the light coming in through the glass casts her face in shadow. There are also two young men, who look to be college age, seated at a table, and a middle-aged couple in a booth two tables behind Jen. She is aiming her watch in the direction of the front of the restaurant when the waitress returns and disaster strikes.

The waitress goes to set the drink on the table and somehow manages to spill the entire thing. The brown liquid flows over the face of the watch, momentarily obscuring our view. And then the video feed goes dark.

"What the hell?" Agent Black mutters.

We hear the waitress start to offer a profuse apology, and then hear Jen say, "Geez, lady, you spilled it all over my new watch. My mom got that for me for Christmas. She had to work extra shifts just to pay for it." There is a whine in Jen's voice that borders on crying, and the waitress continues to offer her apologies. We can still hear even if we can't see anything, and in a moment, it becomes clear that the waitress has retrieved a towel or rag of some sort and is attempting to clean up the mess.

"We lost video," Agent Black says. "If you understand, clear your throat."

Jen dutifully clears her throat a second or two later.

Agent Black lets out a frustrated sigh. "Damn," he says, half under his breath. He looks at his watch, then over at Agent Anderson. "One of us should go in there to get eyes on the scene. We can use a cell phone."

Anderson nods and removes his headset, the apparent presumption that he will be the one to go in.

"Hold on," I say. "You guys can't go in there. Anyone with half a brain will spot you as cops from a mile away." Agent Black starts to object, and I add, "Let me do it. I can walk over there the same way Jen did. At least I don't look like a stakeout cop."

Agent Black purses his lips and looks over at Anderson, eyebrows raised.

"No way," Hurley says. "It's too dangerous."

"No, it's not," I say. "I'll go in there with the cell phone video running and pretend I'm talking to someone. I'll order a pizza to go and during the time it takes for them to make it, I'll walk around a little and keep on talking."

"It could work," Black says.

"I'll do it," Hurley says, his face a thundercloud of emotion.

Black looks at him, then at Richmond. "Sorry, guys, but the lady has a point. You two look like cops, just as much as we do. If this guy is going to show, he'll be a lot less suspicious of someone like your wife here than he will of any of us."

I take my headset off and look at Black, ignoring Hurley's scowling visage. "Should I use my own phone, or do you want to give me one to use?"

Decided on the matter, Black says, "Give me your phone." I do so, and he plays with the settings for a minute, then says, "Yours will be fine. You've got video capabilities and a good battery charge."

"Do you have another one of those ear things, so I can hear you guys?" I ask.

"Don't need one," Black says. "We'll be on the other end of the phone. You'll have to make up a conversation of some sort and not respond directly to anything we say. Do you think you can do that?"

"Easy-peasy," I say with a smile. "I just need one more thing."

Black raises his eyebrows, waiting.

"I don't have my wallet with me. I need a credit card or some cash to pay for the pizza."

"Right," Black says. "Good thinking." He fishes in his pocket, pulls out a wallet, and after rummaging in it, he hands me a twenty and a ten. "That should cover it," he says.

"Thanks." I stuff the money in my pocket.

"I don't like this," Hurley says. "What if this guy is armed?"

"Jen has an ankle holster," Black says. "And if she sees someone who looks like a likely candidate, she can direct Mattie with a nod so she can aim her phone that way. Jen, are you getting all this?"

Jen clears her throat again. "Got it," she says in a low voice. "Someone coming in now." Apparently, the waitress has left Jen's table for the moment.

Black, with a renewed sense of urgency in his voice, says, "Mattie, what's your phone number?" I give it to him, and he saves it in his own cell phone. "Okay," he says. "I'll give you one minute to get to the parking lot, and then I'll call you. You know what to do?"

I nod, put my phone in my pocket, and zip up my coat.

"Okay, if you feel uncomfortable at any point, just leave, all right?"

I nod again. Then I head up to the front of the van, open the passenger door, and get out.

* * *

I pace my stride the best I can so that I reach the restaurant parking lot in the minute Black mentioned. Hurley's glowering face keeps popping into my mind, and I do my best to shut it out and focus on the task at hand. When I reach the parking lot, no call has come and I fear I've walked too fast. I see Jen sitting inside the restaurant and she looks out the window at me, and then quickly dismisses me. Just as I reach the door, my ring tone goes off. I take the phone out, hit the video record button on my camera, and make sure it's working; then I answer the call with a cheery "Hello?" as I open the restaurant door.

I stand by the podium for a moment, phone to my ear, turned so that the camera lens is pointed toward the dining area. I hear Black's voice on the other end say, "Good, is the camera running?"

"Yes, how are you?" I say into the phone, careful to hold it in a way so that my hand isn't covering the lens.

"Okay, try to move around so you can pan the interior, but don't be too obvious about it," Black says.

"That's good. How's William doing?" I say, pretending that it's my mother I'm talking to. A waitress, the same one who spilled the drink on Jen, is approaching me, so I say, "Hold on a sec, can you?" I drop the phone from my ear, and hold it near my injured shoulder, the lens pointed toward the dining area. When I walked in, I saw a man seated at a table alone, someone who wasn't there earlier. I assume this is the new arrival Jen mentioned, and try to aim my phone in his direction.

"I'd like to order a pizza to go," I tell the waitress. "A large with pepperoni and sausage."

The waitress scribbles the order on a ticket, and carries it over to the counter that fronts the kitchen. I take advantage of the moment to return to my call.

"Still there, Mom?" I say into the phone.

"I'm here," Black says.

"Good. Sorry about the interruption. You caught me just as I was entering a restaurant to order a pizza for dinner. Hold on again, I have to pay for it."

Once again, I lower the phone as I fish in my pocket for the cash Black gave me. I hand the girl the twenty—the total is just under seventeen bucks—tell her to keep the change, and then go back to my phone.

"Sorry, Mom. I'm back."

"It will be about fifteen minutes," the waitress says, and I nod.

Black doesn't respond to me this time, so I make up a conversation in my head. What would my mother ask me? I realize the most likely scenario would be a listing of her current symptoms for whatever imagined ailment she thought she had.

"I don't know," I say into the phone. "What are your symptoms?"

As I pretend to listen, I walk around the salad bar, checking out the contents, moving the phone slightly whenever I get close to someone. The woman in the far booth has a bad cold. I hear her sniffling and coughing, and when I get close to her, I get a strong whiff of eucalyptus, probably from some kind of rub.

"That could be any number of things," I say into the phone. "When did it start?"

Reaching the other side of the salad bar, I stop when I'm near the table with the newest arrival. He's a man who looks to be in his thirties, dressed in a sweatshirt with the Packers logo on the front of it, snow boots, and a knit cap. His hooded parka is hanging on the back of his chair, and he's reading a copy of the local paper. I turn slightly to look out the window, acting as if I'm listening to my mother's litany of complaints. From this position, I should get a good shot of the man.

"Have you made an appointment to see your doctor?" I say into the phone. And after a few seconds, I say, "Why not?" in an exasperated tone. Behind me, I hear the door to the restaurant open and turn to see who has come in. Then I realize it's someone leaving: the middle-aged couple who had been seated behind Jen.

"Mom, you can't keep ignoring this stuff," I say into the phone. I see Jen turn to look out the window, and wonder if she is saying anything for the guys to hear. Then I see a car pull into the lot. I walk quickly to the other end of the salad bar and switch the phone to my other hand so that the camera is aimed out the windows toward the parking lot. I don't watch to see who gets out of the car, but a moment later, when the front door opens, I see a woman with two preschool-age kids come in.

"I don't want to discuss this anymore," I say into the phone. "If you're not going to take care of yourself, then I don't want to hear your complaints."

I turn and aim my phone toward the twenty-something guys at a table. They look harmless, and their heads are bent close together, laughing at something that one of them has on his phone.

For the next ten minutes, I continue to wander around the front area of the restaurant, discussing the antics of Matthew, the storm, and then, running out of topics, Hurley's upcoming birthday. I have no idea if Black has his cell phone on speaker, so I'm careful not to get into too much detail, but I do bemoan the fact that I can't come up with a good gift idea for Hurley.

Finally my pizza is ready, and when the waitress hails me up to the register to get it, I'm not sure what to do. No one else has come into the restaurant. I look at my watch, see that it's nearly four o'clock, and say into the phone, "My pizza is ready, Mom. I really need to go."

"Anyone new in the place?" Black asks.

"No, Mom."

"Okay, come on back."

"Bye, Mom. Talk to you soon." I disconnect the call, but keep the phone out, holding it in my hand. I go up and get my pizza from the waitress, and carry it over to a bench near the take-out area. I set the pizza down on the bench and sit beside it, then I type out a text message to Hurley. I'm stalling for a little more time, hoping our man will show, but after several minutes with no new customers, I stop the recording, gather up the pizza, and leave.

I half expect a car to pull into the lot as I'm walking across it, but it doesn't happen. By the time I reach the van, I'm bummed.

"Let me see what you got," Black says, holding out his hand once I'm inside.

At first, I think he means the pizza and I go to hand him the box.

"No, the phone," he says.

"Oh, right," I say with a self-deprecating smile. I set the pizza down on the passenger-side seat, and take the phone out of my pocket, handing it to Black.

"I'll take a slice of that pizza," Anderson says.

I get the box, open it, and hand it around to the others. Arnie, Richmond, and Anderson all take a slice, but Hurley just glares at me and shakes his head when I offer the box to him. I shrug it off, carry the box back to the front seat, and take a slice for myself.

"You did really good," Black says, watching my video. "Unfortunately, it looks like our guy is a no-show." He watches for a few seconds more and then says into his headset, "Anything, Nolan?"

I don't hear the answer, but I can tell what it is by the crestfallen look on Black's face. He looks at his watch. "Okay, let's call it," he says. "Either the guy never intended to show, or something scared him off. Let's hope this was just a test run on his part, to see if you'd be willing to meet him."

Black removes his headset, and the others do the same. Then Black plugs my phone into his laptop and transfers my video. "I'll take a piece of that pizza now," he says, once the data is transferring. I get the box for him and he takes a piece. By the time I return the box to the front seat, Jen has returned to the van.

"Sorry, guys," she says to Richmond, Hurley, and Arnie.

"Hey, it was worth a try," Richmond says.

"We'll have our guys keep looking for your girl," Black says around a mouthful of pizza. "If anything comes up, we'll let you know. And if your online guy offers another meeting, we'd be happy to help out again."

"How should I respond to him?" Arnie asks.

"Just go into your young-boy mode and either e-mail or message him and ask, 'What's up?' Try not to come across too mad, because you want him to think you really want this meeting, those games."

Arnie nods, and then helps himself to another slice of pizza.

Ten minutes later, Hurley and I are back in his truck headed for home. I'm bummed, disappointed that our little sting didn't work, and depressed that we've accomplished nothing toward finding Lily Paulsen.

Hurley, stone-faced and silent, hasn't said a word to me. I can tell he's still angry, and thinking that shoptalk, rather than personal talk, might ease the situation, I say, "What do you think went wrong?"

"Sending you in there was an asinine move," he says, flexing his fingers on the steering wheel. He looks over at me and shakes his head, sighing. "If the guy had shown up, he would have run in a heartbeat. You wandering about in that place, the way you were, would have looked suspicious."

"I don't think so," I argue. "I made like I was checking out the salad bar while I waited for my pizza."

"I don't want to discuss it," Hurley says, and I can tell from the tone in his voice that any attempts to do so will likely result in a blowup.

Resigned to my fate, and hoping that a decent night's sleep will improve his temperament and outlook on the matter, I sit back and stay quiet for the rest of the ride back to Sorenson.

Chapter 29

When Hurley pulls into the police department lot, he turns off the truck, gets out without a word, and storms off into the police station with nary a glance back in my direction.

Hurt and angry, I get out of the truck, slam the door closed, and walk out of the lot toward my office. Let him sulk, I decide. But my determination is waning by the time I reach my office.

Christopher isn't in, and Cass informs me that he is out on a call for what sounds like a routine death, if such a thing is possible. It's an elderly man who was in home hospice care. I settle in at my desk, and find the invoice for Not a Trace's most recent efforts. I toss it aside and lean back in my chair, thinking about Hurley, thinking about the case, thinking about Lily Paulsen out there somewhere, lost and alone, and her grieving father, a walking corpse of a man.

These thoughts remind me of the grief support group Hildy told me about, and I decide to give Michaela Watkins another call. Before I can, my phone rings and I see that it's Emily.

"What's up?" I answer. "Is Matthew okay?"

"He's fine," Emily says. "He is very proud of his first snowman, loves hot chocolate, and is about to sit down to a dinner of frozen pizza and sugar snap peas."

It's an odd mealtime combination, but the peas are one of the only vegetables Matthew will eat, and I keep a stock of the frozen ones on-hand all the time.

"But I'm a little worried about Hoover," Emily says. "He keeps whimpering and licking his belly. I let him outside, thinking maybe he needed to poop some more. He kept squatting like he was trying, but nothing came out."

"Great," I say irritably. "I hope all that stuff he ate last night hasn't blocked him up. Let me call and see if I can get him in to see the vet before they close."

I disconnect the call and place one to the vet clinic. After explaining my situation, they agree to squeeze me in between appointments if I can come right away. "I'll be there in twenty minutes," I tell them.

I dash down to my car, once again impressed with the job Not a Trace has done. By now, the roads have been cleared, and I make it home in good time. I hook Hoover up to his leash, and then tell Matthew I'll have to check out his snowman later because Hoover has to go to the doctor.

I don't quite make it in the promised twenty minutes, but the clinic staff takes us into an exam room right away. Hoover normally hates the vet office as much as he hates baths, and the fact that he's subdued and not looking scared scares me.

I explain the situation to the veterinarian who comes into the exam room, a pleasant young man named Brian Murphy, who is new to the clinic.

"The main concern is whether or not he's obstructed," he explains, palpating Hoover's belly. "We should do an X-ray."

I agree, and he takes Hoover by his leash and leads him into the back area of the clinic. Ten minutes and some worried pacing later, he returns. Hoover looks like a new dog.

"Good news," Murphy says. "No blockage. In fact, he took a rather large dump on the X-ray table and it improved his mood considerably. I suspect he's just got a tummyache from all the sugar he ate last night."

I thank him, pay my bill at the front desk, and load myself and Hoover into the hearse. As I'm preparing to pull out of the parking lot, I glance at my watch and see that it's a few minutes past six. After a brief mental calculation and a moment's debate, I switch my turn indicator in the other direction and pull out. Then I place a call to Emily to let her know Hoover is okay and that I'll be later than planned.

* * *

Forty minutes later, I arrive at the local medical center in Mauston, park, and head inside after telling Hoover to be a good dog. A woman behind an information desk asks if she can help me, and I inquire as to where the grief support group meeting will be held.

"In the basement. It's held in the Nelson Meeting Room," she says. "You can't miss it. It's the only meeting room down there." She directs me to an elevator and stairwell, and I opt for the stairs.

The basement area is mostly offices and storage areas, and the employees who would normally be working them have long since gone home at this hour. Despite that, the hallways are well lit, though eerily quiet and deserted. The Nelson Meeting Room—identified with big black letters over the doorway—is around the corner and down the hall from the elevator and stairs, but is easy enough to find, as promised. The room is open but dark, and after peering into the inky blackness of the windowless space for a moment, I step over the threshold and feel on the wall for a light switch.

"It's on the left side," says a female voice behind me, making me jump. I gasp, whirl around, and see a woman in her thirties standing behind me.

"Sorry," she says. "I didn't mean to startle you." She pushes past me and reaches to the left of the doorway; a second later, the room is flooded with light. I see that it has been set up with a dozen chairs in a circle, and more chairs and several tables folded up and leaning against the far wall. "You're here for the grief support group?" the woman asks.

"Yes, I am," I say, following her inside.

"You're new here." She looks at me, smiling warmly. I nod. "Well, welcome, though I suppose this isn't the sort of thing one wants to be welcomed to, now is it?" She laughs, a nervous titter. "Anyway, I'm Lori Vickers. Widow for almost a year now. Car accident." Her expression sobers as she says this, but quickly turns back to a smile. "Who have you lost?"

I think fast. I'm not normally a superstitious person, but every so often, I hedge on the side of caution, just to cover my bases. I don't want to claim the death of anyone I currently have a relationship with, for fear that it might somehow come true. Even though my logical mind would know it was nothing more than a coincidence, I'd always wonder, and always harbor some guilt.

"My brother," I say. "Cancer. Very unexpected."

"Oh, how awful," Lori says. "How old was he?"

"Thirty-three," I say, using Desi's age, though even this level of connection to a real person in my life makes me a smidge uncomfortable. But Hurley taught me that if you're going to lie convincingly to someone, it helps if you use as many facts and truths as possible. Too many lies create too long a trail to keep track of.

"Well, you did the right thing in coming here," Lori says. "It's a good group."

"How many people typically attend?"

"Oh, it varies. We have some core regulars who have been coming every week for months now, but eventually most folks move on. Or so I'm told. Most weeks it's eight to ten people. And we have folks of all ages and types, old folks and young folks, housewives and career women, one single dad. It's a good mix."

"Who runs the group?"

"There are two people, actually. Michaela and Dennis. Sometimes they tag-team us, and sometimes they take turns. Michaela has a practice here in town, and Dennis is a counselor somewhere. I forget where. But they're both very good."

I hear the sound of someone approaching and the squeak of wheels on a cart. Three people enter the room, one of them a dietary employee for the hospital, who wheels in a cart laden with cookies, coffee, and water. The other two people are an older man and an older woman.

"That's Minnie and George," Lori says to me in a whisper. "They both lost their spouses last year and they've kind of bonded. I think they might even be dating now. Sweet, isn't it?"

"It is," I say. Then I take out my cell phone and start scrolling through the messages until I find what I need. I pull up a picture of Liesel Paulsen, the one from her driver's license, and I show it to Lori. "Do you know this girl? Does she come here?"

Lori looks at me rather than at the picture with a hurt expression on her face. "What are you doing? Are you some kind of investigator or something? Because this group is private. What happens here, who comes here, and what gets said here is confidential."

"No, no," I assure her. "I'm sorry. It's just that her family was friends of my family, and she told us how helpful this group was for her after her mother died."

I watch emotions play over Lori's face, concern, empathy, and curiosity. She finally deigns to look at the picture and I see her eyebrows shoot up.

"You knew Liesel?"

My heart speeds up a notch. "Not well. My parents knew her parents, her mom, before she died."

"A very sad case, that one. I think she—"

Whatever she is about to say is cut off when four more people enter the room. There is a man who looks to be my age, his face stamped with pain, and I guess that his loss is more recent. There are also two more women, who look like they're in their fifties, and judging from the way they interact with one another, I gather that they are friends.

The fourth person is a man, and it's someone I know, or at least recognize. It's Kirby O'Keefe.

"Hello, Dennis," Lori says, bestowing a smile on the man.

He smiles back at her, and then his eyes settle on me. "We have a newcomer," Lori says, looking over at me. "I'm sorry, I didn't catch your name."

"It's Mattie," I say after thinking fast about whether or not my real name will give anything away.

"Hello, Mattie," O'Keefe says. "Welcome to our group."

"Thank you, I think."

O'Keefe smiles understandingly. "Yes, I suppose it's not a place anyone wants to be, but if you need us, it's nice that we're here." He moves on then, chatting with some of the others, while my mind scrambles. What should I do? I don't want to risk clueing O'Keefe on the real reason I'm here, and I don't want him to get away.

"Excuse me, is there a bathroom down on this level?" I ask Lori.

"Yes, just down the hall and around the corner. On the other side of the elevator."

I get up and leave the room, passing two more women on their way in. They smile at me as I pass, an awkward, trying-to-be-friendly-but-sorry-you're-here kind of smile that feels forced. As soon as I'm in the bathroom, I take out my cell phone and call Hurley. He doesn't answer, and I curse under my breath, wondering if he's busy or if he's not answering on purpose because he's so mad at me. I leave a message, letting him know where I am and who I've found, and ask him to call me as soon as possible.

Next I try Richmond's number, but once again, I get voice mail. I leave the same message with him, and ask for him to call. Unsure what I should do next, I decide to return to the meeting room and sit there until someone calls me back. I'm about to head that way, when I hear a toilet flush in one of the three stalls. Belatedly I realize I should have checked underneath the stall doors before placing my calls to make sure I was alone.

The stall door opens and a second before I see who's about to come out, I get a whiff of something that makes my blood run cold: eucalyptus. In the split second before I see her face, my mind argues that it means nothing, plenty of people use eucalyptus-scented stuff for a variety of reasons.

But when I see her face, and the cold, curious smile she bestows on me, I get a sinking feeling that my goose is cooked.

"Hello," she says, stopping in front of me. "I saw you earlier today, at the pizza restaurant."

"Yes," I say, trying to look innocent and unafraid, even though my insides are trembling. "In Necedah."

"Yes. And here you are now in Mauston. What a coincidence."

I can tell she doesn't think it's a coincidence at all, and I back up a step. "Well, you know how it is with these small towns," I say.

She narrows her eyes at me, cocks her head to the side, and stares with a hard glint. "If we met twice in one day in Necedah, or here, I wouldn't think anything of it. But to meet there and here? What are the odds?"

Between the skeptical tone in her voice, and the predatory look on her face, my warning bells are clamoring. I turn around and head for the door, hearing and feeling a rush of movement behind me that makes the hair on the back of my neck stand up. As I'm reaching for the door handle, the woman steps in front of me again, blocking the door.

"I think we need to talk," she says, grabbing my free arm—the injured one—and giving it a yank. I yell out with pain, and it startles her. She steps back and I make another grab for the door, but she slams it shut with the flat of one hand before I can pull it open.

"Who are you?" she says, moving her face in closer to mine. She eyes me with intense scrutiny. "And how do you know Kirby?"

"You two work together?" I say, answering her question with one of my own. "Nice setup. Having a woman involved makes everything look less suspicious."

She doesn't offer me a denial of any sort, but she doesn't respond, either, other than to tilt her head to one side and narrow her eyes again.

"What tipped you off at the pizza place?" I ask. I figure if she is part of a human-trafficking ring, my goose is probably cooked already anyway. If she's not, if I've somehow misinterpreted all of this—and I'm certain I haven't—it won't do any harm to ask.

"It was too easy," she says. "It all happened too fast and a little too perfectly. My gut said sit and watch, and that's what I did. As soon as I saw you come strolling across the parking lot and do that walkabout thing in the restaurant, I knew I was right to be cautious."

She rears her head back and eyes me from head to toe. "Though I have to confess, I never would have pegged you for a cop otherwise."

"I'm not a cop."

"Really? Who, or what, are you then?"

I quickly debate several lies, and decide on the truth. "I'm an investigator for the medical examiner's office in Sorenson. I'm looking into the death of Liesel Paulsen."

"Yes, an unfortunate situation, that one," she says with mock sympathy. She sniffles, sidles her body in between the door and me, then reaches into the bag she has hanging over her shoulder. I'm not surprised when she produces a gun, a cute little snub-nosed number, with pearl on the handle.

I back up into the bathroom, distancing myself from it and her.

"Smart girl," she says.

"Yeah, well, I've already been shot once this week, and have no desire to repeat the experience, thank you very much."

She gives me an amused but skeptical look, clearly wondering if I'm telling the truth. I pull down the sleeve of my top and show her part of the dressing on my shoulder. She nods then and smiles. "Good to see you haven't lost your sense of humor."

Keeping the gun aimed at my chest, she takes a cell phone out of her pocket with the other hand and manipulates the screen with her thumb. After a few seconds, she says, "It's me. You need to leave the room right now and meet me at the elevator. We have a problem." She listens a moment, and her face suddenly contorts with fury. "I don't give a damn how awkward it is. Get here now!"

She stabs at the screen with her thumb and then shoves the phone back into her coat pocket. Stepping to one side of the door, she waves the gun at me, indicating that I should move over to her side. I do so, and keeping me in the gun's sights, she cracks open the bathroom door and peers out into the hallway.

I can see out, too, and at first, the hallway is empty. Then I see O'Keefe come hurrying toward us.

"Let's go," she says, waving the gun hand toward the hall. "No funny business."

I walk past her and step into the hallway, feeling her jab the gun into my ribs. "The stairs," she says to O'Keefe, nodding toward them.

O'Keefe looks from her to me, and then back to her again. "Michaela, what the hell are you doing?"

"Shut up and go," Michaela says in a low but deadly voice.

O'Keefe hesitates a second or two, but the look on Michaela's face convinces him to do as she says. He opens the door into the stairwell and holds it for us. The jab of the gun urges me forward and I enter the stairwell and start climbing.

"Check the hall at the top," Michaela says, and O'Keefe goes sprinting past us to the top landing. Once there, he cracks the door, peers out, then gives us a nod.

"I don't have my coat," I say, thinking stupidly, desperately, that I need to stall for as long as I can. I have no doubt that if I leave with these two, no one will ever see me alive again. Michaela lets me know what she thinks of my protest with another jab of the gun.

O'Keefe leads the way, but instead of going to the right when he exits the stairwell, thus going out the way I came in, he takes a left. At this end of the hallway is a door, and when O'Keefe pushes through it, I see that it is the start of another stairwell, this one going up, as well as an exit—one of those doors you can go out, but can't come in. By exiting the building this way, O'Keefe is avoiding contact with the information desk and anyone using the main entrance, as well as possibly avoiding any security cameras.

It's a good plan for him and Michaela, but not good news for me.

Chapter 30

The exit that O'Keefe leads us through deposits us on a side area of the hospital. There is a narrow concrete path leading around to the front and back of the building, but off to the side, there is a low concrete retaining wall, and beyond that, what appears to be a steep drop down a hillside into a wooded area. I look up and scan the edge of the building, searching for security cameras, but I don't see any.

"Give me your cell phone," Michaela says, sniffling as the cold makes her nose run.

I fish the phone out of my pocket and hand it to her. She sets it on the ground and raises her foot as if to stomp on it.

"You might want to hold off on that," I say.

She gives me that queer smile of bemused amusement again. "Why is that?"

"There's a video recording on there that you might want to look at," I explain. "When I was in the pizza restaurant, I wasn't just observing, I was recording. And the FBI has a copy."

"You're lying," she says, but the ambivalence on her face tells me she isn't sure.

"Check it out," I say with a shrug that makes my shoulder smart.

She stares at me, gauging my honesty, and then sneezes. Sniffling again, she wipes her nose with her sleeve and then bends down to pick up the phone. After swiping at the screen a few times, she apparently finds what she wants. She holds the phone up, watching the screen as O'Keefe looks over her shoulder.

"Holy shit," O'Keefe says after a minute or so. "There you are."

Michaela frowns, then shrugs. "So what? There's no reason for anyone to connect me to her. If they suspected me, they would have nabbed me then and there." She tosses the phone down to the ground again in disgust. "You're the one they're after. That crazy-ass doctor told you so. And I heard this one"—she waves the gun at me—"on her phone leaving a message for someone that said she saw you and wanted to know what to do."

O'Keefe dismisses her claim with a *pfft*, but then casts an angry glance my way. After a moment, he lets out a heavy sigh. "Face it, Michaela," he says, looking back at her and shaking his head. "We're done here. Between Dr. Crazy giving me up, and you getting caught at that restaurant, it's only a matter of time."

Michaela frowns at this. "We can make it work," she says, shaking her head. "The situation here is perfect, and the money is too good to give up. Besides, who else is going to give you another chance with your record?"

"We can't get greedy. We have enough money for now," he says. "We can start over at the new spot. Everything is in place."

Michaela shoots him an angry look and lets out a breath of disgust. "Whatever possessed you to take that girl to a hospital?" she says, a bitter tone in her voice.

The expression on O'Keefe's face is there and gone in a flash, but I see it and it surprises me.

Michaela starts pacing, wearing a circular path in the snow just beyond the walkway.

His face now deadpan, O'Keefe leans toward Michaela as she paces toward him. "It's time," he says in a no-nonsense voice.

Michaela shoots him an irritated look, which then morphs into one of resignation. "I need to think," she says, still pacing. The gun is pointed toward the ground, and for the moment, she seems to have forgotten about me. "Our handlers aren't going to let us just walk away after what happened to that girl," she says. "We know too much. We're a liability." She pauses in her pacing and arches her eyebrows at O'Keefe.

The two of them are staring at one another, several feet away from me, their eyes locked in silent communication. I see something click between them, some understanding that is mentally shared, and then they turn in unison to look at me.

I get a sinking feeling in my gut, realizing they have likely determined me to be their biggest liability. If I'm going to make a move, it's now or never. "It looks like my call for help has paid off," I say, looking past them toward the far edge of the front parking lot.

Both of them whip around, Michaela raising her gun, ready to fight. I take three huge steps to the retaining wall and leap over it. My feet touch ground several feet down, hitting a patch of ice and snow. The next thing I know, I'm on my butt, sliding, frozen snow getting jammed up the back of my shirt. I try to slow my descent a little with my hands, but when I hear the whine of a bullet overhead, I decide to let gravity do its work. My attempts to rudder myself make me turn sideways, and suddenly I'm rolling like a log. I put my arms over my head to protect it, feeling my injured shoulder scream in protest. I hit something with my feet and it spins me around so that I'm headed down the hill headfirst. From this position, I can see the hillside above and faces peering down at me. I also see something that gladdens my heart: the wash of red and blue oscillating lights in the night sky.

My head hits something hard and unresisting, my body comes to a jarring halt, and I see stars where there wasn't any a moment before. I struggle to see what's happening on top of the hill, but my eyes won't focus. My fight-or-flight instinct is at war with my graying consciousness, and it's only with a huge amount of determination that I'm able to keep from passing out.

My nursing instincts take over and I do a quick head-to-toe assessment of myself. I palpate my head with my right hand to see if anything feels soft and mushy where it shouldn't, then move to my neck, running my fingers down the cervical bones in back to feel for steps, deformities, or pain. The wound in my left shoulder is throbbing, but the pain is helping me to stay focused. I wriggle my torso to check for pain in the rest of my spine, and when nothing leaps out at me, I manage to sit myself up and lean against the trunk of the tree that halted my descent.

My focus is better now, and at the top of the hill, I see lots of lights and people moving about. Realizing the immediate threat to me is gone, I let myself relax and the dregs of adrenaline surging through my system make me start shaking, that and the frigid night air. I try to get to my feet, but now I'm trembling so bad that my legs won't work right. Giving up, I lean back against the tree and close my eyes.

"Miss? Miss, are you okay?"

Someone is shaking me by my left shoulder and the pain of it brings me immediately alert. "Ow!" I yelp.

"Sorry," says the male voice, releasing the grip on my shoulder. "Open your eyes."

I do so and see a uniformed young man squatting in front of me, blond hair, blue eyes, and a big smile.

"I'm Trevor, an EMT. What's your name?"

"Mattie. Mattie Winston."

"Nice to meet you, Mattie. Can you tell me what day of the week it is?"

"Thursday, unless it's after midnight and I've been down here a lot longer than I think."

"Good. Let me give you a quick exam." He reaches

up with both hands, prepared to sandwich my head between them.

"No need, Trevor," I say. "I'm a nurse. I've already cleared my own C-spine, I have no lower spinal pain, and my skull is intact. Mostly just some bumps and bruises, a lot of leftover adrenaline, and an old wound on my left shoulder from a bullet wound I sustained before today. I have the shakes, but if you help me, I think I can manage my way back up the hill."

"Actually, we'll go down it," Trevor says. "But let me do my own exam, or my supervisor will have my butt in a sling."

I roll my eyes, but smile, trying to keep my teeth from chattering. "Have at it, Trevor."

He does a quick but thorough exam, agrees with my earlier assessment, and then helps me to my feet. Once I'm standing—hanging on to a branch of the tree that I hit because Trevor is all of five feet tall and probably weighs half of what I do—I look around and realize there is a path about five feet below us. By grabbing from one branch to another among the thick growth of trees, Trevor and I make it down without further incident.

"Let me get a stretcher down here," Trevor says, and I shake my head.

"I'm fine. I can walk." Not giving him a chance to object, I start along the path, heading in what I think is the right direction to get back up top.

"Um, Mattie? That leads to a riverbank and some woods."

I stop, curse to myself, and reverse directions. Trevor wisely opts to simply walk at my side rather than assist me in any way. The walk does me good, and I feel stronger and steadier when I reach the top. My mind is clearer as well.

I take in the scene around me: three cop cars, an ambulance, and twenty or thirty people milling about, some wearing lab coats, some in uniforms, others in scrubs, and a couple of lookie-loos in street clothes. And then a blue 4x4 truck comes tearing up the hill, and I see Hurley come piling out of it and rush up to me.

At the sight of him, I burst into tears, and that gives Trevor a start.

"Mattie? What's wrong? Does something hurt?" He is about to ask me another question, but Hurley rudely shoves him aside and wraps me in his arms.

"Squatch, are you okay?"

"I'm fine," I tell him between sobs. "I'm sorry . . . so sorry."

"Sorry? About what?" he asks, his breath warm on my hair, his arms secure around me.

"You were right, Hurley. I should have listened to you, but I let my stupid stubbornness sway me."

Hurley steps back, holding me by my shoulders and looking at my face. His hand on my shoulder makes me wince, and when he sees it, he eases his grip. "Can I get that statement on the record?" he says with a half grin.

"That's just it," I say, struggling to get a grip on my sobs, my body shaking uncontrollably. Hurley undoes his coat, slips it off, and wraps it over my shoulders. "That recording I did at the pizza restaurant had that crazy woman, Michaela, on it. She's the one behind this, she and O'Keefe. It was the woman. We never thought it might be the woman."

"What woman?" Hurley says, clearly confused.

"I think she means that one over there," says a male voice I don't recognize. It's a local cop, and he's pointing to a spot on the ground alongside the hospital building, near the door O'Keefe led us through not long ago. A large white sheet lies over a mound on the ground, and I see a splotch of red seeping through the covering.

"Is that Michaela?" I say, looking at the cop.

"That's the name she was using, according to her friend over there." He nods in a different direction, and I see Kirby O'Keefe standing beside a cop car, looking morose, his hands cuffed behind his back.

"She's dead?" I say, and the cop nods. "Who shot her?"

The cop gives me a funny little smile, one eyebrow arched. "She shot herself. At least that's what he said," he adds, nodding toward O'Keefe. "Apparently, she slipped and lost her footing when you decided to launch yourself down the hill. She fell and the gun fired. Shot herself right in the chest, probably in the heart."

I look back at Hurley. "They're getting their victims from counseling groups," I tell him. "It's the perfect setup, vulnerable kids looking for emotional support. The two of them were running the grief support group here at this hospital. Liesel Paulsen attended, and I'm betting that's how Kirby and Michaela learned about Lily, too."

I see another car pulling up and recognize Richmond's sedan. He gets out, talks to a nearby officer, then sees us and heads our way.

"I think Detective Richmond can tell you all you need to know," Hurley says as Richmond reaches us. "Thank you for responding so quickly. You may have saved my wife's life."

"Sounds like she saved herself," the cop says. "That was a crazy thing to do, taking a leap down that hill, but it worked."

Hurley wraps an arm around my waist and pulls me close for a moment. "She's a crazy gal that way," he says. He smiles when he says it, but I can't tell if he's being sarcastic or serious.

"We need to get a statement from you, ma'am," the cop says.

Belatedly I read his name tag, which says MONTAG. "I'll do whatever you need," I tell him. Then I look up at Hurley. "Will you stay with me?"

"You couldn't beat me off with a stick," he says, giving me a squeeze.

"Can we go to the station?" Montag asks, looking at Hurley. "It will be easier, and more comfortable." He looks at me then. "That's if you're sure you don't need medical attention of any sort?"

I shake my head. "No, I'm sore, but I'm fine. And I'm alive. That's the most important thing."

"We'll follow you," Hurley says to Montag. Montag turns to head for one of the squad cars, while Hurley and I walk down to his truck, Hurley using his remote start button to get the truck engine going.

A faint sound seeps into my brain, and then I realize what it is. "Hoover!" I say, pulling away from Hurley and heading for my hearse.

I hurry over to my car, but it's locked and I don't have my keys. They're in the pocket of my coat, which is still in the basement meeting room.

"Why is Hoover with you?" Hurley asks.

"I had to take him to the vet, and when I was done, I came straight here."

"The vet? Is he okay?"

"He is. It's a long story. I need my keys, and they're in my coat pocket." I explain to Hurley where my coat is and he sends an officer inside to get it. He returns a few minutes later, coat in hand, and I give Hurley back his coat and shrug into mine. I dig the keys out of my pocket and open the car door.

A stench of dog poop wafts out toward me, along with my dog. Hurley snags Hoover by his collar, and I squeeze my eyes closed after seeing the splotches of doggy diarrhea all over the back of the hearse.

"Oh, for heaven's sake," I moan. I shut the door, lock it again. Hurley has walked Hoover over to his truck and put him in the backseat of the cab. I join him, and say, "Hoover pooped all over the inside of my car."

Hurley makes a face, and opens the passenger door of his truck. "Get in and get warm. We'll deal with that later."

I climb inside, too cold and too frustrated to argue.

"I'll be right back," Hurley says, tossing me his keys. "I need to talk to Richmond for a minute." He shuts the door and walks over to where Richmond is talking to the cop standing beside O'Keefe. I watch as the cop pushes O'Keefe into the squad car and shuts the door.

O'Keefe turns and stares out the back window of the car toward me. He looks scared and vulnerable, his brow furrowed with fear and uncertainty. I recall that fleeting expression I'd seen on his face earlier, and feel a sudden surge of empathy for the man, the truth of the situation forcing me to view him through a different lens than the one I've been using. Then he was the monster, the culprit, the person to blame, the person to hate. Now I realize he's also a pawn in someone else's bigger game, still a scumbag, but not the biggest one, because I now believe he has one redeeming quality.

Can he help us find Lily Paulsen? *Will* he?

I see Liesel Paulsen's dead face in my mind, except in this image her eyes are open and pleading with me. The vision morphs, and Liesel's face is replaced by her father's, his eyes dead and lifeless. How long will these two haunt me?

I climb out of the truck and walk over to Hurley and the other men. "I need to talk to O'Keefe," I say, interrupting them. "Please."

Montag says, "When we get to the station, maybe we—"

I reach over and wrap a hand around Hurley's arm. "Please," I say. "Now." I tighten my grip, digging my fingers into his arm through the fabric of his coat.

Hurley studies my face a moment, and gives me

the faintest of nods. He turns to Montag. "Let her do it here, now. Your car is equipped with a camera, isn't it?"

Montag nods, but he looks unsure.

"She's good," Hurley says to him. "And there are other lives at stake here. One in particular."

Montag waffles, chewing on the inside of his cheek. He looks to Richmond for help, but if he's hoping for someone to take his side, he is disappointed. "It's irregular," he says. "That's not how we do things."

I sigh and roll my eyes. Figures I'd get some by-the-book, small-town cop with a stick up his ass and a fondness for regulations just when I need someone who can bend a little.

"What's the harm?" Richmond says, seeing my frustration. "You read him his rights already, didn't you?"

Montag nods again, but I can tell he's still not convinced.

Hurley makes one last appeal: "If she does what I think she can do, there's a good chance you'll be at the heart of busting a huge human-trafficking ring." He pauses, gives Montag an arch look, and then delivers the coup de grace. "This case is huge," he says with great import. "It's a career maker."

I see a shift in Montag's eyes and breathe a sigh of relief, uttering a silent thanks to both my husband and Richmond.

"Okay, I suppose," he says. "But you can't threaten the guy, or hurt him, or even touch him," he says, giving me a stern look. "I don't want you to do anything that will compromise my case."

"I won't," I promise. Then I smile at him and add, "Thank you."

I open up the front passenger-side door of the cop car and settle myself into the front seat, shutting the door behind me. After shifting around to look at O'Keefe, I smile at him. "Hello again, Kirby."

He stares back at me with angry suspicion, his arms handcuffed behind him.

"I wanted to give you a chance to make a difference here," I tell him. "I think you know that your goose is cooked at this point, but there might be a way to make things better for you." Still, he says nothing, but the look on his face softens to one of nervous curiosity. "You loved Liesel, didn't you?"

He rears back in the seat as if he's been slapped in the face.

"That's why you took her to the hospital, isn't it? Even though you knew your handlers wouldn't have wanted that. When you saw how badly she was hurt, you tried to help her. You bought her that chocolate bar, hoping it would make her feel better, and then, when you realized just how serious her condition was, you drove her to an ER. You couldn't risk hanging around the place, but at least you did what you could for her."

O'Keefe stares at me, unblinking, his face now a mask of wounded emotion. I see tears welling in his eyes.

"You never hurt Liesel, did you?"

O'Keefe squeezes his eyes closed and shakes his head. "They never should have let that guy have her," he says, his voice cracking. "They knew he was violent. The first time was bad enough, but they kept letting him come back, and he asked for

Liesel every time." There is anger in his voice.

"I can't promise you anything, Kirby, but I know there is a lot of interest in breaking up this human-trafficking ring. If you're willing to help the authorities, they might be willing to offer you witness protection. Just think, a whole new life, a new identity, and no prison time."

He opens his eyes, and his expression brightens momentarily, but then he seems to register the unlikeliness of this scenario and the sadness returns.

"You can make the man who hurt Liesel pay for what he did to her," I go on. "And maybe get a new start for yourself. If your own future isn't that important to you, think about the futures of all those young people out there being held against their wills, used and abused. Because one of them is Liesel's sister, Lily. And while there isn't anything more you can do to help Liesel at this point, you have the power to save her sister. Honor Liesel's memory. Honor your love for her, Kirby. Help bring her sister home. Because that was Liesel's dying wish. The last thing she said, the last thing she thought of, was helping her little sister."

O'Keefe drops his head forward and tears fall onto his lap. His shoulders heave, and I hear the faint hiccup of a barely contained sob.

"If you really loved Liesel, Kirby, prove it now. Save Lily."

The man says nothing at first and his only movement is the occasional shudder of his shoulders as he tries to contain his emotions. Just as I'm starting to think that my gambit has failed, he raises his tear-stained face and looks at me.

"Okay," he says. "I'll tell you what I know."

I smile at him in gratitude, lower the window, and wave the men toward me. "Thank you, Kirby," I say. "I know Liesel is smiling down at you right now."

I get out of the car and let Richmond take my place. And as Kirby O'Keefe begins to tell his story, I have a feeling this case will haunt my dreams for years to come.

Chapter 31

The ride home—me following Hurley's truck after a somewhat heated debate over whether or not I should be allowed to drive, an argument I won when I reminded Hurley of what Hoover did, and that he might do it again—gave me more time to think over everything that had happened. I grow inured to the stench inside my car after the first few miles, and bemoan the fact that I will have to call Not a Trace for the third time in as many days.

When we arrive at the house, both kids are in bed asleep, and we settle in at the kitchen island with a late-night snack of hot cocoa and chocolate chip cookies that Emily baked.

"Do you have to go into the station tonight?" I ask Hurley.

He shakes his head. "I wouldn't be much use. I've been up for nearly two days straight and I imagine they'll be at it all night with O'Keefe. Richmond can handle things. He's bringing the FBI back into it."

"I really am sorry," I say to Hurley. "Sometimes I get so caught up in these investigations and my need to solve the puzzle that I don't think things through the way I should."

Hurley leans over and gives me a brief, chocolate-flavored kiss. Then he stares into his mug of cocoa for a minute before he says, "I'm sorry for getting so mad at you." He sighs, then adds, "To be honest, it's not so much what you do that upsets me, because even though some of your ideas strike me as insane and irrational, you always seem to get results. But sometimes those results turn out to be dangerous, and *that's* the part that upsets me. I'm so afraid something will happen to you, and I won't be there to save you."

Though he still isn't looking at me, I see the sheen of tears in the eye closest to me. It both saddens and gladdens me to know that he feels this need to protect me, to save me—sometimes from myself.

I reach over and rub his shoulder. "I never meant to burden you in that way, or scare you. I only want to be a part of the team, and this investigative stuff is so interesting to me. Plus, I'm good at it, I think. I have good instincts."

"You do have good instincts," he says with a sniffle, blinking away the tears in his eyes. "I don't want you to stop being a part of the team. And I definitely don't want you to stop puzzling out the cases." He pauses, and I know there is a "but" coming. "But," he says finally, "I love you. I love our family." He swivels on his stool, reaches over, and then takes hold of my hands, sandwiching them between his. "You make me happy, Mattie. So happy that it scares me sometimes. I don't know what I'd do if I lost you, which is why it makes me crazy when you put your life at risk unnecessarily."

Feeling overcome with love and affection for this man, I lean over and kiss him on his lips, first a gentle peck, then a more earnest one. "Okay," I say after the second, heated kiss, touching my forehead to his. "I get it. I promise that from now on I will only put my life at risk when it's absolutely necessary." I mean this partially as a joke, but I feel him stiffen in response and realize my timing is off. "*And* the definition of that," I add quickly, "will be when my life is already in danger and I have no choice, or the life of someone I love is in danger. Is that fair?"

"No," Hurley says, but with no anger or rancor in his voice. He reaches up with one hand and tucks a stray strand of my hair behind one ear. "I want you to promise me that you'll tell me what you're going to do before you do it."

I start to protest, knowing from past experience that Hurley will likely shoot down many of my ideas and proposed excursions, but he senses it and uses the thumb of his free hand to shush me by tracing it over my lips. "And in return," he goes on, his breath warm on my face, "I promise not to put an automatic kibosh on whatever it is you want to do. Okay?"

Our eyes lock, and at that moment, we are as intimate as two people can be. My heart swells at the sight of those dark blue eyes gazing so lovingly into mine, the erotic touch of his thumb on my lips, and the sweet chocolaty taste of his mouth still lingering on mine. "Agreed," I tell him. "Can we go to bed now?"

We do just that and Hurley wraps me in his arms and falls asleep almost the instant his head hits the pillow. It feels as if everything is right with the world, at least for the moment, and I, too, fall into a sound sleep, curled up inside the safety, warmth, and love of my husband's arms.

Morning dawns bright and sparkly, the sun glinting off the snow diamonds left behind by the storm. It's the sort of deceptive beauty Wisconsin winters are known for. It looks lovely and magical until you step outside and realize it's so cold it hurts to breathe and your nostrils freeze shut.

I'm reluctant to leave the warmth and security of Hurley and our bed, but I hear the sound of Matthew's pattering feet from down the hall. As I rouse myself up, I realize those little feet are moving fast and coming toward me. In the next instant, Matthew flings himself onto the bed, scrambles up, and then flops down between us, making Hurley awaken with a loud *oomph* and a flailing of covers.

"Mammy, Maff-you make a snowman!" my son says with obvious glee.

"A snowman?" Hurley says, rubbing sleep from his eyes.

"Yes. Me made a snowman," Matthew says. Then

he repeats the last word several times in a singsong voice. "Snowman, snowman, snowman, snowman. Wanna see it?"

"You bet I do," Hurley says. "Let's fly to it, shall we?" He grabs Matthew around his waist and holds him aloft, swinging and swaying that little body to simulate flying. Matthew, excited to be enjoying one of his favorite playtime things with Daddy, flings his arms out like wings and starts making motor noises with his mouth. Hurley moves him faster, and soon all Matthew can do is laugh. When Hurley finally lowers Matthew, bringing him in for a landing on his chest, Matthew is giggling and squirming hysterically, flushed with enjoyment. Hurley adds to the mayhem with a few well-placed tickles before finally giving Matthew some time to breathe.

Matthew takes a few seconds to get himself under control, his tummy on Hurley's chest, his head near Hurley's chin. With a look of utter adoration on his face, Matthew looks up at Hurley and says, "I wuv you, Daddy."

"I love you, too, my little man," Hurley says. He kisses Matthew on top of his head. Then in a bad imitation of a cowboy voice, he says, "What do you say we go downstairs and rustle up some breakfast, partner?"

Matthew answers by scrambling off his father's chest and hopping off the bed. He makes a mad dash down the hall, and Hurley rolls over, gives me a quick kiss on the cheek, and then tosses off the covers. A moment later, I am alone, basking in the display of love I just witnessed, happy that I have this family of mine.

An hour and several text messages later, Hurley is dressed and ready to head for work, and Emily is up and ready for school. It's another day off for me, technically, but there are things happening today that I don't want to miss, so I plan to go in.

"The roads are still slick in spots," Hurley says to his daughter, getting up from the table. "You be careful, okay?"

"I will," she says.

Hurley kisses both kids on top of their heads, says "Love you" to each, and then heads for the front closet to don his winter gear.

I spend half an hour in the garage, cleaning the mess in the hearse the best I can. After that, I shower and dress, and then see Emily off to school. It takes me an additional half hour to get Matthew dressed and ready to go, and another twenty minutes after that to drive us to Izzy and Dom's house, listening to Matthew complain about the stink in the car the entire way.

When I carry Matthew inside, I find Dom seated at his dining-room table, giving Juliana breakfast. The wonderful smells of cinnamon and butter are a welcome reprieve to my assaulted sense of smell.

"Good morning," Dom says. "I made French toast this morning, Matthew. Would you like some?"

Matthew nods eagerly and positions himself in a seat next to Juliana. Dom gets up from his seat and the two of us venture out into the kitchen, where we can talk somewhat privately and still see the kids.

"Did Izzy call you about Roger's autopsy?" Dom asks in a low voice as he turns on the burner beneath a frying pan.

"He did," I say. "I'm headed for the police station now to sit in on an interview with Rebecca Haugen, assuming she shows."

Dom mops a piece of bread in an egg mixture he has in a bowl beside the stove, and then drops it into the frying pan. "Darn shame," he says. "I imagine this is going to set the theater group back for a while. It might even be the death of us." He realizes what he has just said and claps a hand over his mouth, his blue eyes wide above it. "Oh, geez, I didn't mean—"

"Don't worry about it," I say. "Nobody appreciates a good death pun more than I do."

The smell of the French toast as he flips the slice of bread over with a spatula is tantalizing, and I must be eyeing it longingly because Dom offers to make me some.

"Tempting," I say, "but I'm going to pass. Thanks, though." I kiss him on his cheek and add, "Not sure how late I'll be. Are you okay to keep Matthew for the day if need be?"

"I'm not going anywhere," he says. "Couldn't if I wanted to. Izzy has my car."

"I noticed neither car was in the garage when I came in."

"They came and towed Izzy's car into the shop," Dom says. "Hopefully, it won't be anything too major, but with these old cars, you just never know." Izzy's car is a restored 1960s-era Impala, a project he lovingly worked on for several years.

"If you need anything, or want to go anywhere, call me," I say. "I'll be happy to come and get you."

"Thanks."

I leave, second-guessing my refusal of the French toast, and arrive at the police station a little before ten. Rebecca Haugen is due at ten, and I find both Hurley and Junior in the interrogation room—a term used jokingly, since it also serves as a general meeting and conference room—seated at the large table, chatting. At one time, suspect or witness interviews were conducted in smaller rooms that were later commandeered to serve as office space as the department grew and the building didn't. The conference room was outfitted with audio- and video-recording equipment, and it has been used as the primary interview space for the past six years or so. The décor is hideous, but definitely not stark, and it often throws people off when they enter the room. They come in expecting to be questioned in some tiny, bare room with one overhead light, a desk, and a couple of chairs. Instead, they find themselves seated in a section of corporate America. It works, oddly enough, because the setting often relaxes people. They let their guard down, and the police are experts at using that vulnerability to move in for the kill.

I greet Junior, and a moment later, Heidi, the dispatcher, comes back to inform us that Ms. Haugen has arrived.

"Send her back," Junior says after Hurley gives him a nod.

The two men are seated on the side of the table near the entrance to the room by the controls that turn on the recording equipment.

"Where should I sit?" I ask.

"Here," Hurley says, patting the empty seat to his left. I settle in, and when Heidi returns with Rebecca Haugen in tow, Junior gets up to greet her. He directs her to take a seat and waves a hand toward the other side of the table. There is a chair located at the head of the table, but almost no one takes it when seating choices are given. Too close to the interrogators, I imagine. There have been exceptions—typically, people who are overly confident and feel superior. So it doesn't surprise me when Rebecca opts to take the head-of-the-table seat, and Hurley's leg nudges mine beneath the table in an unspoken communication.

Junior starts off the interview by stating the date, the time, the case it relates to, and the names of all who are present. He then informs Rebecca that he is going to read her the Miranda warning as a matter of routine protocol. He does so, reciting it from memory. When he's done, he informs Rebecca that the session is being recorded.

"That's fine," she says.

I've never seen Junior handle a suspect interview before, and I'm curious to see what he does. Hurley typically starts out with mundane chatter designed to put the person at ease. Junior, however, opts to go straight to the meat of the matter.

"Ms. Haugen, I've reviewed the statement you made on the day of Roger Dalrymple's death, and

I know that you lied to us. So today we are here to get to the truth."

Rebecca looks askance at Hurley and me. "I didn't lie to anyone."

"Yes, you did," Junior insists. "You told Detective Hurley here that you weren't up on the catwalk the day of Mr. Dalrymple's death, and yet we found evidence on that catwalk that suggests you were."

"Really?" she says, folding her arms over her chest and leaning back in her seat, an amused look on her face. "What evidence was that?"

"We found a smear of theater makeup on the railing near where Mr. Dalrymple went over and it was still fresh. So we know it was left there less than an hour from when we found it. And when our lab tech did an analysis of that makeup, he found some interesting items in it."

Rebecca says nothing, but shrugs to let us know she isn't worried.

"We found a tiny piece of tobacco in the makeup," Junior says. "And you were smoking that day in the theater. You had a pack of cigarettes that you were carrying around with you."

"So? Anyone else could have picked up a bit of tobacco from me."

"Maybe," Junior says, "but we also found a very fine, blue-colored mohair fiber stuck in that smear of makeup, which matches the sweater you were wearing."

While the bit about the tobacco is true, this last bit isn't. But the police are allowed to lie under these circumstances, and ramping up the pressure will often get suspects to break.

"Again," Rebecca says dismissively, "a transfer that could have occurred between me and anyone else."

"Okay," Junior says, looking thoughtful as though he's actually considering this scenario. "Then how do you explain us finding your DNA in the makeup?" he asks.

This, too, is a lie. It would take days, maybe weeks, to test the makeup for DNA, but we're hoping that Rebecca, theater buff that she is, has watched enough TV crime shows to think that it can be done in a matter of hours.

With this last question, Rebecca's composed expression falters for a brief second, but she quickly recovers. She is an actress, after all.

Then Junior delivers his coup de grace with one final lie. "*And* we found your DNA in some makeup smears that were on Mr. Dalrymple's shirt," he says. "We know the makeup was yours because it was a different compound than what Mickey Parker uses on the others. He said you always insist on doing your own makeup. Care to explain that?"

Rebecca frowns and drops her arms to her sides, no longer trying to hide her worry. Her eyes dart from Junior to Hurley, and back to Junior again. And then I see a look of resignation on her face that tells me she has realized the jig is up.

"Look," she says, leaning forward, forearms on the table, "it's not what you think. It was an accident."

"Tell me," Junior says.

Rebecca hesitates, and I wonder if she's trying to decide what spin to put on her words. "He at-

tacked me," she says finally. "He came back after
lunch, all drunk and staggering like some fool. He
went up on the catwalk, and I was worried about
him, staggering like he was, afraid he might fall.
So I went up there to convince him to come down.
But instead, he tried to rape me."

"*Rape you?*" Junior echoes with obvious skepticism.

"Yes," Rebecca insists indignantly. "I was trying
to talk to him, but he kept talking over me, or trying to anyway. He was so drunk, he just kept drooling and slobbering and slurring his words. And
then he just lunged at me. All of his weight fell
against me, like he was trying to push me down,
and so I shoved him as hard as I could to get him
off me." She pauses, and gives us a pleading look.
"I was only trying to get him off me. I didn't know
he'd go over the side." Her expression shifts to
one of determination. "It was self-defense," she
says.

Hurley's phone buzzes, and when he takes it out
to look at it, I lean over to read the text message he
received. I look at him and smile.

Rebecca, watching us, says, "I suppose I need a
lawyer. Are you going to arrest me?"

"No," Junior says. "You're free to go."

Rebecca looks startled, her eyes darting from
his face to Hurley's and back again. "Really?" she
says. "I'm not under arrest?"

"You are free to go," Junior repeats. To prove his
point, he gets out of his chair, opens the door to
the room, and nods his head toward the hallway.

Rebecca gets out of her chair and walks slowly

toward the door, her body tense and ready to spring like some animal on the hunt, or one being hunted. When she crosses the threshold without incident, her pace picks up and she all but runs away from us.

Junior returns to his seat and gives Hurley a reticent smile. "I would have preferred a bust, but thanks for letting me do this part of it at least," he says.

"You did really well," Hurley says. "You'll get to solve a homicide someday. It just won't be today."

"We can't even get her for involuntary manslaughter?" Junior tries, not willing to let go yet.

Hurley shakes his head. "The DA won't go for it. Technically, our victim was dead before she pushed him over the side. The best we could hope for is abuse of a corpse."

"Damn," Junior says. He looks at me with one last glimmer of hope. "Izzy is sure about this?"

"He is," I tell him. "Dalrymple's alcohol level was zero and the tissue studies of the samples taken from his injuries showed little to no bleeding. That means his heart wasn't beating when he fell. He was already dead. Brain bleeds like that can often make people act drunk the way Roger did. Most likely he died when he collapsed against Rebecca, even though she thought he was trying to make a move on her."

Junior digests this info, but he still looks disappointed.

"If you want to get a glimpse of the lighter side of this job," I say to him, "come with us."

"Why? What's going on?"

"Come on. You'll see."

We grab our coats and hats, and walk from the police station to my office. As we come in the front door, Cass smiles at us from behind the desk.

"Where is he?" I ask her.

"In the library. He's alone. Christopher and Izzy had to go out on a call."

I lead the others back there and find Kurt Paulsen seated at the table, staring off into space. "Mr. Paulsen," I say, walking over to him and placing a hand on his shoulder. "It's good to see you again." Off in the distance, I hear the *ding* of the elevator arriving on our floor.

Paulsen looks up at me with dead eyes. "Wish I could say the same," he says in a flat, monotone voice. "I take it you have information on my other daughter, Lily?"

"We do." I can tell from his demeanor that he is expecting bad news. "We found her."

"Do I have to . . . look at her, the way I did with Liesel?" He swallows hard, no doubt reliving that awful moment.

I hear footsteps approaching out in the hall and tell Paulsen, "Yes, we do need you to look at her. But I think you'll find it easier this time."

Bob Richmond walks into the library then. Beside him is a scarily thin girl, pale, with dark circles under her eyes. She stops just inside the doorway and looks at Paulsen. He turns around to see who has entered the room and freezes.

For several long seconds, nothing happens. Then Paulsen, his voice hitching, says, "Is she . . . real?"

The girl bursts into tears and runs to Paulsen. "Daddy," she sobs, wrapping her arms around his neck. She falls into his lap and buries her face in his shoulder, her sobs coming hard, wracking her thin body. Paulsen, still frozen, blinks several times very fast, and then wraps his arms around the girl. With his eyes closed, his face contorts into an agony of pain and relief, love and disbelief. Then he is sobbing as hard as his daughter.

"Lily girl," he says between sobs, raising one hand up to caress her head. "Oh, my sweet Lily girl."

I swipe at the tears running down my own face and glance at the other men in the room, seeing a glistening wetness in their eyes as well.

"We'll leave you alone for a bit," I say to Paulsen, though I'm not sure he hears me. "I think you two could use some privacy."

At the sound of my words, Richmond, Hurley, and Junior all shake off their trances and look at one another. As if they rehearsed it, they each turn away from the other, wiping their eyes and making their way to the door.

I wait until they are out of the room, and then step into the hallway to join them, shutting the door behind me.

"Wow," Junior says, blowing out a breath. "That was powerful."

I smile at him. "It's okay to cry, you guys," I say. "It's an emotional moment."

"I'm fine," Junior says, dismissing me with a shooing motion. "I have some paperwork to catch up on, so I'll see you guys later." He turns and heads back the way we came.

"Yeah, me too," Richmond says, and then he pivots around and starts down the hall toward the elevator. "Lots of paperwork," he adds over his shoulder.

I look up at Hurley, and touch the dampness on his cheek with the back of my hand.

"You did that, Squatch," he says. Then he embraces my face between his hands, gives me a kiss on my forehead, and says, "I'm very proud of you."

"Thanks." I let out a shuddering breath, and glance toward the closed library door. "There's a long road ahead of them," I say. "She's going to need lots of counseling, and probably some drug rehab, too. It won't be easy, particularly with her sister gone."

"It wasn't a perfect ending," Hurley says, "but it could have been a whole lot worse."

"Did Richmond say how many people they've managed to bust?"

"He said the FBI, along with local authorities in several towns and cities, have made about a dozen arrests so far, with more to come. Our Mr. O'Keefe knows quite a bit about the operation because he and Michaela have been working with them for five years now. The two of them go back further than that, but he was starting to get scared of her, so he's not harboring any last feelings of devotion toward her. He said she was the one who snatched both of the girls, and we're inclined to believe him. Liesel was attending the grief support group, and I can't imagine her trusting O'Keefe enough to go off anywhere with him. Once they had Liesel, Michaela drove out to the Paulsen farm to see Lily and tell her she knew where her sister was. Then she snatched her, too."

"Evil bitch," I mutter.

"And you'll be happy to know that they've decided to shut down Dr. Lowe, now that they know about his little black book."

"Good!"

"Plus, it turns out our local intrepid reporter, Irwin Cleese, managed to dig up quite a bit of info on his own. He was about to come to us with some of it when everything went down. And since the local paper comes out tomorrow, he's got the insider scoop. So he's pretty pleased."

"I'm glad. I like the guy."

Hurley kisses me again, on the lips this time. It isn't a long kiss, but it's tender, sweet, and full of unspoken thoughts and sentiments.

"Are you going back to the station?" I ask him once we part.

He nods. "Do you think you'll be tied up all day?"

I shrug. "I want to make sure the Paulsens get the help they need. I've got a few things lined up already, starting with a visit to that social worker, Hildy, over at the hospital. She has a list of resources we can use, and she's already offered to provide some counseling for the two of them, at least initially."

Hurley cocks a wry smile and chucks me under my chin with a finger. "One of the things I love the most about you, Squatch, is that you have a big heart. It's even bigger than your feet." Then, with lightning quickness, he turns and hurries off down the hall. "I'll be home for dinner," he says over his shoulder.

I smile, feeling all liquid and happy and joyful inside. I take a moment to bask in this ball of contentment, and then I tuck it away in a special place, deep down inside my heart, reserved for when I need to take it out again. Then, with a deep, bracing breath, I square my shoulders and go back into the library.

Chapter 32

Another snowstorm beats its way into Sorenson on Saturday night, leaving the town bruised and frozen. Its inhabitants, however, are a hardy bunch, well inured to these sorts of attacks, and they are out in force, shoveling, snowblowing, digging out their cars, and chatting with one another. They aren't fazed by the knowledge that another blizzard is on its way, due to strike late this evening, and likely to tie up rush-hour traffic come Monday morning.

Today is Hurley's birthday party, and Christopher kindly offered to switch weekends with me so I could be free. For Christopher, this means two more nights of sleeping with the dead in our office. I'd feel guilty, except he doesn't seem to mind it, and I suspect it seems like the Ritz when compared to his house.

I get Matthew ready to go early in the morning, planning to head to Desi's house to help with the last-minute details of the party. When I arrive at my sister's place, she is already up and has breakfast cooking on the stove. Bacon and eggs for breakfast is a Sunday ritual in the Colter household, and the aromas smell wonderful. By the time I get Matthew out of his snowsuit and boots, I'm practically drooling.

"Good timing," Desi says. "We're just about to sit down and eat. Want to join us?"

"I have some last-minute shopping to do," I waffle, but my heart isn't in it. "Though I suppose a little extra energy won't hurt," I say, shrugging off my coat.

"There's something I should tell you," Desi says as I turn to go hang up my coat and Matthew's snowsuit.

Her warning comes a second too late, as Matthew suddenly squeals with delight and dashes past me toward the person standing a few feet away. Dressed in boots and a down parka, my father is holding an armload of cut wood. I glance past him toward the fireplace in the living room and see that the beginnings of a fire have been set: some crumpled papers and a small tower of kindling.

"Hi, Pop-pop," Matthew says, wrapping his arms around one of my father's legs and hugging it. This is the first time I've heard Matthew refer to my father by any name. I have no idea where "Pop-pop" came from, and suddenly I feel like an outsider.

"Hi, chief," my father says with a smile, managing to shift his load enough to free one hand, which he uses to pat Matthew on the head.

My father's gaze shifts to me. "Good morning, Mattie," he says with a tentative smile.

"Hello, Cedric," I say, my tone as cold as the air outside. He winces, and I suspect that my use of his first name, as opposed to the title he wants me to use—Dad—has stung a bit. I feel a twinge of guilt, and in an attempt to soften my blow, I smile at him and say, "How are you?"

"I'm doing well," he says.

"We having a birfday party for Daddy," Matthew announces, releasing my father's leg.

"So I heard," Cedric says. "How fun, eh?"

"Matthew?" Desi says from behind me. "Want some bacon?"

"Bacon!" Matthew echoes, and he quickly dashes over to the counter and climbs up on a stool.

Cedric turns back into the living room and deposits his wood load into a bin on the hearth. Then he squats in front of the fireplace and starts stacking logs on top of his kindling.

I look over my shoulder at Desi, who shakes her head in a chastising manner. Sighing, I trudge into the living room and hang up our stuff in the coat closet. Then I walk over to stand next to my father. "Look," I say, "I know that things are, well, kind of strained between us. I'm working on it. I just need more time."

"Take all the time you want," he says, busying himself with the laying of the fire and not looking at me. "I'm not going anywhere. Not this time."

I stand there, chewing on my lip, unsure what to do or say next. This awkwardness between my father and me refuses to go away. Desi, bless her, has somehow managed to put the past and all the deceptions behind her, and she has welcomed my father—*our* father, as it turns out—into her life. And if you get right down to it, she has more reason to be angry about everything that happened in the past than I do. Desi grew up thinking another man was her father, a lie of astounding proportions perpetuated by our mother.

I open my mouth to say something more, but the words aren't there. After doing my best imitation of a fish for a few seconds, I give up and head back to the kitchen. Matthew is happily chowing down on two strips of crispy bacon and playing a game on a tablet Desi has given him, leaving a trail of greasy fingerprints on the screen.

I walk over to stand by my sister, who is busy scrambling eggs on the stove.

"You're still angry with him?" Desi says in a slightly chastising tone.

"Not angry," I say. "Just . . . I don't know . . . uncomfortable. Unsettled. It's going to take time."

"He's really good with Matthew, you know. They adore one another."

"So I've seen."

I'm not sure how I feel about this. On the one hand, I want Matthew to know his grandparents, and have a relationship with them. This has already proven to be a challenge with my mother, who looks at Matthew's runny nose, or food-smeared face, or dirt-covered hands, with something akin to horror. She buys him things, and talks to him on the phone, but whenever they are together sharing physical space, she keeps her distance. Matthew has sensed her reservations, and he tends to steer clear of her.

I realize Matthew has the opportunity to have the relationship with my father that I never did, and the thought cheers me a little. But it also angers me on some level. For my father to casually stroll back into my life after more than thirty years of nonexistence and expect to be embraced and accepted with open arms strikes me as the height of audacity, especially after all the lies that were told over the years.

Granted, I have since learned that those lies were told in order to protect Desi and me, and that my mother was as much, if not more, of a culprit in the duplicity that took place all those years ago. But I spent so much of my life resenting and hating the vague memory of the man I knew as my father, a man who deserted my mother and me when I was four, that I now find it hard to reverse gears and put all that behind me.

I don't know what to say to Desi on the subject, and since my father has now entered the kitchen, it's a moot point.

"I've got the fire going," Cedric says.

"Thank you," Desi says. "These eggs are ready. Shall we eat?" As she carries the pan of eggs to the dining-room table, she hollers for the rest of the family. "Ethan? Erika? Lucien? Breakfast is ready."

The meal goes off smoothly enough with light, conversational chatter about mundane topics like the weather, stuff the kids are doing in school, and Matthew's frequent reminders that we are having a "birfday party with cake and ice cream." My son's fixation with food borders on my own.

* * *

I notice that everyone else at the table seems quite comfortable with Cedric, and I realize that he must be a frequent guest in the Colter house. Even Lucien, who is known for having a terminal case of foot-in-mouth disease, chats amiably with the man.

Once we're done eating, Erika takes Matthew back into the living room to watch cartoons, and Ethan disappears into his bedroom to spend some bonding time with his collection of mostly dead bugs. Lucien excuses himself to go to his home office and finish up some paperwork, leaving Desi, Cedric, and me at the table.

Cedric looks out the window, then at Desi. "I'm thinking I might not stay for the party," he says. "The storm that's coming is due to hit late this afternoon, and I'm not sure I'll be able to get a cab if I stay for dinner like we planned. I should go now."

"Don't be ridiculous," Desi says. "Just plan on staying here for the night. There's a fold-out bed in that couch in Lucien's office."

I watch my father's face as he considers Desi's invitation: pleasure mixed with doubt. Is he considering an early departure because of the weather, or because of me? And I realize then that despite the awkwardness I often feel when I'm around him, I don't want him to go.

"Please stay for the party," I say. "I'd like you to be here."

Cedric looks at me with surprise.

"I mean it," I say. "I know things are strained and awkward at times between us, but I'm trying. And I want to . . . I need to get to know you better."

I see tears glisten in his eyes as he looks at me, and another stab of guilt pierces my heart.

He finally tears his eyes from mine and looks at Desi instead. "Are you sure it won't be too much trouble if I stay?"

"Not at all," Desi says with a smile.

"Okay." He looks at me, and adds, "Thank you."

Erika and Matthew reappear then. "Matthew wants to go outside and build a snowman," Erika says. "Is that okay? I'll keep an eye on him."

"That sounds like fun," I say, and then I get up and fetch Matthew's snowsuit and boots from the closet. While Erika gets herself dressed to face the elements, I help Matthew into his snowsuit, but wrangling him into his boots proves to be an exercise in frustration. As I hold one of the boots so he can put his foot in, he makes a face at it and doesn't lift his foot from the floor.

"Come on, Matthew," I cajole. "Put your foot in."

"I don't like boots," he says with a pouty face.

"If you're going to go outside, you need to wear them. They keep your feet warm and dry."

"They make my feet feel funny," he says in a whiny voice.

I ignore his protest, one I've heard dozens of times, and grab his foot with one hand while I try to maneuver his boot on with the other. Matthew refuses to point his toes, pulling his foot back so it is ninety degrees from his leg and not going into the boot.

"Matthew," I say in my best warning voice. "Knock it off and straighten your foot."

"I don't want to," he whines again, and he pulls his foot loose from my hand.

My father appears at my side then, and he crouches down in front of Matthew. His smell, a mixture of apple-scented pipe tobacco and whatever soap or aftershave he uses, wafts toward me, and it is instantly familiar, transporting me back in time. I have a flash of memory, of me sitting in his lap, looking up at him adoringly, feeling safe, loved, and happy. I shake it off, or rather I try to, but there is some vestige of that warm, loving feeling that remains, refusing to be driven away.

"You need to do what your mother says, chief," my father commands in a no-nonsense voice. "Now put your boots on."

I try to decipher the expression on Matthew's face. It isn't fright, but it's close. More like awe, respect, and adoration, tinged with a tiny hint of fear. After a few seconds of staring at my father, Matthew sticks his foot in the boot and pulls it on himself. Then he does the same thing with the other one.

"Thanks," I say to my father, a bit grudgingly. "I need to bottle that, whatever it is, because he doesn't listen to me at all these days."

"Goes with the age," my father says. "He'll grow out of it."

I wonder how he knows this, given that he wasn't around when his children grew up. Then I realize I'm making some potentially erroneous assumptions.

As Erika grabs Matthew's hand and hauls him toward the back door, I look over at my father. "Did you . . . do you have any other family?" I ask. "Did you hook up with anyone when you were in the Witness Protection Program?"

He looks down at the floor, and his cheeks redden. "I don't have any other children of my own," he says. "Just you and Desi. But I was with a woman for a number of years and she had young children when I met her. So I had some stepchildren for a time."

"Are you still in contact with them?"

He shakes his head. "No, I figured it was safer for everyone involved if I kept my distance. And their mother didn't know about my past, my real past. So when I decided to leave the program, I more or less just . . . well . . . disappeared."

It takes me a moment to digest this. "You mean, you didn't tell her you were leaving?"

He shakes his head, looking embarrassed and ashamed. "I made a clean cut," he says, looking away.

I'm not sure whom to empathize with in this story. I realize how difficult it had to have been for him to do what he did, but I also know that the woman he was with, and her children, must have gone through hell wondering what happened to him, and whether or not he was dead or alive.

"I did send her a letter," he adds. "Just to let her know I was okay and wouldn't be back." He stands, grunting a little, and I hear his knees crack loudly. He extends a hand to me to help me up from the floor. It's a huge hand, and it envelops mine, warm and steady.

"Why did you leave the program?" I ask when I'm standing, pulling my hand back. "Why risk everything?"

He looks at me, his eyes damp with emotion. "Because of you," he says. "I couldn't stop thinking about you. I didn't know about Desi then, and even if I had known about her, I never spent any time with her. I never knew her. But you . . . you were my little girl."

His voice cracks when he says these last few words, and I feel tears burn behind my eyes. I try to swallow, but it feels as if I've swallowed a golf ball that's stuck in my throat.

"Leaving you was the hardest thing I've ever done in my life," he says.

Emotion surges through me, threatening to burst out of my very pores. I feel overwhelmed, vulnerable, and frightened. And I do the only thing that makes sense to me at the time. I hug my father for the first time in thirty-plus years.

Chapter 33

The birthday party goes off without too many hitches, largely because my sister planned it. Not surprisingly, my mother and William fail to show, but it is just as well. Having my mother, her current paramour, and my father all together under one roof would have been the height of awkwardness, and I want Hurley's party to be a fun, memorable occasion.

Desi has whipped up a variety of yummy appetizers, and in addition to the cake and ice cream, there is plenty of soda, beer, and wine. Izzy, Dom, and Juliana come with Sylvie in tow. Sylvie has apparently regressed back to her childhood. She shows up dressed in her party finery, her scant gray-and-white locks in pigtails. After taking the chair closest to the fireplace, she proceeds to ooh and aah over the festivities, periodically clapping her hands together in glee and protesting, "All this for me? You shouldn't have!"

I look at Izzy, who shrugs and smiles. "Is her birthday coming up?" I ask him.

"Not for another two months," he says.

Then Desi, perfect hostess that she is, drums up a party hat that Sylvie happily dons, the elastic band disappearing into the wrinkles under her chin. Then Desi has Erika wrap up some gifts: a lone teacup she found at a yard sale, some hair ribbons, and a sweater that I suspect Desi bought for herself and kindly offered up as a sacrifice.

We let Sylvie unwrap them, and she's as giddy as a schoolgirl with each one, profusely thanking everyone, and then declaring herself ready for cake and ice cream.

At one point during the festivities, I watch my father playing with both Juliana and Matthew. Despite the fact that my father is a huge, dark bear of a man—or perhaps because of it—the kids are drawn to him. They climb on his lap, laugh at his antics, and when he tries to go off and get some more food, they follow him like rats after the Pied Piper. He's a natural with kids, I realize, and I feel a stab of loss over all the years I missed with him during my childhood. How different might my life have been if he had been there?

Hurley, as the true guest of honor, is kept busy throughout the party, visiting with guests, opening presents, and participating in the ritual bemoaning over the passing of years. The gifts are mostly small items: a bottle of his favorite wine, a six-pack of his favorite beer, and a collection of humorous mugs, books, and other items with witticisms about getting old. I bought him a few small things, too: a

mug printed with *World's Best Dad,* some air fresheners for his truck, and a Whitman's Sampler, one
of his favorites. I have a bigger gift for him, but I'm
saving it for when we get home.

The snow starts to fall around three-thirty, and
within an hour, it has already added another inch
to the existing ground cover. It's a signal for everyone to leave so they can go home, get cozied up
for the night, and then start anew in the morning,
tackling Mother Nature's latest fury.

We are the last to leave, and while Hurley and
my father wrestle with getting Matthew dressed for
the excursion home, I hug my sister and thank her
profusely for all her hard work.

"It was my pleasure," she says with a smile, and if
it weren't for the fact that I know she means it, I
might feel guilty. "I take it you never came up with
that big gift idea you were so worried about," she
adds.

"Actually, I did," I say with a smile. "But it's something I want to give him in private." After looking
around us to make sure no one is within earshot, I
tell her about the gift.

My sister's eyes grow huge, and then she leaps at
me, hugging me like I'm a life preserver and we
just jumped off the *Titanic.* "It's perfect!" she says.

Our ride home is in separate vehicles, since I
had arrived at my sister's house earlier in the day,
but we stay together on the roads, driving slow as
the wind hurls a tunnel of snow at us. My hearse,
once again cleaned by Not a Trace, the staff of
which now eyes me with wary concern, smells
clean and fresh. I heard a rumor that the owner of

the company has fled our chilly climes for the Caribbean, using my payments to fund the vacation.

Emily, who came with her father, rides home with me, while Matthew gets to ride in "Daddy's bwue twuck."

I tell Emily about her father's final birthday gift from me, gauging her take on it. "So what do you think?" I ask her when I'm done.

"I think he'll be over the moon with it," she says. "It's the best gift he'll ever get."

When we arrive at the house, I fix dinner, managing to broil steaks for Emily, Hurley, and me, and serving them up with the inevitable "mackachee" for Matthew. It takes forever to get Matthew, who is still revved up on a sugar rush, ready for bed and tucked in for the night. He finally crashes around eight o'clock, falling into a sugar coma, and Emily retreats to her room.

Hurley and I settle in on the couch in the living room in front of the fireplace, cuddling as we bask in the glow of the flames.

"Did you have a nice birthday?" I ask him as he plays with the hair on the nape of my neck.

"I did," he says, kissing me on my head.

"I have one more gift for you."

"Hmm," Hurley says with a hint of salacious interest. "I was hoping you might."

I pull a card out of my pocket and give it to him, and I can't help but smile when he says, "Oh," in a slightly disappointed tone.

I ease up from where I was nestled in the crook of his shoulder and turn to face him on the couch.

"I thought long and hard to try and come up with the perfect gift for you. I hope you like it."

"I'm sure I will," he says, tearing open the envelope. He reads the card aloud, a mushy, romantic thing. Then he reads what I wrote.

"'Our journey of life has been wonderful, though the ride has been wooly and wild. I can't wait to start our next adventure, the making of another . . .'" He pauses, swallows, and looks at me before uttering the last word. "'. . . child.'"

I smile at him, and kiss him on his cheek.

"Are you sure?" he asks, his voice cracking slightly. I see the glistening wetness in his eyes and answer without hesitation.

"Absolutely."

He pulls me into him, and holds me so close that it feels as if we are one person. I relish the solid warmth of him, feeling happier than I can ever remember being.

"What made you decide?" he asks after a while.

Reluctantly I separate myself from him, sitting back and looking deep into his eyes. "Fathers," I say. "Watching my own father come to grips with the losses he endured, the tough decisions he had to make, and how much being a father meant to him. And then there's Mr. Paulsen, all the agony and joy he's been through. It's made me realize how important it is to be a father, what it means. And I can't think of a better way to express the love I feel for you than to make another human being who will get to know the love and wonder that is you."

"God, you're an amazing woman, Squatch," he

says, taking my hand and kissing the back of it. "I love you."

"I love you, too."

As we gaze into one another's eyes, the warmth of our love heats up as the fireplace cools down. "I think it's time to start practicing," I say in a sultry voice.

"Happy birthday to me," Hurley says with a scandalous grin. And then he takes me by the hand and leads me upstairs.

If you enjoyed DEAD OF WINTER,

Don't miss the next installment of

The Mattie Winston Mysteries:

DEAD RINGER

Available in March 2020

In the meantime, please enjoy the excerpt of

NEEDLED TO DEATH,

Annelise Ryan's new series,

A Helping Hands Mystery, featuring

Hildy Schneider.

Turn the page for a quick peek!

Chapter One

I can still see the shadows of death on some of their faces, evident in the droop of their eyes, the taut, thin line of their lips, and the pale, pasty coloring of their skin from spending too much time indoors hiding away from society and life. It's evident, too, in the tentative and wary way they walk, their shoulders hunched over defensively, as if they're expecting another grievous blow to descend upon them at any second.

Some people wear their cloak of grief for a long time. Others shrug it off in good time and good order, eager and able to get on with their lives, even if it's only a few small steps at a time. The people who are with me tonight tend more toward the former group, and it's my job to try to help them become members of the latter group.

I'm about to start the session when a new face enters the room—a woman who looks to be in her mid-to-late forties—and I'm tempted to clap my hands with delight. This would be both inappropriate and unprofessional, so I quickly rein in the impulse and focus on forming a smile that looks warm and welcoming, and hopefully doesn't show the excitement I feel. I hurry over to her, aware of the curious stares coming from the others in the room.

"Hello," I say. "Are you here for the bereavement group?" The question is rhetorical, since this woman is wearing her mantle of grief like a heavy shawl. Her face is expressionless, her shoulders are slumped, and her movements are sluggish and zombielike. She looks down at me—nearly everyone I meet looks down at me in the strictly physical sense, since I'm barely five feet tall—and nods mechanically.

"Well, welcome," I tell her, touching her arm with my hand. "I'm Hildy Schneider. I'm a social worker here at the hospital, and I run this group."

She nods again but says nothing. I suspect her loss is a recent one, very recent. *Who was it?* I wonder. Based on her age, a parent is a good guess if one assumes the natural order of things. But I've learned that death doesn't care much for order.

"What's your name?" I ask, hoping to ease her out of the frozen, deer-in-the-headlights stance she currently has. She looks at me, but I get a strong sense that she doesn't see me. I've encountered this before and suspect she's mentally viewing some memory reel as it plays repeatedly. I tighten my touch on her arm slightly, hoping the physical connection will ground her. It does.

She blinks several times, flashes an awkward, pained attempt at a smile, and says, "Sorry. I'm

Sharon Cochran." Her voice is mechanical, rote, with no lilt or feeling behind it.

"I'm glad you're here, Sharon," I say. "Can I get you something to drink? A water, or some coffee?"

She looks at me with brown eyes that are stone-cold and dull, and then shakes her head.

"There are some cookies, too," I say. "Can I get you one?"

Again, she shakes her head, her gaze drifting away from mine. The others in the room have lowered the tenor of their conversations to soft, whispered murmurs, no doubt so the newcomer won't hear them talking about her.

"Sharon?" I say firmly, wanting to bring her attention back to me. "Have you ever been to a support group before?"

"No."

"Okay. Let me give you a brief overview of how the group works. We meet every week on Thursday evenings unless there is a holiday that falls on that day. In that case, we often meet the evening before. Attendance is totally voluntary. Come as little or as often as you want and come as many times and for as long as you want. Typically, I pick a topic for us to focus on each week, and I talk a little about that topic before opening things up to the group." She is looking down at the purse she is clutching, fidgeting with its clasp, making it hard for me to tell if she's hearing me or not. I continue anyway.

"The members of the group have the option of discussing something relative to their individual grief issues and experiences, and if it happens to be related to the topic at hand, that's great. But it doesn't have to be. Anyone who wants to talk may do so, but there is also no obligation to do so. The others who are here tonight have all been coming for some time, and they do plenty of talking. You might feel like an outsider because of that, but I promise you that if you commit the time and effort to attending several sessions, that will dissipate. It's a very friendly and supportive group of people, and all of them share one thing in common with you. They've all lost someone close to them."

She looks at me then, and I see the first spark of life in those mud brown eyes. "How?" she asks.

I'm confused by the question. "How what?"

"How did the others die?"

"Oh. Well, there's a mix. And rather than my trying to give you any background on the others, I think it will work better if you let them tell you their stories." I again ponder who it is Sharon has lost. Maybe it was a spouse?

"Any suicides?" she asks. Her eyes are scanning the others in the room.

"Yes," I say. "Did you lose someone to suicide?"

She nods slowly, frowning and surveying the other attendees.

"There is someone here who lost her husband to suicide," I say. "She hasn't had anyone else who shares her situation up until now. I can introduce you to her, if you like."

"No." Flat, dead, robotic. "What about homicide?" she says, eyes still roving, though I get the sense that she isn't focusing on anything or anyone.

"What about it?" I reply, unsure where she's going.

"Has anyone here lost someone to murder?"

"No." Something in the back of my brain connects with something in my gut, and instinct makes me qualify my answer. "Well, none of the group members have lost anyone to murder," I clarify, "but I have. My mother was murdered when I was little."

I see a spark of interest soften her face, and she looks me in the eye for the first time. "Did they catch who did it?" she asks, which strikes me as an odd thing to ask before expressing some token condolence or inquiring about the circumstances. Though most people merely make an awkward attempt at changing the subject whenever I bring it up.

"No, they never did," I tell her, feeling a familiar ache at the thought. I glance at the clock on the wall and see that it reads two minutes past seven. "I need to get things started," I say. "But I'd like to talk with you some more after the group ends, if you can stay for a bit."

"Sure," she says, and she gifts me with a tentative smile.

I give her shoulder a reassuring squeeze and then address the room at large, speaking loudly. "Okay, everyone, let's get started."

This command is typically followed by one last dash to the snack table to get another cookie, or to top off a cup of coffee. Generally, I allow a minute or so for people to heed my request, and then I start regardless of what's going on or who might be still hovering over the cookies. Tonight, however, the presence of a newcomer has intrigued everyone enough that things get changed up. The music of the various conversations stops as if on cue and everyone quickly claims a seat as if we are playing a game of musical chairs. I suspect they are eager to rubberneck on someone else's misery for a change.

The dynamics always change when someone new joins a group. Most of the time it's a good thing, if knowing that someone is struggling with grief can ever be considered a good thing. I've been spearheading this group for nearly two years now, and its composition and size has ebbed and flowed, fluctuating with some regularity. This is good because when all the players stay the same, things can get stagnant. A little fresh blood always invigorates the group.

I've had people who came only once, some who came for a handful of sessions, and two regulars who have been here since the group's inception. The average stay is about ten to twelve weeks for most. Some come alone, others with friends or relatives. The size of the group varies, too, having reached twenty-two people at its peak, though for the past two months it's been a core group of nine. We are in Wisconsin, so in the winter months the weather sometimes forces cancellations or keeps the group smaller. Now that it's springtime, I've been hoping the group would see some new blood.

I always arrange the chairs in a circle, and while this configuration is designed to create a feeling of community and equality, people tend to form smaller niches within the larger circle, mini groups where they feel the most comfortable.

My two die-hard attendees (though I should probably try to come up with a less offensive descriptor, under the circumstances), the ones who have been coming since I started the group, are Charlie Matheson and Betty Cronk.

Charlie is in his fifties, a widower, with a full head of gray hair that typically stands like a rooster comb by the end of a session, thanks to his habit of running his hands through it. Charlie works here at the hospital in the maintenance department and fancies himself as some sort of soothsayer or prognosticator. He swears he can "read" people and predict their futures after chatting with them for a few minutes. While I don't deny that the man has accurately predicted the behaviors of some of the group members in the past, it has less to do with any special powers he has than it does his ability to recognize when he has annoyed someone to the point of action. It didn't take a wizard to figure out that Hailey Crane, a teenager who came to the group with her mother when her father died, would decide to leave the group after one session as Charlie predicted. The fact that, despite my attempts to rein him in, Charlie badgered the girl a couple of times to "open up" and "express yourself" when she clearly didn't want to be there helped with that prediction.

I had a stern talk with Charlie after that, and I've had to do so on other occasions as well, since his actions often necessitate a cease-and-desist warning. If I let him, Charlie would take over the group. I've come to realize that he sees himself as my assistant, a coleader or facilitator of sorts, a perception I try hard to extinguish every week. I should probably ban him from the group, but he has a reputation around the hospital of being something of a tattletale. Whenever someone does something he doesn't like, he's quick to run to the human resources department and file a complaint. He knows how to play the system and isn't afraid to do so.

Since I can't steer clear of Charlie, I do my best to control him instead. I don't want to be on Charlie's bad side, so I struggle to balance my occasional desire to kill or maim him with my best professional façade. I don't have the luxury of picking and choosing my clients or patients in this hospital setting, and it's a simple fact of my professional life that I won't like some of them, and some of them won't like me.

Betty, my other long-term attendee, is a widow in her fifties, a stern, hard woman with a sharp-edged face, a tall, lean body, and a no-nonsense attitude. She wears her hair in a tight bun and dresses in drab, sack-like dresses, holey cardigans, heavy stockings, and utilitarian shoes. Betty's husband, Ned, was a quintessential Caspar Milquetoast kind of guy who not only let his wife lead him around by the nose, but seemed to like it. Theirs was a match made in heaven, but when heaven came calling for Ned, Betty found she didn't know what to do with her bossy personality. She and Ned never had any children. Just as well, I think, as I imagine little Bettys running around like creepy Addams Family Wednesdays—and not surprisingly, Betty doesn't have many friends. She came to the grief group because she felt befuddled and confused, a rudderless ship adrift on a foreign sea. And she found the perfect home for her acerbic style.

Unfortunately for me, her style is often at odds with what my group is about, and like Charlie, she can be a disruptive influence. The two of them keep me on my toes, I'll give them that. Tonight, with a newcomer in the mix, I know I will need to be extra vigilant and stay on top of them both lest things get out of control. They're like sharks smelling fresh blood in the water.

Charlie and Betty don't like each other, and they often seat themselves on either side of me—a subtle way, I suspect, of declaring their perceived leadership status. This works in my favor, however, because it's much easier to shut them up if they are within a hand's reach.

Charlie swears I once pinched him hard enough to leave a bruise on his thigh, a mark he offered to show me after everyone else had left for the night.

"Charlie, that would be completely inappropriate!" I chastised as he started to undo his pants.

He paused in undoing his belt and blinked at me several times. Then he smiled and refastened the belt. "Yes, I suppose it would be," he said with a shrug and a smile.

After that incident, I kept expecting a call from human resources, but it never came. Charlie was on his best behavior for a few weeks, though Betty stepped in to make sure my duties as group leader remained challenging. While she tends to ignore the women in the group, she has this seemingly uncontrollable need to harangue the men who come, muttering comments like "Man up, you big sissy" or "Warning, man cry ahead."

Betty would have made a great drill sergeant.

I steer Sharon to a chair and then settle in beside her, earning myself angry stares from both Betty and Charlie, who are seated in their usual places. I tend to sit in the same seat each week, and clearly neither of them anticipated me doing anything different tonight, since they are situated on either side of that chair. I resist the urge to smile, because I have to admit, I enjoy rattling them a bit. It's good not to let them get too complacent.

"Welcome to this week's meeting of our bereavement support group," I begin. "I want to start by reviewing the ground rules first, both as a refresher for those of you who have been here before and to inform our new visitor."

Predictably, most of those who have been coming for a while roll their eyes or shift impatiently in their seats. But reciting the ground rules is a must.

"First and foremost, remember that anything said in this room is confidential and is not to be discussed or relayed to anyone outside of the group. Remember that we are here to share experiences, not advice. Be respectful and sensitive to one another by silencing your cell phones, avoiding side conversations, and listening to others without passing judgment. And finally, try to refrain from using offensive language."

I pause and scan the faces in the group. "Any questions about the rules?"

I'm answered with a sea of shaking heads and murmured declinations.

"Okay then. Since we have someone new here tonight, let's start by going around the group and stating your name and who it is you've lost." I turn and smile at Sharon Cochran. "Sharon, would you like to start?"

I'm pleased when she nods, even though it's an almost spastic motion. My pleasure then dissipates as she completely derails the evening's agenda.

"My name is Sharon Cochran, and I'm here because the cops think my son took his own life two weeks ago. But I know he was murdered and I'm hoping you can help me find his killer."

Connect with Us

Visit us online at
KensingtonBooks.com
to read more from your favorite authors, see books
by series, view reading group guides, and more.

 Join us on social media

for sneak peeks, chances to win books and prize packs,
and to share your thoughts with other readers.

facebook.com/kensingtonpublishing
twitter.com/kensingtonbooks

Tell us what you think!

To share your thoughts, submit a review,
or sign up for our eNewsletters, please visit:
KensingtonBooks.com/TellUs.